The Devil's Angels MC
Book 6 – Pigeon

Lola Wright

Contents

Preface vii
Acknowledgements.. ix
The Devil's Angels MC Family Tree xi
Chapter 1 1
Chapter 2 17
Chapter 3 31
Chapter 4 55
Chapter 5 67
Chapter 6 93
Chapter 7 113
Chapter 8 121
Chapter 9 141
Chapter 10 165
Chapter 11 187
Chapter 12 223
Chapter 13 259
Chapter 14 343
Chapter 15 353
Chapter 16 441
Epilogue... 451
About the Author 457
Also by Lola Wright 459

First published by Lola Wright 2022

Copyright ©2022 by Lola Wright

All rights reserved. No part of this publication may be reproduced, stored, or transmitted in any form or by any means: electronic, mechanical, photocopying, recording, scanning, or otherwise without written permission from the publisher. It is illegal to copy this book, post it to a website, or distribute it by any other means without permission.

This novel is entirely a work of fiction. The names, characters, and incidents portrayed in it are the work of the author's imagination. Any resemblance to actual persons, living or dead, events or localities is entirely coincidental.

Lola Wright asserts the moral right to be identified as the author of this work.

Lola Wright has no responsibility for the persistence or accuracy of URLs for external or third-party Internet Websites referred to in this publication and does not guarantee that any content on such Websites is, or will remain, accurate or appropriate.

Designations used by companies to distinguish their products are often claimed as trademarks. All brand names and product names used in this book and on its cover are trade names, service marks, trademarks, and registered trademarks of their respective owners. The publishers and the book are not associated with any product or vendor mentioned in this book. None of the companies referenced within the book have endorsed the book.

Adult Content Warning: This book is intended for readers 18 years of age and older. It contains adult language, violence, explicit sex and may contain triggers for some people.

First edition

Editing by Pam Clinton @ pccProofreading

Preface

Ivy

When my mother, who suffers from mental illness, leaves my brother and me in the care of our grandparents, my life changes dramatically. Being raised on a large ranch, loved and cared for, I had a great childhood with them. With my grandparents passing, though, things changed. My brother and I have always had a difficult relationship, but it only gets worse now that he's in control of my life.

Working at an animal rescue, FurEver Homes, I have become friends with a few of The Devil's Angels members and their families. When a member of their club steps up to help me get free of my brother's control and abuse, I accept it gratefully, but I want much more than that from the tatted biker with kind eyes.

Pigeon

Watching Ivy on the security cameras at FurEver Homes, I'm intrigued and amused by her. She's young, too young for a jaded, somewhat older biker, but that doesn't change the fact that watching her with the forgotten animals calms my soul. When I spot obvious signs of abuse, I step in.

Spending time with Ivy, her strength and resilience only impresses me more. This young woman is fighting alone for her future and her dreams of starting a therapeutic riding center for kids. Her dream to help others shouldn't have to come at such a high cost to herself. I make a promise to her that I'll do whatever I can to help her succeed, but none of us saw the road that promise would lead us down.

Mature content. Discretion is advised.
Recommended for age 18 years and up.

Contains sexual situations, violence, sensitive subjects, offensive language, and mature topics.

Content warning for some readers.

Acknowledgements

Cover Photographer: Sorsillo @ Dreamstime.com

Cover Design: Nathan Wright

Editor: Pam Clinton @ pccproofreading.com

The Devil's Angels MC Family Tree

Chapter 1
Pigeon

Grand Junction to Denver is normally a six-hour drive using the beautiful Highway 70. Riding a Harley can shave an hour or so off that time and riding at the speed I do, even more. I'm not far outside of Denver before some tension finally starts to ebb from my body. Another visit home that I've survived, so I give myself a mental pat on the back as I finally start to enjoy the ride. Weaving my way around the cars, trucks, and campers sharing the road with me, I twist the throttle. Feeling my bike respond with a growl almost puts a smile on my face. Speed and the wind whipping through my hair can only make up for a little of the hell the last few days have been for me.

I have a lot of things in my life to be thankful for but spending time with my parents is not one of them. I'm not a good son, and I've learned to be okay with that. I've accepted that about myself many years ago, and yet, even at the age of 36, my parents have not. The world changes daily, but my parents never will. Between their old-fashioned beliefs and their strict religious views, I'm not only a disappointment but an embarrassment to them. The fact that they share those views with me—often and loudly—is why I seldom return home to hear it all again. A few minutes in their presence is all it takes before I feel my soul draining from my body. A day or two, and I leave feeling like an empty shell, unworthy of life.

I knew I was different from my family members at an early age. When parents are devout members of an off-shoot religion of the United Pentecostal Church, there are certain expectations for their children. I failed at every single one of them. I formed my own opinions and refused to follow their beliefs blindly. I constantly questioned the teachings of their church. I spoke up and did so often. I scoffed at the church members that spoke in tongues and flatly refused to be anointed with oil. There was no ritualistic foot washing for this kid. I don't know why I was that way, but I just couldn't make myself believe in their faith as they did. The church members seemed fake and overzealous to me, and being a true believer was not in my future. It's not that I didn't believe in

God, or at least a higher power, but I didn't believe as they demanded.

As I got older, things only grew worse. My parents were strict in every sense of the word, and I rebelled at every turn. My father spent countless hours preaching to me and then beating me. When the first didn't work, he resorted to the second. The beatings I endured behind the barn didn't make me conform; they simply convinced me that my dad had a mean streak. He found enjoyment in bringing the belt down hard against his son's body. I knew then that being a man of God, as he called himself, was bullshit. He used his religion as a weapon and a means of controlling his family. My mother and brother both jumped when he spoke and never doubted his word. They were completely brainwashed, in my opinion, and that caused a rift between me and them too. I was the misfit, the black sheep, the misguided soul.

Life was difficult, and I didn't do anything to make it easier. As a teenager, my friends were considered unsuitable by my parents. Unsuitable meant they weren't members of our church. Regardless, I remained friends with them. I joined the high school wrestling team against my parents' orders. I excelled at it and enjoyed the praise I received from the coaches. I was no stranger to smoking, drinking, raising hell, and sneaking out of the house, but nothing too far outside of normal teenage behavior. If they said no, I did it. I was not a good son, but they were not good parents either. Not to me, anyway.

I shake off the old memories as I turn my bike into the security company's parking lot. Coming to a stop, I shut it off and slowly dismount. The security company is the newest addition to The Devil's Angels businesses. Rex, a tech-savvy club brother, manages it. I work for him now and really enjoy the job. The business is closed today, but after the last few days, I need the quiet it'll provide. I need space from humans and a chance to get my mind straight. This job has become my refuge when needed. Sharing a house with Horse Nuts, another club brother, means that my office here has become my alone space.

I enter the silent building, walk through the reception area, down a hallway, and turn left into my office. Along the left wall is a large bank of TV screens. All are off, but I know it takes but a click or two of my mouse to bring them to life. I walk to my nondescript metal desk and flop down in my chair. Leaning to my left, I open the tiny refrigerator sitting on the floor and grab a beer. Opening the bottle, I down half of it. Leaning back, I place my boots on the desk and relax into my chair.

After I finish my beer, I give in to the need to turn on the monitors and find what I'm looking for. Opening my laptop, I type my way through the login procedure and then click on the appropriate icon. Instantly, the monitors come to life with several different camera angles and room views. I turn on the various camera mics, adjust the angle of my chair, and let my eyes search for my target. A full smile finally hits my face when I find her.

Ivy Monroe is currently in the pig barn at FurEver Homes. Walking down the aisle, she stops at each stall to chat with its occupant. My smile grows, and the leftover tension in my body eases as she talks nonsense to every single pig. This is exactly what I needed to shed my thoughts of the past. Grabbing another beer, I settle in for some free entertainment—Ivy-style.

FurEver Homes is an animal rescue that Ava, my club president's wife, donates to regularly. That means, in effect, that my club, The Devil's Angels, does too. It's where Ava adopted her pig, Gee, and where Craig found Bart. They do great work, and we're happy to help where we can. It's not uncommon to see various club members building fences or repairing barns there. When Margie, the manager, called about some missing puppies, it was decided FurEver Homes needed a security system. Of course, Rex being the person he is went overboard. We installed a top-notch system that we control from our offices, and the surveillance footage is stored here. Reasoning that the theft could be an inside job, the cameras are hidden, and only Margie knows that they exist.

Because of that fact, Ivy has no idea how often she puts a smile on my face.

At this point, I should probably explain that I'm not some old-ass creeper watching some young woman with perverted thoughts running through my head. It's nothing of the sort. Ivy is young, maybe late teens or early twenties, but that's not why I enjoy watching the FurEver Homes cameras. It's her interactions with the animals that keep me awed and amused. She treats every one of them as her best friend as if they're as human as she is. She gives them nicknames, special treats, an extra hug, or pat when someone's in need. Her love and connection to the animals are returned tenfold by her furry, feathered, and hooved charges. Without looking, I can usually tell which barn she's in by the sounds of excitement the animals make when she enters.

There's a small part of my brain that says it's wrong of me to watch while she's unaware, but I squash that down. We were hired to keep an eye on the rescue, and that's what I'm doing. To ease that part of my brain, I make a point to review parts of every employee's shifts. It's not as fun, but it's the job.

Hearing the rumble of a Harley, I know Rex is here. Since he seldom surfaces from his office, I was surprised he wasn't here already. Grabbing another beer, I wait. As soon as I see his face, I sidearm throw the beer at him. I smirk as I watch Rex fumble a laptop, cell phone, and papers in his hand to catch the beer before it collides with his chest.

"You fucker! Why do you always have to be such an asshole?" Rex sputters.

"Miss me?" I ask while blowing a kiss in Rex's direction.

"Fuck no. I enjoyed the quiet and not having things thrown at me," Rex replies as he takes a seat across from my desk. "You just get back?"

"Yeah," I answer without looking at my club brother. I know exactly why he's sitting in my office and not his own. Rex is here to gauge where my head's at after time spent with my blood family.

"I'm good," I tell him before he asks.

"What do you need, Pigeon?" Rex asks quietly.

"I'm good," I repeat.

"I'll let Trigger know he can stand down then," Rex says after a few beats. Standing, he walks out.

Sighing, I take one last look at the monitors. Shutting everything down, I head back outside to my bike. A shower, a hot meal, and a shit-ton of alcohol are what I need now.

Rolling out of bed the next morning, I'm regretting a few of my choices from the night before. The beer, the tequila, and the vodka were good friends then but not so much today. Tripping over an empty bottle, I make my way to the bathroom. I avoid the mirror and step directly into the shower. Standing under the hot water, I start to feel almost human again. I enjoy that feeling for less than a minute before my brain registers the sound of a flushing toilet. If my reflexes weren't dulled by a hangover, I might have been able to move my ass a little faster. Instead, as my hot shower instantly turns ice cold, I attempt to bolt out of the shower. I slip, whack my forehead against the tile wall, and crash sideways through the shower door. Landing face down on the bathroom floor, I lie there knowing my boys are going to stay lodged high in my body for at least a day. Sadly, I'm going to have to push through the pain, so I can find Horse Nuts and fuck him up.

"This isn't a good look for you, Pigeon."

Raising my head takes effort, and the grin on Gunner's face is like rubbing salt in a wound. I'm hating my life right now, but it looks like Horse gets to live another day.

"There a reason why you're standing in my bathroom admiring my ass, Prez?"

"Wipe the blood off your face, quit flattering yourself, and come drink some coffee, Sunshine," Gunner orders before tossing a towel at me and walking out the door. I listen to his laugh while his extra-large feet thump loudly down the stairs.

Pulling my sorry-self off the floor, I clean the gash on my forehead and bandage it. After pulling on some clothes, I make my way to the kitchen. I ignore the grins from Gunner and Horse but accept the coffee Gunner hands to me. Planting my ass against the counter, I start the process of replacing the leftover alcohol in my system with coffee.

"Church tonight at 7pm. Everyone needs to be there," Gunner states.

"Something up?" I ask.

"Yeah, we have decisions to be made that can't wait until our regular meeting," Gunner answers while setting his cup down and striding to the door.

I watch Gunner's eyes widen in horror a second before he bolts out the door. For a big guy, he can move fast. Due to his earlier stunt this morning, I feel nothing but joy at his fear. Looking out the window, Horse and I know exactly why Gunner's on the move. I shove Horse out of my way, so I can make it outside to view the carnage that's about to occur.

Watching Tessie's Jeep barrel down our street, I briefly wonder how Gunner intends to protect his Harley from becoming another casualty of Tessie's driving skills. Horse and I've learned our lesson and never park our bikes in the driveway. Or even close to it, in fact. Gunner will never make that mistake again, either.

I watch my President haul ass to his bike, but he must realize he doesn't have enough time to move it to safety. Instead, he places himself between the oncoming Jeep and his bike. Arms in the air, waving wildly, Gunner starts shouting the word "stop" repeatedly. His tactic works to a point and gains Tessie's attention. I can't stop the laugh that escapes me when she grins and waves back.

"Stop that fucking Jeep!" roars Gunner in a voice I've never heard him use before.

With Tessie's attention on Gunner, she takes the turn a little too short. A little too fast, too. Cutting across the corner of our neighbor's yard, she clips the edge of his privacy fence, dragging a section of it behind the Jeep. Sliding the Jeep to a stop inches from Gunner and his bike, I watch a dust cloud slowly roll over my club president. When it passes,

I see a very large man bent over, head hanging, hands on his knees, and I'm sure I hear him give up a little sob.

Luckily, the only damage is to a section of the fence this time. And, quite possibly, Gunner's boxers. I'm laughing too hard to hear what Tessie says to Gunner when she exits the Jeep, but I do witness the pat on the back she gives him as she walks past.

Seeing movement near the Jeep, I watch Mac flutter to the ground and fall onto his back.

"Oh, fuck me! Fuck me!" Mac screeches while flopping around dramatically. He looks like he's having a seizure and swearing nonstop during it.

After clearing his throat a few times, Gunner straightens, levels his gaze on Tessie, and asks in a quiet voice, "Why, the fuck, is Mac in a vehicle that you're driving?"

"Axel told me to drop him off at the bakery," Tessie answers while looking at her phone.

It's probably best she's not looking at Gunner's face. It's a few shades lighter than normal, and it's not a happy face at all.

"You whole, Mac?" Gunner questions.

"Make it stop, Dad!" Mac moans.

"Tessie?" Gunner growls.

Tessie continues messing with her phone and doesn't respond.

Gunner tries again with the same result. Gunner takes a few steps to stand directly in front of Tessie before barking her name at an astounding volume. Tessie jumps, and her eyes fly upward to meet Gunner's.

"Give me your keys," he orders.

"Why?" Tessie warily asks.

"Because if you don't, I'm going to systematically take your Jeep apart with a sledgehammer. Then I'm going to find your brother-in-law and maim him for buying it for you. You are no longer allowed to drive it on club property until you can prove you have the ability to do so in a safe manner," Gunner answers in a deadly voice.

Tessie hesitates but makes the smart decision and drops her keys into his hand. I breathe a sigh of relief that Tessie's smart and knows this isn't a battle she'd win.

Gunner stalks to the Jeep, scoops up Mac's still prone, twitching body on his way, and climbs inside.

"I'll walk!" Mac screams out in protest.

Gunner starts the Jeep and quickly maneuvers it until it's parked properly in the driveway. Exiting the Jeep with Mac, he pockets the keys and heads to his bike. Slinging a leg over it, he sits before looking our direction.

"You working today, Tessie?" he questions.

"Yeah."

"Pigeon, get her to the shop after she apologizes to the neighbor. Horse, get his fence fixed today and get me a receipt for the materials. The cost will be deducted from your pay this week, Tessie. Call Vex and Axel and tell both to meet me at the clubhouse right the fuck now. Mac, hang tight. You're riding today," Gunner states before starting his bike.

"Weeeee!" Mac shouts as they hit the street and roar away.

I pull my phone out and shoot off a group text to Vex and Axel. It's only a few seconds later when I get responses.

Axel: Why?

Me: To kill you. Slowly, painfully and probably twice.

Vex: Something wrong?

Me: Tessie's driving and you buying her the Jeep. Good luck, brother!

Axel: Fuck! Because of Mac riding with Tessie?

Me: He's traumatized for life.

Vex: She ok?

Me: She is. Advice—wear a cup!

Axel: Mac or Gunner?

Me: Both. Can you suggest my name as the next VP? Deathbed suggestions carry more weight.

Axel: Ava know yet?

Me: You're still able to text so I'm guessing she doesn't. Can I be there when she finds you? Please?

Vex: Tessie at your place again?

Me: Yep. I'm taking her to work.

Vex: Do it before Taja finds out she's around Horse. I can only go to war once today over that girl.

Me: Do I have your vote for VP after Axel's funeral?

Vex: Yeah you do. Be nice not to have an ugly VP.

Me: Let Bailey know I'm happy to move in next week. Little Alex needs a daddy.

Axel: Fuck both of you!

Tucking my phone in my pocket, I look up and find two sets of eyes on me.

"Let's go, Tessie. You've caused your limit of drama for one day," I say with a laugh as I walk toward the backyard.

"Where you going?" Tessie asks, bewildered.

"We park our trucks back here. That way, you'd have to drive through the house to hit them. It could still happen, but the way I figure it, the house would slow you down, and the damage to my truck would be less that way."

"That's harsh, Pigeon," Tessie mumbles as she follows me.

"But sound logic nonetheless, little one."

Lola Wright

Chapter 2

Ivy

Bone-deep exhaustion washes over me, but my day is far from over. Working the evening shifts at FurEver Homes allows me to have my days free to work my family ranch. After a full day of ranch work, I make the hour drive from Fort Collins to the outskirts of Denver, where the rescue is located. I work my shift there and then drive the hour back home to sleep a few hours before starting over again.

I eat more often in my truck than at a table. It's done on the run, and it's usually whatever I can grab in a hurry. It's been a very long time since I had a day off and even longer since I've been on a date. My life consists of work and more work. College hasn't ever been an option, not since Nana and Papa passed, even though it was their dream for me. My life isn't easy, but I have goals, and I don't mind working hard for them. I ignore the tired, aching bones and muscles and focus solely on my future plans for the ranch.

Parking my battered truck next to the house, I sit quietly for a few moments. Knowing my brother Ted is most likely still awake, I take an extra minute to gear up my defenses. Ted and I have a difficult relationship, to say the least. I'm the younger sibling by several years and female, both being facts Ted sees as weaknesses. Add that to his drinking, the details of our grandparents will, and our relationship is the perfect storm.

Entering the house through the kitchen door, I cringe at the mess strewn about. When I left this afternoon, the kitchen was spotless. Now the stove is covered in grease, dirty dishes are in the sink, on the counter and table, and beer bottles are scattered everywhere. The only bright spot is my old cat, Tabitha, curled up in her bed in the corner.

I hang my backpack and jacket up on the hook by the door and walk to my faithful friend. Being hard of hearing, she doesn't realize I'm home until I stroke her head. Lifting tired eyes to mine, she begins to purr. I continue petting her, knowing she'll fall back to sleep soon. She's sleeping more and more these days, and it hurts my heart knowing we don't have many left together.

"Ivy! Bring us a few beers!" Ted shouts from the living room.

Straightening, I walk to the fridge and retrieve the beer bottles. Walking into the living room, I hand them off to Ted and our ranch foreman, Todd. Turning around without speaking to either, I head back to the kitchen and start cleaning. Sleep will have to wait because I can't leave Nana's kitchen looking like a disaster area.

When you work a job until 11pm, drive an hour home, and clean a kitchen before going to bed, 4:30am comes early and fast. Shutting off the alarm, I roll out of bed immediately. If I don't move fast, I'll fall back to sleep, and there are hungry mouths to feed. I shower quickly, once again promising myself I'll actually have time to condition my hair next time and finish getting ready for the day. I pick up Tabitha off my bed, carry her downstairs and open the backdoor for her. While coffee's brewing, I stand at the sink, eating a piece of toast while looking out over the barns and corrals. It's still dark, but the familiar shapes show faintly. There's comfort in seeing their outlines. They're the images I've known throughout my childhood. I pull my eyes away and pour coffee into a travel mug, letting Tabitha in the door as I walk out.

Walking into the barn, I breathe the hay and horse smells in deeply. Tossing a few bales of hay into the bed of the side by side, I drive it outside to the corrals. Speaking softly to each of the horses, I get busy with the morning chores. After the horses are fed and watered, I drive back to the barn to get the tractor. There are many more mouths to feed before daylight hits.

I have several hours of work done before I see Ted and Todd standing outside one of the hay barns. I drive past without a glance, park the tractor, and walk toward my truck. Driving it to the tool shed, I load up the supplies I need to start repairing a section of fence. Cody, one of the ranch dogs, jumps into the bed of the truck. It's not often one or more of the ranch dogs isn't riding shotgun with me. Giving him a pat on the head, I try, once again, to get him to ride inside the truck instead. As usual, I fail, so I give up trying and resign myself to driving extra slow again. Putting the truck in drive, I aim it to the north pasture.

Arriving back at the tool shed hours later, I'm putting away the tools when I hear footsteps. Looking over my shoulder, I see Ted approaching. My stomach drops when I see the beer in his hand.

"Did you get the corrals cleaned out? The stalls?" he barks.

"Stalls, yes. Corrals, no. Feeding and watering are done. I fixed fence in the north pasture today."

"Corrals before you leave, Ivy. I shouldn't have to tell you this shit. If you can't get your work done, then you'll have to quit your job."

"I'm not quitting FurEver Homes, Ted. It's my only income since you control the money made by the ranch."

"You'll fucking do as you're told," he growls while taking a step toward me menacingly.

Involuntarily, I take a step back as Cody lets out his own growl. I place my hand on his back to reassure him before Ted takes his anger out on the dog instead.

"I do more than my share of the work around here. I can't do it all, Ted. You and Todd don't …" my voice trails off as he takes another step closer.

"Want to finish that sentence, Ivy?"

I made it to work on time today, but it was close. I broke several traffic laws to get here, but luckily, I wasn't stopped by the police. Rushing into the rescue's employee breakroom, I stow my backpack in my locker after pulling my lunch out of it. I didn't have time to make a proper lunch, but what I grabbed on my way out the door is now in the fridge for later. Heading to the office, I greet Dale as he's coming out.

Dale's a nice enough guy but comes across as a little odd. I don't mean odd in a bad way, just different. He's always polite, good with the animals, and hardworking but has a bad habit of staring for uncomfortably long times. Even if you catch him and make eye contact, he'll continue staring instead of looking away, as most people would do. It's unnerving and happens often.

I say hi, squeeze past him and hurry to the time clock. I make it with less than a minute to spare. Turning around, I see Margie at her desk, frowning. Taking a seat, I wait for her to finish reading whatever has caused the frown. It's not long before her eyes meet mine.

"Hi, Ivy. We had a few intakes today. A friendly little Corgi whose owner passed, and the family doesn't want. He won't be here long, I don't think. It's the other dog that came in that I wanted to speak with you about. Mixed breed but large and very scared. He's obviously been mistreated and was possibly used as a bait dog for a dog fighting ring. Our vet checked him out, treated some older wounds, but his mental state is my biggest concern. A lady found him along a road with a choke collar on with a piece of broken chain hanging from it. Somehow, she coaxed him into the back of her car and came straight here. He's cowering at the back of his kennel and is clearly terrified. Can you work your magic and see if you can get him to relax a little?"

"Of course. I'll spend some extra time with him tonight. Has he shown signs of aggression?" I ask.

"Not yet, but he might if he feels pushed or threatened. Be careful. The vet's going to come back on Monday and should have his blood work back by then. He's going to wait until then to vaccinate and worm him."

"Sounds like a plan. Anything else?"

"Well, the usual thing. Prissy has been voicing her displeasure at you not being here 24/7," Margie states with a laugh.

I grin and stand. I can be dead on my feet, but Prissy can always make me smile.

"I'll go check in with her before I start my rounds. If I don't see you before you leave, have a great night, Margie."

"You too, Ivy. Hope you enjoy your days off, and for God's sake, get some sleep," Margie orders with a kind smile when she catches me yawning.

Leaving the office, I aim myself to the aviary to make my apologies to a very bossy cockatoo named Priscilla. Large birds like her are not always easy to find the perfect home for, so Prissy has been with us for several months now and quickly became attached to me. Cockatoos are demanding, loud attention whores that become depressed or destructive if not given enough attention. Priscilla happens to be a beautiful sulphur-crested cockatoo with a large vocabulary. All white body, with a bright yellow mohawk-looking crest, she came from a home in Savannah, Georgia, and speaks with a southern accent. Another case of an owner passing, Prissy bounced through a few homes before being dropped off here. The bright spot in her life was her original owner, who clearly spent a lot of time with her. Prissy's very intelligent but mischievous and demanding. She gets down with being destructive if left to her own devices too often. She feels superior to all the other birds and berates them often. Dale is somewhat afraid of her, and she loves intimidating him through posturing when he's close to her. When he backs away, she laughs a tinkling little laugh, just like a proper lady. She's not mean at all, just a beautiful brat that I would love to adopt but can't because of Ted.

"Hey!" Prissy screeches from her perch when I enter the aviary.

"Hey, Queen P. How's my favorite lady today?" I greet as I stop in front of her eye-level perch.

With Prissy being nearly twenty inches tall, I must crane my neck to look up at her.

"I's good," Prissy answers immediately. With her southern accent, it sounds like "aah's good," and it never fails to make me grin.

"Want to help me with rounds?"

"Yes, ma'am," Prissy states before stepping up onto my hand, where I then transfer her to my shoulder.

The best part of my day starts now. No Ted, no stress, and surrounded by animals. I take a deep breath and get to work.

Priscilla and I make the rounds of all the barns and enclosures, but I return her to the aviary before I enter the dog area. I want to meet the new guy, and I can't trust Priscilla not to scare him. I greet each dog as I walk past their kennels, making mental notes as to who needs water, food, or something else, and casually ease past the new dog. I watch him out of the corner of my eye and see that he instantly turns his face away while pressing into the back wall. He's terrified, and my heart breaks a little. Moving on, I grab leashes, select a few dogs to take to the outside dog park to let them run, and turn them loose. A few months ago, some of The Devil's Angels members came here and fenced in a few acres for this purpose. They went above and beyond by also installing a small, shallow pool for the water-loving dogs, waterspouts that turn on and off automatically for the dogs to drink from or play in, a large sandpit for digging, tires, and even a few fire hydrants. The dogs love every bit of it, and it's made a huge difference in their attitudes with not having to be in a kennel most of the day.

Returning to the dog barn, I continue to talk to the dogs while completing the necessary chores. I make a point of walking by the new dog's kennel often, but I don't look at him directly. After several trips past, I notice him starting to look my way. After swapping out the dogs in the dog park with other dogs, I gather up food, water, and treats. Making my way to the new guy's kennel, I sit on the floor in front of it. Looking at his info card, I see the vet has aged him at around two years old. Pit bull mix, he's a beautiful gray/blue color with visible scars. One ear is partially missing, there's a jagged scar over his nose, a few on his sides, but he has sad, kind eyes. His life's been hard, but not anymore. We'll find him a home where he'll be loved, or he'll stay here. Either way, he's done being abused. His wounds are not fresh and not serious at this point. It's his mental and emotional wounds that may never heal because humans can be evil. Some days are harder than others when working at an animal rescue.

Softly, in a calm voice, I talk nonsense to the pittie mix. My words don't matter as much as the tone, so I talk about what chores I have to do tomorrow, what groceries I need to buy, and how good his new life is going to be. After several minutes, I move my hand toward the latch and watch to see his reaction. Not seeing anything signaling aggression, I open his gate enough to slide the food and water inside. Relatching his gate, I sit patiently and wait. After a few moments, I see him sniffing the air and glancing toward the food. I remove a dog biscuit, homemade by my friend Ava, and stick one end through the wire. I don't know what she makes them out of, but I know of no dog that's refused them yet. Ava brings a large tub of them and other treats each month, and we save them for this type of situation.

Eventually, either curiosity or hunger overcomes some of his fear, and he starts to inch toward the treat. It takes patience and several minutes, but eventually, he's close enough to stretch his neck far enough to sniff the biscuit. I continue talking softly as I watch streams of slobber slide from his mouth to the floor. He wants this treat badly, so it's now just a matter of time. I wait.

The dog very slowly, while watching me intently, reaches for the biscuit. I let go when he gently tugs on it, and I grin when he rushes to the back of the kennel again. Once there, it's but a few seconds, and the biscuit's devoured. I pick up the small blanket I had sitting next to me and lay it on my lap. Wiping my hands on it, I let it absorb my smell and that of the biscuit. I open the gate enough to slide the blanket, with another treat on top of it, inside. We've made progress, so I stand and walk away to let him enjoy his second biscuit in peace. Returning to the office, I sit at the computer, open his file, and type in a name that fits a brave dog—Thor.

Walking into the cat enclosure, I'm instantly surrounded. I refill food and water dishes, clean litter boxes, and pet furry heads. I also spend a lot of my time unhooking little claws from my jeans. So many cats and kittens to find homes for that some days it's overwhelming. If only more people would spay and neuter, it would make a huge difference in the unwanted cat population. At least the ones here are going to be okay. They're loved, have shelter, and all the other necessities. Hopefully, they'll also have their own home and a family to love them soon. After showering attention on as many as I can, I move on to the rest of the barns and our residents.

After several hours, hunger makes me realize it's time to take a quick break. Grabbing my lunch out of the fridge, I take a seat and dig in. All I had time to grab was a small bowl of macaroni salad I made a few days ago. I seriously need to do some grocery shopping tomorrow. My cupboards are bare, my dirty laundry is piled up high, and the house needs a thorough cleaning. I'm behind on everything, but chores still need to be done, and the ranch doesn't run itself.

When my grandparents were still alive, Todd and Ted did their share of the work. Since then, they do very little and don't do much right. They're too busy drinking to be good at their jobs, and neither care. Papa would never have tolerated this, and it's just sad that his wishes aren't being followed. Losing him and Nana so close together has devastated my life but has brightened Ted's, unfortunately.

I've pretty much always known that I'd inherit the ranch, and Ted would receive money, but I never dreamed it would happen the way it has. Papa and Nana had their will done several years ago, when I was still a minor and was advised to make certain conditions. Conditions that have now made my life a living hell. Nana realized mistakes had been made, but she was already sick when we unexpectedly lost Papa, and the will never got revised before she died too. So now I have to just push through, survive each day as it comes, and put my dreams on hold for a few more years.

I rinse my container, stow it in my backpack, push away my thoughts, and get back to work. A few more hours to go before I'm done for the night. Most people are happy on their last day of work for the week but not me. Two full days around Ted is never a good time. Sighing, I head for the pig barn.

Chapter 3
Pigeon

We're sitting in Church, and Gunner's laying out some new info that's been passed to him. I can clearly see anger and disgust on several of my club brothers' faces. I'm sure my face reflects the same emotions as theirs because I can feel my blood pressure rising. All of our thoughts must be similar, and action is going to be needed because none of us are going to sleep easy until this is settled.

"Of course, we're going to act on this," states Petey emphatically.

"Absolutely. It's not if. It's how that I'm bringing to the table," Gunner answers.

"How? With lead is how!" bellows Trigger.

"Need a little more to the plan than just to end them," Gunner responds patiently.

"Wait a minute. I have a question. Who's Alfonse?" Freddy asks.

"Carmen's brother. Some of us met him when he came here to pick her up after we brought her and Bella to the clubhouse," Cash answers.

"How'd he find out there's another sex ring operating here?" Pooh questions.

"Since his sister was grabbed, and we returned her, their family has made exposing sex rings their personal mission. I don't know all the details, but their info seems solid. Several of them will be here the day after tomorrow, and we'll know more then. They asked if we could put them up somewhere so they can stay under the radar. If no one objects, I'd like to offer them the rooms here. No one will know they're even in town that way. I know several of us have rooms but don't live here anymore. Everyone okay with that?" Gunner explains.

A chorus of yeahs and yeses ring out, and that matter is settled. While half-listening to other questions the members are asking, my mind flits to Bella. How's this going to affect her? She's come so far and put her past behind her, and now this will bring it all up again. Will she withdraw into herself again? Before I can voice these thoughts, Pooh does.

"I don't think Bella should know why these men will be here. I don't want this to bring up all that she's gone through again. What do you think, Petey?"

"She's smart and well-adjusted. I don't know if we could keep it a secret from her with strange men staying here. It might be best to explain what's happening and be available for her if there's fallout," Petey answers but not in a convincing voice. He has doubts too, and that concerns me.

"You need to talk with Trudy before that decision's made, Pops. Bella will have all the support she needs, but Trudy knows her girl and what's best for her. We'll support whatever decision you and she make," Axel states, and he's not wrong.

"She's finally back to being herself after killing that intruder at the Aunts' house. I agree with Petey, though. Bella's going to figure out what's going on, and it's best she's prepared for it instead of being blindsided," Chubs adds.

"Is our involvement in this going to create problems for Livi and James?" Vex asks.

"James is still a prospect, so we can keep him out of it by limiting what he knows and his role in it all. He can work the gate and get supplies. Livi won't ask questions. With that said, both would back our decision on this without a doubt," Cash answers.

"Let's finish up for today and get things ready for our guests. As for now, this info doesn't leave this room. Let us know your decision, Petey, and we'll go from there. Axel, get the prospects to stock up on groceries, and I want one at the main gate at all times. No one except members and family are allowed through the gate without one of us okaying it," Gunner orders before banging down the gavel.

Walking out of our meeting room, Horse and I head straight for the bar. So much for swearing never to drink again. As Toes sets beer down in front of us, Mac lands on the end of the bar. Waddling to the bowl of nuts, he uses his foot to push them around until he finds a cashew.

"Remind me to never eat the mixed nuts here again," I mutter to Horse.

"His disgusting feet haven't killed you yet," Horse says with a chuckle.

Looking at Mac's feet, I bark out a laugh.

"A pedicure, Mac?" I say while nodding my head at his bright pink toenails.

"Yep. Twisted Twins," he answers while digging around for another cashew.

"They do Gee's again too?"

"Yep, and Loki."

"Duffy's?" I ask, already knowing the answer.

"Nooooo!" Mac answers before cackling. "Assman's are gold!"

"Gold?" Horse asks with a snort.

"Sparkly gold," Mac responds with another cackle.

Chubs plops down on the seat next to me and turns to Mac.

"Heard you rode a Harley today, Mac. Like it?"

"Vroooom! Vroooom!" Mac screams before doing a perfect imitation of a Harley engine roaring down the highway.

Vex walks behind the bar and comes to a stop opposite Horse. His face is serious, and I already know what's coming.

"Was there a reason for Tessie being at your place today?" he asks bluntly.

"Collecting rent," Horse replies calmly while taking a sip of beer.

"How often does she collect 'rent'?" Vex questions sarcastically.

"Once a week, Vex. She insists we pay weekly. It's her house, so we do it her way," Horse answers.

Vex's eyes turn to me, and I nod my head in agreement. Tessie's house, Tessie's rules. We all know it's her way of seeing Horse, but nobody's called her on it. That's Vex and Taja's job, not mine.

"Rent is paid monthly and paid to me from here out," Vex orders.

"No problem," Horse responds while I nod my head again.

"Why are you being pissy about this, Vex?" Chubs asks in a serious tone.

"Because I got my ass chewed off today, so I'm just sharing the love. Prez said he's not returning her keys until she's no longer a danger to society. Said he's doing it for the good of mankind, but it's just because she nearly made him piss himself today," Vex answers in a frustrated voice.

"Seems to me, the best way of achieving that would be to make Horse Tessie's driving instructor. Yeah, they'd be spending time together, but it wouldn't be fun for him at all. And, chances are, he wouldn't survive it, and Taja wouldn't have to worry anymore about him and Tessie," Chubs advises with a smirk.

"You rat bastard!" shouts Horse while slamming his beer down on the bar and turning shocked eyes to Chubs.

"You were overheard volunteering me to be her instructor the other day, and that shit's not happening. My solution will give Vex some payback and keep me whole at the same time. What do you think, Vex?" Chubs says with an evil grin.

"I like how you think, Chubs. Horse, you can start her lessons tomorrow in the field behind my house. Be there at 8am and bring your truck," Vex states with a huge smile before he turns and walks off.

"Do I have to do this?" Horse questions while looking at me and Chubs.

"Yep," we answer at the same time.

"Why would you throw me under the bus like that, Chubs?" Horse whines.

"You tried to do it to me. I just play the game better than you. Word of advice, Horse. Don't fuck with The Chubs. I'll win every time," Chubs answers with a chuckle before he too walks off.

"That curly-haired bastard has an evil side," Horse complains.

"Yes, he does. If you die tomorrow, I'm taking your room at the house. It's bigger than mine."

"If I end up brain dead, pull the plug," Horse says with a sigh.

"Happy to honor your last wish, brother," I answer with a grin as I drain my beer and stand.

Meeting's over, and I have a rescue to check in on. I walk out, straddle my bike, and leave the compound.

Watching Ivy make her rounds, I frown. I don't know what's bothering me, but something is. Something seems off with her, even though I can't say what. She's working, as usual, chatting up all the animals, and all seems fine, but at the same time, something isn't. Instead of calling it a night, I settle more firmly in my chair, turn up the volume and continue watching.

"How you doing tonight, Batman?" Ivy asks when she stops in front of a stall containing an extremely large, black pig.

The name card clearly states "Fred," but Ivy often gives out nicknames when she doesn't think the animal's name matches their personality.

The pig grunts several times before heaving himself to his feet and waddling to the front of the stall. He waits patiently for Ivy to hand him a carrot chunk. For as large as he is, he takes the carrot delicately from her hand. Receiving a head pat, he grunts again before Ivy moves to the next stall.

"How's it shaking, Miss Jiggles? You're looking like a superstar tonight," Ivy says to the smaller, black and white pig named Mary.

Miss Jiggles squeals and does a couple of twirls before coming to a stop in front of Ivy. Placing her front feet on the edge of a bottom board, she stretches up for her cuddle and treat. Miss Jiggles is an unusually loud pig. All pigs can be loud, but she can top the best of them with earsplitting squeals.

Ivy spends a few minutes complaining to Miss Jiggles about how much laundry she's got to do and how a new dog came to the rescue today. Miss Jiggles appears to listen closely and adds a grunt or squeal at somewhat appropriate times.

"I'll check back before I leave, sweetie. Thanks for the chat," Ivy states as she moves to the next stall.

When she reaches the final stall, the occupants greet her in a loud chorus of pig talk.

This stall has several piglets from the same litter, and they're bouncing their rubbery little bodies in anticipation. Ivy doesn't disappoint.

"Piggy Smalls, Squealy Dan, Elvis Pigsley, and Piggy Davis Jr.! How's my favorite boy band doing? Who loves you? Who loves your little snouts? I do! Everyone does! You're the kings of the musical world! Sing it out! Sing it to me!" Ivy greets them in an excited voice while clapping her hands.

This sends the piglets into a noisy, frothing frenzy of motion, with each trying to get Ivy's attention first. Each competes with the others in noise level and movement. Ivy opens the gate, walks in, and sits down in the center of the stall. Instantly, she's got piglets climbing on her, rutting against her legs and neck, squealing in delight.

Eventually, the piglets tire themselves out, and each finds a spot to cuddle close to Ivy. She talks softly to each while handing out affectionate pats and scratches. I find myself smiling at how she takes this extra time with the little ones and how much they look forward to it.

I grew up on a farm, so I understand animals too. None of ours were pets, though. If they didn't have a job or weren't there for food, they weren't allowed. My dad wouldn't even allow a barn cat. To him, feeding something that wasn't going to bring him a profit was ridiculous. At first, when a stray cat would appear, I did my best to keep it hidden and fed. After my dad found out the first few times, I quit doing it. I'd scare the cat away even when it seemed cruel to do so. It was a lot less cruel than what my dad would do when he found them. I learned at a young age not to show an animal love, or I'd have to listen to one of my dad's lectures. Lectures that usually involved a beating or two to make sure the point was made.

I think Ivy's love and admiration for animals is the main reason I like watching the rescue cameras. She shows them love unashamedly and without reserve. All the employees are obvious animal lovers, but Ivy takes it a few steps further. She engages with them above and beyond her duties. She has an affinity with them that the others lack. She has a way with the animals that puts them at ease, even the scared and skittish ones. I know Ava and Reno have nothing but respect for Ivy, and that's saying something since both are very particular about animal treatment. Craig sings Ivy's praises every time he visits the rescue with Ava, Reno, or Chubs. I always smile when Craig gets to visit because he can barely stand still wanting to make sure he gets to see every single animal there. He thinks up projects for the Devil's members to do just so he can come along too. The little guy is an ornery little shit some days but never to any animal. Usually, it's just to Axel, and that's always amusing for the rest of us.

Focusing back in on the monitors, I realize what's been bothering me. Ivy seems to be favoring her left arm some. She's moving a little stiff, too. I lean forward and continue watching. After a few more minutes, I realize I'm right. Ivy's injured, not seriously, but now I'm concerned and wondering how it happened. Thinking back, I realize this isn't the first time I've noticed injuries on her. I know nothing of her home life. I only know what I see on the rescue cameras and what little I've heard when helping on a project at the rescue. Now that I think about it, I don't even know if she's in college, single, living with someone, or what her life outside of there consists of. Not that it's any of my business, but now that I know she's been injured again, I'm curious. Bike accident? Car? Fall down the steps or trip over a curb? Boyfriend?

On that thought, I mentally stop myself from thinking about it anymore. I watch her closely for a few more minutes, note that it's not a serious injury, just some stiffness, and I switch off the monitors. Closing down my laptop, I leave the building. Time to head home, eat, and hit my bed. I briefly think about hitting up the club's strip club, but the thought doesn't appeal to me at all. Unless I'm helping out there, I seldom find myself pulling into the lot anymore.

Arriving home, I find Horse sitting in front of the TV watching a reality show in the dark. Grabbing two beers, I hand one off to him and flop down in my recliner. We watch TV for over an hour before he breaks the silence.

"I haven't crossed any lines with Tessie."

"I know you haven't. I know it hasn't been easy either. If she ever finds out for sure how you feel about her, she'll be unstoppable," I reply.

"Will Vex and Taja ever be okay with me asking Tessie out?"

"When Tessie's older, yes, they will be. You're a good man, Horse. They know that, too. Taja's spent her life taking care of Tessie, raising her, loving her, and she's just not adjusting to the fact that Tessie's almost grown up now. It's hard for her to see Tessie that way, and it'll be hard for Taja to take a step back and let Tessie go. I think losing the baby has made Taja hold on to Tessie a little tighter. You've waited this long. Stay the course and continue being patient. When the time's right, you'll need to argue your case to both Taja and Vex. Probably Trigger too, so he'd be a good one to keep on your side. Taja will rebel against it, but she's reasonable and will come around," I advise again.

This isn't the first time we've had this conversation, but I give Horse credit because he's not pushed this matter. He understands about Tessie's age, and he respects Taja and Vex's decisions. He wants to do this the right way, and I encourage him whenever he gets frustrated. Tessie doesn't make it easy for him, and Vex's last decision will only make it harder for Horse to keep his distance. That is if he survives the driving lessons. If not, I'll mourn his loss, pull the plug, and raise a beer to my dead friend.

Axel: You coming to Vex's for the driving lesson?

Me: Yeah

Axel: Horse going to back out?

Me: How much have you bet that he will?

Axel: $100 against Pops.

Me: Pay your dad. Horse left a few minutes ago.

Axel: He might change his mind on the way here. Birds singing/sun shining. All those reasons to live.

Me: Possible. $100 says he doesn't back out?

Axel: I'll take that bet. Bring snacks.

Me: Gunner lock you out from breakfast this morning?

Axel: Fuck you! But yeah, he did.

Me: On my way

I stop at Ava's bakery and load up on treats, small containers of orange juice and chocolate milk, and hit the highway. Arriving at Vex's huge-ass house, I park my bike next to the rest gathered there. Behind the garage, behind a large tree, I leave it in the safest place I can find. I gather up the food and drinks and make my way to the large clearing and bikers standing around.

Before I come to a stop at the picnic table, Pooh grabs a bag out of one hand while Trigger grabs one from the other. When I start to protest, Trigger tosses a chocolate milk my direction. I should say, at my head. Looking around at the crowd gathered, I realize the club has a lot of businesses being neglected today. I spot the Aunts sitting at the picnic table and walk over to drop a kiss on each of their cheeks. One of them gives my ass a pat, and I flash both a wide smile. Cash just shakes his head and drops his chin at their antics, but if my ass hadn't gotten a pat, I'd have been worried.

"You lovely ladies are up and about early today," I say.

"We have nothing else to do but wait for death. Might as well be here enjoying the show," Lola answers with a wicked grin.

"We're here to support Tessie. We tried helping her with her driving, you know, but Cash and Lars put a stop to it," complains Lottie.

"No, you old bat, my garage door put a stop to it when you three crashed through it," mutters Lars, Cash's dad.

"That too," Lottie responds with a shrug.

Looking out over the large field, I watch as Horse walks around placing orange pylons designating a road course. Tessie is standing next to Horse's battered truck with a blinding smile gracing her face while listening to whatever Taja is telling her. Vex is pacing and glancing toward his house, barn, and pool constantly. I'm guessing he's already regretting his decision to have her lesson so close to his home.

"How'd your trip home go?" Petey asks in a quiet voice from next to me.

Glancing his direction, I see the concern in his eyes. Petey's known me for a long time and knows that trips home are always difficult for me. I don't talk about my family much, but after a particularly bad visit and way too much alcohol, I unloaded my past life on Petey and Trigger. They listened quietly, but even a drunken me could feel the anger rolling off both men. Petey always checks in whenever I return from my parents' farm, and his support is always appreciated.

"As expected, Petey. Nothing ever really changes regardless of why I'm there."

"Sorry to hear that, Pigeon. You make the trip there to help out while your dad's laid up, and their heads are so far up their own asses, they don't even appreciate it. You got dealt a shit hand in the family department, brother. Let's hit the road after Tessie crashes, and Horse pisses himself. Go for a ride, grab a burger and beer somewhere. Yeah?"

"Yeah, Petey, that sounds good."

"Count me in. I'm taking the rest of the day off, and riding is the best way to enjoy it," states Trigger as he walks up to us.

"Have you ever taken a day off before, Trig?" I ask in a shocked voice. I honestly can't think of a time that Trigger skipped work for anything other than an emergency.

"Don't remember, but I am today, so you're stuck with me," Trigger responds with a grin.

Trigger's grin disappears as Horse's truck fires up. All heads swing toward the truck, and last-minute bets take on a frenzied pace. I watch in amusement as Horse places his hand on the door handle and appears to be talking to himself. Whether he's saying a prayer or trying to convince himself he'll live through this, I'll never know unless he survives. Turning to Axel, I place my bet.

Predictably, every orange cone is smashed flat as Tessie maneuvers the truck through the course Horse set up. As they pass, at a safe distance, I can see Tessie grinning, Horse hollering with arms flailing, and his tan nowhere in sight. I feel a moment of pity for Horse, but I shake it off because I'm just thankful it's not my ass in the passenger seat. The truck gives a hard jerk before speeding up considerably. When the next turn is taken, we all watch as the rear of the truck slides around until it's in line with the front.

Everyone stills as the truck straightens out but is now aimed toward our group.

"At least she's learning how to pull out of a slide," mutters Rex.

"If that truck doesn't turn another direction, I got Lola, you got Lottie," Cash orders quietly from beside me.

"Done," I reply as my body tenses at the imminent threat that is Tessie.

"I want to be saved by Trigger!" shouts Lottie, obviously overhearing Cash's request. "Not that you aren't a fine-ass man yourself, Pigeon. No offense meant."

"None taken, Aunt Lottie. Trigger's hotter than Hades for an old fucker. Wouldn't mind being rescued by him myself," I reply, knowing my response would set off Trigger's temper.

"Why, for the love of God, do you always encourage that bat-shit crazy cougar?" Trigger barks while jabbing a hard finger into the middle of my chest.

I didn't get a chance to enjoy the moment before Cash shouts, "Go time!"

I race to Lottie, picking her up and cradling her in my arms before running for the barn. Halfway there, I change directions when I see the truck heading in the same direction.

"Head for the trees!" Cash bellows.

I veer that direction and almost drop Lottie when I spot the chaos happening around us. It's harder than you'd think running for your life, carrying precious cargo, and trying not to laugh all at the same time. Lottie had no issue with enjoying the moment, though. She hooted with laughter while shouting out encouragement to all the fleeing bodies.

Just before making it to safety, I watch in amazement as Axel, pushing Lars' wheelchair, flies past me in a seriously impressive burst of speed. Poor Lars is hanging on for all he's worth, but he's still bouncing around like a rag doll. A few bruises are minor compared to what damage the truck could do.

I make it to the first tree, thankfully a very large, sturdy one, and duck behind it to find Cash, Lola, and Gunner. I set Lottie on her feet and watch as she fist-bumps her sister, both giggling like teenage girls. Trigger's right—bat-shit crazy through and through.

The truck veers sharply away from the tree we're cowering behind and makes its way back the way it came. After a sigh of relief, I look around at the others hiding from a one-way trip to the E.R. and do a headcount. I note that Axel, along with Lars and Trigger, are behind a large boulder, and Lars is still upright in his wheelchair. Petey, Chubs, and Rex cautiously step out from behind the barn, and I grin when I see that the near-death experience didn't diminish Chubs' appetite any. One hand holding an iced coffee, the other holding a large cookie, Chubs calmly continues with his snack while watching the truck wreak havoc with the edge of Vex's manicured lawn.

Shooting a glance toward the house, I spot Taja, Vex, and Reeves on the deck. A smile graces my face when I see Vex's hand protectively, most likely unconsciously, cupping Taja's large baby bump. It shouldn't still make me grin every time I see him doing that, but it does. After what they went through, Vex's protectiveness is way over the top this time but totally understandable. The entire club holds their breath with every doctor's appointment they have until we see them smiling afterward. Ava and Gunner are expecting again too, and both babies are due within a week of each other. That will be a celebration of epic proportions when both are born, and everyone is known to be healthy.

Hearing an unnatural sound, I look back to see Horse's truck balanced perfectly on top of the picnic table. After a moment of stunned silence, the table collapses, setting the truck back on three of its four tires. Correction—it's sitting on all of the tires it still has left attached. I'm not sure where tire number 4 is, and I scan quickly to make sure it's not headed my direction. A second after that, the passenger door opens, and Horse bails out.

"No! No fucking way am I getting back in there again! Fuck this, Prez! I'll take a beating in the ring with you instead! Fuck this! I'm out!" Horse shouts as he storms our direction.

Halfway to our tree, Horse looks toward the deck, stabs his finger that way, and continues his rant.

"Your sister, your problem, Vex! We can meet up in the ring too, but I'm not taking this hit for you! Fuck this shit!"

"You know, Horse, you're not a prospect anymore. Vex can't make you do shit for him," Axel says with a wicked grin.

Horse's angry face swings my direction, then he aims the look at Chubs.

"You said I had to!" Horse bellows accusingly.

"Yeah, about that. I lied," Chubs answers with a careless shrug before popping the last bite of cookie into his mouth.

While the crowd of spectators laugh at Horse, Chubs gives him a perfect salute and strolls away. With the cookie gone, I'm guessing he's planning on raiding Vex's fridge while Horse realizes that no smart man crosses Chubs.

"That went pretty good. Who's riding shotgun now?" Tessie shouts out the truck window.

That girl might not know how to drive worth a shit, but she's an expert at clearing out a crowd.

Lola Wright

Chapter 4

Ivy

After morning chores, I make a quick trip to town for groceries and to run a few errands. That done, I return to the ranch and start the laundry. While that's going, I give the house a quick cleaning and start cooking. I try to get a few things cooked ahead of time that make quick, easy meals throughout the week. When I have the laundry caught up and a few things cooked, portioned out, and placed in the freezer, I head back out to the barns.

I have no idea where Ted or Todd are or what they're doing, but it doesn't matter. I know what I need to get accomplished today, so I get busy. After unloading the heavy bags of grain I picked up in town, I gather the medical supplies I need and saddle my favorite horse, Junior. Whistling for the dogs to follow, we head out for the pastures.

I relax as soon as I can no longer see the house or barns. Alone with just Junior and the dogs for company, I'm now in my element. I can't see a single man-made structure, and I think again how fortunate I am to have this life. Not the part that includes Ted, but the opportunity to live with the kind of peace that this land provides. It settles my mind, replenishes my soul, and I know it could do that for others too.

My view from atop my horse is of beautiful ranch land dotted with cattle in the distance and a creek winding its way through grass that lightly sways with the breeze. Spring brings new life, and it's my favorite season. It's still early, but the grass is getting greener by the day, and wildflowers are starting to pop up. Calves and foals have been born and while the workload increases, so does the joy of watching them begin their lives.

I've always felt at one with nature and animals and less so with people. Animals are honest and usually give love when they receive it. Humans aren't as easy to understand. Working with the animals at the shelter, I'm often left at a loss for words at how many have been mistreated. Humans can be cruel, and I'll never understand why. Being kind is free, whether it's to a child, an animal, or an adult. What I do know is that someone who's mean to animals is usually a bully with humans too. Ones that are smaller or weaker than them, of course. Bully or coward, the words can be interchangeable.

Sensing Junior's restlessness, I pull my ball cap down tight over my unruly hair, lift the reins, and lightly give his sides a squeeze. He breaks into a lope, and my heart lightens even more. The dogs break into a run on either side of us as we race toward the creek. Just before reaching the edge, I slow Junior enough to let the dogs hit the water first. Then slowing to a trot, Junior happily splashes his way to the other side and leaps up the bank in a graceful move. Heads lift from grazing to watch horse, rider, and dogs approach the herd.

Riding quietly around and amongst the cattle, I check for injuries or illnesses of any kind. Taking an extra look at each of the calves, I'm happy to see all are doing well in this pasture. With another whistle to the dogs, I turn Junior north to check on the next herd.

After checking on two different herds, it's time to return to the barn. It's been a beautiful, if somewhat crisp, day for a ride, but there's more to accomplish before I'm done today. When the buildings are back in sight, I realize how tense my body is becoming when Junior starts tossing his head. Making a conscious effort to relax, I pat his neck reassuringly and sigh. A few more years, and I won't have to dread coming home.

"Get dinner on the fucking table, Ivy!" Ted shouts from the living room.

I ignore his voice and continue filling dishes. When everything is placed on the table, I turn to grab the iced tea pitcher and find myself shoved against the counter's edge instead. Wincing from the pain in my wrist from Ted's grasp, I shift my eyes to his bloodshot ones.

"When I speak to you, you answer," Ted growls.

Pulling my head back to escape his breath laden with beer, I jerk my wrist free. Placing both palms in his chest, I shove hard. Caught off-guard, Ted stumbles back a step.

"Don't touch me, Ted. I warned you before about putting hands on me, and I won't warn you again," I say in a low voice.

Taking another step back, Ted crosses his arms over his chest and smirks down at me.

"And what are you going to do about it, Ivy?" Ted asks while tossing a grin at Todd, who's standing in the doorway looking uncomfortable.

"When the terms of the will are met, you're gone, Ted. You'll never step foot back on this ranch, and neither will you, Todd," I reply firmly while avoiding the real question he asked.

"A lot can happen in three years, Ivy. A lot," Ted warns, his voice turning menacing.

Pushing past Ted, I grab the pitcher and fill my glass. Taking my seat, I don't respond. After a moment, Ted kicks the leg of my chair then takes his own seat. Todd sits and immediately starts filling his plate. It's several minutes of silence before Ted breaks it.

"I'm hiring a full-time cowhand. Todd's cousin is taking the position and will be here in a week or so to start work. He'll be staying in the bunkhouse but eating with us most days. Plan on that."

I stare at my brother, wondering how we were raised by the same set of grandparents and yet so fundamentally different as people. We didn't need another ranch hand except during certain parts of the year. What we needed was for Todd and Ted to do their jobs as they did when our grandfather was still alive. Todd had been a decent ranch foreman then, and Ted did his share of the workload. Papa wouldn't have tolerated anything less, and it hurts my heart knowing how disappointed he'd now be in Ted.

"I think it's a waste of money that could be put to better use," I state while drawing in a breath in preparation for Ted's reaction.

"Take a good look at my face, Ivy. Does it look like a face that gives two shits what you think?" Ted responds in a much calmer manner than I expected.

"No, Ted, I know you don't care about anything I say. I'm saying my piece anyway, though. If you and Todd did the job the way you used to do, we wouldn't have to pay for another hand. Papa only hired extras during haying and calving. In less than three years, the ranch will solely be mine, and it would be nice if you and Todd didn't run it into the ground before then. You can take your inheritance, leave now, and leave me to deal with the ranch," I say in a quiet voice.

This is a conversation we've had many times but to no avail. Ted is determined to control the assets of the ranch and my life regardless of how much I want him to leave. His inheritance is his to take, but why dip into that when you can spend the ranch's money? Why leave a home where you have a roof over your head, money in your pocket, food on the table, and not have to work for any of it?

The blow to the side of my face isn't a complete shock. My head snaps back, but I fight down any show of pain. I calmly look at my brother and feel nothing but disgust. Since our grandparents have passed, Ted's real personality has risen to the surface. The mean streak he's always had is now emboldened by alcohol, and there's no need to hide it anymore.

Glancing at Todd, I note that he's got his eyes on his plate. Todd is a weak man, and I learned that a long time ago. There will never be help or sympathy coming from that corner. I was never a big fan of Todd, but over the last few years, I've come to despise him. The feeling isn't as strong as it is for Ted, but it's not mild either. The day I take control of the ranch will be the last day I have to see him, and I look forward to seeing his taillights.

Having lost my appetite, I rise and take my plate to the sink. Standing there for a moment, I look out the window at the land I've called home for most of my life. I feel trapped, and in essence, I am. If I move out, the ranch won't survive, and I'll lose everything I have left to love. If I stay, I'm a slave and a punching bag to my only sibling. Not able to stay inside for another moment, I turn abruptly and walk to the door.

"Where do you think you're going?" Ted says in a raised voice.

"Fuck you, Ted," I say as I pull the door open and walk out.

Breathing in the clean, crisp air, I stop at my truck long enough to grab a hoodie. Cody appears at my side as I break into a jog. Entering the barn, I head directly to Junior's stall, grabbing his bridle on the way. Slipping it on him, I lead him outside and use an upside-down bucket to stand on to mount. Words aren't needed, and neither are cues. We've done this so many times in the past, Junior knows what to do. Wrapping my hands in his mane, I lean down, and we're off.

Dusk is settling over the land as I let Junior have his head. We race past the house and Ted screaming from the deck and hit open land. One with my horse, I allow him to pick our route, and I simply breathe at the freedom of riding. Junior picks up speed for a short time before slowing to a gentle lope. My mind blanks of all worries, and my body relaxes as I allow myself to enjoy the ride. After we're quite a distance from the ranch buildings, Junior slows to a walk. We walk aimlessly for over an hour before we make our way down a gentle incline. Reaching the edge of a creek, I loosen the reins so Junior can drink.

The only light is moonlight, and luckily, it's close to a full moon. We pick our way across the creek and up the bank before stopping. I slide off and lead Junior, Cody by my side as I think about my options. Give it all up and leave or tough out my situation for now. I know what my grandparents wanted for my future, but they didn't have a clue as to the path it would take for me to get it. I'm not a quitter, but I'm having a lot of days where I'm exhausted from the fight. I drop to my butt on the ground and drape my arms over my raised knees. Cody sits quietly beside me as Junior takes advantage and grazes next to us.

I sit until my butt becomes numb, and my mind is too tired to think anymore. Rising, I lean into my horse and breathe in his scent. Knowing it's time to return home, I lead Junior to the slope that leads down to the creek. Standing on the high side, I swing up on him and settle against his broad, warm back. Lifting the reins and taking another settling breath, we head home to face the consequences of my abrupt departure.

Ivy: Can you swing by the rescue tonight?

Gunner: Yeah. Around 7 or 8pm ok?

Ivy: Yes.

Gunner: Is this going to make Ava happy?

Ivy: She's going to love them!

Gunner: Them? As in more than 1?

Ivy: Bonded pair that can't be separated. Once bonded, they should never be separated. They're perfect though.

Gunner: See you tonight.

I slide my phone into my back pocket and smile. At least this aspect of my life is going well. Giving the two donkeys each a quick cuddle, I make my way through the barn and outside. Walking to the outdoor dog area, I again smile when I see Thor. Even with his battle scars, he's a beautiful dog. He's not at the point where he can have other dogs in the fenced area with him yet, but he's starting to show interest. His tail gives a quick wag, and he makes eye contact with me. I watch as he trots in my direction and then slows to a stop before reaching the fence. He's still very cautious, but he's making huge strides in the right direction. I speak quietly with him for a couple of minutes before tossing him a biscuit. Catching it out of the air, he drops to his belly before devouring his treat.

I decide to let him have a few more minutes playing outside, so I make my way indoors. I can hear Priscilla berating some poor bird in the aviary, so I make my way to the door. Walking in, I see her presiding over the rest as usual. Sitting on her favorite perch, she's on a rant.

"Someone's got their feathers ruffled. What's up, Prissy?" I ask.

"Fools. Damn fools. Fools!" she screeches while wildly flapping her wings.

"They're not following orders, are they?" I ask, already knowing the answer.

"My perch. Mine!" Prissy shouts in her perfect Southern-Belle accent.

"Come hang in the office with me and give the others a break from General Prissy, okay?" I offer while lifting my arm.

After another show of feather-ruffling and posturing, Prissy takes flight and lands on my wrist. We close the door behind us, walk down the hall, and enter the office. Prissy immediately flies to the perch by the desk and lands gently. I ignore her muttering and take a seat at the desk. Pulling up the donkey's info, I reread everything, so I'm prepared for Gunner's visit.

Lola Wright

Chapter 5
Pigeon

Hearing my name shouted, I look to see Gunner walking out of his office. When he nods toward the main door, I stand up and follow. Once outside, my club president turns to me.

"You were raised on a farm, right?" he asks.

"Yeah," I answer while wondering why that's important to him.

"What do you know about donkeys?"

"Ava about to own another ass, Prez?" I ask, grinning because I think I know where this is going.

"Maybe and quit grinning at me. I'm not soft, pussy-whipped, or any of those other names you and Axel have tossed out. I just like making my woman happy, and apparently, animals do that for her. I swear to fucking Christ, Pigeon, if you keep smirking at me, I'm going to remove your face," Gunner threatens heatedly.

I can't help it and start laughing out loud. I'm poking a very large bear, but it always makes my day to annoy the guys in the club. Not having a woman makes it easy for me to taunt the ones that do. After a minute of enjoying his annoyance, I quiet down and answer his question.

"Donkeys are smart. Smarter than horses and are incredible animals. They're very protective and will outright kill things they take as a threat. You don't want to cross one because they'll never forget or forgive that shit. Ava and your kids would love one, no doubt. You should always have two, though, and best yet a bonded pair. They form bonds that last their lifetimes. That's not to say that they won't form tight bonds with people or other animals too, though. You give them kindness, it gets returned. They're cheaper to own than horses and less likely to get sick. Tough, durable, and protective. You thinking standard size, mammoth or minis?"

"FurEver Homes has a bonded pair of minis that I'm going to look at tonight. Can you come and tell me what you think? If we think they'd work out okay for Ava and the kids, I'll take Ava there tomorrow and let her decide before the kids know anything about it. Vex said we can set them up at his barn until I get one built," Gunner answers.

"Yeah, Prez, I'll go with you," I reply while giving him a slap on the shoulder.

"I'll go too," Axel announces as he appears next to Gunner.

"Didn't your dad ever teach you it's wrong to eavesdrop?" Gunner asks with a scowl.

"No, and it's not eavesdropping when your voice carries like it does," Axel replies with his own scowl.

"Why the frown, my little bald princess?" I ask Axel.

"Fuck you, Pigeon."

"Either Bailey has left with Alex, or Bailey's still refusing to get pregnant again. Which is it, VP?" I taunt Axel now that I'm done taunting Gunner. For now, anyway.

"Bailey's pissed at me. Pointing out that she can work, take a few art classes, and be pregnant at the same time is apparently a bad thing to say. Fuck me, I might as well buy the whole damn flower shop and own it myself. I'd make a mint and stay in business for fucking ever," Axel answers in a disgusted voice.

"You'd go broke because you'd be your only customer. Maybe you shouldn't have pointed out that Ava is pregnant, runs a business, and has three kids already," Gunner advises but does so with a huge grin. It's so wrong, but he's loving Axel's misery. "Women aren't big on being compared to other women."

Hearing this, I wince. I'm single, no woman other than the occasional stripper or one-night stand, and I know better than to say something like that to any woman. What the hell, Axel? It's like he wants to die a slow, painful death, and he's chosen Bailey to aid him in that endeavor.

"I didn't mean it the way it came out, but she didn't wait long enough for me to explain. She went nuclear, and I thought it best to give her some space," Axel mumbles.

"At least out here, if she comes at you with knives, you'll see her coming," I add.

"If you're coming with us, keep your mouth shut. I don't want Ava and the kids knowing about the donkeys until I've had a chance to see them and to talk with Ivy some more," Gunner orders.

"I might eavesdrop, you dick, but I'm not a gossip," Axel argues.

I leave them to their arguing and return to the clubhouse. Entering the kitchen, I stare at Ava until she notices me. As soon as she does, I give her my best puppy dog look and take a seat at a worktable. I grin when I hear her sigh because I know I'm about to get fed. Minutes later, Ava slides a large bowl of homemade soup, slices of still warm buttered bread, and a sleeve of crackers in front of me.

"You know you're my favorite, Ava," I tell her.

"I know, Pigeon. How you doing, honey?" she asks softly.

"I should be asking you that instead of sitting here waiting for you to feed me," I answer with more than a twinge of guilt hitting my gut.

"I feel great. I keep telling Gunner that too, but he still worries. But honestly, I think my body likes being pregnant. I have more energy and get a lot done each day. Everything is ready for this baby, and I'm not ready to just sit and wait yet. When I am, I'll hunker down and let the rest of you handle things," Ava says with a serene smile.

While eating, I chat with Ava as she continues cooking and stacking containers of food on the counter. When I look around, I'm amazed at how much food she's cooked today.

"Why all the food?" I ask.

"Gunner told me about the visitors we're getting. When I heard their plans changed and they wouldn't be here for another week, it gave me time to stock the freezers and fridges for them. He said they'd be lying low, and this way, there'll be enough food prepared to feed however many come. The other women cleaned the rooms and put out fresh bedding and towels. After today, we have the clubhouse stocked and ready," she answers.

"Reeves and Cam are staying with Horse and me, so their rooms are available. What else do you need done? I had Cam make a liquor run, and he and Toes have the bar well-stocked," I tell her something she probably already knows.

"As soon as I finish in here today, we're done. Trudy asked for the kids today, so it freed me up to get this finished. We're good, Pigeon."

"You get the food into the containers how you want it, and I'll get it all put away. Toes can clean up the kitchen tonight. That work for you?" I ask.

"Sounds good."

Gunner and Axel join us, and we help Ava finish up for the day. Gunner walks Ava home and sends Toes in to clean up the kitchen. When he returns, the three of us mount our bikes and point them toward the animal rescue.

Ivy opens the door and grins up at each of us as we enter FurEver Homes. I notice I'm not the only biker that stiffens at the bruise that covers the majority of the left side of her face. Her cheekbone took the brunt of whatever caused the bruise because it's darkest in that area. After closing the door behind us, Ivy turns to face three large, unsmiling bikers. I watch as her own smile fades, her eyes drop, and her hand makes a quick waving motion at the bruise.

"It's nothing. Really, it isn't. Head bop from a horse," she mumbles unconvincingly before pushing past us and walking quickly down a hallway.

My eyes meet Gunner's then Axel's, and I know they're not believing her any more than I am. Pushing past them, I follow Ivy through another door and outside. She subtly positions herself, so the bruised cheekbone is on her opposite side from where we're walking beside her. I let her have this play, but it's only temporary. Eventually,

I'll be asking questions I'm already positive she's not going to want to answer.

Entering the large horse barn, Ivy stops at the second stall. Glancing inside, I see two mini donkeys. One brown with the faint marking of a cross on his back. A Bethlehem donkey or at least a mix. The other is white with brown spots. Both are no more than 34 inches, if that, at the withers. They're definitely minis, and I know instantly that Ava is going to fall in love again.

"Damn, they're small, Gunner. Isn't Ava a little big to ride them?" Axel asks seriously.

Ivy laughs at the same time as I do before explaining patiently that the donkeys aren't to be ridden. They're pets, not rideable animals. Axel looks confused at first but listens closely to Ivy. After that, she explains to Gunner about their history, temperaments, housing, and care requirements. She's knowledgeable and knows her equines.

Glancing back to the donkeys, I look into their intelligent eyes and know they're going to be living near the clubhouse soon. As Ivy answers questions from Gunner and Axel, I open the stall door and slip inside. Holding the back of my hand toward them, I wait. Donkeys are cautious animals and won't allow anyone or anything to rush them. They're curious, but they need time to think things through before they react. Knowing this, I continue to wait. After a few moments, the brown donkey slowly approaches, neck stretched out, to sniff my hand. When he survives our encounter, the white-spotted donkey does the same.

"What's their names?" I ask in a quiet voice.

"Brown one is Moose. The spotted one is Matilda. He's a treat-seeking donkey and lets his stomach determine his wariness level. Matilda is the more cautious of the two but tends to enjoy affection more than treats once she's decided she likes someone. Both are friendly, affectionate, and love being groomed. Moose will never walk away from someone with a brush in their hand, especially if they are willing to scratch his rump. He's pushier for attention than she is. Matilda is less pushy but waits patiently to be noticed. Neither have ever been abused or neglected, and in fact, were cared for and well-loved. Because of that, they've never shown aggression to humans and love kids," Ivy answers as she enters the stall to stand beside me.

"So, you think they'd do well with kids? Small kids?" Gunner questions.

"Absolutely. They've been here for about a month, but I waited to call you until I'd spent time with them. I wouldn't recommend them if I didn't believe they'd do great with your little ones. Most donkeys don't like dogs at all, but they've done fine with the dogs I've introduced them to. So far, neither has shown aggression to any other animal. They were raised with goats. That's a huge plus because goats are naughty, and yet the donkeys are patient and get along well with them. They lead, tie, trailer, and are great about having their hooves trimmed. I've introduced them to the various types of animals here with no problems. I'd adopt them myself if my situation were different," Ivy answers, saying the last sentence in a quieter voice.

Gunner and Axel enter the stall and follow my example of letting the donkeys approach them when they're ready. It's not long, and Moose is using Axel's leg to scratch his ass against. Gunner soon finds Matilda quietly leaning against his leg, thoroughly enjoying the neck scratches he's giving her. Aiming my eyes to Ivy's, I see the soft look in hers as she watches two bikers bonding with two donkeys.

"I wanted to get a look at them and talk with you before I told Ava about them. Now, I wished I had brought her with us. I think these two are exactly what she's always wanted," Gunner says to Ivy before swinging his head toward me. "What's your thoughts on them, Pigeon?"

"They're perfect and will be well-loved by your wife and kids. I trust Ivy's assessment of them. Maybe you should call your wife, Prez," I answer honestly.

Ivy's eyes meet mine, and I see the question in them. I answer it before she asks.

"Gunner asked me to come along tonight because I was raised on a farm. I know animals, and I know Ava and his kids."

Ivy nods in understanding and gives me a small smile before turning back to Gunner.

"I'm here until midnight if you want to call Ava. If you want to wait until tomorrow, anyone here can help you with the paperwork, or I'll be back at 4pm. If you decide you want them, I can help with transportation whenever you're ready for them. I have to go bring a dog in from the outside run, but I'll be back in a couple of minutes. It's a big commitment, and I get that, but I know your wife too. If you call her, you've as good as signed your name on the adoption papers."

Ivy flashes a knowing smile at Gunner before she leaves the barn. I turn back to look at Moose and Matilda, and I know what she just said is the truth. So do the other two men standing in the stall. I watch as Gunner pulls his phone out and makes the call.

Following Ivy to the office, we pass the aviary on the way. Axel and I stop in front of it and stare inside. Birds of all sizes and colors, most in large, elaborate cages are chattering, singing, and generally being noisy. There are a few that look like Mac, but most are smaller birds with several to a cage. My eyes are automatically drawn to a large, white cockatoo. It's standing on a perch looking directly at Axel.

"After having to put up with Mac, this room is the stuff of my nightmares," Axel states.

I bark out a laugh at my VP, knowing he's speaking the truth. Mac goes out of his way to make Axel's life difficult, and we all get to sit back and enjoy the show they put on.

"Are you the one Mac complains to me about?" Ivy asks from behind us.

Axel and I both turn to look down at her smiling face, and Axel nods his head.

"Last time Ava brought Mac with her, he asked me if I could have you adopted out," Ivy informs us with what sounds suspiciously like a small snort. "Like we do with the pigs, he said. He offered cashews as payment." This time there was no doubt. She laughed, snorted a little, then outright laughed again at Axel's look of disgust.

"Mac's a pain in the ass that needs to disappear," Axel informs Ivy.

"Did you know he calls you Assman?" Ivy says with a large grin aimed at Axel's scowling face.

"Mac's got a big mouth that needs to be taped shut," Axel replies in an irritated voice.

A loud wolf whistle pierces the air, and we all turn to look at the culprit. The same white bird is still staring at Axel when it lets loose another whistle. Seriously, this bird could rival any construction worker that's ever whistled at a passing female.

"Hot man alert!" the bird coos in what can only be called a sexy, sultry voice.

"Priscilla! Behave yourself, little lady," Ivy admonishes on a laugh.

"Sexy man!" the bird states while talking over Ivy.

"Finally! A bird with brains and good taste," Axel exclaims while opening the aviary door and walking up to the bird.

"Huge yamagurgle!" the bird informs Axel while leaning close to his face.

"Huge what?" Gunner questions Ivy.

"I have no idea," Ivy answers as we walk through the door and stop next to Axel.

"Very big yamagurgle," the bird now says in another cooing voice.

"Must be bird slang for cock," Axel informs us with a grin.

Turning back to the bird, Axel reaches up and strokes the yellow mohawk-type feathers on the top of the bird's head. This is beyond strange to watch. I swear this bird is flirting, and Axel's eating it up. I look at Gunner to see his expression of confusion that has to match my own.

"Name?" the bird asks with a head tilt and while never taking its eyes off Axel.

"I'm Axel. What's your name, you gorgeous thing?"

"Priscilla," she answers in what I'm positive is a beautiful southern drawl.

I turn to Ivy to see she's amused at this odd encounter.

"Priscilla's a female?" Gunner asks with humor in his voice.

"Yes, Prissy is a female cockatoo who originally lived in Savannah, Georgia. She's, um, well, she can be a handful," Ivy answers in a hushed tone.

"For shame, Ivy. For shame," Prissy admonishes.

"Love you, Prissy," Ivy states quickly, and it was the right thing to say. Prissy's feathers smooth out a bit as she continues staring at Axel.

Before this bizarre meeting goes any further, I hear a buzzer ring in the distance.

"That must be Ava. I'll go let her in," Ivy says and then disappears out the door.

"Do you like the other birds, Prissy?" Axel asks.

"Fools. Dumb-ass fools," Prissy answers immediately.

"Do you know who Mac is?" Axel continues questioning.

"I's prettier," Prissy responds while raising her head feathers until they are standing nearly straight up.

I shake my head at this weird-ass conversation and exit the aviary. Gunner follows me out and closes the door on Axel and his new love interest just as Ava and Ivy come into view. Ava's face is beaming, and I can feel her excitement. Rushing up to Gunner, she plants her hands on his biceps and raises up on her toes to wait for the kiss he drops on her mouth.

"Where are they?" Ava asks excitedly.

Gunner doesn't respond, but I watch as he grins down at his wife. After a moment, he points to the door and then rushes to get his arm around his wife before she can break into a run. Tucking her into his side, he slows their pace to a more fitting one for a pregnant lady. I watch as they exit the building then glance back at Axel. He's still carrying on a conversation with a flirting bird, so I walk off.

I find the building that houses the dogs and enter. I stop and pet a few on my way down the long aisle, but I already know where I'm going. At the end is the kennel that has the new dog in it that Ivy's been working with. Stopping in front, I watch as Thor stiffens then shuffles back a few steps. With slow movements and speaking to him in a quiet voice, I take a seat on the floor in front of his kennel. I wait until his curiosity wins out over his fear, and he inches closer. It takes time, but I have nowhere else to be, so I wait him out.

Noticing the scars and the half-missing ear, I beat back the anger that tries to rise in my chest. Animals sense those things, and I don't want to scare him. Breathing slow and even breaths, I succeed, and he continues inching closer. When he's within a foot of the front of the kennel, he drops to his belly. His eyes never leave mine, and I know he's waiting to see if his show of trust will be abused.

Slowly, I put the back of my hand against the kennel and wait. After a few long moments, he leans close enough to sniff it. Still not moving, I wait. Eventually, I feel his wet tongue lick my hand before pulling back to a safe distance. I tell him what a good boy he is and watch as his tail gives a small wag.

"Hey, Thor. What a brave boy you're being today," Ivy says in a soothing tone as she takes a seat next to me.

I heard her enter the room but hadn't taken my attention off Thor. Looking at her now, I'm again fighting back anger when my eyes land on her bruise. Ivy's eyes meet mine, and she shifts somewhat to obscure my view of the battered side of her face. When she hands me a dog biscuit, I let the questions I have for her drop for the time being. Taking the biscuit, I hold it through the wire toward Thor. Once again, it takes a moment, but he leans close enough to carefully take the treat from my hand.

"Ava bakes those treats and drops them off regularly. Dale, a guy that works the day shift, swears they smell good enough that he's always tempted to eat them himself," Ivy says on a small laugh.

"Knowing Ava, they're probably made from the best ingredients and are safe for human consumption. I'll ask Chubs when I see him because chances are, he's had a few already," I say. "Is Gunner going to be a donkey dad now?"

"No doubt. At least he seems happy about it too," Ivy responds.

"Gunner's happy anytime Ava's happy. Doesn't matter why, he just is. The donkeys will have a good life with them. Their kids will spoil them rotten, and the girls will be painting their hooves and adding ribbons to their tails for sure. You chose well by thinking of Ava," I say.

"I've seen you here before, but I don't think we've met. I'm Ivy."

"I'm Pigeon. You have a phone on you, Ivy?" I ask.

Giving me a questioning look, Ivy pulls her phone out of her pocket.

"I want you to add my number to your contacts, Ivy," I tell her.

"Okay. Can I ask why?" she asks as she opens up her contact list, finger hovering over her phone.

I gently take the phone from her and add my name and number. Handing it back to her, I say, "I want you to call that number the next time that horse head bops you. When you do, I'll come. I can, and will, do whatever level of intervention you want or need. I'll get you to a safe place or make the place you're at safe. I also have no issue with putting the horse down in a permanent manner. Your decision, but I'll come no matter when you call."

I watch her face as my words sink in, and I catch the fleeting look of hope, possibly relief, as they do. She quickly ducks her head, and when she lifts it, the look is gone, and her expression is of resignation. I wait, knowing she'll speak when she's gathered her thoughts. I expect a denial or anger, but instead, I get truth.

"If I do that, I'll lose everything my grandparents worked for and wanted for me," Ivy answers in a soft, defeated voice, shoulders slumping.

"I don't know your circumstances, Ivy. But I do know no woman deserves whatever you're going through. I also know there is always a way, even if it's not obvious at first. I'm willing to help however you need it, and I have a club brother whose woman is an expert in this kind of thing. She can help you figure out anything you need to and come up with a good solution. You don't have to deal with this alone if you don't want to. Use that number, yeah?"

Ivy hesitates for a moment before looking at me again. Another moment, and she gives a small nod.

As much as I want to fix this problem right now, I know she needs to be the one to make that decision. Standing, I reach down, grasp her hand, and help her to her feet.

"Thank you, Pigeon," Ivy whispers just before the door opens, and Ava comes rushing in.

I release her hand and step back as Ava and Gunner approach. I partially listen to their conversation, but I turn back to Thor. I find he's laid himself as close to the door of the kennel as he can physically get. While Ivy and I were talking, he relaxed and placed himself close to the humans. Huge step for a scared, abused dog. Crouching down, I slide my hand through the kennel and run my finger over his head. I get a tail wag and a slight body wiggle before he turns to lick my hand. I think I made a new friend tonight. Maybe even two new friends.

"Did I see a look? I'm sure I did. I saw a look," Axel says again.

Again, I ignore him and continue sipping my beer. We're back at the clubhouse after leaving the animal rescue, and while Gunner and Ava headed home, Axel stayed to have a beer with me. I'm contemplating buying flowers for Bailey myself just so Axel feels it's safe to head home.

"What kind of look?" asks Horse as he takes a seat next to Axel.

"Don't encourage him, you dick," I mumble before downing the last of my beer and reaching over the bar to grab another.

"A look that said there's some interest there," Axel answers.

"That true, Pigeon? You having dirty thoughts about the lady at the rescue?" Horse questions with a smirk. "Isn't she a little old for you? I would've never thought you'd go for the cougar type."

"Not the lady who runs it. The young one that works evenings there. Ivy. The very young one," Axel replies, emphasizing the words "very young."

"You're listening to a guy who spent the evening flirting with a bird," I inform Horse.

"Prissy is gorgeous, has great taste, and is intelligent! Who wouldn't flirt with her?" Axel argues.

"Wait a minute. I thought her name was Ivy. Who's Prissy?" Horse asks, clearly confused.

"Prissy is a cockatoo who lives at the rescue. She's smart and very vocal. Ivy is the young lady that works evenings and is the best with the animals. Why are we talking about them?" Chubs asks as he and Lucy join us at the bar.

"Ivy called Gunner about a couple of donkeys she thought Ava would like. We went to look at them, and Axel met and flirted shamelessly with Prissy while we were there. It was beyond disturbing, to say the least," I say, bringing them up to date on this strange conversation.

"And I saw a look between Ivy and Pigeon. It was definitely a look, and he's now trying to deny it, but I saw it. I did," Axel insists.

I groan when I see Chubs and Lucy both turn to focus in on me. Lucy grins, but Chubs just stares at me for a minute before speaking.

"Ivy's great. She's nice, takes exceptional care of the animals, and I like her. Something bothers me with her, though. Do you know her, Pigeon?" Chubs asks in a quiet, serious voice.

"No, not really. What bothers you, brother?" I ask because Chubs has great intuition about people, and he notices the little things that others miss.

"I stop by there a lot, dropping off treats and donations for Ava, and usually go in the evening after work. Ivy seems to have a lot of little accidents, you know? Bruises, moving stiff, those kinds of things. I've tried chatting her up, but she's reserved most of the time. I know she's single and doesn't have a boyfriend because I point blank asked her. But some of Ivy's mannerisms remind me of the women at New Horizons. Maybe I've spent too much time helping Pippa and just see every bruise as abuse now, but I don't think so," Chubs answers.

"Her face was bruised tonight. All of us noticed it, and she was clearly uncomfortable that we did," Axel adds, all joking aside now.

"I gave her my number. Told her to call, and I'd come. I don't know her story, but someone is clearly mistreating her. She did admit that but didn't say who it is. I was going to speak with Pippa tomorrow to see what else can be done," I say, and even I can hear the underlying anger in my voice. "You're at New Horizons a lot, Lucy. What do you think I should do?"

"Giving her your number does a couple of things, Pigeon. It gives her an out, and it lets her know she's not alone anymore. There's someone willing to help, and that's huge in the mindset of women that are being abused. They almost always feel alone and unable to change their circumstances. You did the right thing by doing that and by not pushing for details," Lucy answers immediately. "Pippa will know the best way to handle this, but unfortunately, there usually isn't a lot anyone can do until the woman reaches out. Might be a good idea to chat with Livi and James too. They're also trained in this type of thing."

"Ivy reaches out to you; you call me. You don't go alone unless absolutely necessary. We'll help in any way we can, but we don't know her situation and having a brother at your back is safer for everyone," Axel orders.

"Any way we can keep closer tabs on her in the meantime?" Lucy asks.

"Yeah, we can. We monitor the rescue at the security company. I'll let Rex and Reeves know, and we can keep a closer eye on the cameras. At least while she's at work, she'll have eyes on her," I answer.

"Let them know tonight, Pigeon. With our visitors coming, the club's going to be stretched thin for the next few weeks, but there's enough of us to help Ivy, too, if needed. The club will back whatever play you think is best. I'll speak with Gunner and bring him up to speed on this," Axel states as he stands to leave.

"Will do, VP," I reply.

Axel is a character, full of life and attitude, but always the first one to offer help. While I love giving him shit, I also appreciate him as a brother.

I stand, give Lucy a one-armed hug, and walk out. When I'm sitting astride my bike, I pull out my phone and make the calls. I make another one and will be meeting up with Pippa at New Horizons tomorrow.

Lola Wright

Chapter 6
Ivy

I'm happy about how things went tonight with Ava. I know I've found the perfect family for Moose and Matilda, and that's the best part of my job. I stop at the aviary, make sure everyone is tucked in for the night, and shut down the lights. Heading to the office, I drop into the desk chair and bring the computer to life. I work until all my notes are done on the various animals and then write a note for Margie about the upcoming adoption.

Caught up for now, I go to the breakroom and heat up my dinner. Eating in the silence, I think back to my conversation with Pigeon. His words gave me a rush of hope before reality crashed back down on me. If Ted was a boyfriend or husband, I'd leave. But if I leave the ranch, there will be nothing left of everything my grandparents worked so hard for. My future and dreams are centered around the ranch, and I can't just walk away from it.

Papa and Nana took Ted and me in and raised us with love. Our mother, their only child, was unable to care for her young children due to mental health issues. As Mom's mental state deteriorated, and with our father a distant memory, Nana took over more and more of our care. Eventually, my grandparents had to make the heartbreaking decision to have our mother committed to a mental institution. They packed us kids up and moved us to their home. I was only five years old and yet so grateful for the security and simplicity of ranch life.

Mom improved somewhat over time but still needed supervision with her illness and medications, so my grandparents had her moved to a long-term residential care facility. It's nice with great staff, and Mom does well there. So well, in fact, that she doesn't want to leave. I visit as often as I can, but I don't think Ted's been there in years.

Ted's always been quick to write off anyone that is no longer capable of doing things to benefit him. When Nana became sick, I watched in horror as Ted's attitude toward her changed too. He was careful to hide it while Papa was still alive, though. After Papa died, Ted no longer had a physical threat to keep him in line. It broke my heart watching the realization dawn on Nana that her beloved grandson wasn't the man she thought she raised. It seems horrible to say now, but I'm glad she passed before she saw the true extent of Ted's mean side.

Dragging my thoughts away from Ted, I let them go to Pigeon. Tall, built, longish black hair, and heavily tatted, he's exactly what a mind conjures up when thinking biker. Worn jeans, scuffed boots, black hoodie under his leather cut, knife sheath on one hip, and he wears the biker gear like he was born in it. It's his voice that caused shivers to run up my spine, though. Deep, yet soft, sincere, and concerned. There was a promise in his words that I instinctively know he'd never break.

When the club members have come to the rescue to help with projects, I've seen Pigeon. Always laughing, teasing the other men, and enjoying himself. Being female, there's no way I wouldn't have noticed him, but tonight was the first time we've spoken. I'm not sure why it was so easy to admit the truth to him when I've denied it to others, though. Maybe because he didn't ask, he already knew the truth. No judgment, only an offer to help. Kindness when he owes me nothing. A good man, and that's something I haven't been around in a while.

After eating, I finish up my duties and then hang with Thor until the end of my shift. Making the drive home, I dread reaching the place that used to be my sanctuary.

Over the next few days, I do well at avoiding Ted. I keep busy, get ahead on a few things, and do a disappearing act when I hear Ted or Todd's voice. I also have several phone conversations with Ava, then Gunner, about the donkeys, barn plans, fencing, and feed. Ava's done her homework and knows what to expect. Gunner is being more practical than most husbands and understands that this barn needs to be built for more than the two donkeys they're currently adopting. Planning ahead, he knows that eventually, the donkeys won't be the only barnyard animals using the barn and land.

I promised Ava I would meet her at the clubhouse before my shift today to look at the temporary accommodations they've set up on land adjacent to theirs. I hustle through my chores, hit the shower, and then the road. Singing loudly and badly along with the radio, I follow the directions Ava provided. Pulling onto the road to the clubhouse, I'm stopped by a large gate. A large black man steps outside from a small building next to the gate and approaches my truck.

"Hi. Name?" he asks while flashing a friendly smile.

"Ivy. I'm here to—"

"Meet with Ava. She said to send you up. Just follow the road. You'll see the clubhouse," he says before I receive another blinding smile, and he reenters the building.

I wave as I drive through the gate, follow the road and before long, see the clubhouse. Even if I didn't notice the very large building, I could never have missed the crowd waiting outside. Grinning as I exit my truck, I drop to my knees just in time for Gee to crash into me.

"Hey, Gee! How you doing, you sexy little pig beast?" I ask him as I hug his chubbiness.

Pig snorts of happiness erupt from the happy little guy as I sit back on my heels. Noticing his shirt, I start to laugh, then give a snort that sounds a lot like Gee's.

"Data Hog" is emblazoned across his back in bright purple print on a black shirt.

"Ivy!" my name is screeched as I look up to see Mac coming in for a landing. Getting my arm up in time, he lands on it before he starts making kissing sounds.

"Mac Daddy! Still love me?" I ask.

"Yep!"

"Okay, guys, let Ivy up," Ava orders.

Mac moves up my arm and onto my shoulder. I give Gee another quick hug then stand. I grin when I see the twins near their mom, vibrating with excitement. Luke is standing behind them, shy smile in place. He gives me the sign for hello, and I return it. I only know a few basics of ASL, but I try to learn more each time I'm around Ava and Luke. Glancing at the rest of the crowd, I see several familiar faces and a few that aren't.

Ava makes quick introductions, and I nod to each one. We decide to load up in Gunner's truck, and he drives Ava, me, and the kids to their house. Gunner takes some time and shows me the layout of their land and where he was thinking of putting the barn. He explains how a club brother owns the land behind his, and that they're working out a deal on Gunner buying some acreage from him. I smile up at him because he's smart to realize he's standing on a slippery slope. Wives and little girls will always want more animals. More animals mean more land will be needed, and he's thought ahead. After I offer some suggestions, along with explanations, we load up again and take a road through trees and open land to his club brother's house.

Stepping down from the truck, I stare open-mouthed at the house. It's almost indescribable in its size and beauty. I hear the twins giggle at me, but I slowly spin to take in the lawn, pool, large decks, and then the barn. Being a ranch girl, the barn draws my attention even more than the house. The phrase "work of art" comes to mind as I walk toward it. I know what works with a barn and what's just for show and whoever built this knew horses. They cared about their horses and built their barn to what they needed more than trying to make a statement. I'm not even inside yet, and I'm totally in love. I don't notice the kids racing ahead of me, but I do hear the amused voice behind me.

"Barn orgasm incoming."

"Vex! Be nice!" Ava says with a laugh.

Turning, my mouth drops open again, and I stand looking like an idiot, I'm sure. I'm staring at another work of art, this time in male form. Nearly gold eyes watch me in amusement while I fumble for composure. Before I gain any, I feel a blush sliding up my face. Abruptly, I turn to Ava and silently mouth the word "wow."

"Yeah, yeah, yeah, we know," Gunner grumbles. "Vex is too fucking pretty for words. Whatever. Vex, this is Ivy."

"Hey, Ivy. Welcome. Don't mind Gunner's attitude. It's not his fault he was born ass ugly and bitter about it," Vex states with a large, white smile.

"Nice to meet you, Vex," I say now that I've found my voice again.

"Take a look around and see what you think. Anything that should be changed to make things safer for the donkeys, let us know. They'll be staying here for a while, so we'd like them to be comfortable," Vex says with a wave at the barn.

After another moment of simply staring at him, I turn and walk away. I ignore the male laughter, but when Ava slings her arm through mine, I grip it. Stepping through the side door of the barn, I turn to her, releasing her arm.

"You should have warned me!" I whisper-shout.

"I'm so sorry, Ivy. I've gotten used to him and didn't think to be honest. If it's any consolation, every single one of us women in the club have embarrassed ourselves over him at one point or another," Ava answers with a grin. "Well, all of us except Lucy, that is. She sees nobody but Chubs."

Taking a deep breath, I release it and grin back at Ava.

"Chubs is the best, so I get that."

"Yeah, he is. Let's walk around and see what you think."

Arriving back at the clubhouse, Gunner invites me inside for coffee before I have to leave for my shift. Entering, the first person I see is Pigeon. He's sitting at the bar, back against it, facing the door. Standing next to him is the guy from the gatehouse only now he's in a police uniform and a pretty female cop. Sprawled out asleep next to her foot is a chubby English Bulldog.

"Has Denver P.D. switched from German Shepherds to bulldogs now?" I ask while grinning down at the dog.

"Lord, I hope not! I'd have to chase suspects on foot while carrying his fat ass," laughs the male cop.

"Ivy, meet James and Livi. Snots is the slumbering princess, and it's by far his best skill," Pigeon states.

"Hi, Livi, James. Nice to meet you," I respond before bending down and giving the dog a pat on the head. He doesn't move but does start giving up little doggie snores.

"Did the twins get a hold of him?" I ask while meeting Pigeon's eyes.

"If you're referring to the pedicure and leg warmers, then no. That's all Terry's doing," Livi answers with a laugh.

I have no idea who Terry is, but I'm getting the sense that pedicures are common in this club. I nod like all of this is normal when it's really not and turn to accept a cup from Gunner. When Pigeon nods to the stool next to him, I take a seat.

"Ivy? What are you doing here?" I hear Craig's voice before his face appears on the opposite side of the bar. I instantly recognize his voice, but it takes my eyes a moment to recognize his face under all the dirt and grime covering it, though.

"Hey, Craig. I stopped by to help Gunner and Ava with where to put their barn," I answer, having no idea that I'm about to unleash Craig on society.

"Their barn? Their barn for what?" Craig asks while aiming his look at Gunner.

I have to admit to being impressed that someone Craig's size shows zero fear of someone Gunner's size. The look Gunner received was one of a young boy just realizing he's the only one who doesn't know something, and he's not happy about that fact.

"Before this turns ugly, Craig, are you sure you're okay with babysitting Snots for me?" Livi asks quickly as she grips James by the shirt sleeve and starts pulling him toward the door with her.

"Yeah, Livi, I got him. Go make Denver safe," Craig answers while keeping narrowed eyes on Gunner.

As Livi and James bolt out the door, I hear Pigeon snicker. Looking at him, I see his amused face watching Gunner.

"Gunner and Ava are adopting a couple of donkeys from the rescue. They asked Ivy for some advice on a barn for them. I can't believe the twins or Luke didn't tell you. They're so excited about it," Pigeon says, and I realize he's loving the fact that he's stirring the pot.

"And nobody told me? No one?" Craig asks in a voice that can only be described as an alpha bear in training tone.

"And they didn't ask you to go to the rescue with them when they went to see the donkeys either," Pigeon interjects.

"Shut it, Pigeon. You're not helping," Gunner states.

"Not trying to, Prez," Pigeon answers nonchalantly.

"I know all about donkeys. Chubs helped me while doing our learning things. I learned about goats too, so if Miss Ava got some, I would know how to help her with them. I learn all these things, but I don't know that donkeys are going to be living here. How come? Huh? How come?" Craig demands in a rising voice.

While Craig's talking, I see a biker walking up from behind Gunner and Craig. I've seen him before, helping Trigger build the dog park at the rescue, and I think his name's Pooh. Next to him is Axel with a tiny, female version of himself riding on his shoulders. I can't help the grin when Pooh stops abruptly, cringes at Craig's words, and turns to make an escape.

"Hey, Brother Pooh!" Pigeon shouts as Gunner's head swings around to where Pooh's trying to reach the door before he's noticed.

Turning back to face us, Pooh shoots a dark look toward Pigeon before saying, "You suck, Pigeon."

"Maybe I should get going," I mutter.

"And miss all this fun?" Pigeon asks with a wicked grin while slinging his arm over my shoulders and pulling me tight to his side.

"Hell, even I went and saw them at the rescue already," Axel states while turning fake, sad eyes to Craig.

"Why would you take Axel and not me? I love going to the rescue, and you left me out of that too! I babysit all the animals, and I take good care of them!" Craig shouts with anger rising.

"Craig, honey, it was a spur-of-the-moment visit there and kind of late in the evening. And yes, you do babysit, and all the pets love you because you're so good with them," Ava interjects while trying to soothe the little boy's hurt feelings.

"I met a gorgeous bird named Prissy when I was invited to go," Axel says in a clear attempt to goad Craig's anger.

"Axel, stop!" Ava says, shooting a look at Axel.

"What? I did, and she loved me," Axel defends.

"Prissy's cool, but she would never like you. She's very fussy about who she likes," Craig says with a small sniff of disdain.

"She did too! She flirted with me and everything," Axel answers smugly. "Even told me I had a big dick."

My eyes go wide at this statement and the fact that it was made in front of kids.

"You're a project, aren't you?" Craig asks Axel while dropping his hands to his hips and shaking his head.

The adults, minus Axel, all laugh at Craig's comment, but the little boy is still in a snit. He feels left out, and his feelings are hurt. My soft side responds to him immediately.

"Craig, if your parents agree, I would love to have you spend a shift with me at the rescue. We have some new piglets, a couple of tiny goat kids that have to be bottle-fed still, and I could use the help," I offer.

Craig's entire face goes from angry to happy and excited.

"Really, Ivy? I could come for hours?" he asks.

"Absolutely. I'd enjoy having the company," I assure him, and I realize I mean it wholeheartedly.

"You have no idea what you're getting yourself into, Ivy," Axel says with a hoot of laughter. "Hide the Sharpies is my advice."

"Shut it, Assman. Can I go, Pooh?" Craig asks excitedly.

"I'll double-check with your mom, but I'm sure it'll be fine," Pooh answers while Craig throws his arms around Pooh's legs for a moment before racing around the bar, coming at me.

At the last moment, Pigeon removes his arm from around my shoulders and throws his hand up, landing it on Craig's forehead. It stops Craig's forward motion and saves me from whatever is now all over Pooh's jeans. Craig steps back, glares at Pigeon but then turns a beaming, dirty face to me.

"When?" he asks.

"Talk to your mom, and we'll work it out. I promise," I tell him.

"I can't wait! Thanks, Ivy!" Craig shouts, fist-bumps Pigeon, and turns to Snots.

It takes effort and determination, but the dirty little boy gets the lazy dog to his feet, and they walk out.

"If he swears like a sailor while he's with you, it's because his mom has a potty mouth," Pooh says with a grin.

I get home that night to find that Ted and Todd have left the ranch for the next few days. I feel like a huge weight has been removed from my shoulders, knowing they're gone to a cattle auction in New Mexico. It's like being a prisoner and finding out you just got paroled. I pick up Tabitha, cuddle her close while letting Cody in the back door. Turning on some music, I drop into a kitchen chair and simply relax. Looking around, I groan at the mess the guys left in the kitchen. I set Tabitha down, grab a garbage bag and make a round of the house picking up beer bottles. It takes time, but eventually, the downstairs looks like it did when I left today.

It's late, and I need to get to bed, but I decide to take a bath first. I've only taken showers for ages now, partly due to lack of time and partly because I'm not comfortable taking one with the men in the house. Sad, maybe a bit paranoid, but true. I don't trust them. Grabbing a Coke and my phone, I gather clean jammies and make my way to the bathroom. Closing the door behind me, I twist the water on and search for some bath salts. Finding a tiny bit left, I add them to the water and strip. I remove my contacts and slip on my glasses. Sinking into the warm, fragrant water, I sigh at how good it feels.

While shaving, I hear the door rattle. Two of Tabitha's paws, upside down, are poking under the door. She hates it when I close any door on her, and she's letting me know. She continues rattling the door and now adds some pitiful meows. After another moment, I step out of the tub and crack the door open. Walking in, tail swishing, she gives me an earful of cat attitude. I slide back into the water and finish shaving before scrubbing my body clean. Leaning back and relaxing, I close my eyes. I could get used to this kind of pampering.

I must doze off because the sound of a text jerks me upright. Looking for my phone, I find it on the floor with Tabitha batting it around.

"No, Tabby, don't," I say while leaning out of the tub to grab it.

Just as my fingers get a grip, the phone starts ringing. Startled, I fumble it, and it makes contact with the floor. Tabitha pounces, pushing it with two kitty paws further away while it continues ringing. Leaning way over the edge of the tub, I finally get it away from the cat. Hitting the accept button, I hear a deep male voice shouting my name.

"Hello?" I say, confused as to who it is and why someone's calling me at this hour.

"Ivy? You okay?"

"Uh, yeah, I'm fine. Who's this?"

"Pigeon. You texted, but it didn't make sense. I got worried," he answers in a somewhat calmer tone. "Can you talk? Are you alone?"

"Oh God, Pigeon, I'm so sorry! Tabby was playing with my phone, and your contact must have still been up," I answer while shooting dagger eyes at my cat.

Tabitha shows zero shame at her behavior as she stares back at me while cleaning her paw.

I listen to his deep laugh before sitting my rear back down in the tub.

"No worries, Ivy. When I got a text that was all jumbled words and couldn't figure it out, I was worried. You sure you're okay? No one's standing nearby, right?"

I swear I feel my heart do a slow somersault at his concern. The man doesn't even know me, not really, and yet called immediately when he thought I might be in trouble. My own brother would walk past me without a backward glance if I was sitting in the yard on fire. Yet, this man with the gorgeous brown eyes and beautiful tats was worried. About me—Ivy Monroe—and I'm having trouble wrapping my head around that.

"No, Pigeon. I'm fine, really. I'm home alone, in fact, and the only problem I have at the moment is a naughty cat," I say while feeling the heat of embarrassment hit my face.

"Tabby, I'm guessing," Pigeon says with a laugh.

"Yeah, Tabby. I hope she didn't wake you."

"I'm good. Was just getting into bed when the phone went off. By the way, you made a small, dirty little boy very happy today. Nice of you to do that."

"I'm happy to have him hang out with me. He's really good with the animals, and he listens great," I answer, honestly.

"He's so excited that he made the rounds to everyone's houses tonight to let them know. Pooh and Pippa's only concern is that he's going to try to bring home another pet," Pigeon says with a quiet laugh.

"The way he loves Bart, I wouldn't be surprised if he tries," I answer on a yawn.

"You sound tired, Ivy. I'll let you go so you can get to bed," Pigeon says.

"Okay, and thank you for calling," I reply, feeling disappointed that our conversation is ending.

"Sweet dreams," Pigeon says softly before disconnecting.

"Sweet dreams, Pigeon," I say to dead air.

Chapter 7
Pigeon

Sitting in my office, I grin at the screen on the wall. Turning up the sound, I laugh out loud. Ivy's in the aisle that runs the length of the barn she's in, singing Blake Shelton's version of "Footloose," off-key and loudly while shaking her booty. She turns and dances down the aisle, followed by several large white ducks. When she shakes her booty, so do the ducks. When she trots back down the barn, they follow in formation, waddling awkwardly, quacking the entire time. I zoom in a little to see several goat faces peeking over their stall watching the show. When they add their voices to the mix, I have to turn the volume down a little. I'm still watching the antics of woman, ducks, and goats when Rex walks in.

Rex looks at the screen, grins, and takes a seat in front of my desk. Propping an ankle on the opposite knee, he continues watching the rescue sing-along. After another moment, I mute the monitor.

"I watched a few minutes of the rescue the other night. Ivy was doing goat yoga, and all went well with the little ones. When a large goat decided to join in, Ivy was flattened," Rex says with a grin. "When's Craig going there? That's a shift I want to see."

"He said he's going on Saturday because Ivy's working a day shift. Guess she's filling in for someone, and Craig can stay the whole shift that way," I answer.

"Did some digging around. Ivy and her brother were raised, for the most part, by their grandparents. Both are dead now, but Ivy lives on her grandparents' ranch with her brother. From what I can find, he's got to be the one hurting her. He's several years older than her and likes his beer. As in a lot," Rex says in a quiet but angry voice.

"What the fuck, Rex?" I respond in disgust.

"Yeah, I know. I haven't had a lot of time to look into this yet, but I will. I've been busy with gathering intel for our incoming guests, but I'll dig further on Ivy's brother as soon as I can. Also, I need you to do something, but it has to stay between us," Rex warns.

"It will. What do you need done?"

Rex sets a tiny box on my desk that I hadn't even seen in his hand.

"I need you to place that on Chubs' bike."

My eyebrows shoot upward when I pick the box up and realize it's a tracking device. Looking at Rex, I order, "Explain."

"Livi's getting pressured to talk to the Feds about Chubs again. You knew that, but she's worried they're going to scoop him up regardless of his refusal to talk to them. Try to force his hand or something. He's not talking to any of us, so we're still not sure what's going on. This is just a precaution in case we need to find him. It's not a foolproof plan, but it's a start," Rex explains.

"I'll get it done tonight. I'd feel better if I could stick it on him instead, though," I answer. My good mood suddenly soured.

"Heard. Maybe we should insert it in a piece of pie," Rex says without any real humor in his voice. "Let me know when it's in place."

"Yep."

Rex walks out, and my head turns back to the monitors. Not even Ivy's antics can help my mood out now. Closing down my office, I head to the clubhouse.

Mission accomplished, I text Rex, then enter the clubhouse. Toes is behind the bar and slides a beer bottle toward me as soon as I take a seat. Chubs and Lucy are sitting at a table, chatting quietly, while Chubs eats a hoagie. Axel is sitting in the middle of the floor with Alexia and a huge pail of Legos. Craig strolls in through the kitchen, Bart's backpack on his back, being trailed by Luke and Cain, one of Loki's pups. Both boys give me the hello sign before joining Axel and Alexia.

Pooh and Pippa take the stools next to me a few minutes later. Turning to Pippa, I speak.

"We're pretty sure it's her brother. Her own fucking brother. The person who should be looking out for her the most, and he's putting his hands on her."

"Unfortunately, that's not as uncommon as people think. Lots of siblings abuse the other. Do you know why she's staying with him if he's the abuser?" Pippa asks in a quiet voice.

"No. She made a comment that she'd lose everything her grandparents worked for and what they wanted for her if she left, but that's all she said."

"Could be some stipulation in their will. People add conditions to their wills but don't update them as time passes. Not that it really matters, though. All that matters is that Ivy's safe," Pooh adds.

"We're taking Craig to the rescue on Saturday. I wanted to meet Ivy even before you and I spoke about this because Craig thinks she's the total shit. Ava and Gunner do too. I'll give her my number, but I can't question her about her brother. That's a decision she has to make when she's ready to share. Knowing she has people she can reach out to is the best we can do for now," Pippa advises. "If things change for her, she's always welcome at New Horizons."

"Thanks, Pips. Appreciate it," I reply.

"Anything new on Carmen's family?" Pooh asks.

"Rex is working on intel for them. That's about all I know, really."

"I'm not sure I can see another child in the situation that Bella was in and not kill every single person involved," Pooh says in a brutal tone.

Pippa instantly slides both arms around Pooh's middle and lays her cheek against his chest. I watch as Pooh takes a deep breath and then pulls Pippa tighter. Bella's rescue was hard on all of us but Pooh especially. Pooh never shies away from doing whatever needs to be done for the club but seeing sex trafficking of a child up close damaged his soul. He's made it a point to check on Carmen, the woman rescued with Bella, regularly. By doing so, her family knew if they ever needed help, the club would have their backs.

"Not sure any of us would have a problem with that, brother. You have a family to look after now, though. Why don't you sit this one out and let me do whatever needs done," I suggest in a careful tone.

The look I receive from Pooh tells me what I knew he'd think of my suggestion. I nod in understanding and stand. No way in hell that Pooh would sit out the possible rescue of more victims. Slapping a hand against his shoulder, I remind him of something he already knows.

"I don't have a woman or kid needing me if something goes sideways. I'm not anyone's whole world. You are. Just saying, I'm fine with doing the wet work and you keeping your hands clean."

"You have Ivy," Pippa says quietly.

My head jerks to face her to deny this claim, but she speaks again before I can.

"You made her a promise, and you're her lifeline right now. Even if she never calls, she knows she can, and that's important. Also, don't even think about standing here saying that you have no one who would miss you if something happened, Pigeon. Every single one of us would, and your loss would be devastating. What you guys are going to do will most likely be dangerous. Us women get that and back you 100% because someone needs to help the victims. But none of us are okay with you getting hurt so our man is safe. Pooh will go with you at his side, and I'll be here worried sick until you both return."

Staring at Pippa for a moment, I lean down and kiss her cheek. Giving Pooh a chin lift, I leave the clubhouse and ride to the security company. I feel a need to check on Ivy, and I'm a little unsettled as to why the feeling is so strong.

Lola Wright

Chapter 8

Ivy

I take the time to make two large lunches for work today. Craig will be hanging out with me, and I want to make sure he has a good meal. I had to get up really early to get the animals fed before leaving for my day shift, but I got it done in time to drive the speed limit for a change. Pulling into the parking lot, I see Dale's car. I groan a little, but I should have checked the schedule to see who I was working with when I agreed to the shift swap. I'll stay busy with Craig and can hopefully avoid Dale for most of the shift. He'll cover the front desk, and I'll take Craig with me to the barns, so it shouldn't be too awkward working with him for one shift.

I drop my backpack and lunches off in the breakroom and make my way to the front desk. On my way past the aviary, I pop in long enough to scoop up Priscilla. Riding on my shoulder, she waits until I'm closing the door behind us to shout to the other birds, "Haha suckers!"

Grinning at her, we enter the doorway to the front desk area. Dale, who's sitting at the desk, turns in time to watch us. He continues to blatantly stare as I take a seat, and Prissy jumps off my shoulder to land on the desk.

"I have a volunteer spending the day with me, so if you're okay with it, we'll work the barns. Anything new I need to know?" I ask.

"That's fine with me. No new intakes. Had a few adoptions of cats and one dog. A lady was here yesterday and might be interested in the emu. Said she might be back today," Dale answers while still staring.

I boot up the computer in front of me and do a quick check as to who was adopted. I can feel Dale's eyes, so I continue looking at the computer so I don't have to make conversation. Prissy struts the length of the desk between the two humans, muttering to herself. Each time she gets near Dale, she stops, extends her head at him, and stomps a foot. Each time, Dale gives in to his nervousness around her and leans back. Prissy holds her pose for a few beats, then cackles and struts away. When I hear the buzzer announce the front door opening, I sigh in relief at the chance to end the awkwardness in the room.

Standing, I see Craig race into the reception area. Behind him are Pooh and a beautiful, black-haired woman that must be Craig's mom. Walking out of the room, I enter the reception area and brace. Craig rushes to me and throws his arms around my hips, his little head tipped back. I smile down to see his excited face. I lean down and give him a quick hug before looking at the two adults.

"Hi. You must be Ivy. I'm Pippa," the woman says while extending a hand.

"It's nice to meet you, Pippa. Thank you for letting Craig come today," I tell her while shaking her hand.

"No, Ivy, thank you. He's been so excited about today. This is like Christmas to Craig," Pippa states with a smile.

"My pleasure. We can always use volunteers, and Craig's great with the animals," I assure her before turning to Pooh. "Hey, Pooh, thanks for bringing him."

"No problem, Ivy. Here's a few numbers in case you need to reach one of us. Mine, Pippa's, her mom Tammy's, and Trigger's. If you need one of us to pick him up early, you can call any of those numbers. Otherwise, we'll be back around 4pm," Pooh says while holding out a small square of paper to me.

"I brought some treats!" Craig interrupts loudly while letting go of me and picking up a backpack.

"Thanks, Pooh. I'll hang onto them. That's great, Craig, but I brought lunches for both of us," I answer both at the same time.

"The treats are for the animals," Craig replies with an eye roll.

I suppress a laugh at his obvious "adults aren't too bright" eye roll and turn to Pippa when she speaks.

"If it gets to be too much, please, call. One of us will come right away."

"Standing right here, Mom. I'm not too much. I'm just right. I remember our talk and the rules. Listen to Ivy and do as she tells me. No swearing. No hiding pets in my backpack to bring home. You guys can go now," Craig responds in a slightly sarcastic tone.

"We'll be fine," I reassure her with a grin.

"Okay. Craig, go help Pooh bring in the other things, please," Pippa orders and watches as Craig and Pooh leave the building before turning to me.

"You have my number, Ivy. If you ever need anything, please use it," Pippa says in a quiet, sincere voice.

I nod but get the feeling she's talking about more than if Craig wants to leave early. My mind flashes back to Pigeon's comment about a club member's woman being an expert in abuse. Looking at Pippa's expression, I know it must be her. I'm not sure how I feel about Pigeon mentioning my bruise to her, but I know instinctively he didn't do it to embarrass me or just as something to gossip about.

"Thank you, Pippa," I tell her while looking her in the eyes.

"Everyone can use another friend, and everyone needs help sometimes," she adds before turning to the door as the guys come back through it.

"I brought some phone books and catalogs. Mac loves to tear them up, so I thought the birds here might like some too," Craig says as he and Pooh set down several thick books on the counter.

"That's a great idea, Craig! Prissy especially likes to destroy things," I reply. "How about if we drop those at the aviary and get busy in the barns?"

"Bye! See you tonight," Craig says with a wave over his shoulder before he grabs his backpack in one hand, my hand in the other, and pulls me to the door.

Pooh and Pippa shout their goodbyes as the door closes behind us.

We often have volunteers at FurEver Homes, and they're invaluable. Without them, we couldn't stay open. Margie usually assigns their duties, and I pretty much do my own thing, answering questions when needed. Having Craig volunteer for the day was a stroke of genius, though. He has boundless energy, full of compassion for the animals, and way more knowledge than I expected. What I was expecting was that getting dirty wouldn't be a problem for him, and it's not. He hasn't shied away from any of the duties, including cleaning stalls. While he's not strong enough to push the heavy wheelbarrows, he's found ways to be useful. He uses his head, reasons his way through a problem, and comes up with solutions. No complaining about dirt, manure, or the sometimes unpleasant smells. This is fast becoming my favorite shift ever.

"Ready for a break?" I ask as I watch Craig spread wood shavings on the floor of a stall.

"I could use a drink. Can we take our break in here?" he asks.

"Absolutely. I'll go get us drinks if you'd like to turn all the goats loose in here. We'll sit on the hay bales over there, and they can run up and down the aisle. That'll make it easier to clean their stalls too when we're done with our drinks."

I walk out while Craig's opening stall doors and greeting each goat as they exit. I grab two bottles of root beer and return to the barn. I find Craig running the length of the barn with the goats. His giggles blend in with the goats blatting. Some are tossing their heads while others appear to be racing each other. Boy and goats are having a blast, and I love seeing the look that's on Craig's face. I totally understand his love of animals because I've always been the same way. I take a seat on a hay bale and wait for Craig to make another pass down the aisle. When he returns, he drops down next to me, breathing hard.

"How'd you know?" Craig asks as I hand him his bottle.

"Know what?"

"That root beer's my favorite," he responds with a wide smile.

"I didn't know that. It's my favorite too, though," I answer while taking a long drink.

"Axel said that Prissy likes him. That true?" Craig asks.

"Yeah, it was kind of funny. She took to him right away," I answer.

"He went on and on about it. I think he has a crush on her. Want to hear something funny, though?" Craig asks with a mischievous smile.

"Sure."

"Axel said she told him he has a big yamagurgle, and he thinks that means he has a big di… uh, well, he thinks it's about his boy parts." Craig laughs loudly for a few seconds before continuing. "Me and Chubs googled it…" Craig pauses again to laugh. "Yamagurgle is slang for forehead! Prissy thinks he has a big forehead! Probably because he's bald!" At this point, Craig's bent over slightly, kicking his legs, laughing uncontrollably.

I think back to Axel and Prissy's conversation, and I start laughing along with Craig. This makes him laugh even harder, and even the goats quit bouncing around long enough to look his way.

"Oh my God! Did you tell him what you found out?" I ask.

"No! It's too funny to ruin by telling him! Chubs, Lucy, and I just laugh when he tells someone all about Prissy," Craig answers, wide smile still in place.

"I've met Chubs and several of the others in the club. You're lucky to have so many nice people in your life," I tell him sincerely. "They've done so much for the rescue, and it's very kind of them."

"Yeah, I'm very lucky. My real mom didn't want to be a mom, so Pips adopted me. She loves me, and I have a whole family now. Luke, Bella, and even Ava are all adopted too," he answers with all humor gone.

Looking at his face, I expect to see sadness, but I don't. His face is soft, full of love, and I realize how secure he is in his family. He knows who he is, and he knows he's loved. My heart swells for the confident little boy and that he's landed in a safe place.

"That's really cool, Craig. My mom was sick a lot and couldn't raise me and my brother. We were lucky too because our grandparents wanted us to live with them. They gave us a good life."

"Trigger is my Papa now. He takes me and Luke fishing sometimes. He's building a bike for Luke, so we can ride together, but that's a secret. Luke doesn't know about it yet. Pooh and Pippa are getting married this fall, and then he's going to be my dad because he's adopting me too. Did your grandparents build you a bike and take you fishing too?"

"We fished together on the ranch, and they taught me a lot of other things. Like how to ride a horse and how to rope. How to care for the animals, and how to cook. I can drive a tractor, doctor sick animals, and know when and how to cut the hay. They bought me my first horse when I was a little younger than you," I answer.

"You lived on a ranch?" he asks with wide eyes.

"I still live there."

"Did you rodeo?"

"Yep, I did breakaway roping, barrel racing, and goat tying. They let me join 4-H, and I showed steers, horses, and pigs."

"I want to learn how to ride horses. Ava said she's going to get a couple someday, and I want to be able to ride them," Craig says with a sly grin aimed at me.

"Yes, before you ask, I'll teach you if your parents agree," I say with a grin at the way his whole face lights up.

"Thanks, Ivy! I can't wait!"

"Ready to get back to work?"

"Yeah, we better before these goats eat my other shoelace," Craig answers while holding up a booted foot that's missing its lace.

"Hey, Craig, Ivy! How's it going?" Chubs says with a grin as he approaches Craig and me by the dog park area.

"Hi, Chubs!" Craig shouts excitedly.

"Hi, Chubs. Want to meet Ava's donkeys?" I ask.

"Absolutely," Chubs answers.

We just put several dogs in the outside yard, and we're getting ready to go to the horse barn when Chubs appeared. Craig couldn't wait to see Ava's donkeys, so we went there earlier today, but now we have a few minutes, and he wants to learn how to groom them. Chubs falls into step beside us as we enter the barn.

I hand Craig two lead ropes and wait beside Chubs as Craig enters the donkeys' stall. A minute later, he exits, leading Moose and Matilda just like I showed him earlier. Both donkeys look Chubs over carefully, decide he's not a threat and walk past. Using an extra lead rope, I show Craig how to tie the donkeys using a quick-release knot. He practices it a few times, and I'm surprised at how quickly he learns. I explain why that knot should be used, and Craig nods in understanding. Once he's ready, I let him tie the two donkeys to the rings hanging from the outside of their stall.

Once secured, I hand Craig the bucket of brushes. I explain about each one, how to use them, and give a quick demonstration. Craig listens closely and follows my instructions to the letter. Looking over at Chubs, I see his smile and the pride he has for this little boy.

Chubs and I step back and let Craig get to work. I smother a laugh when Craig starts talking to the donkeys while grooming them. He's telling them about his day, the other animals, and how excited the kids are that they're coming to live with them. He even explains about Bart, his skunk, and how they don't need to be afraid of him, and how Loki's just a large teddy bear.

"He's amazing with the animals," I tell Chubs in a low voice.

"Yeah, he is. He's amazing, period. Smart as hell, takes great care of the animals at the clubhouse and looks out for the other kids. He's learned more sign language than any of the adults have or even Lucas has. He learns words and then teaches them to Luke. I would love to know his IQ, but I'm afraid it might be higher than mine," Chubs says with a chuckle.

"Are you here to take him back home?" I ask, hoping that's not why Chubs showed up.

"No, I dropped off my IOU donation and thought I'd come out and say hi before leaving," Chubs replies. "I've heard so much about the donkeys. I had to get a peek at them."

"I told Ava I'd deliver them whenever she's ready."

"Expect a call in a day or two. She wants to get them settled long before this baby's born."

"I told her I'd take care of them when she's having the baby," Craig adds.

"And after today, you'll know everything you need to know to do that," Chubs praises. "You guys have fun. I've got to get going because it's snack time."

Chubs grins, gives a salute, and walks away.

"It's always snack time for Chubs," Craig says with a laugh.

"I've heard a little about that. His IOU donations add up to a tidy amount each month. We're grateful for him raiding Ava's bakery so often."

While eating our lunch, Craig teaches me some more ASL and is patient while I'm learning them. He also entertains me with stories of The Devil's Angels members, including one about a hand-to-hand combat scene in a toy store. I'm laughing hard, but I haven't decided yet if he's telling tales or if Axel really did get his ass handed to him by a female store employee. Craig swears it's a true story and has promised to show me the video when Pooh shows to pick him up.

"Staring is rude and a little creepy," Craig states with a bite to his tone while looking behind me.

Turning my head, I see Dale standing in the hallway with just his head showing. My first thought is, where are his hands, and what exactly are they doing. Pushing that thought from my mind, I watch his face disappear and then hear the door closing to the office. Turning to Craig, I see his eyes are on mine now.

"He's been doing that all day. He just stares at you, and I don't like it. You should have Pigeon kick his ass—uh, backside—so he stops doing it," Craig informs me while cleaning up his lunch items.

"I don't think he means anything by it. I think he's just awkward around females," I respond while putting away my lunch containers.

The Devil's Angels MC

"Pigeon would explain to him how it's creepy and not to do it again. I can have a chat with him for you, but Pigeon would do it better," Craig explains with a small laugh. "Any of the guys would do it, but Pigeon should be the one you ask. I heard Pippa tell him he has you, so I'm guessing that makes you his to protect."

"Thank you, but it's okay. I don't work with him very often. You like Pigeon, don't you? You've mentioned him several times today," I ask while deciding not to ask how I've suddenly become Pigeon's problem.

"Yeah, he's my friend. Pigeon's fun because he lets us kids get away with a lot because he says that he gets to give us back to our parents when we get out of control. He doesn't even care when we get dirty or forget to take our shoes off at the door. He's been teaching me how to play poker too," Craig says with a wicked grin.

"He sounds like a good friend to have," I answer.

"He is, and that's why he would tell Dale to quit being a weirdo for you. Pigeon's single. No woman or kids. Did you know that?" Craig asks with fake wide-eyed innocence.

"No, I didn't," I murmur as we walk out of the breakroom.

"The women all say he's hot. You should ask him out on a date. I can ask him for you if you're too shy to," Craig offers as we enter the dog shelter. "Axel says that Pigeon needs a keeper, and I think you'd be perfect at it. The guys all want Pigeon to find a woman, so they can give him back the sh… uh, crap that he gives them for having a woman."

"No, that's okay, Craig," I say hurriedly. "I'm pretty busy right now and don't really have time to date anyone; not that Pigeon isn't great."

"You think he's hot too, don't you?" Craig says with a giggle.

"Of course, I do. He's gorgeous and very nice. Tall, muscled, beautiful eyes, and tats. What's not to like?" I stop when I realize I'm giving away that I've thought about Pigeon. After a few beats, I finish by saying, "I just have a lot on my plate right now and have to stay focused on my future."

"What's on your plate?" Craig asks, thankfully changing the subject.

We're standing in front of Thor's kennel, and we both take a seat on the floor. Thor's ear perks up, and his tail starts wagging before he crawls over close to us. Laying down on his belly, he pushes his nose through the wire at Craig. Craig opens his backpack and pulls out a few dog biscuits and feeds them to Thor. I'm so proud of Thor when he very gently takes them from Craig's hand before eating his treats.

"I work here, but I also work the ranch during the day. One day, it'll be all mine, and I want to make some major changes then. Both jobs, though, don't leave me a lot of time to myself," I answer while watching Thor bump Craig's hand for attention.

Craig instantly starts petting Thor through the kennel. After another moment of judging Thor's attitude, I reach up and open the kennel door. Thor walks out and drops down to lay between Craig and me. He lays his scarred head on Craig's lap and waits patiently for the affection he's starting to crave. Craig doesn't disappoint.

"What kinds of changes?" Craig asks.

"I want to sell off most of the cattle, not all, and use the ranch as a therapeutic riding center and possibly an animal rescue for animals that can't be adopted out," I answer quietly.

Craig is the first person I've ever really explained my dreams for the ranch to, and I'm almost nervous that speaking them aloud may somehow keep them from happening.

"What's a therapeutic riding center?" Craig questions then gives a small laugh as Thor all but climbs into his lap.

"I want to teach kids how to ride a horse. How to care for them and other animals. Kids with special needs, or what the world calls disabilities, because animals help them in so many ways. Animals love but don't judge anyone for missing a limb or having autism. Animals don't bully kids that may be somewhat different from the others like humans so often do. I'd love to be able to share the peace and solitude of the ranch with people who need that in their life. Even if it's for a weekend or a few days a week," I explain.

"That's so cool, Ivy. Lucas is deaf, and I know everyone is worried that others may treat him differently because of it. I won't let them if I'm around, though. Neither will Ava or Gunner. You're right, though, about animals. They love anyone who's nice to them, and they don't care if you're dirty or not. You should talk to Pippa about the ranch. She runs a home for women and kids that need to hide from their husbands or fathers. That's how she got me. Lucy's dad is the governor, and he helps my mom get money to run New Horizons. He could help you too. Is your ranch far from here?" Craig questions.

"About an hour's drive."

"Might be a good place to hide people too," Craig says, almost as if he's thinking aloud.

"When I'm ready to make the changes, I'll speak with your mom if you think she wouldn't mind. She could probably answer a lot of questions for me."

"She wouldn't mind. She loves helping people. She even got shot one time trying to save two little kids," Craig answers in a subdued voice.

Reaching over Thor, I give Craig a quick hug. He smiles up at me, but I can tell he's still affected by the close call his mom suffered.

"I heard about that. She saved those kids, and that makes her a hero," I say as I let him go.

"She was a hero even before that. She saved me too."

Thor gives a soft whine before lifting his head and rubbing the side of it against Craig's cheek. Craig's arms wrap around the dog's neck, and both seem to settle. Another sign that animals are the perfect cure when someone needs one.

Lola Wright

Chapter 9
Pigeon

My mind is still screaming, "what the fuck" while my hand absently picks up a half-full beer can and tosses it at Rex. Rex ducks but continues laughing his dumb ass off at me. Reeves is standing in the doorway to my office, gripping it to stay standing while he does the same as Rex. Ignoring them, I hit mute on the cameras at FurEver Homes. Instantly Rex leans over and unmutes them. I breathe a sigh of relief when I hear Craig's voice, and it's not trying to be a matchmaker anymore. Fucking kid should get a job at Tinder.

"Craig's setting your ass up!" crows Reeves.

I glare but refuse to respond.

"Kid's smart. Probably thinking long-term for the benefits he'd gain. Horses, dogs, cats, and cows.

Craig's version of heaven, and it'll only cost you your freedom. That, and you'd have to give up some ass but to only one woman. For forever," Rex adds before leaping out of his chair and making a run for it.

Too bad for Rex, Reeves blocks the doorway long enough for me to tackle him to the floor. After a few seconds, I push off him and stand. It's no fun pounding on someone's face when they're laughing uncontrollably. I turn, shove Reeves out of the door, watch as Rex hurriedly rolls clear, and then slam the door behind them. Turning my eyes to the monitors, I see Ivy hugging Craig.

I shut down the cameras from the rescue and try to concentrate on some paperwork I need to get done for Rex. It's Saturday, my day off, but I came in because I wanted to watch Craig with Ivy for a few minutes. Then Rex and Reeves showed up, and we sat around drinking beer and watching the free entertainment. Up until Craig decided to marry me off, I was enjoying the show. Now, I'm regretting a few things. One, that Craig has the ears of a bat and hears things he shouldn't. Second, that I showed my shock at his words in front of the guys. They'll get a lot of mileage out of that, and I know one of them has already sent out a group text. My phone will start buzzing soon with brothers wanting to give me shit.

Later, when the guys aren't here, I'll go back and review more of the video. I want to pay more attention to what Dale was doing and to hear the part about Ivy's plans for the ranch. I missed it since I was pinning Rex to the floor, but I'm curious about everything concerning Ivy. I groan, run both hands through my hair before scrubbing them over my stubbled face. I should close down my office and leave, but I know I won't.

When my phone vibrates on the desk, I glance at it to see Pooh's name. I click the accept button, bark a loud "fuck you" into it before disconnecting. A minute later, I repeat the same action. After the third time, I shut my phone off and slide it into my pocket. At a loud knock on my door, I start looking around for something to throw at Rex, but it's Reeves' voice I hear.

"Pooh's trying to reach you. Answer it, asshole. He needs a favor."

Pulling my phone out, I turn it on and hit Pooh's name.

"What's your problem?" Pooh asks in an irritated voice.

"You calling to give me shit?" I ask in the same tone.

"About what?" Pooh asks in a now curious tone.

"About your damn kid trying to sacrifice me for his own gain."

"I need to get Craig waivers written up and make everyone sign them agreeing that I'm not to be held responsible for whatever havoc he creates," Pooh answers with a laugh. "What'd he do?"

"Reeves said you need a favor. What's up?" I ask while ignoring his question. Word will spread quick enough without me being the one to tell Pooh.

"Pippa's headed to New Horizons for a new intake and wants me there if possible. They've had trouble with the woman's boyfriend before, and I don't want her there alone. Can you pick Craig up from the rescue for me? Around 3:30-4:00?"

"Yeah, no problem. It'll give me a chance to beat your child and hide the body," I answer.

"He'd haunt your ass, you know. He can be an ornery little fucker but take your chances if you feel brave enough," Pooh says with a laugh. "We should be home by 5:00pm, I think. Thanks, brother."

I disconnect, drop my head into my hands, and offer up a short prayer.

"Please, God, don't let Craig volunteer my ass for something it's not ready for," I whisper before standing and leaving the building.

Stopping at the clubhouse, I find Chubs sitting alone at the bar. Not eating, drinking, or watching the TV. I feel a chill run up my back as I take a seat next to him. It takes another moment for him to notice he's not alone any longer, and that's very unlike him. Nudging his elbow with mine, I speak first.

"Don't know what's going on with you, but I'm here for anything you need."

"Know that, Pigeon. Appreciate it, too, but nothing's wrong," Chubs lies while not meeting my eyes.

"Where's Lucy?" I ask.

"She left with her parents and sister for Washington D.C. Her dad has some meetings, and her mom wanted some daughter time. They'll be gone for a week," Chubs answers in a monotone voice.

"You want to go riding tomorrow? Get away from here for a few hours?"

"Thanks, but no. Got things to do," Chubs replies in the same flat voice.

"Worried about you, Chubs. Everyone is."

"No need to be," he answers before suddenly turning to face me fully. "If something did happen, I'd want you and the others to take care of Lucy. Keep her close, and don't let her put herself in danger on my account. No matter what happens, just know that I'll be fine, Pigeon."

I feel alarm hit my chest, but I nod my head, agreeing. Before I can say anything else, he stands and walks out. I pull my phone out and call Cash. He's the club enforcer and needs to know that whatever's up with Chubs, it's heating up. Feeling unsettled but not having answers, I leave the clubhouse to go retrieve Craig's helmet.

"Hey, Pigeon! Guess what I got to feed today?" Craig asks excitedly.

"What, little man?" I ask.

"An opossum! A baby one, and they're called joeys! It's so cute and cuddly!" Craig shouts while bouncing around on his feet.

A full day at the rescue, and his energy level is still high. Reaching out, I ruffle his hair and grin down at the little menace. The desire to throttle him disappeared on the ride here because I know he didn't mean any harm. I will, although, be more careful about his hearing abilities and what I say if he's nearby.

"That's cool, Craig. Have fun today?" I ask, already knowing the answer.

"Yeah, I did. I got to feed all kinds of animals, and I hung out with Priscilla too. Hate to say this, but I think Axel's right. I think Prissy has a crush on him. Birds are strange," Craig informs me.

"Tell Ivy thank you, and we'll hit the road. Pooh and your mom will be home soon, but we can stop and get something to eat on the way. Whatever you'd like," I tell Craig.

"Fuc… uh, flipping awesome!" Craig shouts before turning to Ivy. "Thank you, Ivy! I had a lot of fun today, and it was nice you let me come here. I'll talk to my mom about learning to ride a horse."

"You're very welcome, Craig. I had fun too," Ivy responds with a smile.

"Thanks, Ivy. Have a good day," I say.

"Hey, how about you come eat with us, Ivy?" Craig asks as I turn to leave.

"Oh, no, Craig, I better get home. I have some things to get done yet," Ivy refuses politely.

"But you're going to have to eat all alone then, Ivy," Craig says while aiming sad, puppy dog eyes in my direction.

I open my mouth to tell Craig that Ivy's busy, and we need to leave when she speaks.

"I won't be alone, Craig. My brother's home now," Ivy reassures Craig, but I'm positive I hear a wobble in her voice. Concern or fear maybe?

"Buying you dinner's a small price for the smile you put on the little man's face, Ivy. We'll go somewhere quick, so you can get home at a decent hour," I insist, changing my mind instantly.

Without waiting for her to refuse, I turn to Craig and ask, "Got everything?"

"Yep, and Ivy's already put her things in her truck. We on the bike, Pigeon?"

"Yeah, we are. Follow us, Ivy. How's pizza sound to everyone?" I ask as we exit the rescue.

"Pigeon, you don't have to…" Ivy starts to protest when I cut her off.

"You have something against eating pizza with bikers? Two handsome, charming bikers?" I ask with a raised eyebrow.

"No! Of course not. I just don't want you to feel—" Ivy attempts to say before I cut her off again.

"What I feel is grateful to you because I didn't have to put up with Craig today, and that's more than worth some pizza," I tell her with a wink.

"You think you're funny, but you're really not," Craig tells me with a glare as Ivy gives a small laugh.

"Okay, then. Pizza it is," Ivy concedes.

After giving the server our order, I watch Ivy quietly while she answers questions from Craig. She's patient and never talks down to him. She's realized how smart Craig is and answers the questions accordingly. I take this time to also study her features. As many times as I have watched her at work, I've never consciously thought about how cute she really is.

Average height, curvy in all the right places, lightly tanned skin, hazel eyes with light brown, nearly blond hair. Her curves are perfect because she's a few pounds overweight, and that's not a turnoff for men. Certainly isn't for this man anyway. Hair that ends mid-back and is a bouncing mass of curls. I like that she doesn't straighten it because the curls frame her face perfectly. The fact she wears little, if any, makeup is a nice change from the women that hang around the strip club and the clubhouse. Ivy's attractive in the girl-next-door-type, but it's her personality that draws you in first as it should be.

"What the fuck, Craig?" I snap when he kicks me hard in the shin under the table.

"Sorry about that, Pigeon. Accident," he replies in a sickly-sweet voice. "But since you're listening to me now, I wanted to tell you about how that Dale guy stares at Ivy all the time."

"No, Craig, I told you it isn't a big deal," Ivy hurries to say before turning to me. "I don't work with him very often, so it's no problem. Craig was concerned, but it's okay."

"Is that all he does, Ivy? Just stare?" I ask.

"Yes, he's never gotten out of line. Never. He's just odd, is all."

"I told Ivy that you should have a chat with Dale about it," Craig volunteers.

"If it becomes a problem, I will," I answer while making eye contact with Ivy.

Our food arrives at that moment and saves Ivy from answering. I slide a couple of slices of pizza on each of our plates and pass the chicken wings to Craig. When the server sets the plate of breadsticks on the table, Ivy and I reach for them at the same time. I raise my hands in surrender as she helps herself, grinning at me. She places one on Craig's plate, takes some for herself, and then passes the plate to me. No one talks for the first few minutes as we dig into our meal. When Ivy moans, my eyes rise to meet hers.

"Good, huh?" Craig asks. "This is my favorite pizza place."

"Yes, it is. I can see why it's your favorite," Ivy answers.

"You haven't eaten here before?" Craig questions before stuffing half the breadstick in his mouth.

"No, I haven't. I don't eat out very often, but I'll be coming back here now that I know how good their food is," Ivy responds.

"How come you don't eat out? We do a lot because Pooh says it's safer than having Mom cook, and he says he needs a kitchen break sometimes," Craig says.

"Don't have time. I usually just grab something out of the fridge and eat it on the run."

"Do you know how to cook? Miss Ava's really good at it, but my mom can only use the microwave," Craig informs her.

"Yeah, I can cook. I like to but don't have a lot of time for it."

"Maybe when you teach me how to ride, Pigeon and I can take you out for dinner again. Right, Pigeon?" Craig asks with his fake innocent look plastered to his matchmaking little face.

"Yeah, sounds like a plan," I answer, shocking myself and, most likely, Ivy too.

"I have to use the little boys' room. Be right back," Craig announces before jumping out of his chair.

"Wash your hands!" I shout as he walks off.

"He's adorable," Ivy states with a smile as she watches him weave his way to the restroom.

"Not sure anyone has ever described him as adorable before."

Ivy laughs before slipping her straw into her mouth to sip on her drink. I wait until she's done before bluntly asking, "How old are you?"

"22, going on 23, why?"

"You're older than I thought. I was thinking you look closer to 18," I answer honestly.

"You thought I was a teenager. Is that why you were worried about my bruise?" Ivy questions in a quiet voice while setting down her fork.

"No, your age has nothing to do with that. I'm worried because I know you have someone mistreating you, and I don't like it. You, at any age, should never be hurt by a man. I want your promise that you'll call me if that ever happens again," I insist.

Ivy studies my face for a moment before giving me a silent nod. Without thought, I reach across the table and wrap my index finger around her pinkie. Giving it a slight tug, I give her what I hope is a reassuring smile before saying, "Thank you."

I release her hand when I see Craig coming toward the table, but when I see his eyes light up, I realize I didn't release it quick enough. Hopping onto his chair, surprisingly he goes back to his meal without comment.

Walking into the clubhouse, I head straight to the bar and take the seat next to Axel. Little Alex is sitting on the bar in front of him, and they're playing some pattycake-type game. I watch, silently laughing at my VP, as he patiently shows her the pattern again. Little Alex has the tip of her tongue sticking out of her mouth and a serious look of concentration on her cute little face. After she successfully completes the beginning sequence, Axel shows her the rest of the game. When the large, bald biker gets to the point of mimicking the rocking of the baby, my laughter is no longer silent.

"Shut it, Pigeon," he growls my direction before starting at the beginning of pattycake again.

"Can I request you sing 'The Muffin Man' next?" I ask and then dodge the elbow he throws my way.

"I'm ignoring you now," he replies without missing a beat.

"Hello, pretty lady. Uncle Pigeon wants a hug," I say to Alexia while holding my hands toward her.

As expected, her bright smile flashes in my direction before she launches herself at my hands. I catch her and pull her close. I shoot a grin at Axel over her shoulder while she winds her arms around my neck.

"Got your hug, now give my daughter back," Axel orders.

"I'm ignoring you now," I retort while hugging Alex tighter. She giggles, Axel scowls, and Craig interrupts my taunting.

"You were right about two things, Axel."

Sufficiently distracted, Axel turns to face Craig and asks, "I was? About what?"

"Prissy has the hots for you. We chatted today, and she asked about you a lot," Craig answers.

"I knew it! She's the only smart bird I've ever met!"

"Heard that, Assman!" Mac hollers from across the room.

"Doesn't change the fact it's true, you feathered jackoff!" Axel shouts back before turning to Craig again. "What else was I right about?"

"There was a look," Craig answers nonchalantly. "Pigeon. Ivy. A look."

"I knew it! I'm two for two!" Axel crows.

It takes me a minute to realize what Craig's talking about and then another one to digest the fact that the little brat just tossed me under the bus. Axel's never going to stay off my ass now. Shooting a death glare at Craig, I hand Alexia back to her father. Staring Craig down, I rise off my stool and break into a run at the same time he does. He makes it across the room and behind a couch before I can reach him. He gives me an arrogant grin with raised eyebrows. The grin disappears when I vault over the couch. My hand grazes his shoulder, but he ducks under it and makes a break for it. Leaping back over the couch, I run him down, grab the waistband of his jeans, and pull him to a stop. Looking over his shoulder, our eyes meet.

"Gonna beat me now?" he asks in a voice I should have paid attention to.

"Yep," I answer.

"I think not," he calmly replies before letting loose an ear-splitting scream. Deep breath and another scream.

I freeze and quit breathing when I hear the low, threatening growl coming from directly behind me. When the second growl is even closer, I release my fingers, one at a time, from his jeans. Not moving anything else on my body, I wait to see if today's date is going to become the anniversary of my death. I ignore the smug look on Craig's face, Axel's howling laughter, and Mac's singing of "Who Let The Dogs Out."

When I survive a full minute, and there's no more growling, I slowly turn my head to see Lucas, Loki, and Cain standing behind me. Luke is giving Craig a thumbs up. Loki is eyeing me but seems relaxed now that the threat is gone. Cain's ruff is still standing up, and I can see small flashes of his teeth. After a moment, he settles down and walks off. Breathing for the first time in what feels like forever, I turn back to Craig.

"What's going on?" asks Pippa as she and Pooh enter the clubhouse.

"Pigeon's trying to become a chew toy," Axel wheezes out.

"Loki's bird hunting!" Mac shouts.

"Why? Or should I ask, what's Craig got to do with it?" Pippa says while shooting a mom look at her son.

"I did nothing. We're good; all's good. It's a guy thing, Mom. Pigeon and I now have an understanding, though, don't we?" Craig asks with a smirk.

"Yeah, we do. All's well," I answer while thinking of ways to make Pooh pay for his kid's antics.

"Oh shit. You're going to take whatever this is out on me, aren't you?" Pooh whines.

"Yep."

"Fuck me," Pooh says, accepting his fate. "Knew I should've gotten those waivers printed up."

"Thanks for picking Craig up for us, Pigeon. Let's go, Craig. You can tell us about your day, but first, you need to apologize to Pigeon for whatever you did to have him contemplating murder," Pippa states.

"Sorry, Pigeon," Craig responds immediately and not very sincerely. "Thanks for dinner."

"Before you tamper with my bike's brakes, remember that he did apologize," Pooh tells me as they walk out the door.

Returning to my seat, I grab a beer and turn to Axel.

"Where's everyone at?"

"Ava had a doctor's appointment, so Gunner took the girls and met her there. They're eating dinner somewhere and then will be back. Luke wanted to stay with me and Alex, so we came here since Bailey is drawing. Pops and Trigger just left before you got here. I have no clue about anyone else except Livi and James because they're on shift," Axel answers. "Carmen's family will be here tomorrow. They're positive the trafficking ring is making a sale this coming week. Rex is working on locations and names."

"We ready for them?" I ask.

"We're ready," Axel answers before changing the subject. "Sounds like Craig had a good day. Everything okay with Ivy?"

"Yeah, he did. I don't think anything will be okay for her until her brother has a come to Jesus moment."

"You get the chance to make that happen, I want to be there," Axel says with a wicked grin.

"Sounds like a plan."

Walking into the clubhouse the next afternoon, I look around at the men gathered there. My club brothers, along with several unfamiliar men, have pulled several tables together and are sitting around them. Taking a seat next to Horse, I signal Toes for a beer. After he places it in front of me, Gunner points to each club member and states their name. When he's finished, Carmen's oldest brother, Mateo, does the same with his men.

"Tell us what you know," Gunner says.

"Since your club returned our sister to us, we've been working to bring an end to more sex rings. We tried working with law enforcement but have found their hands are tied most of the time. They have rules and laws to follow, and we do not. We appreciate any help you can give us but don't expect any of you to risk yourselves doing that," Mateo states.

"How's Carmen doing now?" Petey asks.

"Much better, but she has scars, inside and out, that will never heal. Our sister went from being a young, confident woman to being scared to leave the house. She's quiet, reserved, and not the woman who terrorized her brothers when they were younger. What you did for her can never be repaid, but we're trying to do the same for others that are in the position she was once in. Can you tell me what has happened with the young girl that Carmen was with? Bella?" Mateo asks.

"My wife and I adopted her, and she's doing great. Therapy and a lot of love has worked wonders for Bella," Petey answers with obvious pride in his youngest child.

"That's great to hear. Really, it's amazing and gives us hope for the young girls we've gotten back so far. Carmen will be happy to hear that Bella's safe and happy," Mateo states with a warm smile.

"Carmen mentioned that Bella couldn't speak. Was that because of the trauma?" Luis, another brother, questions.

"Bella can speak just fine and started to within a few days of being brought here," Pooh answers. "We're assuming it was the trauma that silenced her because there was no medical reason for it."

"That's understandable. Since we rescued our first victim, we've seen some women and young girls in horrific conditions. The fact that they survived attests to their inner strength," Luis replies in a low, angry voice.

"Recently, we found out about a sex ring that's operating out of Seattle. Our contact told us they will be transporting a few women to Denver at the end of this week to meet up with their new owner. We don't know how many women this involves, but we may need a place to bring them to for immediate medical attention, food, and clothing. After we know they're healthy enough for travel, we'll take them to Chicago with us and locate their families then," Mateo informs the room.

"I've found a few locations where I think the exchange might take place. Nothing definite, but I'll continue looking into them. We don't know much about the buyer other than his online name. I'm still trying to trace his online presence backward to find where he's coming from and where he plans on taking the women," Rex states.

"What do we know about how many men will be in on the exchange?" Trigger asks.

"Nothing yet. What we've found so far is that there are usually two men with the women and another one that handles the business transaction itself on behalf of the seller. The buyer usually brings his own bodyguard and a couple of extra men to transport the women. That way, the buyer can see what he's paying for but doesn't have to travel with the women in case they're caught. The buyer doesn't always come, but if he's there at the exchange, it's the only time we'll catch him along with the rest. The guys that do the transporting are scum and should pay for it, but it's the buyer we really want. We're hoping if we can catch him, he'll give up the seller to save his own ass. Not that it will," Mateo explains.

"Rex will continue looking for the location while the rest of us can help in any way you need us to. We have a club nurse, Vex's wife, and she's stocked a spare bedroom here with basic medical supplies. We'll gather up additional items, like clothing, and have that ready, too. Kitchen and bar are well stocked, freezers full. You're welcome to it all, and we'll keep the clubhouse closed to just your crew and us," Gunner says.

"Thank you. We'd like to scout out the possible locations over the next few days. Not being familiar with this area, it would be helpful to us if some of your guys could help with that?" Mateo asks.

"Absolutely," Gunner answers immediately. "Pigeon, Horse, and Cash can help with that. Need more, let me know."

After discussing a few more details, the meeting ends. I make sure each of Carmen's family members have my number, and I leave. It's as I'm riding out the main gate that I realize Chubs wasn't at the meeting. Pulling to the side of the road, I pull my phone out and call Cash.

Lola Wright

Chapter 10

Ivy

Today's the day to deliver the donkeys to Ava. It's a huge day for her, and yet I'm dreading it immensely. When I got up this morning, the first thing I did was contemplate calling her to postpone. Instead, I did my chores and hooked the horse trailer to my truck. I owe Ava this, and I won't disappoint her because of my own issues.

I make a point to get my work done early today, and at the same time, I avoid Ted at all costs. Placing my backside into my truck, I begin the long drive down the ranch driveway. I call Margie and let her know I'm on my way, so I know the donkeys will be ready to go when I get there. Reaching over, I crank the radio as loud as my ears can take, and I slowly relax into the familiar drive.

Lying in bed last night, I admitted some truths to myself. I can't continue to live with the way things are with Ted. I certainly can't do nearly three more years of this. That was truth number one. Truth number two was harder to admit, but I finally did. I'm developing feelings for Pigeon. Maybe it's because he's shown me kindness after such a long drought without any? Maybe it's because he's so different from anyone I've ever known and gets to live his life free? Maybe it's the gorgeous face and eyes combined with all the tats? I don't know the exact reason for my feelings, but I know they exist. What else I know is that we're complete opposites, there's an age difference, and while I'm confident in myself, I'm sure I'm certainly not someone that would be on his radar. So, what in the hell am I supposed to do with these feelings?

Arriving at the rescue, I push these thoughts aside and focus on what I need to do. I stuff my mass of curls into a ball cap, keep my sunglasses on, and I meet Margie by the horse barn to load the donkeys. Once accomplished, I climb back into the truck and pull out. Calling Ava, I let her know I'm on my way. She gives me directions different from before, and I realize I'm going directly to Vex's house and not passing through the club's compound. I cross my fingers and silently give up a small prayer that none of The Devil's Angels members are at the barn, but I realize that God's ignoring me again when I see the crowd gathered.

Parking the truck, I step out and am immediately swamped with excited kids. After greeting them and receiving several hugs, I watch Ava approach with a blinding smile. Quickly glancing around, I note that Pigeon isn't present. A sigh of relief, a tight squeeze from Ava, and it's time to unload her new babies. Before I do that, I explain to the kids that the donkeys will be nervous with the new surroundings and that they should stand back and let the donkeys check things out on their own. They all agree, including Craig, and race over to stand with the bikers near the barn.

Unloading the donkeys, Ava and I walk them around to let them check out their new surroundings. Moose, as usual, was more concerned with finding food than exploring. Matilda, being the more protective one, studied everything and everyone around us. After she deemed the area safe, we took them into their new enclosure and then walked the fence line. The donkeys settled quickly, partly because Ava had everything well prepared. Another successful adoption done right.

While everyone gathers near the fence to check out their new family members, I return to my trailer and secure the door. When I turn around, I find Petey standing quietly nearby. I flash him a smile that's not returned, and I feel a moment of unease. That feeling triples when he speaks in a low voice.

"Sunglasses cover the bruise, but not the real damage."

"I'm—" I start, but he continues speaking.

"Don't say you're fine. Don't say you're not hiding a black eye or worse. You don't owe me or anyone an explanation, and don't ever let anyone force you into giving them one. Just know, Ava and Pigeon aren't your only friends here, Ivy. You have help when you're ready for it."

With that, he gives my elbow a gentle squeeze and walks off. I take a couple of deep breaths, settle my emotions, and walk the paperwork over to Ava. After answering a round of questions, mostly from the kids, I give Ava a hug, Petey a small smile, and leave.

My shift ended 15 minutes ago, but I'm exhausted and not in a hurry to make the drive home. Due to staff shortages, two nights a week, there's no human here until 4:30am, so staying late isn't a problem. Deciding to take a break from life, I grab a bottle of water, put a leash on Thor, and go outside to sit in the dog park while Thor races around. Leaning my head against a fence post, I think about Petey's words.

I need to schedule an appointment with my grandparent's attorney. There's got to be a way around the wording of the will and a way out from under Ted's control. I don't want to lose the ranch and my dreams, but I can't keep going on this way either. Ted having so much control over my life wasn't the intent of the will, but it's gotten twisted over the years.

Deep in thought, I absently notice that Thor's went completely still. When I hear his low growl, though, he gets my full attention. When we came outside, I didn't turn on the lights because the moon is bright tonight, and I knew Thor could see just fine. Now, seeing him watching something behind me, I wish I had turned on the floodlights.

Turning my head, I see two men walking toward the barn that houses the dogs. The rescue is closed, has been for hours, and these men did not come from the parking lot direction as visitors would have. They haven't seen me sitting on the grass in the dog park, but one of them turns to face Thor's growling.

"He's locked in there. Someone must have forgotten he was outside. Let's get this done," the man says as the two of them enter the barn.

As soon as the door closes, I whistle softly to Thor and place his leash on his collar. Walking quietly to the door of the barn, I peek through to see the men placing puppies in two large burlap bags. I place my hand on Thor's head to calm him while I pull my phone out. Without thought, I hit Pigeon's contact and wait while it rings. No answer, and the call goes to voicemail. Disconnecting, I dial 911.

When the men finish stuffing puppies in the bags and the police haven't shown up yet, I know I can't let them leave. Scared out of my mind and doubting myself, I open the door and hit all the light switches. The room floods with light as both men jerk around to face me. Thor hits the end of his leash, but I hold tight and stand between the men and their only exit.

"Put the bags down, and I'll let you leave," I order.

"You'll *let* us leave? She'll *let* us leave," laughs the man closest to me.

"Get out of our way, and we'll let you live," counters the other man while hefting the bag over his shoulder.

I cringe when I hear the whining and cries of the puppies, but I don't move from my position. Several of the dogs in the kennels are now barking, growling, and the noise is nearly deafening. Staring the men down, I pray the police show soon.

When my phone rings, I glance down to see it's an unknown caller. I ignore the call. It disconnects and then starts ringing again. Still ignoring it, I repeat my order to the two men. When all I receive from them are evil grins, I brace because things are about to get ugly.

When both men start walking toward me, carrying their bags, Thor leans into his collar. Holding on for dear life, he drags me in the direction of the men. Thor's flashing teeth must finally penetrate their tiny brains because both men stop, slowly lower the bags to the floor and hold their hands out in a placating manner. Maybe what convinced them was me dropping my phone and slowly losing my grip on the leash. It doesn't really matter why, but I'm grateful that there's still some distance between us.

Puppies of all sizes spill out of the bags and run every direction, crying and howling. Thor eases back, and my feet come to a stop. Unfortunately, I'm wrong when I think the men are going to leave without a fight. When a young terrier mix puppy scoots past the men, one of them scoops him up. Holding the crying puppy by the scruff, the man lays out his idea of how this is going to go.

"Take the dog and get inside a kennel. Do it right the fuck now, or this puppy's going to get its skull caved in."

"God, no, don't do that!" I beg as I back toward the closest kennel that happens to have a friendly collie in it. "Please don't hurt the puppy!"

"Do it, or the puppy won't be the only one getting its skull caved in," the man orders.

"By the looks of her face, this bitch doesn't follow orders well," states the other man with a sneer. "Somebody try to teach you a lesson you were too stupid to learn?"

As my back hits the kennel door, and I reach behind me to fumble with the latch, the door to the barn opens. All eyes swing that direction as two more men enter. While I was hoping to see a couple of uniforms, I don't. What I do see is just as reassuring, though. Both are large, angry-looking men, but the part that almost makes my knees buckle in relief is that both are wearing Devil's Angels cuts and aiming handguns at the other men.

"Go outside, Ivy. Take the dog with you and call Rex. Tell him we're here, and you're safe," orders the extremely large, pissed-off Viking slash biker-looking dude.

I pull Thor behind me, grab my phone off the floor, then bolt through the door the other biker is holding open for me. Once outside, I lift my phone and call the unknown caller number from before. I have no idea if this is the right number or not, but I'm too shaken to think clearly.

When a man's voice answers, I ask, "Is this Rex?"

"Yeah, it is," answers a calm, soothing deep voice.

"This… uhh, this… I'm Ivy," I stutter before calming enough to talk coherently. "Sorry. This is Ivy. A friend of yours told me to call and tell you he's here and that I'm safe."

"Yeah, that's good. You okay, Ivy? Did they hurt you?" he asks.

"I'm good. No, they didn't touch me. Should I maybe let him know that I called 911? I'm only asking because the cops should be showing up soon, and there's noises coming from inside that might be hard to explain."

"Cops will be there in about a minute, and no, you don't need to tell Cash that. He's aware. You might want to go to the parking lot and show the cops how to get to the barn. Keep Thor with you, Ivy, and I'll stay on the phone with you too."

"Okay, I can do that," I answer as I take the outside route to the parking lot, arriving at the same time as the police car. "Cops are here. Thank you, Rex."

"Chat later, Ivy," Rex answers before disconnecting.

Two female officers emerge from the patrol unit as I approach them. Quickly explaining who I am, they follow me to the dog barn. Motioning for me to stay back, they cautiously approach the door, look inside and then relax.

"I love these fucking guys," the tall officer says with a laugh.

"Livi's a lucky bitch for sure. Should we take a coffee break and let them finish? No, that wouldn't be right. We have to at least appear to be needed," says the shorter officer before opening the door and entering.

I crouch down next to Thor and wrap my arms around him. Body stiff, his eyes are alert and active, but he's quit growling. Several minutes later, the two officers emerge with the two men, cuffed and looking like they're rethinking their life choices. Thor snarls and lunges at them, but I hang onto him and pray I have the strength to continue doing so until the men are gone. Luckily, the officers escort the men around the building and out of sight. The two club members stop in the doorway and eye Thor carefully, but he ignores them completely. Dogs know who can and can't be trusted, and this just proves it again.

"You got him?" the Viking slash biker asks in a quiet tone.

"Not sure, to be honest. Hope so, though," I answer with a grunt as my knees smack hard on the cement.

"Was hoping you'd say a definite yes to that," replies the other biker.

"Anything we can do? Without getting mauled, that is?" asks the Viking biker with a small grin.

"Uh, maybe move so I can get him back inside," I answer while wrapping the leash, dangerously, I might add, around my hand several times.

Both men move several feet away and stand still. I stand while talking in soothing tones and coax Thor back inside. I hear the door close behind me, and I almost smile. Thor calms down but is still antsy, so I get him into his kennel and close the gate behind him. The door to the barn opens, and both men reenter. Surprisingly, Thor's tail begins to wag when the men stop in front of his kennel.

The dogs are starting to quiet down, but the puppies are cowering in different corners, on top of each other and behind anything they can find. Dropping to my knees on the floor, I start trying to calm them down with reassuring tones and words. Not long, and I have puppies swarming me. Making sure each one gets a hug and a few soft words, I get to my feet and start returning them to the kennels they belong in. Once done, I turn to face the two bikers. I watch as both of their faces harden as their eyes take in the damage to my face. Dropping my head for a beat, I raise it back up and make eye contact with one and then the other before speaking.

"They didn't do this. They never got close enough to touch me, thanks to Thor and you guys."

Both men give me a quick nod but continue examining my face. After a moment, the Viking holds out his hand to me without speaking. Without uttering a word, I open my contacts and hand my phone to him. I'm beginning to understand how these things work with protective men. When he's done, he hands it back to me. I see four new contacts—Livi, Cash, James, and Horse.

"I'm either going to gain a roommate or lose the one I have," states the one with a patch that reads Horse. One mystery solved.

"Yep," the Viking one agrees, and I look to his patch to see the name Cash. Second mystery solved.

"Pigeon and I need to have a chat about that."

"This wasn't his fault. I didn't think when I called him first. I just panicked and hit his contact. I should have called 911 to begin with," I insist while having no idea what they're talking about but knowing I need to defend Pigeon.

"Yep, losing or gaining. Either way, this is going to be entertaining as hell."

"Yep," Cash agrees with a grin.

"Can I go now? I'm pretty sure I've reached my limit of drama today," I ask, and even I can hear how tired my voice is.

"You won't be driving home tonight, Ivy. Pigeon is on his way here to pick you up," Cash says as he opens the door and flips off the lights.

I follow him outside, lock the door behind us, and then speak, but I have to do it while trying to keep up with the long strides of the men.

"I have to go home. Nothing will get done, and nobody will get fed if I don't. I'm fine to drive. I'm used to it."

The men continue walking but neither respond.

"Guys, listen. Thank you for the help tonight, but I need to go home."

"Plead your case to Pigeon," Horse says with a chuckle.

With rising panic, I blurt, "It'll be bad for me if I don't!"

Both men stop dead in their tracks just as we hit the parking lot. Turning, Cash levels his gaze on mine.

"In this way?" he rumbles out while indicating my face.

Before I can explain, a motorcycle roars into the parking lot. Stopping in front of us, I watch as Pigeon shuts it off and swings his leg over the seat. Standing next to his bike, hands on his hips, feet planted wide, he stares at me.

"Thanks, Cash, Horse. Appreciate the help," Pigeon states while keeping his eyes on me.

"Did you talk with Rex?" Cash questions.

"Yeah, he explained."

"I added some numbers to her phone. Need anything else?" Cash asks.

"No, I got this," Pigeon answers.

"Should I make up the guest room or…" Horse asks with another laugh.

"You sleep like the dead. Would be easy for a motivated person to make their life easier by eliminating yours," Pigeon calmly answers.

"Noted. I'm out of here. Nice meeting you, Ivy," Horse says before walking away with a smirk on his handsome face.

"Thank you, Horse. Have a good night," I tell his retreating back.

"See ya," Cash mumbles before following Horse to the two bikes parked a short distance away.

Their bikes roar to life, and the two men ride out of the parking lot. Turning back to Pigeon, I realize I'm at a loss for words. It's been a long, stressful, terrifying day, and I'm emotionally, mentally, and physically spent.

"Let's go. You need to sleep and heal, and I need to know you're safe," Pigeon tells me in a low tone.

When I shake my head in protest, words still not forming, he gently pulls me to his chest and wraps his arms around me. I lean into him and accept his comfort. Wrapping my arms around his narrow waist, I soak up his warmth and win the battle against the tears forming from his kindness. We stand this way for several minutes before he pulls back, takes my hand, and leads me to his bike.

After Pigeon takes a seat, I sling my leg over and slide on behind him. Reaching back, he pulls my arms around his stomach and waits until I clasp my hands together. As we're leaving the rescue, I lay my cheek against his back and enjoy the ride.

Instant panic sets in when I open my eyes and recognize nothing. Bolting upright, I look around the room I've been sleeping in and briefly wonder if genetics have set in, and I've went over the edge like my mother did so many years ago. It only takes a moment, though, before I realize where I am and how I got here.

After arriving at a home not far from the rescue, Pigeon silently led me through the house and up the stairs to his bedroom. Handing me a t-shirt from a dresser drawer, he pulled my head toward his and laid a sweet, gentle kiss on my forehead. When he reached the doorway, he turned to me and spoke.

"Wear that and get some sleep, Ivy. I'll be downstairs if you need anything. You're safe tonight, and we'll talk tomorrow on how to keep you that way."

I stood in the room for only a moment before doing exactly as he requested. Slipping into his shirt, I folded my clothes and laid them on a chair.

Climbing into his big bed, I snuggled into the sheets that smell like him and fell asleep way quicker than I expected to. Now it's morning and time to face Pigeon and then Ted. I'm afraid of both encounters but for very different reasons.

Dressed, I let myself out of the room and walk the hallway looking for a bathroom. Finding one, I use the facilities, use the toothpaste and my finger before attempting to tame my curls. Giving up on that endeavor, I leave the bathroom and find my way to the stairs. Following the low voices I hear, I enter the kitchen and stop silently in the doorway.

Horse is sitting at the table with Gunner, Axel, and Cash while Pigeon is leaning against the counter, coffee cup extended my direction. I walk to his side, accept the cup, and mimic his stance. Taking a healthy swallow of the steaming black coffee, I close my eyes in appreciation. There's nothing better than that first cup of God's brew, especially after a rough night. Opening my eyes, I watch the men exchanging money.

"Thanks for the payday, Pigeon. I knew I could count on you," Horse says while counting the bills in his hand.

"Yeah, thanks," Axel adds while doing the same as Horse.

"You both suck," grumbles Gunner as he puts his wallet in his hip pocket.

"Agreed," says Cash as he follows Gunner's example.

"It's your own damn fault, you sore losers. I told you I saw a look," Axel gloats.

"What's going on?" I mutter to Pigeon.

"You sleep okay?" Pigeon asks from my side while ignoring my question.

"Yes, thank you."

"You took on two guys, possibly armed, with nothing but a half-wild dog and a phone. Have you lost your fucking mind?" Axel asks in a calm, conversational tone.

"They were going to steal the puppies," I answer in the same tone, though I'm somewhat bewildered as to why he's questioning what I see as an obvious action.

At the time, no other action came to mind. Now, in the light of day, it might not have been my smartest decision. Would I make the same decision if faced with the same set of circumstances? Yeah, I probably would. If that makes me certifiable, then so be it. I've been called worse, and at the end of the day, I have to live with myself and my decisions.

"Only my crazy-ass sister, and maybe Craig, will understand why you did what you did. Even so, mad respect, Ivy. More guts than brains, you're going to fit in like you were raised a Devil's Angel," Axel states while the other men chuckle.

Tilting my head slightly, I ask, "What would you have done?"

"He'd have done the same as you, but don't take that as a compliment. No one has ever accused Axel of being sane," answers Gunner before asking his own question. "The men never got close enough to hurt you, and yet someone has. Who?"

Knowing the time has come, I have to make some decisions about my life. Shuffling my feet, uncomfortable being the center of attention, I hesitate. Glancing up to Pigeon's kind eyes, I open my mouth and tell my truths.

"My brother. Since Nana and Papa died, he's gotten worse. He was always mean, a bully, but his drinking and control over the ranch and me have made him worse. Our grandparents didn't see this side of him until Nana was sick, and it was too late to change anything. Their will grants him a large sum of money, so he could afford to start a new life, but the ranch goes to me on my 25th birthday.

If they died while I was still a minor, it stated that Ted would have control over the ranch, drawing a healthy wage, until I either married or turned 25 years old. Nana passed two weeks before my 18th birthday, putting that condition into effect. If I give up and leave, the ranch would still be mine, but there wouldn't be anything left to receive. Ted's drinking and bad business decisions would ruin my future plans for the ranch. Also, Ted wouldn't use the ranch income to take care of Mom, and I can't afford the residential care facility on my own if I have to pay rent somewhere."

Silence reigns in the room for a minute before Gunner breaks it.

"Do you have a copy of the will? We have a club attorney that I'd like to take a look at it and see if there's any wiggle room in it."

"Yeah, I can get it to you. This isn't your problem, but I appreciate the help. I don't think I can do this for another couple of years," I admit quietly.

"You're done doing this, Ivy. We'll find a way out for you whether it's polite or bloody, legal or not," Pigeon states with a small bite to his voice.

"When Ava finds out about your brother, I guarantee it's going to lean toward the bloody side," Axel adds.

"Ava's pregnant and not getting involved in this," Gunner barks, and I agree wholeheartedly.

All heads turn to the door when it opens, and in walks Chubs. I feel the room go wired, but I don't know why. Staying silent, I watch Chubs walk to the coffee pot, pour a cup, refill mine, then take a seat, all without saying a word.

"Shit's been happening, brother, and apparently your phone's broke," Gunner says in a frigid voice.

"Here now, Prez," Chubs answers while taking a sip of his coffee.

Even being an outsider, I can read a room. There's tension radiating from every man in the room except Chubs. It's time to make an exit.

"I need to get home and get chores done before my shift. Thank you—" I start but get cut off.

"You called in sick this morning. Margie's aware of what happened last night and has agreed to get your shift covered. Also, your brother's been calling your phone all morning. A few of his voicemails indicate that at least one of us will be going home with you. Looks like you get some free ranch hands for the day," Pigeon informs me with a beautiful smile.

"I called in sick?"

"Axel did since he has the most feminine voice in the club," Cash states with a grin.

"Nobody appreciates my raw talents," Axel grumbles.

"I'll take Ivy home. I can stay there with her or bring her back. Whichever you want done," Chubs offers while looking at Pigeon.

After a few seconds, Chubs holds a piece of paper out to Gunner.

"There's the location Rex is looking for."

"Are you sure about this?" Gunner questions.

"About 95% sure," Chubs answers while standing and placing his cup in the sink.

"Chubs and I'll be taking you home, Ivy. After chores are done, you'll be coming back here, so you'll need to pack a bag," Pigeon informs me before reaching for my cup.

"Ted's not going to like that idea," I warn him. "He might get physical about it."

"God, I hope so," Chubs states emphatically before walking out the door.

Chapter 11
Pigeon

The drive to Ivy's home is a typically beautiful Colorado drive. Not much about this state to not like, though. Even with the views, Ivy's tense, understandably so, but Chubs keeps the conversation flowing with questions about the ranch. When he asks about her future plans, though, that's when she gets animated. As she talks, my admiration for this woman grows. Wanting to return the ranch to a place of peace, solitude, and growth for others less fortunate, as it was for her when her young life was turbulent, is a dream I can get on board with. It angers me to know that to achieve it, she's been living a life of hell brought on by her own family member. Having been raised on a farm of horrors, I can relate to her current life.

Driving down the long winding driveway, I spot large herds of cattle in the distance on both sides of us. To the right is another large pasture with several horses grazing peacefully. Up ahead, I get my first glimpse of the homestead.

Large, white two-story farmhouse with black shutters opened next to each window. Wraparound-style deck runs the full length of at least two sides of the house. Beautiful flower beds, all in bloom, line the front of the house, and the square-shaped lawn is a deep green. In the distance are several ranch buildings, including barns, a few well-maintained sheds, what's most likely a machine shop, and another smaller one-story home. Stopping Ivy's truck to the side of the driveway, I watch as a few blue heelers race toward us and two men step out of a barn. The men start walking our direction, and one has an angry face. Guessing that's the brother.

"Fucking paradise, Ivy. I can see why you're willing to fight for it," Chubs says as he opens his door and steps out.

I do the same on my side and wait for Ivy to slide across the seat and step out next to me. I slam the door shut, place my hand on the small of her back and wait for the dogs to reach us. Ivy greets the dogs by name, and I give them a chance to sniff me before encouraging Ivy forward.

"Where the hell have you been, Ivy? You forget there's a ranch full of hungry animals here?" the angry-faced man barks loudly.

I feel Ivy's flinch, but she keeps her eyes trained on her brother. Chubs stops in front of him and holds his hand out, saying, "Hey, Ted. I'm Chubs."

Ted hesitates before taking his eyes off his sister but eventually turns to Chubs, accepts the handshake, and asks, "Who are you?"

Suddenly realizing where this is going, I order Ivy to stay back, and I move to stand beside my club brother.

"Glad you asked. As I said, my name's Chubs, and this good-looking dude is my club brother, Pigeon. We're members of The Devil's Angels MC. Want you to remember our names and the name of our club, okay, Ted?"

Even though it's not close to noon yet, Ted reeks of beer. He's either still drunk from last night or getting an early start on today's binge.

"Yeah, fine, whatever. What's my sister doing with you two?" Ted questions irritably.

"We'll get to that. What you need to focus your pickled brain on right now is that I'm about to flatten your lazy, abusive ass, and I want you aware of it so you can't whine later that you were suckerpunched. Yeah?" Chubs explains patiently while a huge grin breaks across my face. Savage Chubs, my favorite version of him, is now in play.

With that said, Chubs pulls back and lands one hell of a punch to Ted's face. Ted staggers back, Ivy gasps, and I land the second punch when Ted steadies himself. This time, there's no staggering. The two consecutive blows put Ted on his ass in the dirt.

"We brought Ivy home so we can have a chat with you about her bruises. How she's never going to receive another one. Fucking ever, Ted. Now, stand up and prepare yourself to land there again. We've got all day to teach this lesson, and I missed my workout this morning," I say while grabbing Ted's shirt and hefting him to his feet. He cowers, tries to cover his head, and pull away. He fails.

"Question, Ivy. That other guy—has he ever laid a hand on you?" Chubs asks in a voice that sounds almost hopeful.

"No, Todd's never put his hands on me," she responds immediately, and I almost laugh when Chubs seems to deflate a little. Then she adds, "But he's stood by while Ted did."

"I couldn't intervene! He's my boss!" the other man shouts while throwing up his hands and backing away.

"Not a good enough excuse, fuckface," Chubs responds while he starts after the man.

"Ivy! For the love of God, call the police!" Ted orders.

"I have animals to feed, remember, Ted?" Ivy says calmly before walking away, dogs in her wake.

I hear a thump and watch Todd's ass plant in the dirt, similar to how Ted's did. Got to love Brother Chubs.

We teach our lesson, give Todd a time limit on packing his belongings and take Ted to the back deck of the house. There, we sit like civilized people and explain his new life to him. Once Chubs and I are convinced Ted understands, we find Ivy and get to work. Deep down, I know men like Ted can't handle losing their power over someone, and I know this isn't the end of trouble with him. What else I know is that Ivy's no longer his to control, his to abuse, or his life will end. Violently, painfully, and without a drop of remorse from me.

After the animals are fed and watered, the trailer disconnected, and the basics done, I tell Ivy to pack some clothes because she'll be staying in town at night. Chubs and I hang out in the kitchen, Chubs raiding the fridge while we wait for her. When she comes down the stairs, I watch as an older cat trails behind her, protesting loudly. After setting her bag on the floor, Ivy picks the cat up and cuddles it close.

"Bring the cat," I tell Ivy.

Shocked eyes look my direction, but I only shrug. I already live with a Horse. Why not a cat too?

"Are you sure? Tabitha's old, and Ted hates her, so I hate to leave her here, but I can take her to the rescue for a few days," Ivy offers.

"Pack what you need for her, Ivy. She's welcome at the house. What about the dogs? Will he hurt them?"

"No, he keeps his distance from them, and they stay in the barn with the horses."

When Ivy's ready, she carries the cat while Chubs and I carry the bags to her truck. It irritates me that Ted roared out of here earlier in a new, super-duty pickup, decked out with every option available while Ivy commutes daily in an old, battered truck. I'm surprised it still runs, but it fires up immediately, and we're on our way back to town.

At some point during the drive, Ivy's head leans against my shoulder, and she falls asleep, cuddling her cat. Looking down at her delicate features, I feel a tug low in my gut. She hasn't earned the life Ted's been giving her, but she still has a smile for everyone around her. Living in hell, she goes out of her way to brighten the day for abandoned and abused pets. She sings with piglets, dances with ducks, makes a little boy feel needed, and shares her food with a forgotten dog.

"She'll be fine, Pigeon. She's strong. She'll bounce back and push forward. It takes more than a shithead brother to break someone like her," Chubs says quietly but firmly.

"You're right, but I hate that she's had to go through any of it."

"Life's not fair. We've all had to make tough decisions and live with them regardless if they were the right ones or not. All we can do in this life is make a choice, hopefully for the right reasons, and push forward. Not everyone will understand why she stayed, but to her, she did it for the right reasons. I respect that," Chubs explains while staring out the side window of the truck.

"You have a tough decision to make, Chubs?" I ask.

"I fucking make it every single day," he mutters before dropping his head back and closing his eyes.

I know without saying another word that our conversation has ended. Chubs has said what he's going to say, and that's it. I lift my right arm, wrap it around Ivy's shoulders and pull her tighter into my side.

"Can you cook?" Horse asks as we walk into the house.

I don't even have the door shut, and he's got a stupid grin plastered to his stupid face and asking stupid questions. I shoot him a dark look which only makes his grin widen. Pillow, his sleeping face—I need to start making the plan.

"You have food here?" Ivy asks as she sets Tabitha on the floor.

"After you guys left, I went shopping," Horse answers while aiming hopeful eyes at Ivy.

"Ivy's not here to cook for you, dick splat," I remind him.

"That's not a nice thing to say in front of a lady, Pigeon," Horse corrects me with an innocent look.

"I don't mind, Pigeon. I like to cook, in fact. Nana and I cooked together a lot and being in the kitchen with her are some of my favorite memories," Ivy says in a soft voice before taking a seat next to Horse on the couch.

"Most of my favorite memories involve food too," Chubs adds with a wicked grin.

"I've heard things about that. Your, um, your appetite is kind of legendary," Ivy says with a smile.

"Thank you! I think I'll hang out with Horse and honor you with my presence for dinner then," Chubs responds. Turning to Horse, he asks, "What did you buy?"

"A huge fucking roast like the ones Ava buys. Potatoes, carrots, and some other veggies," Horse answers enthusiastically.

Shaking my head at the two men, I carry Ivy's bags upstairs to my room. Spotting my guitar leaning against a chair, I place it in the closet and shut the door. Walking back downstairs, I find Tabitha curled up on the couch, alone. Walking into the kitchen, I grab a beer, take a seat at the table next to the other two assholes, and take a long drink.

When I see Ivy standing at the counter staring at my hand, I look down to the beer bottle.

I move my eyes to her face and wait for hers to meet mine. When they do, I lift the beer bottle slightly and shake my head.

"Beer isn't his problem, Ivy. He's a dick, even sober. Nobody sitting in this kitchen will change their behavior toward you because they've had a few beers. Nobody in our club either. Words are cheap. I know that, but you'll see that for yourself in time."

Her eyes soften, and she gives a quick nod before turning back to the food she's prepping.

A few hours later, the smell of the roast in the oven is making my mouth water. As a club, we eat very well. Ava makes sure of it, but there's nothing like kicking back on the couch, watching a game, and having dinner in your own home. Glancing down at my thigh, I smile when I see Ivy curled up with her cat, her head on my thigh, both sound asleep. I'm beginning to understand just how hard her life has been in recent years.

I run my fingers through her soft curls and watch them shape themselves around my finger before springing back to their original shape when my hand pulls free. I can only imagine how cute she was as a child with those big hazel eyes and bouncing nearly blond curls. Riding her horse, dogs following, around a ranch that saved her from a life of uncertainty. The land, the home, and her grandparents gave her confidence, a sense of belonging, and safety. I want her to have those things again.

"Dinner's done," Chubs says while standing from the chair he was just napping in.

"You're not the cook. How do you know it's ready?" Horse looks up from his phone to ask.

"It's a gift," Chubs replies with a grin before bolting for the kitchen.

"Shit! Wake Ivy and get her out there before Chubs eats our share too!" Horse blurts as he too takes off for the kitchen.

Giving Ivy's shoulder a nudge, I call her name.

Sleepy eyes look up at me before she places her hand on my thigh to push herself upright. Setting Tabitha on the end cushion, Ivy yawns then stands. Hearing the clatter of plates and utensils, a few swear words, and what sounds like a struggle, Ivy looks toward the kitchen before realization dawns. She bolts out of the room, and a minute later, I hear her ordering the men to stand down.

Following her, I enter the kitchen to see Horse blocking Chubs from the roasting pan sitting on the stove. Chubs is not deterred, but Horse is using his size to win this battle.

"Jesus, you two! You've seen food before!" I shout into the fray but to no avail.

Seconds later, Ivy lifts the large pan, oven gloves on her hands, and sets it on a towel near the sink. Lifting the lid, steam rises, and along with it, more aroma. Chubs literally groans loudly while keeping his eyes glued to the pan. Horse takes advantage of the distraction and places Chubs in a headlock. Stepping between the two idiots and Ivy, I stand guard while she cuts the roast.

"Remember the last time you crossed me, Horse? Driving lesson with Tessie. Do I need to call Gunner and make sure that lesson isn't the last one?" Chubs asks in a muffled voice.

Horse instantly steps back while releasing Chubs from the headlock. Chubs grins before his eyes find the roast again. I step sideways to block his view and shake my head at him.

"You have nothing to threaten me with, Chubs. You want to eat, sit your ass at the table, and wait for Ivy to serve the food. You too, Horse."

Both men take their seats, bitching me out, and I turn to help Ivy get the food plated. When I notice her shoulders shaking, I frown, concerned the men scared her. Instead, I see tears in her eyes but from silent laughter. Nudging her elbow, those eyes meet mine.

"I'd heard things, but I honestly thought they were exaggerated! Now I understand why Chubs makes such large donations to the rescue each month!" Ivy says during a fit of giggles. Gathering her composure takes a minute, but she does and then asks, "How is he not 500 pounds?"

"We have no idea. It's unexplainable. He says it's a gift, but I call bullshit. It's a fucking nightmare for anyone wanting a late-night snack at the clubhouse. That fucker can hear a potato chip bag opening from a mile away. I mean that in the literal sense. I was once lying in my bed in the clubhouse, door shut, watching a movie, and made the mistake of opening a bag of chips. My door busts open, and Chubs bounces himself across my bed, leans on his elbows, and asks, "What'cha got there?" I explain while shooting her a grin.

"Harsh, but true," Chubs agrees amicably.

Ivy starts laughing again before giving a snort then laughing even harder. I watch in amusement before taking the fork and knife from her hands and ordering her to take a seat. Chubs jumps up and pulls a chair out for her, then slides it back to the table. Horse rolls his eyes and flips Chubs off. Normal dinner time with The Devil's Angels.

"I think I should hang around here to help keep an eye on Ivy," Chubs says while lounging in a recliner.

"You're only saying that because you heard her say she's making fried chicken tomorrow, you lying bastard," Horse counters from his chair.

"That confirmed my thoughts, yes, but I also like to be helpful," Chubs insists.

"Ava not feeding you?" Horse asks suspiciously.

"Ava's busy bonding with Moose and Matilda. Kind of Ivy's fault, really," Chubs complains.

"I work tomorrow evening, but I'll leave dinner in the fridge. Dessert too if I have time after I get back from the ranch," Ivy says.

"You'll have time because you'll have a few ranch hands to help get the work done," Chubs replies. "Pigeon's going to be busy with club stuff, so I've wrangled James into coming with us. He's a prospect, so it'll be fun to torture him with all the dirtiest chores."

"If I knew Ted wouldn't be there, I'd ask Craig if he'd like to come too. I don't want Craig around Ted at all, though. I promised Craig that I'd teach him to ride if his parents agree, but that should wait for now," Ivy quietly says.

"On your next day off, we'll take Craig to the ranch with us. Pippa and Pooh will want to go too, so there will be enough of us I'm guessing Ted will make himself scarce," Pigeon states.

"Craig said Trigger likes to fish with the kids. Papa stocked a pond with trout and other fish years back. I take fish pellets to it a few times a week. The creeks have walleye, bass, salmon, perch, and trout too. If Trigger would—" Ivy informs us before getting cut off by Chubs.

"Trigger's going to hound you daily if he finds that out. If we tell him, though, we can have a fish fry of epic proportions," Chubs says excitedly while pulling his phone out.

While Chubs makes the call, Ivy turns to me.

"I needed help with dealing with Ted. I know that, and I appreciate all you guys have done, but I can't stay here for much longer. There's just too much to do at the ranch to be making the extra trips back and forth. The guys didn't pull their weight, but I managed to get by with what they did do. I'm going to have to hire some help once I talk with the attorney tomorrow."

"Let's find out what the attorney says, and then we'll go from there. Unless Ted leaves the ranch for good, you won't be staying there alone with him anymore. We'll find a way for you to be safe and still keep the ranch running, Ivy."

"Trigger squealed like a little girl seeing her first pony. Wish I'd have recorded that sound for future leverage," Chubs moans while putting his phone down in disgust. He perks up quickly, though, and then announces, "But he's all for a fish fry!"

I pull my sore ass off the couch at 4am and start a pot of coffee. Taking a quick shower, I knock on the bedroom doors on my way past, waking the occupants. I walk to the back door and open it to greet a blurry-eyed James as he stumbles past me, making a beeline for the coffee cups. Once seated, both of us drinking our coffee, we wait. It's not long, and Chubs comes bounding through the door with boxes in his hands. Ava's bakery logo is printed on them, so that explains why he wasn't in the recliner when I woke up. Horse punches me in the shoulder on his way to the coffee, and I return the favor when he takes a seat next to me.

Ivy walks into the room and does the same as James did. She's dressed in worn, comfortable-looking jeans, work boots, t-shirt, and hoodie. Hair pulled up in a knot with a makeup-free face, she looks younger than usual and ready for a day of labor. A warm feeling settles in my stomach when I notice that her black eye is fading. On impulse, I stand and walk to her. Using my finger, I tilt her face up to mine and drop a light kiss on her perfect lips. Pulling back, I watch her eyes go wide, and I grin before asking, "That okay?"

Nodding slightly, she keeps her eyes on mine. Without words, it seems like we have a whole conversation. I run the back of my finger across her cheek before speaking.

"Chubs brought donuts. Better get what you want before they're gone."

"Okay," Ivy answers before making her way to the table and picking up a donut.

"Horse and I are heading to the clubhouse now. The attorney will be here around 2pm to meet with Ivy, so have her back in time for that. I'll be here if I can, but if not, one of you need to follow her to the rescue for her shift. I'll come there as soon as I can. Margie's aware that Ivy will have a volunteer with her today, so she's expecting one of us," I say as I stand and drop my truck keys on the table in front of Chubs. "Take my truck. It's filled and has more room."

"Will do, brother," Chubs responds.

As Horse walks outside, I stop in front of Ivy.

"Work their asses off and keep one of them in sight at all times. If Ted decides to hang around, stay even closer to Chubs or James, yeah?"

Ivy nods in agreement before saying a quiet thank you. I turn and walk away, and it's way harder to do than I ever thought it could be.

Arriving at the clubhouse, Horse and I head straight to the room we use for Church. Taking our seats, I wait for Gunner to start talking.

"Chubs and James got Ivy today?" he asks while looking at me.

I nod.

"Anything happens to her on our watch, Ava's going to disembowel each of us with a dull knife," Petey states. "Starting with you first, Pigeon."

"Petey and I had a conversation with Ava last night and explained what's been going on with Ivy.

Needless to say, she's fucking furious that she didn't pick up on it and intervene long ago. If Ivy would rather stay with us, she's not only welcome, but something Ava may try to insist on," Gunner adds.

"She's staying with me," I state firmly.

All eyes in the room are aimed at me, but nobody says a word. A minute goes by before Gunner nods and says, "Whatever you need, let us know."

I nod again, and Gunner changes the subject to our guests.

"From everything we can confirm so far, Chubs gave us the most likely location for the exchange. Alfonse Morales has a contact in Seattle that called him late last night and said that a large, black van left the warehouse he's been watching, and he believes the victims are inside. That means they're on their way, and it's roughly a 20-hour drive, so that's why this meeting was called so early today. Also, he doesn't believe all the victims are adults. Some appeared too young, too small to be adults. We each need to get our heads straight with what we may find," Gunner orders.

"We're going to break into groups, mixed with the Morales family members, and cover a few other locations also. Just in case we're wrong about this one. Do what you need to do today to be ready because we're going to be sitting on the locations starting at 3pm. We'll rotate shifts, if needed, and hope we're right on where this will take place. Toes and a couple of the Morales people will be watching the smaller airports just in case they use a private plane, but that's doubtful," Axel states.

"Get with Axel for your assignments and get done whatever needs to be done because if we get lucky and break this shit up, we're going to be busy with the victims for at least a few days," Gunner adds before slamming down the gavel signifying the end of Church.

Taking a seat at an empty table in the main room, I wait my turn to speak with Axel. The Morales family members are milling about, some eating, some just drinking coffee, but the room is filled with energy. Everyone here is ready for this to get done. Trigger sits down on the opposite side of my table and scrubs his hands down his face. I wait because I know he has something to say, and Trigger's always worth listening to.

"I've spent a lot of time working on projects at the rescue. Been around Ivy and watched her with the animals on several occasions. Ava and Craig think she can walk on water, Reno claims she has a God-given gift, and I can't disagree with any of them. Feeling safe in her own environment, there's no telling how much she'll accomplish in her life. How much good she'll do for others. If you're serious about her, then focus on those things and not her age. She's young in years but has an old soul, Pigeon. Not many in this world has her capacity to give back to those in need, whether they're human or animal. Craig told me about her plans for the ranch, and I, for one, want to see her succeed in making them happen. I never met her grandparents, obviously, but I'm sure they'd be proud of what she wants to do with their ranch because who the fuck wouldn't be?"

I think about his words and hesitate a moment before speaking. Meeting his eyes, I seek advice from someone I trust and admire.

"I'm worried I'm too fucking jaded from life to be with someone like her. I'm older, far from innocent, and we both know she's too good for the likes of me. Right?"

"I don't deserve a classy lady like Tammy, and yet I have her. Axel certainly doesn't deserve Bailey. Nobody will ever be good enough for Bella or Tessie in my opinion. None of that matters in the end. What matters is the life you give her. The freedom to be herself and to pursue her dreams while having the security and safety of having you standing strong behind her. Don't let the shit your parents pounded in your head as a kid determine your future. You're a far better man than your dad's ever been regardless of his claims of being a man of God."

I listen closely, then promise to think about all he said. Trigger stands, prepared to walk off, but turns back to me.

"We get this shit done, Ivy gets a game plan to get rid of her brother, have her meet with Bailey. Bailey wants to do an audit on the ranch accounts, and it's a great idea. Her brother's probably been skimming for a while now, and he needs to answer for that. I volunteer now to help make him answer for every cent he's misplaced."

I grin at the visual but agree it's a great idea to have Bailey go over the books. I make a mental note to bring it up to Ivy and another one to speak with Ava about Ivy's new living arrangements.

Lying flat out on the ground next to Axel, we wait. Pooh's on the other side of me, and he's been quiet and withdrawn. I didn't get home in time for Ivy's meeting with the attorney, but Chubs reassured me he's sticking close and will be going to work with her later. James was called in to the police department for an overtime shift, along with Livi, so that keeps him clear of anything that happens tonight.

"I want to have a chat with Ivy," Axel announces.

"What about?" I ask.

"I want to adopt Priscilla. She deserves a good home, and while I've never owned a large bird before, I've been around Mac long enough to know how to care for one. Bailey agreed and is excited about it too."

"Seriously? I thought you hated birds because of Mac," I respond skeptically.

"Nah, I don't even hate Mac. I just like tormenting the little feathered asshole. Prissy's been living at the rescue for quite a while now, and that's not fair to her. Her owner loved her and did her best by her, but shit happens, and Prissy's been living in limbo. Ivy said she's not aggressive with kids, so I think she'd do good with a stable home. I have Ava across the street if I need help or advice."

Looking at Axel's profile, I see how serious he is about this. He's usually impulsive, but he's obviously put some thought behind this decision.

"I'll have her call you."

"Thanks, Pigeon. Did you hear what Gunner did?" Axel asks while flashing a wide smile. "Apparently, when he was at the rescue checking out the donkeys, him and Ava walked through the pig barn while discussing the donkeys and building a barn. Big, badass MC President saw a tiny piglet, the runt of the litter, and contacted Margie the next day about adopting it. I'm guessing it was some kind of love at first sight thing. He hasn't told Ava or the kids yet, so Freddy has a tiny pig living in his back bedroom at the moment."

"Our Prez has grown a vagina. Not sure why he hasn't told Ava. She's not going to be mad about another animal," Pooh speaks for the first time before giving a hoot of laughter.

"No, dickhead, she probably won't be mad, and no, you pissy little fuckface, I have not grown a vagina!" comes a deep voice from directly behind our position.

"Fuck me," moans Pooh before lifting his head toward the new threat behind us.

When I hear a thump and a painful moan from Pooh, I laugh along with Axel.

"Turns out, not all pigs stay on the small side like Gee did. Apparently, I just adopted what will become a large farm pig, and I'm not sure Ava's going to be okay with it being an outdoor pig. Hoping the barn gets built soon so it can move there instead of my fucking home," Gunner admits while I try to stifle another laugh. "Fucking Margie could have told me that before I signed the papers. Serves me right for not going to Ivy about it first."

"Got a name yet?" Axel asks, clearly fighting to keep the laughter out of his voice.

"Yes, I'm calling him Little Axel. Anything else you three want to gossip about instead of paying attention to what we're here for?" Gunner responds in a snarky tone.

All laughter dies when we spot headlights coming down the deserted road that leads to the gravel pit we're lying on the brim of. Gunner disappears while we drop lower to be out of view. My stomach knots when the vehicle is close enough to see that it's a black cargo-type van. It comes to a stop, not 30 yards in front of us, and shuts off. The passenger door opens, and a scruffy-looking guy emerges. Stretching first, he then relieves his bladder on the van's tire. Reentering the van, the driver's door opens, and another guy does the same as the first.

Axel pulls his phone out, reads the text before carefully holding it so Pooh and I can read it too. It's been decided to take control of the van now, get the victims clear of the area before the buyer shows up. Our lookouts have confirmed that there isn't another vehicle on the road, so now's the time to do this. We move in from the direction of the van's blind spots. Matias and Santiago Morales move to the driver's side while Axel and I take the passenger side. Pooh ducks low and inches in front of us. He'll step to the front of the van to cover the rest of us when Axel gives the signal.

Things go off perfectly as planned with no hitches. Doors are jerked open at the same time Pooh pops up in front of the van, rifle trained on the windshield. I drag the male passenger out at the same time as the Morales team does the same on the other side. We ignore the screams from inside the van and quickly secure the two men. Once it's done, Petey slides the side door back while Gunner covers the interior with his handgun. When he lowers the gun, I know these two men were the only threat we were facing.

"Get them the fuck away from the van," Gunner orders, and I hoist my guy to his feet and march him across the clearing to a small stand of trees along the edge. Securing both men to the trees, I gag them before leaving them alone with the two Morales brothers. Returning to the van, I stand near Pooh while Gunner and Petey explain what's happening to the victims inside the van.

"Did anyone bring bolt cutters?" Petey asks in a quiet voice.

"There's a pair in the van with Reeves. I'll get him up here," I answer while making the call.

We wait until Reeves and Rex show up with our van. Reeves jogs to Gunner's side with the bolt cutters while Rex approaches with several blankets in his arms. After a moment's discussion, Reeves climbs inside. Listening to the bolt cutters doing their job, I feel my stomach tighten and Pooh fidget beside me. Glancing at his face, I can tell he's holding on by a thread.

When Reeves steps out of the van, we stand silently as victim after victim steps outside, accepting a blanket from Rex on their way past. Rex runs out of blankets long before we do victims. In all, I count 11 humans that had been crammed in the back of the van, chained to its walls like animals. My stomach does a slow roll when I see how young most of them are. Only a few might be considered adults. One black-haired girl can't be over eight years old. The men standing around start handing out their hoodies and sweatshirts to anyone who doesn't have a blanket. It hits me suddenly that with all the people standing around in such a small area that the silence is deafening.

Finally, a young girl, maybe 14 years old, speaks.

"There's one more in there, but she's dead. She wouldn't stop crying, so the guy in the passenger seat shot her in the face. He put her inside that toolbox thing at the back."

Nobody moves for a few seconds before Gunner aims his flashlight in the van then climbs inside.

When he emerges, the look on his face proves the girl is telling the truth. Gunner takes a moment, then calmly orders Rex and Reeves to load the females into our van and to head for the clubhouse. After the van leaves, he turns to the rest of us.

"Pooh, you're on the hill with your rifle. You'll provide cover. Axel and Pigeon, you're in the van, taking the place of the two men. Lose your cuts first. When the buyer arrives, we'll let them think the van's still holding their merchandise."

Axel and I nod, remove our cuts handing them to Petey before taking the seats at the front of the van. Neither of us speak as the rest of the men move to their previous positions. Only exception is the two Morales brothers taking the two men out of sight of the van. After several long minutes, Axel speaks in a near whisper.

"I'm so sorry, little girl. I'm so fucking sorry we didn't get to you sooner. I'm so fucking sorry."

My heart breaks in half hearing his words and knowing that we're sitting in a van with a murdered child. A child that should be sleeping in a bed, in a room decorated with unicorns, dreaming of puppies, and not be lying dead in a filthy toolbox.

"We'll get justice for her tonight," I tell Axel while not believing my own words.

"There's no justice for this. No matter what we do to these men, nothing will give her justice or make this right in any way."

I nod but don't respond because he's right, and there are no words that will help either of us or her.

Nearly an hour goes by before we get a text that two vehicles are approaching. A very long, endless hour knowing what we need to do but wanting to do so much more. When I started getting antsy a while back, Axel said exactly what I needed to hear at that moment.

"We're guarding a tiny angel, gone too soon, until she gets her wings, Pigeon. No better place for us to be right now."

I stilled immediately, and no words have been spoken since.

Now, it's go time. We watch as the two vehicles come to a stop and two men step from the van. As they approach, Axel and I step outside and close our doors behind us. Coming to stand beside me, Axel and I wait.

"Boss wants to see the merchandise," the taller guy states while waving a hand at the car parked nearby.

"Got the payment?" Axel asks simply to stall so our guys have time to block the entrance to the gravel pit.

"No pay until he views the merchandise. He's been burnt before and isn't paying for sick or older women. He's only paying for underage girls this time. Open the doors so I can get video of them, or we leave."

"You can get video but no touching the property until we receive payment," Axel says while moving to the sliding van door.

Opening it, both men move closer to peer inside. Axel and I strike at the same time, taking both men down. As soon as we do, the driver throws the car into gear and tries to roar off. A loud shot rings out, and a tire explodes, making the car spin in a tight circle. When it comes to a stop, I see Cash standing directly in front of it, gun aimed at the driver. Trigger's next to him, in the same position, as several of the Morales members swarm the car, yanking the doors open. Three men are pulled from the vehicle, but it's the one pulled from the backseat that gains everyone's interest.

He's wearing an expensive suit but having money can't disguise the evil inside of him. He's obviously scared at this turn of events, but as his eyes take in the clothing of the men holding him, he wilts. Yeah, blue jeans, hoodies, and cuts don't scream cop, so he's smart enough to realize he'd have been better off being grabbed by law enforcement who have laws to follow. We don't, and that realization is draining his face of all color. Predictably, he starts begging for his life and offering payment to be released unharmed. He's under the misconception that we're a dirty club looking to steal his money and the women. He couldn't be more wrong and knowing that gives me an overwhelming sense of pride in myself and my club. We might ride bikes, swear a lot, and drink more, but we're the good guys in this scenario.

"Shut your fucking mouth," Gunner barks loudly as he stops in front of the man.

"I can pay. I have money, and you can have the girls. Just let me leave, and you'll never see me again," the man tries again.

"We, too, have money and already have the girls. You are right about one thing, though. They'll never see you again, but neither will anyone else," Jorge Morales answers with rage thickening his voice.

"Shake them down, load everyone into their van, and head to the clubhouse. Decisions will be made there," Gunner orders and turns to walk off. At the last second, he turns back around and plants his fist dead center in the face of the buyer.

When everyone's ready to leave, Axel turns to me and says, "You're riding with me and our angel. Let's take her home."

Walking to the van, we climb in and head for home. Upon arriving at the clubhouse, the prisoners are stripped and placed in the holding cell in the basement. Pooh roughly chains each one to the walls, with the buyer being chained to the ceiling. Reeves takes a seat outside the door and hangs his head. He's drawn the first guard duty of the night.

Discussions take place between our club and the Morales family, and when the decisions have been made, Axel and I head outside. Stopping just outside the main door, I pull a pack of smokes from my pocket and hold them out to Axel. Neither of us are regular smokers, but this occasion seems to call for it, so we light up while leaning our backs against the building.

A few minutes later, Pooh joins us. He's holding a bottle of Jack and passes it around. We have one more thing to do yet before this night of horrors has ended. When Gunner, Petey, and Trigger join us, I note their faces show the strain of what's got to get done.

"Most of you have kids. Let me do this alone," I say into the silence. "Where do I take her?"

"Vex called Taja to ask her for a number to a nurse she knows because our doctor isn't in town. Didn't work out like we were hoping, and she's on her way. Ava and Trudy are coming too and bringing clothes to put her in. Fuck me, none of them should see this. The girl is about the age of our twins and looks similar," Gunner says in a low, tortured voice.

"I don't like it either, especially with two of them being pregnant, but let them do this for the little girl. She deserves a woman's touch and care. We'll pick up the pieces later if needed," Petey advises.

"Take her to my room," Gunner mutters.

Taking the blanket Trigger hands me, I walk to the van. Opening the back doors, I take a deep breath before opening the toolbox. Inside is a tiny child, laying on her side, dark hair spread across her face. The smell of blood assaults my senses, but I ignore it. Carefully gathering her small body, I place her against my chest and then wrap the blanket around her, tucking her in gently. I drop my head back and stare at the black sky for a moment. Sending words to the God I'm not sure exists anymore, I ask for safe passage for a young girl who didn't deserve the cruelties of this world. When I'm done, I turn and stop abruptly.

Standing on both sides of the sidewalk is a long line of men. Different nationalities, beliefs, ages, different in a lot of ways, they're standing united for her. Heads bowed, standing in silence, I walk between them, staring straight ahead. Vex opens the door for me, and I pass through, going directly to Gunner's room. I gently lay her on the bed and place the blanket over her tiny form. When I turn, I see the women waiting at the door. Each face has its emotions tightly under control except for the resolve of what needs to be done. I walk past and make my way to the silent main room.

"You're done tonight, Pigeon. Head home. We got this from here," Axel orders.

I nod and do as I'm told.

The house is silent when I enter through the kitchen door, but there's a light on above the stove. Reading the note left there, I ignore it and instead make my way upstairs to the bathroom. I strip and take a long, hot shower. Head hanging, I watch as a child's blood washes off my hands and down the drain. When the water starts to cool off,

I step out and dry off. Pulling on a pair of sweatpants, I towel dry my hair.

Cracking open the door to my room, I see Ivy curled up in my bed with Tabitha lying on the foot of it. As I'm closing the door, Ivy lifts her head and looks my direction. Changing my mind, I push through the door, shut it behind me, and make my way to the bed. Sliding in beside Ivy's warm body, I pull her close and place my chin on the top of her head. After a moment, she pushes in tighter to my chest. We lay together in silence for several long moments before she speaks.

"You okay?"

"I don't know yet, honey. Probably not, but I'll get there. Do you mind if we don't talk, and I just hold you tonight?"

"I'm good with that," she answers before wrapping an arm around my middle.

I run my hand along her arm until it finds her hand. Clasping my fingers with hers, I close my eyes and pray for the sleep that takes hours to come.

Lola Wright

Chapter 12

Ivy

I lean over Pigeon to reach his phone when the alarm goes off. When it's silent again, I stay propped up on an elbow and look at the man next to me. Beautiful tats stand out even in the dim available light. Muscled chest, arms, and abs, Pigeon has a lean build. He's not bulky in muscle like Axel but has definition, and it's obvious he works out. I let my eyes roam his body and tats before returning to his face. I find sleepy, hooded eyes staring back at me.

"Go back to sleep. I have to get to the ranch, but Chubs said he'd take me. James is coming again for another day of more disgusting torture. His words, not mine. He said Livi wanted to come too, so he's picking her up and meeting us there. We'll be back before my shift," I tell him.

Pigeon lifts a hand and runs it through my hair before pulling my face into his neck. Holding me there for a moment before releasing me, he continues to silently watch me. I slide out of bed, grab my clothes, and make my way to the bathroom.

I find Chubs in the kitchen pouring travel mugs of coffee. As I'm screwing the lid on mine, Pigeon walks in. Bare-chested, sweatpants barely clinging to his hips, he looks delicious. When I realize I'm staring as bad as Dale does, I turn to grab my hoodie and pull it on.

"Spoke to Axel this morning. Church this afternoon. Anything you need, brother?" Chubs asks.

"No, I'm good."

"You're not, and that's okay, Pigeon. I got Ivy today, and I'll keep a close eye on things."

"Find anything out from the attorney?" Pigeon asks, looking at me.

"She's looking at the will and will get back with me if she finds anything helpful," I answer with a small shrug.

I don't have a lot of faith that she can find a way around the will, but it is worth a try. Meanwhile, I have to keep the ranch going.

Pigeon nods his head before saying, "You're not alone anymore, Ivy. We'll deal with this one way or another. Your ranch will continue to be just that. Your ranch. Look to the future and what changes you want to make. Start working on those plans because Ted's reign there has come to an end."

I want to smile and feel relieved, but the sadness lurking in Pigeon's eyes keep that from happening. I don't know what has put it there, but I want it gone. As Chubs makes his way to the door, I hurry over to Pigeon, go up on my tiptoes, and brush my lips across his. When I pull back, his dark eyes stay on mine.

"Stay close to Chubs, James, and Livi today. We'll talk tonight."

I nod and follow Chubs out the door.

"I don't know the rules of an MC, Chubs. I was only asking because Pigeon seems off since last night. If I don't ask questions, I can't fix that for him," I answer in frustration.

"MCs are generally pretty secretive because we don't like outside interference. We make our own rules and laws and live by them, not society's. Not that you're considered an outsider anymore, but still. Pigeon will tell you what he wants you to know, and you have to find a way to be okay with that. I tell Lucy everything, but others don't. Each member has to decide how much to share with their woman. Another thing to remember is if Pigeon shares something with you, that doesn't mean everyone has done the same, so keep it to yourself. It's about trust and who can handle what. All I'll say is that the club helped some people fix a wrong last night, and it was an ugly situation. Pigeon did his job, but there's a price that goes along with that. Be patient and give him time."

"I can do that. Thank you, Chubs."

A few minutes after we stop beside the barn, James and Livi pull up beside us. I swallow my laugh at the disgruntled look on James' face and the excitement on Livi's. Chubs hands James a pitchfork and points to the horse barn. James walks off, muttering to himself while Livi taunts him about his soon to be green manure-covered, white sneakers. Flipping her off over his shoulder, James disappears into the barn.

"I don't mind cleaning the stalls, Chubs. James can load the wagon with hay instead," I insist.

"He won't be a prospect for much longer, and I won't be able to torture him then. Let me enjoy this while I can," Chubs counters before heading for the hay barn.

Turning to Livi, I ask, "What would you like to do?"

"Anything with baby animals!" she shouts.

"Let's make up the bottles. We have a few orphaned calves that need to be bottle-fed. You'll love this chore. It's the best one."

Placing the large bottles into a milk crate, Livi all but skips next to me as I lead her to the calf enclosure. Waiting impatiently are four hungry adorable calves. Instructing her to hang on tight to the bottles, I hand her two. Taking the other two, I lower them to calf height and wait for the hungry mouths to find them. Livi does the same and then squeals in delight when two calves latch on.

"Oh my God! They're so freaking cute!" she whisper-shouts at me.

Laughing, I agree while thinking of the list of things to get done today. It's not long before the calves have drained the bottles, and I check that off my list.

"Now what?" she asks enthusiastically while we rinse the bottles and then refill them for later.

I smile, give her a rundown of what needs to be accomplished and then laugh out loud at the widening of her eyes. Then, we get down to work.

Riding in the side by side with Livi, I take mental notes of the hay pastures. I have to hire a few neighbor guys to help soon because haying season is about to be here. I can do anything that needs to be done on the ranch, but I can't do it during haying season. Haying season is a full-time job in itself, and that's why I take my vacation time from the rescue during it each year. It's time to talk with Margie so she can prepare for me being gone for a week to ten days.

We get back to the barns in time to meet up with James and Chubs and hit the road back to Denver. Rushing into Pigeon's house, I crash into an unmovable object. Bouncing backward, I look up and see it's Horse I ran into. Turning his head, he grins down at me. I grin back, dart past him, and take the stairs two at a time. I grab a change of clothes from Pigeon's room and hurry to the bathroom. Not paying attention to anything but getting to work on time, I walk in without realizing the shower's running. Jerking my head toward it, I see a perfect male silhouette, water running down a tanned, hard body.

Whirling back to the door, I hear an invitation issued behind me.

"Would rather you join me, honey, but it's your choice," Pigeon's deep rumble slides over my body.

Keeping my back to him, I ask, "Is that a good idea?"

"Best idea I've ever had. Been pretending for a while now, and I'd rather get back to being real."

"Pretending? About what?" I question while my stomach tightens.

His answer is incredibly important to me, and my body tenses, worried that it won't be what I need to hear him say.

"That you're just Ava's friend. That I'm amused by you; I admire you, but I'm not attracted to you. That maybe I am good enough for someone like you. I'm tired of pretending that I don't want you naked, under me, for hours while I dirty your mind and mark your body with me."

The last sentence is muttered, lips pressed to my ear and hands sliding up my sides. Being so intent on his words, I didn't know he'd left the shower.

"If any of that's more than you want, walk out that door, and we'll continue as if this conversation never happened. You'll still have mine and the club's help and protection. If it isn't, then I'm going to strip you, shower with you, and I guarantee you're going to be late for work."

Reaching down, I pull my t-shirt over my head. That's all the answer Pigeon requires before he makes my bra disappear and then quickly eliminates the rest of my clothing. Turning to face him, I lift my face to look into his eyes, but his mouth crashes down on mine with intent. After a deep, sensual kiss, Pigeon pulls me into the shower with him.

Placing me under the spray, Pigeon steps back. Instinctively, I move my arm, intending to cover myself, but he stops the move. Clasping his fingers with mine, he lowers our arms, and his eyes begin to devour me. They roam my body, heat evident in them, and then lock on my breasts. My nipples harden under his gaze, and my throat offers up a low moan. Pigeon's eyes rise to mine, then he grins, dimples and all.

"Fuck me, Ivy. You've been hiding all of this under baggie hoodies and loose t-shirts?" Pigeon groans out before releasing my hands.

"Pigeon, please," I mutter in what could easily be taken as begging.

"Please what? Please kiss you? Please touch you?" he teases before finding my mouth with his.

"Yes," I answer against his lips.

Pigeon slides his hands up my neck to cup my face and head with his long fingers. He deepens our kiss, tongue sliding against mine before he pulls back enough to lightly nip my lower lip. Placing his forehead against mine, I hear him take in a long breath before slowly releasing it.

"My first time of being inside you isn't going to be in a shower that's going to turn fucking cold soon. My first time making you come will be, though," Pigeon says before turning my body around, so my back is resting against his chest.

Warm water spraying down on me, I lean against Pigeon and watch his hands land on my breasts. Cupping them, he flicks his thumbs across my nipples several times before one hand goes south. When I feel his finger sliding between my folds, I arch my back in pleasure. Gently circling my clit, I move one hand behind me to grip his hard thigh and the other upward to grip his neck.

Feeling his hardened cock pressed against my backside, I push back against it. Pigeon moans close to my ear before saying, "Yeah, honey, just like that."

Pinching my clit between thumb and finger, Pigeon slowly slides another finger into my wetness. My body gives a small jerk at how much I like what he's doing, and he lightly bites the top of my shoulder close to my neck.

It's been a long time since I was this close to a man. My body has been craving Pigeon's touch, so it responds quickly. Grinding hard against his cock, I feel it slide downward between my cheeks. Pigeon releases my clit and moves his hand so his finger can delve deeper inside of me. His other hand continues torturing my nipple, and I want more of him.

"Need you inside of me," I say on a gasp of pleasure. "Want to touch you."

"You'll get both. First, I need you to come for me, Ivy. Don't hold back."

Removing his hand from my breast, he slides it across my chest, up to my chin before turning my head to meet his mouth. At the same time, his finger is replaced with two, and he presses down on my clit with his thumb. Our mouths clash, tongues finding each other, and his hand picks up its pace. I feel the tingle low in my belly. Arching my back again, I press down on his hand.

"That's it, baby. Fuck my fingers. Come on, Ivy. Give it to me," Pigeon whispers against my mouth.

I slam my head back against his chest as my orgasm crashes through my body. Pigeon doesn't stop. He increases the movements of his hand and draws it out gloriously long. I'm panting as the feeling slowly starts to subside, and my body relaxes its muscles.

Pigeon waits a beat before sliding his fingers out of my body and wrapping both arms around me while he buries his face in my neck.

"Fucking perfection, baby," he whispers against my neck.

After a moment of being held, Pigeon pulls back and reaches for the soap. Looking over my shoulder at him, I raise an eyebrow.

"Water's going to turn cold. Let's get you clean before I take you to bed and let you do filthy things to me," he answers my unspoken question with a wicked grin.

I try to wash quickly, liking his answer, but Pigeon keeps pushing my hands out of the way so he can soap my body. I give up and let him have his way, but I don't make it easy for him. Placing kisses on his broad chest, sliding my hands across his abs, I direct one hand south. Pigeon grabs my wrist before I get to my target and laughs at the look I give him.

I understand his rush, though, when the water starts to cool. Rinsing body and hair quickly, I step out of the shower and into the towel Pigeon's holding up for me. Squeezing as much water as I can from my hair, I turn to view the sight of Pigeon's hard, tanned body with a towel barely covering the parts I want to explore. Again, I get a grin and flashing dimples before Pigeon bends and tosses me over his shoulder. Giving my rump a swat, he exits the bathroom and strides down the hallway.

My eyes go wide, and my body goes taunt when I hear a voice that doesn't belong to Pigeon.

"Fucking Axel is making a mint because of you, brother. I'm going to owe him a week's pay!"

Not knowing if my ass is covered or not, I try to swing a hand back there to hold the towel down. Pigeon's hand brushes mine away and covers the area I was worried about, so I use both hands to hold the towel to my chest instead. Hanging over his shoulder the way I am, the blood is rushing to my face, so I bury it against his back.

"Pay up. Axel was right," Pigeon answers with a laugh before continuing down the hallway.

"Called the rescue for you, Ivy. Told your boss you'd be late today. Car trouble and all that," says the unfamiliar laughing voice as I continue keeping my face and boobs hidden.

"Thanks, Reeves. Now leave," Pigeon orders as he closes the bedroom door behind us.

A second later, my body is flying through the air. I land on my back on the mattress with a bounce that loosens my towel completely. When it falls open, Pigeon pounces. Landing on his knees on either side of my hips, he grips my wrists and holds them against the bed near my head. Moving my eyes downward, I see his towel is gone. The tip of my tongue touches my bottom lip in anticipation, and Pigeon groans at the movement.

"I'm clean, but I have condoms. You on birth control?" Pigeon questions.

"Yes, I am, and I was tested after breaking up with my last boyfriend. I want to feel you, Pigeon, not latex."

"Same. No more talk of boyfriends, though. Ever. I'm selfish that way."

The words no more than leave his mouth before it finds my breast. Nipping lightly at my nipple, he glides his tongue in a circle around it. After a minute or so, he moves to give the other breast equal attention.

I tug on my hands, wanting them free, but Pigeon doesn't release them.

"Want to touch you," I say while pushing my breast closer to his talented mouth.

"In time, baby. Let me play for now because once your hands land on my body, I'm going to need to be deep inside of you."

How do you argue with that logic? I don't, so instead, I relax into the bed and watch Pigeon play.

Sitting back on his heels, he releases my wrists but shakes a finger at me when I go to move them. Tracing his finger between my breasts, down my stomach, he stops it at the top of my pubic bone. He leans down and places a sweet, soft kiss just above his fingertip. Sitting back up, Pigeon's eyes meet mine.

"I'm a bossy bastard and like things my way. I want to see every inch of you, touch, and taste all that I see. I like to play with my food, so to speak. If you're okay with that, I need you to lay still and let me do my thing. I meant it when I said your touch would push me over the edge, and playtime would end. Can you give me this?"

I nod, afraid I couldn't use words even if I tried. To prove I can do what he wants, I place my hands over my head and grip the slats on the headboard. Doing so makes my breasts rise, and his eyes zero in on them instantly. The heat and hunger I see in them makes me feel incredibly sexy and wanted.

"While I explore all of you, please know that sounds make me hard. Don't be silent if you like something I'm doing. Don't be afraid to say no if I do something you don't like."

I give a small nod and watch as he drops his head to my stomach. Closing my eyes, I concentrate on the feel of him and the feelings he evokes in my body.

Tongue moves slowly across my abs while his hands land on my ribs. Neither hands nor tongue stay still. He literally explores my body, and the feeling of it is incredible. When he lifts up on his knees and moves further down my body, I nearly stop breathing. Using a gentle hand under my knee, he lifts my leg until the bottom of my foot is resting on the bed. Doing the same maneuver with the other leg, he slides both hands from foot to knee, then to hip, and back down to my knees. Placing a soft kiss on the inside of both my knees, he pushes them outward, then pauses.

Knowing where his eyes are looking, I don't even attempt to stifle the shiver or the moan. I feel my pussy involuntarily clench then relax with his increased breathing.

"You're fucking perfect," Pigeon whispers in a harsh tone. "Pink, wet, and so fucking ready for me."

When a hand leaves my knee, I clench again. Running a soft finger the length of my labia, he circles my opening twice before running the finger up the other side to my clit. My clit hardens, stiffens, and his fingertip brushes it from side to side before making the trip south again. This time, after circling my opening, he pushes a tiny part of his finger inside. Removing it, he spreads the wetness across my clit. Leaning down, his tongue takes the path his finger has been traveling.

My breath hitches, I moan and fight the need to move. Lifting his head, he repeats the erotic torturous trip again with his finger. Again, he dips his finger inside me but goes deeper. Removing it, he again spreads the wetness on my hardened clit before using his tongue to torment it. Repeating this maneuver several times, each time pushing his finger deeper inside me, I'm on the verge of coming.

"Pigeon, please," I beg. "I need to come, honey."

"Take a deep breath, relax, and let it build. I want to watch you come, hard, and then I'm planting my cock deep inside of you," he orders in a soft voice.

Dropping his head again, I feel his tongue and lips explore me as I do what he ordered. When his lips suck on my clit, one finger goes deep inside my sex. I start to pant. Pumping his finger, lips and tongue in play, his other hand spreads my parts open wide. Showing no mercy, Pigeon ups his game. My hands grip the headboard, my body bows off the bed, and an intense orgasm washes through my body. Before it ends, Pigeon moves quickly. Moving his hips between my spread thighs, he covers my body with his. Pushing slowly, stopping, then pumping slightly, he fits his length deep inside of me.

I let go of the headboard and wrap my arms around his neck, burying my fingers in his hair.

"Harder, Pigeon! Please, God, harder!" I beg while moving my hips to meet each of his thrusts.

Grasping my hip in one hand, Pigeon leans up on the other elbow and thrusts hard and slow. Our faces are close, so I lean up and brush my lips across the bottom of his chin. He drops his forehead to mine and picks up his pace. My orgasm had peaked and started to subside, but Pigeon changes his angle, and it brings my orgasm back to full life.

Slinging my leg over his hip, I use the leverage to push my hips harder into his driving cock.

"Fuck, Ivy. You're so fucking perfect," Pigeon groans before moving quickly.

In one smooth move, Pigeon's on his back, and I'm astride him. Grasping my hips, Pigeon uses them to drive me up and then down hard on his cock. Eyes on my bouncing breasts, he grinds my lower body against his before thrusting into me again. I lean back slightly, and Pigeon's thumb finds my clit. Shaking my head, I tell him, "I can't. Not again."

"Fuck you can't. You're coming with me, baby. Give it to me."

Between thumb and cock, Pigeon gets his wish. When I shudder from the rush of feelings, he groans and slams my body down hard on his. Holding me still, I feel his body harden and twitch slightly, riding out his orgasm. When his body finally relaxes, he pulls my upper half down to press against his chest.

After a couple of moments, I feel him soften inside of me. Our breathing is slowly returning to normal, but Pigeon doesn't release his hold on me. Lifting my head enough to see his gorgeous face, I drop my mouth to his. When I feel him smile beneath my mouth, I open my eyes to see his on me.

"Looks like we need to start over with another shower," he mumbles against my lips.

Dropping my face into the crook of his neck, I let out a small laugh.

I finally make it to work, and I'm only two hours late. Margie waves off my excuse, gives me a smile, and leaves. I say hi to Dale, ignore his staring and get to work. He'll only be here for another hour, so it'll be easy to avoid him. Heading straight to the aviary, I listen to Prissy explain loudly to the other birds why cockatoos are the superior birds.

"Hey, Miss P. You want to help me with rounds?"

"Yes, ma'am," she replies before landing on my shoulder.

I turn my face to hers and wait for her to make her usual kissing sounds. That done, we leave and head for the dog kennels.

Taking some time, I eventually get all the orphaned puppies into the dog park along with a few of the quieter older dogs. Stopping in front of Thor's kennel, I smile when he rushes to the front for some attention. Even with Prissy as my co-worker, it seems quiet today, not having a Devil's Angels member with me. They had a meeting, they call it Church, and I assured Pigeon I was fine at work without one of them here.

A few minutes later, I hear the intercom click on and Dale's voice letting me know I have a visitor in the reception area. Assuming Pigeon didn't believe me, Prissy and I make our way to the office area. Instead of one of the guys, I see Ava, Pippa, and a few other women waiting for me.

"Hi, ladies. What can I help with? The donkeys are okay, aren't they?" I ask when I enter the room.

"Yeah, they're great. Thank you for helping with them, Ivy. They're exactly what I always wanted. The kids love them," Ava answers with a small smile.

"They're being spoiled more each day. Both currently have blue sparkly hooves," says the lady standing behind Ava while smiling and rolling her eyes a little.

I grin back because I totally expected that to happen.

"Is there somewhere we can talk?" Ava asks in a quiet voice.

Sensing something's not right, I nod and open the door that leads to a small conference room.

Closing the door behind the last woman, I take a seat and wait.

Pointing to each lady, Ava introduces them.

"Trudy, she's Petey's. Tammy is Trigger's. Bailey owns Axel and always has our sympathies," Ava says with a grin while the others laugh. "Taja is the lucky one who gets to see Vex naked and Pippa you've met before, I believe."

I nod while trying to remember each name and the face it belongs to.

"We're here for a few reasons, actually. First, did you know Gunner adopted a pig?"

"Uh, no, I didn't. I know that a farm piglet got adopted, but I didn't look at the paperwork. Why? Is it a problem?" I ask, concerned.

"God no, I'm happy as hell about it. But the overly large man is hiding it from me, and I don't know why. Do you?" Ava questions.

Thinking about it, I think I know the answer.

"Other than Gee, is Gunner knowledgeable about pigs?" I ask.

"No, not at all. Why?" Ava asks with a wariness to her tone.

"The piglet I think he adopted is a Mangalitsa. They're super cute as babies, and they grow slower than some of the other breeds, but they end up large. As in 800 pounds plus for a male. They are also wooly, like sheep. Friendly, they make great pets, but not indoor pets," I inform her while fighting a smile at the look of pure glee on her beautiful face. "How do you know he adopted one and is hiding it?"

"Because if Axel knows, everyone knows. He's a gossip," Bailey answers with a huge smile.

"Poor Gunner. He's afraid you're going to want to keep it as an indoor pet!" laughs Trudy.

I shake my head before explaining more about the breed.

"They have wooly hair and do great in colder climates. Once he starts to grow, you'll want him to be outside where he can just be a happy pig. The breed nearly disappeared years ago, but it's making a comeback. There aren't many in the U.S. yet, so if you decided to breed, you'd have buyers. The only reason this one ended up here is because he was the runt. The farm he was raised on went out of business, and the owners simply gave up and moved away. They left their animals behind, so many were brought here. The others in his litter were adopted out quickly. It will be easy to build a shelter for him because they don't require much.

Or you can adjust your barn plans to include a stall and enclosure dedicated to just the pig. He would do well with goats, too, if you're still planning on getting some."

Ava's eyes are bright with excitement about having gained a new pet. I would be too because the Mangalitsa is a great breed.

"I'm not breeding him. Too many unwanted babies in this world as it is. I'll contact my vet and make arrangements to have him vetted and neutered as soon as Gunner gives up his secret," Ava says.

"Another reason we're interrupting your day is that Craig told me about your plans for your ranch. I hope that was okay, but he was so excited, he just spilled the beans," Pippa explains.

"It's perfectly fine. Did he talk to you about learning to ride?" I ask.

Every one of the women laugh and nod their heads. Craig's more excited about it than I realized if he's told everyone he knows.

"Absolutely okay with me if you're sure about doing it. I have to warn you, though, that once Craig sets his mind to something, he won't stop until he's mastered it," Pippa warns.

"To be good at riding, that's the attitude you have to have. Falls happen. Horses are large and can be scary, even when they're behaving perfectly. They're not for the weak, that's for sure. I think Craig will do great at it because of his determination, but also because of his compassion with animals. Horses are incredibly sensitive animals and pick up on people's emotions. If they sense fear in their rider, they start seeing monsters behind every rock. If their rider is calm, it calms them and so on," I explain.

"That's all good information to know, and thank you for explaining. If you're up for it, I would love to pay for his riding lessons," Pippa states.

"There's no charge, Pippa. Craig wants to learn, and I love teaching people with that attitude. Sharing my love of horses and riding isn't a chore, but something I love to do," I answer sincerely before I turn to meet Ava's eyes. "Your kids are always welcome, too."

"That's another reason we're here. Craig said you want to work with kids that have challenges. To work with them with horses and other animals to hopefully instill confidence and a sense of belonging. Can you explain that a little?" Ava asks softly.

"We live in a western state that has ranches sprawled across it. I was a ranch kid, proud of it, still am. Going to school, though, there were different groups that hung together. The city kids, the ranch kids, the rich kids, and so on. Even living in Colorado, I got picked on by some of the kids in the other groups for being a ranch kid. They saw my Wrangler jeans as a sign of being poor instead of being a smart choice in clothing when you work with livestock. The bullies destroyed more of my hats than I can count. They made fun of my shitkickers, as they called them, even though my Roper boots cost hundreds of dollars a pair.

"Kids can be cruel. Parents don't take the time to correct them or give them a better sense of how someone being different from them doesn't make that person someone it's okay to mistreat. Kids with challenges paid the biggest price in school. I hated that words from a bully could make them shrink into themselves and their confidence flee.

"I never fought back when someone made fun of my jeans because I was fine with who I was, but I got into several fights when a kid picked on someone with a challenge. When Nana grew tired of picking me up from the principal's office, we had a chat. She explained how bullies operate and how I could fight them every day, but they'd never change their ways. She said I needed to ignore them and instead put my energy toward helping the one being picked on. When I explained to her that I thought that was what I was doing, she said she'd never be angry with me for standing up for another but that we needed to find a better way.

"During this time, we had a neighbor whose son was on the autism spectrum. He didn't speak much but seemed to come alive when riding his horse. Their ranch bumped up to ours in one section, so he'd ride over often. He was a totally different kid away from school and near animals. He was confident, spoke occasionally, and was completely different than when he was around people.

"Nana and I were talking about it one day, and she gave me a magazine that had an article about animals and kids with special needs. Since then, I've done a lot of research about it and believe that animals can help a lot more than just humans can, especially by instilling confidence and a sense of belonging in this world. Animals don't judge a person by what they can't do, but how a person treats them. Animals don't mind a missing limb, autism, challenges of any type, unlike so many humans do."

"Pregnancy tears! Don't mind me!" Taja shouts while waving a hand in front of her face.

"Pigeon's luckier than he realizes," Bailey quietly says while aiming a beaming smile at me.

"We'll make sure he knows that too," Trudy responds while swiping a finger under an eye.

"I'm sorry. I shouldn't have preached all that to you, but—" I start before getting interrupted.

"But you're passionate about this, and it shows. Nothing wrong with that, Ivy," Tammy murmurs with a soft smile.

"I think New Horizons has some residents that could use time away from the world. Tucked away on a ranch, letting animals heal their wounds. I love where you're going with this, Ivy. Tammy and I are willing to help in any way we can," Pippa offers sincerely.

"Yeah, Ivy, you're onto something, and being passionate about it is the first step to making it happen. When Craig comes to ride, I'd love to bring the girls and Luke, too. After this baby's born, I want to plant my ass in a saddle and spend the day doing nothing else. Would you give me that opportunity in exchange for bakery items and damn good coffee?" Ava asks with an impish grin.

"Coffee? I'm an addict, so yes, I'll make that exchange," I answer with a laugh.

"Pecans too," Priscilla places her order and startling me in the process. I was so engrossed in the conversation I forgot she was still on my shoulder.

"You scared me, Prissy!" I admonish while she cackles.

The women all laugh before I watch Bailey's eyes go wide.

"Is that Priscilla?" she asks.

"I is," Prissy answers while giving Bailey a side-eyed look.

"Oh my God, you're beautiful!" Bailey gushes.

"Bless your heart," Prissy answers in her slow drawl.

"Axel loves you, you know. He talks about you all the time," Bailey says.

"My man!" Prissy shouts while fluffing her feathers wildly above my head.

I watch as a loose one floats to the table before I move my hand close to Prissy for her to step up on. When she does, I lower her to the table and wait for her to step off. Waddling toward Bailey, Prissy stops in front of her.

"Axel's hot. Chingalinga!" Prissy shouts.

When questioning eyes look my way, I shrug. I have no idea what Prissy's saying, but she's adamant and repeats it several times.

"Sorry, but I don't speak southern belle," I explain to the laughing females.

"We'll get out of here and let you get back to work, Ivy. Thank you for taking the time to talk with us. Pigeon told Petey that you're swamped right now with the ranch and work, so if we can help, please call one of us. When we left the clubhouse, Pigeon was rounding up some future ranch hands for you, I think. Good luck turning bikers into cowboys, but if you can make that happen, I want to see it," Ava says, laughing as the women stand and walk toward the door.

After saying our goodbyes, I take Prissy back to the aviary under protest from her and make my way to Thor's kennel. Sitting on the floor, Thor's head in my lap, I realize Pigeon's right. I'm not alone anymore. I have people, and that feels amazing.

Walking through the kitchen door, I smile. Unlike going home when Ted and Todd were there, the kitchen is spotless. Moving into the living room, I smile again when I see Tabitha curled up on Pigeon's lap while he's kicked back in a recliner.

Leaning down, I place a kiss on his lips when he says nothing but aims a finger at his mouth.

"That what you wanted?" I ask.

"For now, yes. Want more later. Made you a plate. It's in the fridge and just needs to be nuked," Pigeon mutters while running a hand up my thigh and across my ass.

"Who was in the hallway this morning? Reeves, I think you called him," I ask while stepping back and plopping down on the couch.

"Club brother. He works with Rex and me at the club's security company. He doesn't live here but was staying for a few days to clear out his room at the clubhouse," Pigeon answers while muting the TV.

"I met some of the women today," I offer.

"I heard. Heard you impressed the hell out of them too. Not an easy feat with Trudy, but you did it, honey. I also had the length of my cock and life threatened if I don't do right by you," Pigeon says with a dimpled grin.

I feel my eyes go wide before I laugh at the mental images of Trudy threatening Pigeon.

"I'm guessing it was Trudy."

"You guess right, but she had her posse as backup, just in case. Please don't let them remove that particular part of my anatomy. I like him attached and functioning. We've become good friends, and nobody wants to lose a friend in the manner she described."

"I want to be just like Trudy when I grow up," I tell him with a wink.

"God knows one Trudy is enough. Axel might run away from home if another one appears."

I laugh and stand to go heat up my dinner but stop at Pigeon's next words.

"Flash me, Ivy."

"Flash you?" I ask, confused.

"Show me my girls," he orders in a low voice, eyes glued to my breasts.

"Let me guess. You're a breast man," I say sarcastically.

"Nope. I'm an Ivy man. But I would never be upset if you wanted to flash me those beautiful girls," he responds before pulling his eyes up to mine.

I have no idea what comes over me because my next behavior is very unlike the Ivy I know.

Pigeon's playfulness pulls something dirty out of me, so I reach for the buttons on my shirt. Pigeon's eyes brighten, and he sits straighter, probably in shock that I'm complying with his ridiculous request.

Unbuttoning one at a time, I enjoy his complete attention and anticipation. When my shirt parts, I unclasp the front enclosure on my bra and push it aside. Cupping the bottom side of each breast, I ask, "This what you wanted?"

"Fuck me," Pigeon says in a low, guttural growl.

"Oh, fuck me!" shouts a voice from the kitchen.

Jerking my shirt closed, I feel the heat of mortification hit my face. Pigeon bolts out of the chair, Tabitha jumping clear of the commotion as I turn my back and fumble with my shirt buttons.

"What the fuck are you doing here?" Pigeon shouts as loud thumping and banging sounds erupt in the kitchen.

"Ouch! Stop that, you demented bastard! Quit it! No, don't go near my dick! I forgot my fucking phone!"

"Get it and get out. Don't return," Pigeon barks, and then more disturbing sounds can be heard, along with more swearing.

I don't wait around for another chance to embarrass myself. I bolt up the stairs and slam the bedroom door behind me. I walk to the bed and faceplant on it. After a minute of contemplation, I start laughing into the pillow I have my face buried in.

Hearing the door open and close behind me, I try to stop but can't. The bed depresses next to me, and I feel Pigeon's gentle hand brushing my hair back.

"Ivy, honey, I'm so sorry. I didn't know Reeves would walk through the door when he did. I, shit, I'm sorry. Don't cry, baby. Please," Pigeon all but begs while misunderstanding the muffled noises I'm making.

Lifting my head, I look at the beautiful face next to mine. His brow is creased, and he's obviously worried that I'm devastated by flashing my goodies at his friend. When another laugh busts out of me, his face clears before breaking into a relieved smile.

"I never want to meet that man. You're going to have to kick him out of the brotherhood because there's no way I can ever face him. Oh my God, Pigeon! I flashed him my best parts!" I holler, somewhat hysterically, before snorting a little, then falling silent.

"You only flashed him two of your best parts. Let's keep the other ones just between us, though, yeah?"

"If he came up missing suddenly, would anyone notice or care?"

"Probably not," Pigeon answers with a laugh. "Sorry that happened, but don't let it deter you from flashing me anything, anytime you feel like it."

"Like now?" I ask as I roll to my back and letting my shirt fall open again.

"Now works for me," Pigeon agrees while circling one nipple with a fingertip.

"You asked me to let you play this morning. I did. Is it my turn yet?"

"For future knowledge, if you ask me for anything in that voice and while semi-undressed, your wish will be granted," Pigeon informs me quietly while still engrossed in watching his fingertip continue the circling.

"Then strip, Pigeon," I order.

Eyes meeting mine, he grins, both dimples showing before standing and complying with my order. I find out that Pigeon has less patience for playing when he's not the one doing it. His hands did not stay attached to the headboard like mine did, and he likes to be bossy. Not that I listen well. Using fingers, tongue, and lips, I explore many tats and the skin under them. I taste, lick, and nibble my way down his body before taking his erection in hand and giving it a slow stroke. I swipe my thumb across the head of his cock then suck the drop of liquid off my thumb. That's when his patience ended, and I smiled into the pillow I was suddenly facing. We both got to play, and the results were earth-shattering.

Lola Wright

Chapter 13
Pigeon

On the drive to the ranch, I pull Ivy close and let my fingers play with a few escaped curls. It's been a week since the Morales family left the clubhouse to go home, and I've leaned on Ivy's strength to get me through it. Not that she knows it, but she's the reason I'm still standing.

During that week, a lot of decisions had to be made. When Rex explained that the dead girl was like Bella and had been sold by her mom, tempers flared. Things got destroyed, and it took time for men to get their emotions under control. Finding out that no missing person's report had ever been made, and the mom was now living off the money she received for committing the worst crime a mother could commit, reignited our anger. Unfortunately, it made the decision as to what to do with the child easier. We no longer had to contact a devastated mother and tell her that her child was dead.

Vex volunteered a secluded spot on his land for her burial site. We named her Angel, placed her in the beautiful wooden box Trigger made for her along with a doll that resembled her that Taja provided, and had a quiet burial. We marked her grave with a large, odd-shaped rock, and she will not be forgotten. Not by any man here and not by the women who came together to lovingly wash and redress her in a cute, fluffy dress. She was loved, but it came too late. Axel and I stood shoulder to shoulder, jaws tight, while Petey said some words and a few Morales brothers pushed the dirt over her new resting place. Not really surprising, the women that helped her are holding strong. They couldn't save her either, but they gave her what they could.

With Petey and Trudy's consent and under their watchful eye, Bella came to the clubhouse. She spoke quietly with the victims about her experience and how she's healed from that. She listened, gave advice, and did amazing at getting through to them. Bella stayed strong, eyes dry, and offered support and understanding to those who were in desperate need of some. During this, Pooh paced outside the clubhouse, worry and concern contorting his face. I joined him, expecting him to snap, but he didn't. When Bella walked out, Pooh pulled her tight and held on. With shaking hands,

Bella hugged him back before telling both of us that she was fine.

"I think I needed that. Not just to help them, but for myself too. Talking about it makes it easier to deal with. Knowing that others have went through similar things helps me get rid of the feeling of being alone."

"You're never alone, Bella. Never," Pooh reminds her as he finally releases her.

After Bella walks off, Pooh's whole body relaxes, and he starts to breathe normally again. I believe Bella's words to the victims and to us has helped Pooh just as much as her and them. Bella has calmed Pooh's mind and soul, just like Ivy does for me.

The victims of the trafficking were mostly in the foster care system or living on the streets. The Morales family was overwhelmed in the beginning, having rescued way more than expected, but they rallied quickly. None of the street kids will be returning to that way of life. They'll be going home with the family that did so much to save them. They'll be accepted as family and treated as they should have been all along. As valued human beings. Arrangements for the others completed, additional cars rented, the Morales family pulled out of the compound. The last van in their convoy contained the battered but mostly alive bodies of the men involved in the transporting. We didn't ask what their future held because none of us cared to know. The look on Jorge and Gael Morales's faces, the two in charge of the men, spelled it out pretty clearly.

Axel put his fist through a window before stalking home to cuddle his beloved daughter. Minus the window, Gunner did the same with his kids. I left, drove straight to the rescue, found Ivy, and pulled her surprised body to mine. Standing amongst a dozen quacking ducks, a swan, and several curious goats, I buried my face in her neck and stood still, soaking in her warmth and comfort. Ivy wrapped her arms around me and let me have my time. When I finally pulled back, running my hands over my head and through my hair, Ivy waited in silence.

"It's been a hard week, and I needed that. Thank you."

"My hugs are free, and you're welcome to as many as you want. How about a ride when I get out of here tonight?"

I nod, relieved that she understands without needing an explanation.

"Today's my last day until hay is done. We can go to the ranch, spend the night there and disappear for a while," Ivy suggests quietly.

I nod again, suddenly liking the idea of getting away from humanity for a while.

"I've got to go wrangle an uncooperative emu. Want an experience you'll never forget?" Ivy asks with a small smile.

"How do you wrangle an emu?" I ask.

"Very carefully while walking on the dangerous line between life and death."

Ivy was not wrong. Emus and I are never going to be besties after the experience I went through tonight.

Riding my bike with Ivy tight against my back is heaven. Placing my left hand on her knee, I relax and let myself enjoy it. Not enough time has passed when I see the ranch driveway come into view. Making the turn, I realize I should have rode slower, drawing out the pleasure. Parking my bike near the house, I wait while Ivy steps off before I follow suit. When I start toward the house, Ivy grabs my hand and leads me to the barn instead.

"What are we doing?" I ask as we enter the dark, warm barn.

"Going for that ride I mentioned."

"Thought we just had it."

"When my mind is too busy, and the world has let me down, my form of riding involves a horse. It's therapeutic in ways nothing else is. Trust me. This will settle your mind and reboot whatever's broken inside."

Ivy disappears inside a stall and returns leading a large, muscled black horse. Slipping a bridle over his head, Ivy moves to his side and waits for me to give her a leg up. Landing softly on his broad back, she looks down at me, waiting. It's been years since I've ridden a horse and even longer since I did it bareback. Grabbing a handful of mane, I swing up behind Ivy and slide forward until her ass is cradled between my thighs and my front is plastered to her back. Wrapping an arm around her waist, I refamiliarize myself with the motion of a walking horse. Once clear of the barn, a couple of blue heelers show up beside us, and the horse breaks into a smooth, effortless lope.

After we've covered quite a bit of distance, Ivy speaks quietly to the horse, and it slows to an ambling walk. Moving off the small road we'd been on, we make our way down a slight slope. Words aren't needed, and the complete silence is welcoming. Splashing through a creek and up the other side, Ivy stops the horse near a tree. I slide off and wait while she does the same. I walk to the tree and take a seat with my back leaning into it.

Ivy sits in front of me, slightly sideways, and rests her cheek against my chest. The dogs lay nearby while the horse grazes next to us. We sit in silence for several long moments before I tell Ivy about the Morales family, how we know them, and what we did with them. I leave nothing out, and she never interrupts. When I run out of words, she raises her head, tears evident in her eyes, and shares her thoughts.

"I wish Angel had met you and your club years ago. She needed a protector, a friend, someone to love her the way she deserved. That didn't happen, but you still saved her in a way. Saved her from whatever other indignities they would have done, like tossing her out like trash. She was taken care of and loved in the end. I'm sorry you had to deal with that, but I'm glad at the same time that she had men like you and Axel looking out for her."

I nod then pull her head back to my chest. Resting my chin on top of her head, I hold her that way for a long-ass time. We make the ride back to the ranch in silence, and I notice that the weight in my chest has lightened. Whether it was talking with Ivy or riding the horse in the dark, I don't know, and it doesn't matter. Either way, Ivy has had a hand in starting the healing process.

Waking up slowly, I roll enough to pull Ivy's body tight to mine. It's still dark outside the window, but I know morning can't be far away. Ivy's hair smells like clean mountain air, so I bury my nose in the curls. When that doesn't wake her, I move my face enough to run my tongue up the side of her neck, then nip her ear lobe. Still not waking up, I let my hand drift down to the waistband of her panties. Sliding a finger inside them, I flick my finger through her pubic hair. Going further south, I find wetness. Lifting my head, I look down at her face to see a smile gracing her lips.

"You're awake," I accuse.

"Of course, but I was enjoying your method of waking me, so I played along."

"You're wet," I growl close to her ear.

"You're in my bed, naked, and you have your hand in my panties. Of course, I'm wet. I've been that way since you dropped your clothes last night," she admits with a small laugh.

"Me getting naked gets you wet?"

"You breathing gets me wet. You naked makes me needy," Ivy corrects as she places her hand over mine and slides my finger up and down the length of her slit.

"You're a dirty girl, and I want you to tell me more," I tell her as my finger circles her opening.

"Keep doing that, and I'll spill all my secrets and dirty thoughts."

Pulling my finger away, I slide my hand around to her ass, give it a squeeze before pushing my hand back between her thighs from behind and finding her wet opening. Pushing my finger deep, Ivy moans low in the back of her throat.

"Use your words, Ivy. I want to hear those dirty thoughts," I whisper in her ear while pumping slowly into her. My head falls back, enjoying this immensely when my eyes land on her dresser across the room.

"I want… what the heck?" Ivy asks in dismay when I leap out of bed and back away, holding my hands up in front of me.

"Get it the fuck out of here, Ivy! Now!" I bark.

Ivy sits up and looks at me like I've lost my mind. She's confused as hell, and I know that, but I'm about to have the panic attack of a lifetime. When she doesn't move further, I grab my shirt off the floor and fling it across the room. It doesn't make it to the intended target, so I rip the quilt off the bed and heave it instead. It hits her dresser, knocking items off but covers the fucking smiling clown statue sitting there. I feel a shiver run up my spine, and I hear a muffled laugh come from the vicinity of the bed. Turning to face Ivy, I give her my best glare.

"Oh my God! You have coulrophobia!" Ivy shares while covering the bottom half of her face with the sheet.

I know she's hiding a smile behind the sheet, and it makes me want to spank her ass red.

"I have no clue what the fuck you're talking about. I don't like clowns. They're creepy as hell! How can you sleep in a room with that thing staring at you?" I shout louder than I intended to.

Ivy continues staring at me, sheet held tight to the bottom half of her face, but her eyes scream laughter. After a moment to compose herself, Ivy lowers the sheet, raises it quickly, then tries again. When my hands hit my hips, she wins the battle.

"I'm sorry. I didn't know, and I shouldn't have laughed. Phobias are real. I'll get rid of it and, um, the one behind you."

I screech, hopefully in a manly-type way, and bolt away from the wall, whirling to find a clown picture hanging a few feet from where I was just standing. Pulling my eyes away from it, I grab my jeans, slip them on and bolt out the door. As I'm taking the stairs three at a time, I hear Ivy's laughter follow me. Fuck me.

After a few deep breaths and some distance between me and the clowns, I move to the coffee pot. Flipping it on, I pop in a k-cup and wait impatiently. When one cup's done, I start another. Hearing footsteps, I glance up, expecting Ivy but find Ted instead.

"What are you doing here?" he asks in a rude voice.

"Keeping an eye on you and your fists."

"Ranch is still under my control, so I'm telling you to fucking leave," Ted states as he reaches for the cup of coffee I made for Ivy.

Blocking him from reaching it, I pick it up and move away so he can make his own.

"I don't think I want to, Ted."

"And I don't want him to. Ranch isn't yours, Ted. I own it. You don't," Ivy states as she accepts her cup of coffee and leans against the counter next to me.

"Pretty mouthy now that you have backup," Ted mutters while glaring at his sister.

"I always spoke my mind, Ted. Only difference now is that you can't make me pay for that anymore," Ivy calmly answers.

"You have chores to get done. Take your biker and get to them," Ted spits out before stalking out of the room.

"He's just a bundle of sunshine and roses, isn't he?" I mutter.

"Yeah. He's a bully, drunk or not, and always was. My grandparents just didn't see it in him because they only saw what they hoped he'd be and not what he really was. They were so happy to have us living with them, and it kills me knowing he was never the grandson they deserved."

"Did he hurt you when you were kids?"

"Yeah, when he could get away with it. I didn't want my grandparents to know and have it break their hearts, and he took advantage of that. When he broke my left arm, I was about six. I said I fell off my horse. When I was around 10, he broke a couple of my ribs. Again, I blamed the horses. Black eyes, fat lips. When Nana started questioning me on all the injuries, Ted started putting them in areas less visible. I was too young to realize how dangerous it was, but I tried warning one of his girlfriends about his temper. She told him what I said, and things got ugly for me. When she turned up a few months later, beaten to hell, my grandparents didn't believe her, and neither did the police. I should have spoken up then, but I didn't. I was so wrong to keep his secret. She left the area, and then Nana became sick," Ivy admits in a low, quiet voice.

"You were a kid, Ivy. Not to blame for his behavior."

"I enabled him by staying silent. I'm done doing that, though."

"I'm feeling the need to take him apart piece by piece, so maybe we should hit the barn now," I mutter.

Ivy moves to the coffee pot and makes a couple of cups. Pouring them into travel mugs, we head outside and to the barn. Working together, we get the morning chores completed quickly. Feeling my phone vibrate, I pull it out and answer it.

"We're on our way," Axel says. "Heads up, but Ivy's getting a larger work crew than expected."

"How much larger?" I ask, smiling because I did expect this.

"Nearly every swinging dick in the club, the kids, and a few of our lovely ladies who are dying to see a working ranch," Axel says the last six words in a high-pitched female voice.

"You bringing food? Not sure Ivy can feed that many without stocking up first."

"You think my sister would do that to her? I'm driving a fucking SUV because of the amounts of food the women made," Axel says before shouting loudly, "Fuck you, Trigger!"

I laugh because I know the men well enough to know that Axel's pouting because he's in an SUV and not on his bike and that Trigger, most likely, just passed him on his. I'm sure someone got flipped off too.

"Ivy's brother's in the house doing God knows what, so don't send the women or kids in there without one of the men. We're down by the horse barns checking on the foals. I'll watch for your convoy," I say before disconnecting when Axel starts shouting at Gunner this time.

"Convoy?" Ivy asks with a raised eyebrow.

"You're about to receive more help than you can imagine, and most of it won't actually be helpful but will be well-intended."

"Huh," Ivy says noncommittally.

"One last thing before they roll in. The clown thing—that stays between us, woman. None of my club brothers need ammo to use against me. We clear on that?"

"Our secret, Pigeon."

I almost believe her except for the mischievous twinkle in her eyes.

"You mean that?" I ask warily.

"Why would I give up my best leverage so quickly? I may need it somewhere down the road," she replies.

"Leverage? Seriously? What the fuck, Ivy? Blackmail is such an ugly thing," I tell her before walking off, grinning at her audacity.

Turning around while I continue walking backward, I tell her the one thing that will get her mind off clowns. "Reeves will be here soon. Please don't flash my brother again." I turn back around and stroll away, smiling huge when I hear her gasp, and I know if I were to look at her, her face would be blazing red right now.

Cutting hay will start tomorrow, so Trigger is checking over each of the tractors and making sure the equipment is in good working condition. Gunner and I changed a few tires on the hay wagons and greased the axels. Most of the hay will be done in large round bales, but square bales are needed for the stabled animals, so the wagons need to be ready. Ivy takes an inventory on twine, makes sure the large diesel tank is full, and a million other things to be prepared.

Kids are running around and peeking in barn doors and stalls, oohing and aahing, while Axel does his best to keep them corralled. When a flashy paint mare trots past me and Gunner, we laugh, knowing that Axel's abilities are being tested. His loud swearing confirms it. Ivy calmly walks toward the mare, gives a loud whistle, and waits. The heelers immediately come to attention and wait impatiently for the signal to herd. Tossing her head a few times, the mare prances to Ivy and then follows her back to a gate. Ivy opens it, lets the mare pass, then closes it behind her. I laugh again when I see the two dogs deflate, knowing their moment has passed.

After giving Cash a quick lesson in operating one of the large John Deere tractors, he's been busy moving round bales so the new hay can go to the back of the hay barns. Livi's been kept busy opening and closing gates to save everyone time as we move the equipment around. Everyone is helping in one way or another, coming together for one of our own. It's obvious as hell to me that's exactly how my club views Ivy now. She's mine, so by extension, she's one of theirs too.

I saw Ted watching out the window a few times before he made his way to his truck and left. It was a smart decision because I'm not sure Trigger would have kept his hands to himself. Petey stood in the middle of the driveway, laughing loudly, and flipped Ted off as he roared down it.

After a few hours of work, I look around for Ivy. Not seeing her or Livi, Gunner and I walk toward the barns and find the two women tossing square bales of hay around like they weigh nothing. Laughing and chatting while they work, they've moved a large stack of hay already.

"Why the hell are you two doing that when you have a yard full of men?" I holler up to the two women standing at the top of the next stack.

"Uh, because we don't want it fucked up?" Livi responds with a smirk. "No sense in moving all this hay just to have it topple over later."

Ivy gives a loud snort of laughter before turning her head away, picking up another bale, and giving it a hard toss.

"Really, Ivy?" I ask in disgust, but I have to bite back my smile at my little ranch girl. Not that I'm dumb enough to use that phrase out loud. Nope, only Axel would make that mistake and only once.

"Your women have muscles," Axel says, and I look to see the men standing behind me, grins in place. "Mine are bigger, though," he adds before flexing his biceps at the women. "Jealous yet?" he asks with a smirk.

"Why would they be jealous? You have muscles, but they're show muscles. Ivy has work muscles. Work muscles are always better. Everyone knows that," Craig informs Axel with a serious look on his face.

"Show muscles? What the hell are you talking about, Craig?" Axel asks.

"It's like show horses versus horses that do actual ranch work. You have muscle from lifting weights in a gym. Ivy has them from years of working hard. Show muscles look good but are fairly useless except for appearances. Muscles made from working hard know their job and get things done. Work muscles are better to have when there's real work involved. Muscle memory and all that. Why do I always have to explain these things to you?" Craig questions with a sad shake of his head before walking off.

"Kid makes sense," Petey adds with a chuckle.

"Kid's a pain my ass," Axel retorts. "Climb down, ladies, and let us men get our workout in."

Shrugging, both women climb down and step back. An hour later, I'm wishing Axel had kept his mouth shut. Every muscle in my body is aching, so I know his are too. Gunner tosses another bale but aims it at the back of Axel's knees. When Axel's large-ass body hits the hay again, he doesn't get up as quickly as he did the first few times Gunner put him down.

"I'm refusing to admit that Craig might be right, but fuck me sideways, this shit is hard!" Axel moans to the ceiling. "I have show muscles, obviously. They're pretty, but that's about it."

Laughing, Gunner, Cash, and I take seats on the nearest bales of hay. Reaching for the bottles of water the women tossed up to us a while ago, we all drink to remove the dust from our throats. After a few minutes of silence, Cash speaks.

"How'd she keep up with all of this? Doesn't sound like she had much help, yet the ranch is well-cared for, and everything is as neat as a pin. It's fucking beautiful here."

"During haying season, she said she'd hire a few neighbor men to help. Otherwise, I have no idea," I answer the best I can.

"She busted her ass nonstop to make her grandparents proud and to honor the work they put into this land," Trigger says quietly and most likely, accurately.

"There's a million other things that need to be done year-round too. Fencing, calving, foaling, breeding, feeding, planting, the list goes on and on. I grew up on a small farm, nothing this size, and the work was endless," I add. "And yet, it's like she's one with the land and animals. No place she'd rather be, and she's not afraid of the hard work. I think the only thing she fears is her brother and not doing right by the gift her grandparents gave her."

"We'll deal with the brother if needed. As for the ranch, I'm willing to help whenever she needs it. I love this fucking place," Cash states.

"Really?" I ask, surprised.

"Fuck yeah. Way the hell away from people, quiet, beautiful country. Grazing animals, streams, ponds, and did I mention away from people? I'd love to have Liam grow up out here and not in a city. I want to bring my dad out and drive him around in the side by side. Hell, I'm tempted to ask Ivy about a job, quit the gym, and make the move tomorrow."

Listening to Cash speak, I realize why Ivy has considered herself lucky regardless of the struggles with her brother. She was born to be on this land. This is home to her in the truest sense of the word. Standing, the others following my lead. We finish moving the hay in silence. When we're done, we go looking for the kids and women.

Finding them putting food out, we file past filling our plates before finding seats on the deck, in the shade, overlooking the ranch. Even the kids seem a little in awe of the view while eating their meal. Ivy sets her plate on the arm of my chair, turns, and pulls another one close before sitting and retrieving her plate.

"No idea how I can thank you all for the help today and the women for the food," Ivy says while looking at each of the men in turn.

"No need to, darlin'. Getting out of the city for the day has been thanks enough," Petey replies between bites.

"Ava and Pippa mentioned that you're going to give the kids some riding lessons. I have two little girls that haven't shut up about that since," Gunner says, and both twins giggle loudly. "Luke wants to come too, and Ava and I want that for him. What you're planning on doing with this ranch is amazing, Ivy. Anything we can do to help make that happen, count us in. Kids deserve the best life they can get, and you wanting to help make that happen for them, yeah, count us in."

"Thank you, Gunner. I have a lot to get done before any of that can happen, but I'm hopeful the attorney will have some good news for me soon."

"Good news or not, start getting things in order, Ivy. I think we can help with the brother situation," Trigger states.

"Unfortunately, he controls the ranch's money until I meet the terms of the will. I have a few years to go before that happens. In the meantime, I can't afford to make the changes I need, and he'd never give me a cent to help. Heck, I don't even earn a wage here."

"You do all this work and don't draw a wage from the ranch?" Cash asks in a dangerously angry voice.

"No. I work at the rescue for my income in the meantime. I started there in my teens simply because I liked working with animals but have stayed because of the pay."

"A lot of places to hide a body on this ranch," Trigger mutters.

Ivy grins, but probably because she doesn't know that Trigger wasn't making idle conversation.

"What's that building over there?" Axel asks while pointing.

"That's a bunkhouse. It was built years back, but Papa had it updated before he passed. Bathroom, kitchen, several bunk beds. It can sleep eight comfortably, more if needed. The ranch hands used to live in it back in the day when they worked the summers here. I plan on using it for the kids and adults that come from out of town."

Conversation flows for a while, people asking Ivy questions about ranch life and her future plans. Once we're done eating, Ivy turns to Trigger.

"If you have a few minutes, I wanted to show you something."

Trigger's eyes light up, and he nods, standing eagerly. The kids abandon their plates and stand too. Laughing, I tell Ivy to take them and go, and we'd put the food away. Ivy pulls the side by side up to the deck and helps seatbelt the boys and twins in the rear seat. It's a tight fit, the twins sharing a seatbelt, but they make it work. Little Alex is placed between Trigger and Ivy in the front seat, dogs in the bed, and they're gone.

"She's going to make Trigger a fan for life," laughs Petey as he gathers up paper plates and carries them inside.

The rest of us clean up outside before entering the house to put away the food and raid the fridge for cold drinks. Taking them back outside, we take our seats again.

"Why didn't Chubs come today?" Livi asks.

Everyone looks at everyone else, and I get that chill up my spine again.

"I thought he was already out here," Gunner states with a frown.

"When's Lucy coming home?" I ask.

"Tomorrow, I think," Petey answers.

Pulling out my phone, I call Chubs. No answer, and it goes to voicemail. Waiting a few minutes, I try again with the same result. Looking up, I notice everyone is watching me. Livi looks worried, so I speak to her first.

"What do you know?"

"Nothing, really. Feds were in the department waiting for me and James yesterday, but we blew them off. Didn't answer any questions, didn't ask any either. We left and stayed out on the street for the rest of our shift," she answers.

When I don't receive an answer on my next call, I call Rex.

"Where's Chubs?"

"Thought he was at the ranch today. He's not there?" Rex questions as I hear his fingers typing furiously on a keyboard.

"No, never showed."

"Okay, wait. His tracker is showing his bike on 70, outside of Eagle. Any reason why he'd be going that direction?"

Repeating the information to the others, no one has an answer.

"I'll keep an eye on it and let you know if anything changes," Rex offers before we disconnect.

"Rex is checking into it. He'll let us know when he finds something out."

"Care to explain how Rex knows this?" Gunner asks.

"Because I asked Rex to put a tracker on Chubs' bike," Cash admits. "I would rather have had one implanted into his arm, but since that would have caused a fight, I went the bike route instead."

"Smart as long as he sticks with his bike," Petey murmurs.

"Best we could do considering the curly-haired bastard won't talk," Cash replies.

Heads nod, and the conversation moves to other topics, but it's obvious everyone is concerned about our buddy Chubs.

"Toss in the fish pellets, and they swarm the surface. Fucking unbelievable. I can't wait to drop a line," Trigger says when the group returned.

"You're welcome anytime, Trigger," Ivy assures him and smiles at the huge grin that comment puts on Trigger's face.

"I don't want to catch fishies. I just want to eat them," Mia, or Zoe, states as she climbs into my lap for some uncle cuddles.

"Trigger, Luke, and I will do the catching. Miss Ava can do the cooking, and we all score," Craig states.

I look to the tapping on my arm to see Luke standing there. When he sees me looking at him, he quickly signs, "When?"

Before I can answer him, Axel signs back. "Whenever Trigger comes out next."

Luke grins and nods enthusiastically before turning to give Ivy a shy smile. Signing "horse," Ivy nods her head and signs back, "when you come to fish."

Luke tosses up a victory sign and takes off across the lawn with Craig and the dogs.

"I'll be here early tomorrow, Ivy. That okay?" Cash asks in his quiet rumble.

"Not fair! I have to work," Livi says with a pout before Cash pulls her down into his lap.

"Weather forecast is perfect for cutting hay, so I can't thank you enough, Cash. We should be able to get several fields done," Ivy answers.

"I'm going to work at the shop tomorrow, but that leaves Petey free," Trigger says.

"I'm riding out with Cash. Horse, Pooh, and Toes will be with us, too," Petey confirms.

"What needs to be done before we leave?" Gunner questions.

"Nothing, really. We're ready to start hay, and evening chores won't take long. The dogs and I will push the unneeded horses out to pasture tonight, and that frees up time from cleaning as many stalls. I think we're good," Ivy answers.

"Then it's time for us to get out of your way and head home. Love your fucking place here, Ivy," Gunner says before brushing a kiss across her cheek. "I'm as excited about the kids spending time here and learning to ride as they are. Thank you. Anything you can do to help Luke with his shyness and confidence, I can't even tell you how much it'll be appreciated."

The kids are gathered up, and everyone heads for home. Turning to Ivy, I pull her into my lap and hold her close.

"I hope I haven't gotten Ava and Gunner's hopes up. I just know that animals, horses in particular, can help with a kid's confidence. I just hope Luke is receptive to it," Ivy says in a concerned voice.

"They're not expecting a miracle, Ivy. They just want Luke to see that he's no different than the other kids, and his challenge shouldn't hold him back from doing the same things they do."

"I look forward to working with the kids. I like kids, and they listen better than adults, especially when you're teaching them to ride. Adults tend to worry more about falling than about learning how not to. Kids are more fearless, willing to try something new, and they trust what you tell them."

"Those kids are going to love you," I tell her before adjusting her body, so her mouth is accessible to mine.

Acting like teenagers, we spend long minutes making out before heading back to the barn to start the evening chores.

"You okay by yourself for a while?" Ivy asks while shifting from foot to foot.

"Yeah, I'll keep watching the game. Why?" I ask, confused by her behavior more than her words.

Ivy takes a deep breath and then lets it out slowly before sitting on the couch next to the chair I'm in. Wringing her hands a few times, she speaks in a quiet, subdued voice.

"I want to take a bath."

I'm at a complete loss as to why this seems to be a big deal to her. Watching her, though, I know that it is, and I feel my temper start to rise.

"Why's that an issue, Ivy?" I ask while trying to keep my voice calm.

"I don't get to take them very often, and I'm enough of a girl to enjoy the hell out of them," she responds, first surprising me with her words but also that she said "hell." I've noticed that Ivy doesn't swear, or if so, very seldom.

"You take your bath for as long as you like, and I'll hang out down here. When you get done, do you trust me enough to explain what you're not telling me?"

I watch Ivy's body give a small jerk, but after a minute, she nods her head.

"Enjoy your bath, Ivy."

She grins, jumps up, plants a kiss on my mouth before rushing up the stairs. I wait until I hear the water running before pulling out my phone. I hit Pippa's contact.

"Hey, Pigeon," she answers.

"Question for you, honey."

"Ask me anything," she offers with a laugh.

"Why would a woman be nervous about taking a bath?" I ask before explaining the conversation and odd behavior that Ivy displayed.

Pippa's humor disappears immediately, but she stays quiet, thinking for a moment.

"A naked woman is vulnerable, or at least, can feel they are. Baths take time. Showers are quick. You're in and out and dressed in a few minutes. Baths, especially if you like them, take much longer and leaves you vulnerable longer. Has she mentioned any reason why she avoids them?"

"No, this is the first I've heard of it. She was obviously excited about taking one, though."

"Why not take them if she enjoys them so much? Most likely, it's because she knows she's safe with you there. Maybe she wasn't safe or didn't feel she was before. Don't push for answers. She'll tell you when she's ready," Pippa advises.

"Thanks, Pips."

"You're welcome, Pigeon."

Over an hour passes before Ivy comes downstairs, walks to my chair, and sits down on my lap. Pulling her close, I pretend to still be watching the game. Ivy settles against me and watches the TV. When the game ends, we head upstairs to her room. Walking inside, I glance around to make sure there are no more ugly-ass clowns waiting for me, ignore Ivy's muffled giggle, and strip down.

Leaving her shirt and panties on, Ivy slides in bed from the other side but pushes in close to me. Wrapping an arm around her, I stroke her arm with my fingertips. Lying in the complete darkness, I wait to hear something that I'm positive I don't want to hear. A long time passes before Ivy speaks in a barely audible voice.

"I avoid baths because I'm not comfortable with Ted and Todd in the house and me sitting in a tub. I shower long before either are awake because they stay up late drinking. If you weren't here, I'd be wearing a lot more clothing right now, too. Since you are here, I knew I could spend time in the tub, shave, condition my hair, and basically pamper myself because you'd keep me safe if they showed up."

"Has either touched you inappropriately?"

"Todd hasn't, but I still don't trust him," Ivy whispers.

Thinking about her answer, I realize that what she didn't say is where the damage lies. Gritting my teeth against the stream of obscenities I want to shout, I hesitate before speaking.

"Here's our rules, Ivy. I'll keep you safe, however you need it, and you learn to live your life free. Bath, shower, or swimming naked in the pond, your choice. Need someone's ass kicked? I'm your guy. Need a place to bury a body? Again, I'm that guy for you. All you need to understand is that I'm not going anywhere in this world without you next to me."

"Will you still feel that way when I tell you I have developed very strong feelings about you?" Ivy asks in the darkness.

"Fuck, Ivy, knowing that, I might not even let you out of my sight now," I respond a second before rolling on top of her warm, pliant body.

"Can we put the rest of this conversation on hold for now? I need you in me," Ivy asks.

I don't answer her question, but I honor her request. Several times over.

Ivy spends some time showing us guys which fields we'll be cutting in today, and it's then that I realize how massive this ranch is. Four large tractors, going most of the day, and there will still be hay standing. Cash grins when I mention this, and I'm still surprised at how much he's taking to working on a ranch.

"Looks like Axel's going to be running the gym alone for a while yet," he mutters before swinging into the cab of the tractor. When he drives off, Petey walks to his tractor and does the same. Pooh flips the rest of us off, starts his tractor, and leaves in the direction of his fields.

"Work their asses off, Ivy. Anything heavy, assign one of them to it. I don't know about Toes, but Horse has ridden before so put his ass on a horse if needed. Don't hesitate to video anything that would be amusing for the rest of us, though. Both guys have a tendency to entertain us whether they mean to or not," I say before giving her a quick kiss and climbing into my tractor. Before shutting the door, I look at Horse. "We haven't seen Ted since yesterday morning, but he might pop up again. Keep Ivy close if he does." Horse nods, and I fire up the tractor.

It's been many years since I have done this type of work on a daily basis. This tractor, though, is nothing like the small, older ones my dad owned. This thing is a work of art, and I find myself excited to be here doing something as simple as cutting hay. I flip on the radio, find a station I like, and find the corner to the first field of hay I'm cutting today. Temperature-controlled cab, plugins for my phone and other electronics, satellite radio, cup holders, and an extremely comfortable seat. This is the right way to ranch.

Not long after I get started, my phone rings. It's Rex, and my stomach tightens.

"Yeah?"

"We can't find Chubs any fucking where," he barks.

"His bike?" I ask.

"Still where it was yesterday when I checked the tracker. Called Gunner and Axel. They sent Freddy and Vex with the wrecker to pick it up and to see what they can find there. Waiting to hear back from them. James and Livi are sniffing around at work to see if they can find out if the Feds were involved. The worst part's that Lucy is flying in today. Gunner's going to pick her up at the airport and see if she knows anything. Fuck, this is a mess," Rex states in a frustrated voice.

Without seeing his face, I know he's showing the signs of exhaustion. Rex can be like a dog with a bone when he's working on something, and Chubs missing is a huge something. Rex won't stop, eat, or sleep until he has answers. Gunner has had to order him to step away from his computer and go to bed before, and I see that happening again if we don't find Chubs soon.

"His phone?"

"It's off, broken, or at the bottom of a fucking well is my guess. Goes straight to voicemail. GPS on it puts it with the bike," Rex answers.

"What do you need me to do? Several of the guys…"

"Nothing yet. I'll keep you all updated. Can you let the guys at the ranch know what's up for me?" he asks.

"Yeah. Let me know if you need us to head back to town."

"Will do."

I let the others know what's up, and we all agree to continue working the fields until we hear something definitive.

About an hour later, I spot two riders pushing a small herd of cattle at the opposite end of the field I'm cutting hay in. As I get closer, I recognize Ivy on Junior immediately. The ragdoll bouncing wildly on the big buckskin horse next to her has to be Horse. I probably should have asked him to explain better about his riding experience before volunteering him to saddle up today. People always say they've rode but never explain that usually means being led around at a county fair for $10. Big difference between being a rider and having rode.

I watch Ivy and the dogs push the small herd of what I can now see are bulls down a slope. It's not a gentle incline either. It's steep, and I have a sudden stroke of genius. I whip out my phone, hit the camera app, switch to the video mode, and aim it at Horse. No way am I going to miss videoing what's about to become a total wreck.

Shutting the tractor down, I step outside the cab but stay on the steps, so I'm in an elevated position. I can hear Ivy giving Horse instructions, but I know him well enough to know that he's past listening. The male ego can screw us in more ways than a female can ever imagine.

The herd of bulls work their way carefully down the steep slope, as does Ivy's horse. Horse doesn't listen to Ivy and doesn't give his horse its head, so it can safely pick its way down, though. As if it's happening in slow motion, I watch Horse pull back hard on the reins in panic when his horse slides a few steps. Worst thing you can do because a horse will fight to stay on its feet even if that means unseating its rider. Shaking its head hard, protesting the too-tight reins, the buckskin sidesteps then gains control of its head. Lowering its head immediately while Horse is not leaning backward to balance his weight, Horse's ass parts ways with his saddle as expected. Horse does a perfect swan dive over the horse's head, cussing loudly, then connecting with the ground hard before rolling. Rolling, bouncing, and more rolling all the way down to the back feet of the last bull in line. The 2,000-pound bull is not impressed with having a human slam into its hind feet and whirls instantly. Bulls are generally bad-tempered, ornery fuckers during their best moments, and this one's not having a good time.

I have a moment of fear for my club brother's life when he lifts his head, and it's not five feet from the bull's lowered one. Another moment of fear when the bull paws at the ground before bellowing, shaking its huge head, slobber flying through the air. Those are classic signs that bulls give before they fuck you up for life or unalive you.

I clearly hear his "Oh, fuck me!" before he tries to scramble backward. I also hear Ivy bark an order to the dogs as Junior and her fly across the uneven ground at breakneck speed. Barreling between Horse and bull, Ivy slaps the bull's shoulders with her rope, and it distracts the bull long enough for the dogs to arrive. Sliding to a stop, Junior executes a perfect roll-back, and woman and horse return to the scene where a grisly murder nearly occurred. The heelers tag-team the pissed-off bull and push it several yards away. Keeping it distracted, the heelers prove that the Australians know how to breed a great cattle dog.

Ivy stops next to Horse, holds her hand down to him in a clear sign that he should grab it, jump up behind her, and save himself. Instead, Horse shakes his head wildly in a no gesture before he turns and starts limping back up the slope, one hand gently cupping his balls. Ivy sidles over to the buckskin, who's standing calmly nearby, picks up its reins, and follows Horse to the top of the slope.

When Horse notices me, he flies his finger high as he turns his limping body in my direction. Ivy leads the buckskin as she and Junior walk behind Horse. When Horse gets close, I can see the rips in both his shirt and jeans, and I don't even try to stifle a laugh. Small scrapes and a few bruises are evident, but he's going to survive, and his pissed-off face just makes me laugh harder.

"Talk to your woman! She put me on that four-legged devil in disguise! Oh, he's super gentle! Oh, he's the quietest horse I own! He's such a sweetheart! All fucking lies, Pigeon! That thing is evil! My nuts will never make another appearance in this lifetime! He beat the fuck out of them!" Horse screams, then winces, and rubs his hand over his abused balls.

I'm still videoing this awesome turn of events when I aim my phone at Ivy. Her head is lowered, but her shoulders are shaking. No sound is coming from her, but I grin because I know she's battling that hard.

"I used to like you, Ivy. Now I hope your horse bites you in the ass!" Horse barks before moaning again.

"I still like you, Horse. Even if you overstated your riding abilities and are as graceful on horseback as… well, I can't think of anything less graceful at the moment. And even though you refused to listen or take advice from, how did you word that? Oh yeah, a mere woman. Sorry today's been so rough on your girlie parts, but it's time to cowboy up. Get back on your horse, listen to what I say, and learn or die. Your choice, but I got things to do," Ivy says in a hard voice to Horse's back.

The whole time she's laying into him, she's grinning at me. Horse got instant karma for making a "mere woman" comment to someone who can ride circles around any man I know. The grin disappears when Horse whirls around to face her.

"Girlie parts? You do know they call me Horse Nuts for a reason, right?" he asks sarcastically.

"Yes, I know that Horse, and I know why. Go, Ava!" Ivy responds, tossing a fist in the air before turning her horse and riding back to the slope.

I end the video and lean against the tire for support while I laugh my ass off at the look on Horse's face.

"You told her about Ava kicking me?" he asks in dismay.

"Fuck no, wasn't me. Did you really say the words "mere woman" to her? Are you fucking suicidal?"

"I was joking. I didn't think she'd put me on a fucking jackhammer on steroids for it," Horse complains.

"She didn't, you dick wad. I rode that horse last night, and he's fucking awesome," I say while swinging back up to the cab, still laughing.

"Guess I'm riding with you now," Horse says before putting his foot on the bottom step.

"Think again, girlfriend. As Ivy said, time to cowboy up. Only pussies don't get back on the horse after they fall off. Try moving with the horse and not against him. Oh, and believe me, ice will be your friend tonight," I answer before slamming the door shut and starting the tractor.

I'm already forwarding the video before Horse even realizes how limited his options are for getting back to the ranch.

Walking into the house with Petey, Pooh, and Cash, we all stop dead at the sight before us. Ivy is at the stove, stirring something in a huge pot and laughing to herself. Toes is setting the table, looks at us, and starts laughing too. The sight that stopped us, though, is through the doorway into the living room. Crowding through the door, we come to a stop in front of the couch.

Laying on his back, knees cocked and supported by pillows, Horse looks like he's waiting for some kind of fucked-up gynecological exam. A large bag of frozen peas is tucked over his balls, large glass of what's most likely whiskey is cradled in one hand and balanced on his abs, while the other arm is thrown over his eyes. Mumbling, almost incoherently, the words to "Mamma's Don't Let Your Babies Grow Up To Be Cowboys," it's obvious this isn't his first glass of liquid pain reliever.

Pooh pulls his phone out and does the honors this time. Walking back to the kitchen, I lean down and kiss the side of Ivy's neck.

"Clearly, we'll be having a guest tonight. He found one of Ted's bottles of booze, has been hitting it hard and has repeatedly told me that there's no way his ass is sitting on anything that moves until his balls heal. I'm going to have to sleep with one eye open, I'm afraid," Ivy manages to say before dissolving in laughter again, Toes joining her.

"He tried to make Ivy promise to make Axel ride the same horse," Toes says.

"Oh, fuck yeah! Can you do that for us, Ivy?" Pooh asks as he joins us in the kitchen, Horse's glass in hand, loud snores following him from the couch.

"Lucky's not to blame for Horse having bruised boy parts," Ivy defends her horse.

"No, cockiness is, so to speak. And stupidity as it usually is," Petey states with a booming laugh.

"Afraid to say this, but Horse is going to hate me even more when he finds out that Lucky's the horse the kids will be learning to ride on. Difference will be, the kids will take advice and listen," Ivy says.

Our phones all ping at the same time with an incoming text from Gunner.

Gunner: James said they didn't find anything out at work. Chubs' phone was lying next to his bike, smashed. Bike was parked along the highway, keys still in it. No blood, no tire marks. If there was a struggle, it wasn't much of one. His cut wasn't there though. Gun in his saddlebags was still there. Church at 8am tomorrow. Pigeon stays at the ranch with Ivy. We'll put him on speaker during church.

Petey: How'd Lucy take it?

Gunner: Hard to tell. She listened to what we found, face went red and she went silent. Asked to be dropped at the bakery and Trudy said she went directly to the apartment and hasn't come out since. Won't answer the door or her phone. Bailey's on her way there now.

Cash: Where do we go from here?

Gunner: Fuck if I know.

The guys eat quickly, say their goodbyes, and leave. Horse remains asleep, occasionally whimpering, on the couch. Ivy makes coffee, and we take our cups to the deck to relax.

"Any sign of your brother today?" I ask.

"No, never showed. Look, I know your club has things happening with Chubs, so I'm fine here if you want to head to town to help. Horse is here, and while he currently wishes evil to fall upon me, he'd never let anything bad actually happen. Raking the hay is the easy part, and I can still call my neighbors for help if I need it," Ivy says.

"They need me, they'll call. Problem is that we're not sure where to start looking for him. There's no reason that any of us knows of for him to have been where he was."

"I like him. The kids all rave about him. I don't know him as well as you do, but is he the type that would walk away from his woman that easily?" Ivy asks.

"No, he's not. Not at all. If he's missing because he wants to be, then that was a hard decision for him to make, and he'd only do it to protect someone. The club or Lucy, I'd guess, but I don't know for sure. If he didn't choose to leave, then someone's snatched him up for some reason I don't know anything about. Not sure anyone does. Rex probably has the best chance of any of us to finding something, though. Hopefully, we'll know something by tomorrow morning."

Sitting on the deck, sipping coffee, and looking over the peaceful ranch, my mind won't stop replaying the conversation I had with him when he told me if anything happened to take care of Lucy. Chubs knew, and several of us suspected, that things were about to go sideways for him. But what?

With the guys' help, haying is done for now. Ted's popped up a few times before leaving again. A few sarcastic comments to Ivy are the worst he's accomplished, and like the coward he is, those were only made when he didn't think I'd hear him. After he and I had a conversation about his attitude toward Ivy, he's kept his mouth shut. Surprisingly, he's helped around the ranch a little, even though he chooses what he wants to do and not necessarily what needs to be done.

Horse recovered enough by morning to ride back to town but not before he apologized to Ivy. She brushed it off good-naturedly and then laughed her ass off when Horse very gingerly set his on his bike.

The search for Chubs has gotten us nowhere, and everyone is on edge. Ivy's back to work at the rescue tonight, so we'll be back to commuting between the ranch and town, but at least that way, I'll be able to help give Rex a much-needed break.

Taja and Ava's pregnancies are progressing without problems. The kids are bugging the adults constantly about their riding lessons that have been put on hold. Ava has been uncharacteristically moody and quick-tempered since Chubs disappeared. Lucy has been angry but silent. Gunner has spent a considerable amount of time trying to get Lucy to tell him any little thing she might know about Chubs, but to no avail. After the last conversation, Gunner walked out of his office while Lucy stormed out and admitted that he was a little afraid of the tiny woman. While we all laughed and teased him. Not one of us offered to take his place.

Walking into the security building, I stop in the doorway to Rex's office. It's a mess with fast food bags tossed everywhere, empty water and pop bottles, and the garbage can overflowing. Rex has the side of his face resting on his desk, one hand still on the keyboard, the other hanging toward the floor. He's sound asleep while still sitting at his computer.

I walk to the supply closet and retrieve some garbage bags. Using my phone, I order two meals, including drinks, from a nice restaurant nearby and then return to Rex's office. Working quickly but quietly, I empty his garbage can and bag up the trash lying around. After returning his office to its normal state, I walk to the main door to retrieve our dinner from the delivery guy, then return to his office.

Setting the food out on the small table, I wake him and point to our meals. Without speaking, Rex stands, walks to the table, and takes a seat. Sitting across from him, I watch as his eyes glaze over before he shakes his head hard and finally appears to be aware of his surroundings.

"This smells amazing," he mumbles while opening the various containers.

I take a minute to study Rex. Being the best tech guy any of us have ever came across, the club leans heavily on him for more things than I can count. Rex is a genius when it comes to anything in the computer field and technology, but he never knows when to step back and take a break.

As a teenager, Rex got in trouble with the authorities on numerous occasions for hacking into things he shouldn't have been able to hack. Sometimes, he would hack a secure system just for practice and the thrill of outsmarting others. Other times, he hacked to benefit someone he cared about. That type of hacking motivates him more than anything else and how he eventually made his way into the club.

Meeting Axel while both were in jail, a friendship developed. Axel was doing seven days for not being faster than Gunner and getting caught by the cops while Gunner got away. Axel refused to give up the name of his accomplice, so the judge gave him a few days to "think over his decision making." Instead of pondering his criminal behavior, he met Rex.

Rex was doing a few weeks for getting caught trying to hack into the college of his choice and to give himself a full-ride scholarship. What the two young men learned from their time in jail was simple and, no doubt, the opposite of what the judge intended. Rex learned to cover his tracks while using the black web, and Axel learned to commit his future bullshit crimes with someone slower on their feet than him. Axel brought Rex to the club, and he's been here ever since.

"You look like shit, brother," I say.

"Thanks for the honesty. It's why you're my favorite," he answers while shoveling food into his mouth.

Hair standing on end, several days' worth of scruff covering the lower half of his face, and a wrinkled shirt, I know he's been working nonstop on finding Chubs.

"Finish your meal, then go home and sleep. I'm going to be here all evening, so if any alerts come up, I'll call," I order, even though Rex is technically my boss and not the other way around.

"I can't find a fucking thing that tells us shit," Rex says in a tired rasp.

"Tracks were covered well by someone, but you still have to sleep. We can't afford to lose you too."

"I'll go home for a few hours."

"While you're there, test out your shower. A change of clothes would be nice too," I say while shooting him a grin.

"Fuck you," he answers with no heat in his voice.

When his meal is finished, Rex leaves, and that in itself shows how deep his exhaustion runs.

Hitting up my office, I sit at the computer, turn on the monitors for the rescue, and get to work. Looking over the installs Reeves and I have scheduled for the week, I keep one eye on Ivy while she goes about her shift. Turning up the sound to the rescue cameras, I listen to Ivy and the animal conversations while I work.

When I hear a familiar voice chatting with Ivy, I look to see Axel at the rescue. Turning up the volume, I grin at what I'm hearing.

"I turned in the application a few days ago, and Margie called today. Bailey and I are set up and ready to adopt Priscilla. Can I go see my girl now?" Axel asks with the biggest smile I've seen on his face for a while now.

"Let's go see what Prissy thinks about that. If she's resistant to the idea, we may have to re-think this, though," Ivy answers in a serious voice, but I know she's just torturing Axel a little.

"Priscilla Taylor will love this idea! Don't try to fuck with the master of fuckery, Ivy," Axel retorts before striding away.

Moving my eyes to the aviary, I watch as Axel walks in, and Prissy immediately notices him. She lifts off her perch and lands on Axel's raised arm before leaning close and rubbing the side of their faces together. Axel's smile has got to be hurting by now, but when Prissy purrs like a cat, it grows wider.

"Hey, Miss P., Axel wants to know if you'd like to live with him?" Ivy asks.

Prissy's screech is painful, even to my ears, and I laugh as Ivy flinches before covering hers with her hands.

"Yes, please!" Prissy coos.

"I stocked up on pecans today. Anything else you like because I plan on spoiling you, you beautiful thing?" Axel asks his new best friend.

"Goldfish," Prissy answers immediately.

"She means the cracker-type ones, not the ones that swim," Ivy explains at Axel's surprised look.

"Good to know," Axel mutters before turning back to Prissy. "Bailey wants to know what chingalinga means."

"Hottie. Hot man alert," Prissy announces in her southern accent.

"I knew it! Please use that word all you want, beautiful lady," Axel encourages. "Especially in front of Mac, but not about Mac."

I roll my eyes, knowing Axel's going to be using that term constantly now.

"Have you ever rode a bike, Prissy?" Axel questions.

"Nope."

"Want to learn?" he continues.

"Of course."

"We were made for each other."

"Are you taking her home tonight, or do you want to come back tomorrow?" Ivy asks.

"I'm not leaving my girl here another night. No offense meant, Ivy, but she's got a home now, and we all want her there. Alex is so excited about this, and so is Bailey. I come home without Prissy, I could be kicked out."

"Whoop whoop!" Prissy shouts.

"Then let's get her things gathered up. Any problems, you know you can call me anytime," Ivy tells Axel. "You said you bought some stuff already, but do you have everything you need?"

"I have way more than Prissy will ever need. We're well stocked up, and Ava helped with the food items, so Prissy gets all the vitamins and minerals she'll need to be healthy. We're ready," Axel answers confidently.

"Did Margie warn you that, um, some birds can be destructive?" Ivy asks carefully.

"Telling tales, Ivy!" Prissy barks.

"Quit worrying. We're ready to give Prissy a great home."

"Okay, Axel. Going to miss you around here, Miss P.," Ivy tells the bird that I know she's become attached to.

"Loves you much," Prissy responds.

Axel and his new friend leave the rescue shortly after to start Prissy's new life. I watch as Ivy waves them off with a grin, then finds a quiet corner and sinks to the floor. Concerned, I watch her bow her head and lay it on her crossed arms supported by her raised knees. A few minutes later, I see Ivy raise her head, wipe the tears from her cheeks, and stand. She gets back to work, but the normal bounce in her step is missing. It finally dawns on me how attached Ivy gets to the animals she cares for and the cost of letting that happen.

Lying in bed in the darkness, Ivy's head against my chest, she speaks. I knew she wasn't asleep, and I also knew she'd talk when she was ready, so I waited. The subject she decides to talk about causes my body to tense and my temper to flare, but I remain silent so she can say what she wants me to know.

"Once my grandparents passed, Ted would barge into my bedroom or bathroom anytime he chose to. He caught me half-dressed a few times, and the look on his face scared me. He's groped my breasts and other parts before, and once, I punched him in the face for it. I paid for that, though. Some of his comments made me sick to my stomach, especially when he was drunk. I learned to pick my times carefully as to when I'd shower. I usually slide a chair under the door when I do. I didn't feel safe in the home I grew up in until you stayed there with me. He's got problems, Pigeon, and they're the kind that I can't fix for him."

I listen carefully to every word that leaves her mouth, and not one of them makes me think Ted is redeemable. Ted isn't only a bully. He's a pervert. I personally feel that the only way to fix someone like that is with lead.

"Would you hate me forever if I killed him?" I ask into the silence.

Ivy gives a small laugh before going still. After a few seconds, she asks, "You're serious, aren't you?"

"Yes. Absolutely."

Ivy takes a long breath before speaking again.

"He's sick, Pigeon. I'm not sure if that means he should be put down for it, though."

"We have different beliefs about that, Ivy."

"My mom's sick, but she deserves the best life I can give her," Ivy whispers.

"Different kind of sickness, honey. She doesn't know right from wrong when her illness takes over. Ted most certainly does but chooses to do what he wants instead. He's selfish and strikes out when he knows there won't be consequences for himself."

"True. I just wish he'd leave the area, and I could get on with my life without looking over my shoulder."

"You say the word, and I'll make that happen. In the meantime, you're supposed to be learning to live free and without fear," I remind her.

"Can we change the subject now?" she asks.

"Yep."

"I've told you my biggest secrets, things that I'm embarrassed about and ashamed of, but I know next to nothing about you except that you love to play," Ivy states.

"You have nothing, absolutely nothing to be embarrassed or ashamed about, Ivy. Ted's crimes, not yours. Let him carry that responsibility because it's not yours," I say firmly before softening my tone and asking, "What do you want to know about me?"

"Everything," she says with a laugh. "How about your name? I'm having dirty sexual thoughts about a guy who I only know as Pigeon."

I bark out a laugh at her wording, ignore my initial reaction of wanting to hear more about these dirty sexual thoughts she's having, and give her what she's asking for.

"My legal name is Elijah Hayes, but I only answer to Pigeon. My dad named me Elijah, and I have no use for him, so shedding it was not a hardship. My parents are religious fanatics, and we don't see eye to eye on anything. I have no issue with religion, but the way my parents live and breathe it, we never got along. Dad uses the parts of his religion that suit him and reinterprets the parts that don't, so they excuse his behavior. He spent years trying to beat his beliefs into me and the devil out. My mom is a sheep and does everything she's ordered to do. My brother is as much of a dick as my dad is but hides it better."

"I'm so sorry you grew up in that type of family. My grandparents gave me an amazing life, and I know how lucky I was to have them. Do you have any contact with your family now?"

"Not much. When they need something, free labor or money, they call. Otherwise, no. I helped them out early this spring with planting because Dad had broken his leg. Didn't stop him from being a dick, though. They expect and demand things but never appreciate anything. I avoid them as much as possible."

"Then I'm not missing out on not having met them. Family can be a blessing or a nightmare. Sounds like we've had both," Ivy says while grazing her lips against my skin.

"I got my first tattoo when I was 17 years old. I knew the reaction I'd get at home for it but didn't care. My body, not theirs and all that. When my dad exploded, I knew I was done with being his whipping post. He grabbed his favorite whip, and the fight was on. Even at that age, I was pretty muscled up with all the hard labor from working a farm. I wrestled the whip away from him and pinned him to the barn wall. I never hit him, wanted to but didn't, but I told him that he'd never hit me again. Things changed a little for me after that, but only because my dad knew I would win a physical fight. I left soon after. Worked various jobs, anything that kept me in food, and bought a bike. Eventually made my way to Denver, met the Angels, and have been here since."

"I'm glad you found your club," Ivy states. "Kind of wish you had hit your dad, though."

"I like this vicious streak you've been hiding, woman."

"Thank you for sharing with me," Ivy says before flicking her tongue against my nipple.

"Share anything with you, honey."

"How'd you get tagged with Pigeon as your new name?"

I laugh out loud before sharing that too.

"My first bike didn't have a windshield. I took a pigeon to the chest while riding next to Trigger, swerved, hit his back tire, and put both of us on the ground. Neither of us were seriously injured. We were slowing to make a turn, but both bikes had some damage. Trigger didn't know I'd been hit by a suicidal bird and thought I just hadn't been paying attention and hit his tire. He started ranting at me about being careless, and I kept trying to interrupt him to explain. The rest of the guys ran up to make sure we were okay, and Petey turned to Trigger and said 'pigeon' before yanking off some feathers that were stuck to my clothes. Tossing them at Trigger, Petey teased him, saying he was wiped out by a pigeon. Trigger was still spitting mad but started calling me Pigeon after that. It stuck and became my road name. I'm still grateful to this day that it wasn't a woodpecker or a yellow-bellied sapsucker that hit me."

Ivy laughs hard before gliding her finger to a tat of a feather on my forearm.

"That a pigeon feather?" she asks with a giggle.

"Yep."

"I much prefer calling you Pigeon to those other choices. Not sure I could moan yellow-bellied sapsucker during sex and not have it ruin the moment," Ivy chokes out.

"Smartass. How about you show me how well you can moan Pigeon then?" I ask as I pull her body on top of mine and plant my hands on her ass, grinding her hard onto my cock.

"Can I play first?" she asks with a sly smile.

"Fuck yeah," I groan.

Ivy stands on the bed over me and pulls her shirt over her head. Wanting to enjoy the view, I lean over and flip the bedside lamp on. Lying back down, I point a finger at her panties. Grinning, she slides them down, lifts one foot and then the other out, and tosses them to the side. Grasping her calves, I stop her from moving. Taking my time, I let my eyes roam.

"Cup your breasts," I rasp.

She does, and I feel my cock harden and rise.

"Take one hand and slide it down to your pussy, Ivy. Open yourself, so I can see everything."

Once again, she complies with my wishes. I slide down the bed a little and toss my pillow to the floor.

"On your knees, baby. Straddle my face."

"Thought I got to play this time," Ivy whispers but does so while doing as I ordered.

"You'll get your turn," I answer while wrapping my arms around her hips and pulling her against my mouth.

It only takes a few swipes of my tongue before Ivy's gripping the headboard and rocking against my mouth. A few more swipes, and I stab my tongue into her opening, listening to her moans of Pigeon. I quit thinking about anything but making her come, and it happens sooner than I expected. Nipping her clit, her body jerks in pleasure.

Moving quickly, I slide out from under Ivy and kneel behind her body. Pushing her down to her elbows, I slide my hand through her wetness, finding her clit, and pressing on it with my thumb. Her body jerks in response.

"Need to fuck you," I mutter while gliding my cock between her folds.

"Please," she moans.

Pulling back, my cock finds her wet opening and slides in. Pushing deep, I hold still for a moment, fighting for control. Being inside Ivy is always a battle to last longer than a teenager. I win against my body's urge and stroke slowly in and out of the body I crave to stay planted inside of. Reaching forward with one hand, I find a breast and tug on her nipple. Using the other hand on her hip for leverage, I up the strength and speed of my strokes. When I get close to exploding, I stop again and wait for control.

"Pigeon, please!" Ivy almost whines as she tries to push back against my cock.

Holding her still, I tell her, "Want more time inside you, honey. Need a minute."

She quits moving, but I can feel the shiver that runs through her body.

Pulling my hand off her breast, I pop my thumb into my mouth, wetting it. Placing it gently against her other hole, I push it slightly inside. When Ivy gasps, I still my hand and wait.

"That okay?" I ask while praying she says yes but prepared to remove it if the answer is no.

"Yeah, it's good. Not something I've done before," she answers, and I do a mental fist pump getting to be her first at this experience.

"Going to fuck you again now, baby, in both holes. Relax, and don't fight it," I encourage as I start pumping my cock deep inside of her.

When I feel her body relax into my thrusts, I push my thumb deeper and circle it inside. Ivy's head drops to the mattress when I order, "Play with your clit."

Ivy immediately moves a hand to her clit, and I feel it brush against my cock as I glide in and out of her. Her breathing turns to panting at the same time as mine does. Picking up the speed of my thrusts, I push my thumb in as deep as I can. Ivy explodes with mewling sounds coming from deep in her throat. Her body seeks mine, pushing hard against me, and I follow her with my own hard release. I pull my thumb out and lean down to cover Ivy's back with my chest. I give a gentle thrust occasionally until I feel her body settle and the quivers stop.

"You okay?" I ask quietly.

"God, yes," Ivy answers in a soft but sincere voice.

Slowly pulling myself out of her, I step off the bed and gather her in my arms. Cradling her close, I take us to the bathroom and set her naked body on the vanity. Turning to the tub, I turn on the water, adjust the temperature, and turn back to find Ivy's eyes following my movements.

"What are you doing?" she asks.

"We're taking a bath together and for as fucking long as we want to. I promise I'll make taking a bath a whole new experience for you."

Ivy grins, hops off the vanity, and approaches me. Placing her hands on my hips, she leans up, and brushes a kiss along the side of my neck. Turning, she steps into the tub and sits down in the water. I slide in behind her, pull her against me, place my lips on her neck, and return the kiss.

Reaching for the pink nylon thingy she has sitting in a cup, I lather it up with soap. Taking my time, I wash every inch of Ivy that I can reach. I, being a man, make double sure that certain parts of her are extra clean before using the cup to rinse the soap away. Leaning against my chest, Ivy is relaxed and smiling. I realize suddenly how much I like knowing I'm the one who's giving that to her.

"The attorney is meeting us at the clubhouse tomorrow before your shift," I tell her.

"Okay," Ivy murmurs without moving.

"Prissy will probably be there, so you'll get to see her. You were happy she found a home, but it was hard seeing her leave, wasn't it?" I ask, already knowing the answer.

"Yeah, it's hard to explain. I'm always happy to find homes for the animals, but that means I can't spend time with them anymore. I work most of my shifts alone and having her there was like having a co-worker. I'll miss Prissy, but I know she's found a great home. I miss Moose and Matilda too, but I know they're better off now."

"You'll see all of them and often. They just have a new address, Ivy. What about Thor? You've gotten attached to him too. How are you going to deal when he gets adopted?" I question.

"I'm not sure that's going to happen for a while, though. He's come a long way, and he's doing great with socializing with the other dogs now, but most people won't give a pit bull mix a chance. Especially one with scars proving what type of life he had. He obviously wasn't used for fighting. His personality doesn't lean that way. He was most likely a bait dog. But the scars will scare most away, and they'll find a cute lab to adopt instead. I'm not criticizing them because, at the end of the day, you have to feel comfortable with your choice and what works with your family. I'm afraid Thor may spend the rest of his life at a rescue in a kennel," Ivy answers with sadness evident in her voice.

"What if I adopted him? I don't have a dog, always wanted one, and he and I get along well. Would he do okay with your heelers and the other animals here?" I ask.

I jerk my head back to keep from getting it smashed when Ivy swings hers around to face me. Staring silently into my eyes, I realize she's trying to gauge whether I'm serious about Thor. What she sees must reassure her because a smile spreads across her face.

"I think he'd do amazing with the other animals as long as he's introduced in a safe way. The heelers get along with everything except unruly cattle. The barn cats are smart and know when to stay or when to hide. Tabitha gets along with everything. Using caution, I think Thor would eventually form a friendship with the pets at the club, too. Are you sure you want to take on a dog that needs a little extra help over one that doesn't?"

"Thor and I have a violent past in common. I was that kid that needed a little extra help for the same reasons he does. I understand his hesitancy to trust again, but I know how far he's come. He's a beautiful dog, and I think as his confidence grows, he'll only become a better dog and deserves a life to go with that."

"I'm so glad you found the club," Ivy repeats her earlier statement.

"Me too, honey. We'll meet with the attorney, then talk with Margie tomorrow when I drop you off at work, yeah?"

"Yeah."

Sitting in the clubhouse's main room, Ivy and I are waiting for the attorney to show. When the door opens, it's Tessie and Bella that stroll through it. Spotting us, they walk to our table and take a seat. All the while, Tessie is staring at Ivy.

"You're Ivy, right?" Tessie asks with a small frown.

"Yes, I am. And you are?" Ivy responds politely.

"Tessie. Taja's sister, Vex's favorite sister-in-law, Trigger's apprentice, and Axel's favorite Uber driver," Tessie replies absently.

"I'm Bella. Petey and Trudy's daughter, Ava and Axel's sister, Pooh's best friend and babysitter of the young and old," Bella explains with a laugh. "But please don't tell the Aunts I said that."

"Nice to meet you both," Ivy says.

"How much time do you spend at Pigeon's house?" Tessie asks with what I've come to know as a glint in her eye that usually spells trouble.

"Um, a few nights a week usually," Ivy says in a confused tone.

"Hmmm. I think we're going to become good friends, Ivy. Glad someone stepped up and put an end to Pigeon's whor—" Tessie says before I cut her off.

"Tessie!" I bark quickly, not wanting the rest of that word to leave her mouth.

"Calm yourself, Pigeon. She must know you've not led the life of a saint," Tessie retorts.

"Maybe we should get moving, Tessie," Bella advises while pulling Tessie out of her chair.

"I was only trying to point out that it'll be nice having Ivy at the house instead of a steady parade of—" Tessie starts again.

"Please warn Vex that you've created another debt, and I'll be looking for him later for payment," I order. "And I will be mentioning to him how happy you are that Ivy's at the house I share with Horse," I add while emphasizing Horse's name loudly. "I'll have to speculate on the reasons, but I'm sure I can come up with a few that will interest your sister and her soon to be beaten husband."

"Pigeon! Don't you dare!" Tessie shouts.

Bella continues pulling on Tessie's arm, trying to save her friend. I can see when the realization of her fuck up hits her face. Shrugging Bella's grip off, Tessie walks back to our table. During this, Ivy has sat silent with a blank face. No reaction whatsoever, and that worries me more than whatever Tessie's about to say.

"Is there anything I can say to fix this? I didn't mean to cause a problem. I spoke before I thought it through," Tessie says in the humblest voice I've ever heard her use.

"What did you do now, Tessie?" Vex says in a resigned voice as he walks through the kitchen door.

"Earned you another ass beating," I answer with a grin at my beleaguered clue brother.

"Fuck! I'm still carrying the bruises from my round with Gunner! Do you hate me, Tessie? Is that it? Please, for the love of all that's holy, remember that your niece or nephew is going to need their father," Vex says on a groan.

Glancing at Ivy, my eyes narrow when I see her staring at Vex like every other fucking woman has done at one time or another. Waving my hand in front of her face, I point to mine when her eyes jerk in my direction.

"Keep them here, babe. Ignore all that is Vex, and remember, I'm the awesome one who knows how to drive a tractor," I order, then watch her grin at me.

"Ivy!" shouts a voice, and I duck just in time for Prissy to miss my head as she lands on Ivy's raised arm.

"Nearly earned a name change to cockatoo," Ivy murmurs before winking at me. "Still a better choice than yellow-bellied sapsucker."

I shoot Ivy a look, but she's already getting kisses from an excited Prissy. Turning back to Vex, I nod my head at Tessie and ask, "After I drop Ivy off at work, we can meet at the gym."

"Why the fucking gym? Why not just go out back now? I'll let you get a few punches in, and then we can all go our separate ways?" Vex argues.

"Let me get a few punches in? Let me?" I ask in disgust while Vex shoots a dirty look at Tessie, who's now standing with a hanging head. "The gym because Pooh, Cash, and Axel will want the entertainment."

"Axel loves to be entertained, but Axel is here today," Axel says while making his way to our side.

Sitting on his shoulders is Alex, grinning, as usual, eyes on Prissy.

"Why are you here today and not at the gym?" I ask.

"Because my boys are powerful swimmers, and Bailey's at the doctor's office to find that out," Axel crows.

"She's pregnant again?" Vex asks with a big smile.

"I hope so but won't know until she gets back. She keeps saying that birth control is stronger than my wishes, but we'll see," Axel explains.

"Why aren't you with her?" Bella questions.

"Because she's not in the mood to see my face right now. Her words, not mine," Axel answers unconcerned. "And with Prissy being so new here, I didn't want to leave her alone already."

"Couldn't Prissy stay at Ava's for a few hours?" Bella asks.

"Mac! Ick!" Prissy shouts.

"Love you more and more, Prissy!" Axel returns.

"Trouble in bird paradise?" Ivy asks.

"Apparently, Mac has a thing for Prissy. Prissy only has room in her life for one man, though, and that's me," Axel says while very nearly preening like Mac does.

I shake my head at how many times strange-ass conversations have taken place in this room. Too numerous to count, but this one's near the top. Saving us from more weird bird and man relationship talk, the attorney walks in.

Ivy and I greet her while the others step away, taking Prissy with them, so we can talk. Ivy waves at Craig and Luke when they enter the room, then at Ava and Trudy. While listening to the attorney talk about the various conditions of the will, I notice several more members enter and find seats.

"So, in short, there isn't much I can do to help. Ted may be keeping his distance now, but he does still control the money and the ranch. I'm sorry, Ivy. I wish there was more I could do," the attorney states before standing, saying her goodbyes, and leaving.

After a long minute of silence, I watch as Ivy's shoulders droop in defeat.

"Well, that's that. It was worth a try, but I didn't really expect to hear anything different than what she just said. I think I'm going to have to find my own place and move off the ranch. Hope for the best, but I know Ted won't do the ranch any favors. Or me, for that matter," Ivy says quietly.

"We can keep doing it how we've been doing it, Ivy. Work the ranch during the day, come to town when we can. The two jobs are too much for you, though, so maybe think about quitting the rescue," I say while thinking out loud. "The guys and I can take turns being at the ranch when you are, so you stay safe."

"I need the income from the rescue. I need—" Ivy starts, but I cut her off.

"No, you don't. I got us covered on that front," I say but watch Ivy shaking her head no at the same time.

The others approach and stand by quietly. I know they're all trying to come up with a solution, but Ivy's options are limited.

"Would Ted let you buy him out?" Axel asks.

"He doesn't own the ranch. I do. He manages it and makes the decisions, though," Ivy answers.

"And probably skims a fuck of a lot of the profits into his own pocket," Gunner adds.

Ivy nods in agreement, and the room falls silent, the vibe angry.

"Easy way to fix this," Craig speaks as he stands next to my leg.

"Not sure Ivy's okay with Ted having a life-ending accident," I answer while giving him a pat on the head.

Swatting my hand away, Craig glares at me. I watch as his ornery side comes out to play and bite back a grin.

"I'll say this slow, so you Boomers can keep up. Mar-ry her," Craig says while dragging out the separate syllables.

Shocked silence hits the room before I turn to look at Ivy's open-mouthed stare aimed at Craig.

"The lawyer lady said that Ivy has to be married or wait until she's 25 years old to get the ranch back from her brother, right?" Craig asks when no one speaks. "Simple then. Get married. Boom!"

"How did you hear their conversation when I couldn't, and I was trying to?" Axel asks in disgust.

"I have bat ears, remember?" Craig retorts while directing his ornery look at Axel.

"He's right, as much as it hurts to admit it," Axel murmurs.

"I appreciate the help, Craig, really I do. But that's going too far," Ivy insists.

"Why is that too far? I'd marry you tomorrow if you'd say yes," I blurt, surprising Ivy, myself, and every person in the room.

Holy fuck, what did I just say? I think I just proposed! Watching Ivy's eyes widen, I realize that I didn't lie to her. I would marry her tomorrow and not look backward once. I jerk in surprise when I also realize that I would do that whether the ranch was involved or not.

"Pigeon! No, I'm not letting you do that just to help me out of a tight spot!" Ivy shouts while standing.

"Ivy, you like Pigeon, right?" Craig asks in a reasonable voice.

"Well, yeah, I do. A lot, in fact, but that's even more reason not to let him do this to himself," Ivy answers with a small amount of panic in her voice.

"Almost a good answer, Ivy. You need to work on it a little bit, though. Pigeon, you like Ivy too, right?" he continues his questions.

"Fuck yeah," I answer immediately and sincerely.

"Then I pronounce you biker and rancher. Ta-da!" Craig says with a laugh before walking away.

"The kid's not wrong. Get married, fulfill the will's requirements, get Ted out of Ivy's life, and see how married life treats you. You want to part ways? It's your choice. You decide not to, better yet," Ava encourages with a small smile.

"You have something against marrying a biker?" I ask Ivy.

"I have nothing against marriage or bikers, but I'm not marrying one that feels pressured to help me out!" she shouts while running her fingers through her hair in a nervous gesture.

"Pigeon doesn't look pressured to me," Gunner says. "Don't know of many bikers that would allow themselves to be pressured into a marriage they didn't want."

"Should we start making wedding arrangements?" Trudy asks with a hopeful smile.

I answer yes, loudly and firmly. At the same time, Ivy all but screeches no. Everyone in the room laughs and walks away, leaving us alone. Standing, I pull Ivy's tense body against mine and hold her there. After a few moments, using my hands, I tilt her head back, so I can see her face. It's white, drawn, and I feel a moment of concern that she's going to be stubborn about this. I've never forced someone into marriage, so I'm not confident of the method needed.

"Please say yes," I implore.

"You don't want to marry me, and I'm not going to steal your freedom for a ranch," Ivy whispers in a tortured voice.

"I do want to marry you. I just hadn't thought about it yet. You're not going to steal my freedom. I'm not giving that up for a ranch. I want to share my freedom with you, honey. When you have time to think about everything, I'm pretty sure you're going to realize that eventually, marriage was going to be in our future anyway. I already told you that I wasn't going anywhere in this world without you. I meant that then, and I mean it now. You're mine, Ivy. Have been since that first kiss. I'm yours, and that's not changing. So, the marriage license does nothing to change us or who we are to each other except to get Ted out of our lives. Say yes, Ivy. I can propose in a lot better way, and I will if that's something you need, but I need your answer to be yes," I beg softly.

"Pigeon, I—" Ivy starts.

"Do you see me when you look to your future?" I ask.

"Of course, I do. I can't even envision what my life would look like without you anymore."

"Will it help if I tell you a secret? One I shouldn't have kept but have because I'm an idiot sometimes," I question with a grin.

"What secret?"

"That I'm in love with you. Have been for a while now. Probably before we even officially met, but I'll explain that another time. Will you marry me, Ivy?"

Ivy's eyes grow soft, and she leans her body further into me.

"Pretty sure I love you too, but since I've never been in love with anyone before, I'm not positive yet," Ivy responds.

"Is that a yes?"

"Will you promise to divorce me if you hate being married to me?" Ivy asks in a tiny voice.

"Not going to happen, but yeah, I promise."

"Then yes, I'll marry you," Ivy answers with a nervousness to her voice that I vow to change to happiness.

The kitchen door flies open, and everyone rushes back into the main room.

"Geesh, took you long enough, Ivy," Craig admonishes with a laugh.

"Only proposal I've ever heard that included a promise of divorce," Trudy says before pushing me back and hugging Ivy. "Welcome to the family, honey."

"Does this mean we can postpone the ass whooping you had planned?" Vex asks me before giving me a one-armed hug and a hard slap to the back. Before I can answer, Ivy does.

"Depends on what Tessie was trying to say before Pigeon shut her down. Anyone want to explain what 'the steady parade of' means? Because if it's what I think she was saying, the ass whooping will commence, and I'll be putting money on Vex winning it."

"Why would you think he'd win?" I ask, astonished that my own damn woman would bet against me.

"Because you'll be starting off already injured and not walking straight," Ivy replies sweetly. "Remember, I grew up on a ranch and can castrate a 1,200-pound bull in 18 seconds flat. You won't take nearly that long."

Every man in the room groans, and most drop a hand to cover their favorite muscle. I give Ivy an innocent look, then explain.

"Tessie lies! She's a shit-stirrer, and you shouldn't spend time in her presence! She's evil!"

Tessie glares at me, but the rest of the room laughs.

"As long as that phrase is in the past, I'll use my skills on the ranch only," Ivy says as she leans into me.

Thank fuck my woman is a reasonable one. Probably helps that she likes my cock, too.

When the women of The Devil's Angels get busy on something, things happen fast. Within a few days, we have a marriage license, a pastor, and Ava's working on a cake. I know Ivy's overwhelmed with everything going on, so I try to keep things as close to normal as I can, but that's not easy.

Ivy did put her foot down firmly, though, when it came to some aspects of our wedding. Cake has to be chocolate, steaks on the grill, no fancy menu. Ranch food and in large quantities she ordered. She insisted the wedding be small and not formal because she said nobody should stuff themselves into clothing they hate to wear just to watch us get married. She asked Ava to stand up with her, and I asked Rex. She asked the twins to be the flower girls and Luke to be the ring bearer.

When Craig's face went slack in shock of being left out, Ivy asked him the big question, one I didn't know she had been planning on all along. She asked Craig if he'd walk her down the aisle and give her away because she doesn't have a dad and that if she could have picked a brother for herself, she'd have picked him. Craig solemnly nodded his head but told her, "I'll walk with you, but I'm not giving you away. Not until Pigeon proves he won't mess this up."

We're having the wedding and reception at the ranch, and Ted was informed he's not invited to attend. He was also told, by me, to start packing because the day of the wedding is his last day living on Ivy's land. Ivy's grandparents' attorney has been notified of the impending marriage and has started the paperwork to move everything into Ivy's ownership.

I went with Ivy to visit her mom. Carol was smiling, crying, and happy to see her girl but refused our invitation to the wedding. She explained that she's not comfortable leaving the premises, and we explained that we understood. Before we left, she grabbed my arm and asked, "Will you please take good care of my Ivy?"

"I promise that I will," I answered before accepting her hug.

After returning to my house, I sat Ivy down and told her we were going ring shopping tomorrow. I expected excitement, but Ivy sat quietly for a moment before stating, "Nana gave me her rings when she knew she was terminal. Would you be upset if I wanted to wear them instead of buying new ones?"

There is a part of me that's disappointed because I want to see my ring on Ivy's finger, but I understand her feelings about this.

"How about a compromise?" I ask instead of answering her question.

"Like what?"

"You wear your grandmother's rings because I know what those two people meant to you. You and I get ring tats like Vex and Taja did, so something of mine is on your body."

"I like that idea. A lot. When can we get the tats?" Ivy asks with a smile.

"After the wedding. We'll get Bailey to draw something up for us."

"Thank you for understanding. You're going to be really good at this husband thing," Ivy says quietly before we seal our agreement with a kiss.

"You two aren't going to start dry humping each other, are you? Because I'd really like to watch some TV and not porn," Horse mutters as he flops down on the couch.

Laughing at his words, Ivy goes to the kitchen to make a few more calls for the wedding.

"You sure you're okay with us still staying here for now?" I ask Horse.

"Long drive to the ranch. You two are always welcome to stay when you don't want to make it. As long as you pay your share of the rent, that is," Horse answers before throwing a pillow at my head, laughing.

I toss it back, and Horse throws one of his boots instead.

"Knock it off, you two. This isn't romper room," Ivy shouts from the kitchen.

When we quit acting like teenagers, Horse asks, "Anything new on Chubs yet?"

"No, nothing. Lucy's way calmer than I would have expected her to be, so that makes me suspicious. Ava seems to be taking his disappearance harder than her. Either Lucy knows something, has had communications with him, or she's got the best poker face ever."

"I have never figured out what it is about Lucy and strange things happening when she's around, but a few of us have noticed that those things are occurring more often since Chubs came up missing."

"Really? I've been too busy lately to notice that," I answer.

"Snots won't even come into the same room with her now. She walked through the clubhouse yesterday, and a table leg fell off, a picture fell, and Toes screamed, grabbed his back, and has been icing it since. All within seconds of each other. He swears that Lucy is cursed, and if we're not careful, her head is going to do a 360 or blood's going to seep through the walls," Horse says before laughing hard, probably at the look of Toes face while he explained his thoughts.

"Toes isn't wrapped too tight," I answer but laugh at the havoc Lucy can wreak.

"After she left, the main gate quit working, and James walked into the clubhouse while kissing the cross necklace that he always wears. When I asked why, he said he just got a feeling that it was the thing to do. He was spooked. Funny shit to see," Horse explains between laughs.

"Speaking of James, the club's got to make a decision soon about him. No doubt, he'll get voted in, though."

"Yeah, it's time to make him a patched member," Horse agrees.

Chapter 14

Ivy

Looking at the club women, I shake my head no. I'm not wearing some huge white, puffy dress just because it's the tradition. I don't mind wearing the occasional dress or skirt, but I'm not a wedding gown type of girl. Livi grins and gives me a wink. She completely understands because that's not the type of girl she is either.

Bella comes into the large changing area, dress over her arm, and gives me a smile. Holding it up for me to see, I nod immediately. Simple, cream-colored, and the length will hit just above the knees. It's exactly what I had in mind. I don't like fancy, and this dress isn't. It's elegant but not so much that it can't be worn for a ranch wedding. The shoes Tessie holds up are the same color, low-heeled and look comfortable. That's good enough for me, and I'm grateful to be done shopping.

With my new posse, I make one more stop. I wanted to get Pigeon the perfect wedding gift, and Bailey gave me the perfect idea. When I'm done here, I'll be driving to the ranch with James as my escort. Pigeon's spending the night at his house and will make the drive with Rex in the morning. Rex promised that Pigeon will be on time and not hungover, but I was never worried. Pigeon has proved repeatedly over the last few weeks just how much he's looking forward to our marriage. When the guys started talking about a bachelor party, Pigeon shut it down. Said he didn't need or want one. He just needed to make me legally his. The guys made several whip-cracking sounds, but Pigeon wouldn't budge.

I get up early and get the chores done before heading upstairs. James is using the downstairs bathroom to get ready, and I know I'm safe to take my time today. A short time later, I hear cars and bikes arriving but continue working product into my curls. When there's a knock on my door, I open it to find Ava and Trudy looking gorgeous and holding up a makeup bag. Entering, they set me down and get to work.

"Should I pull my hair up?" I ask.

"No! Pigeon loves your curls. I'd kill for them myself. We're going to let them frame your face, be stunning and natural," Ava answers.

"We're going light on the makeup too because Pigeon was quick to remind us that you don't need 'all that shit' on your face," Trudy says with a laugh.

Dressed, hair and makeup done, I sit quietly in front of my mirror, wishing with all my heart that my Nana and Papa had met Pigeon. They would have loved him and having them miss today is painful. Taking a deep breath, I dab at the wetness in my eyes and try to concentrate on the good things in my life instead. I remind myself how lucky I was to have had them for the time that I did and ignore the feeling of loneliness of having no family of my own at my wedding.

"You have your Nana's rings for your something old. Trudy gave you your blue garter as your something blue. Tammy gave me her pearl bracelet for you to wear as your something borrowed. Pigeon bought you this as your something new," Ava says before placing a delicate silver necklace around my neck.

Looking in the mirror at it, tears rise again. Hanging from the necklace is a hammered silver disk with a feather engraved in it. The feather matches the tat he has on his forearm, and I smile while waving my hands in front of my eyes.

"Knew that one was going to bring on the tears. It's beautiful, Ivy. That man is all kinds of in love with you," Trudy says softly.

"I'd love to see his face when he gets a look at your gift to him," Ava says with an impish grin.

I return the grin but don't offer to video the upcoming moment.

The simple ceremony goes off without a hitch. Pigeon smiled wide, both dimples showing when he saw Craig walking me toward him. The kids did their parts perfectly. Craig handed me off to Pigeon, but not before I bent low to give him a hug and a kiss on the cheek. After I straightened, Craig leveled a look at Pigeon. Clearly a look of warning, and Pigeon acknowledged it with respect by giving a small nod to Craig. Satisfied that his look was received correctly, Craig stepped to the side.

After repeating our vows, Pigeon pulled me close and kissed me, sealing our marriage vows. Turning to the crowd, he held our clasped hands high and let out a howl. The bikers in the crowd returned it, and the reception was underway.

It wasn't long before I ditched my shoes, and Pigeon got rid of his jacket. Looking gorgeous in all black, he leads me to the makeshift dance floor, otherwise known as the deck, and pulls me close. Music starts playing, and I recognize "Unchained Melody" and then Ava's voice as she sings the lyrics. Pigeon keeps me close, barely moving our feet but loving every second of our first dance.

Close to the end of the song, Pigeon steps away and leaves me standing alone in the middle of our friends. Ava continues singing the ending of the song as Pigeon takes a seat, then pulls a guitar from behind it. As Ava finishes her song, Pigeon starts playing. Shocked gasps and a few "what the fucks" can be heard around me. I guess I'm not the only one who didn't know he had this hidden talent. Just as my mind thinks that, Craig says loudly, "I told you he could play, Axel! Pay up!"

My hands fly to my mouth when I realize Pigeon's playing Ed Sheeran's song "Perfect." When he adds his voice and sings the words, his eyes meet mine. They stay locked together, forgetting for a few moments that we're not alone. Tears well up and spill over, but I don't bother with them. When the song ends, Pigeon sets his guitar down and walks to me. Cupping my face, he whispers, "Perfect. You're fucking perfect for me."

Pigeon kisses me slowly and thoroughly before pulling back to smile down at me.

"Love you," I admit.

"Okay, yeah, whatever, you two. What the fuck, Pigeon? How come we didn't know you played? And you can sing, too!" shouts Axel in accusation from beside us.

"Because I don't play for the likes of you dumbasses. I only play for my wife," Pigeon answers, still staring down at me.

"Thank you, husband," I murmur.

"I have another gift for you, but we have to pick it up tomorrow," Pigeon says with a grin.

"I have one for you that you'll get to unwrap when our guests leave," I return with my own grin.

"Fuck, I think she wants us gone already," Axel complains while Pigeon and I share a laugh.

The reception continues with good food, great company, and flowing booze. Hugs are freely handed out, and I receive a lot of official welcome to the family comments before Trudy started rounding people up to leave. When Axel stops next to us, I listen while Pigeon gives him a hard time about Bailey's doctor's appointment not turning out the way he was hoping it would.

"It'll happen when it happens. Hopefully, that's soon because that woman has to get busy if she's going to give me all the kids I want," Axel complains as Bailey slips under his arm and hugs his waist.

"Not having a dozen babies, Axel," Bailey says while rolling her eyes at me.

"But I like you pregnant. You're extra sexy when you're fa…" Axel stops suddenly. He hesitates then rewords his sentence. "When you're carrying our child."

"Nice save, biker boy. Time to head home. I'm driving so you can conserve your energy so you can apologize thoroughly tonight," Bailey retorts before walking off to retrieve their daughter from Petey.

"I'm hoping she means apologize with sexy time and not by making a trip to the flower shop," Axel whines before following Bailey.

After the last guest leaves, Pigeon and I make our way to our room. As Pigeon undresses and climbs into bed, I take my time. I know his eyes are on me and my every move, so I slowly remove my dress and hang it over the back of a chair. Leaving me in just bra, panties, and a short slip, I walk to Pigeon's side of the bed. His dark eyes continue to follow me as I slowly remove my bra then slip. When Pigeon reaches for me, I step away. Eyebrows rising, I smile at his confusion and impatience.

"Remember, I told you I had a gift for you that you had to unwrap?"

Pigeon grins before nodding.

I turn until my right side is in Pigeon's view, my nipples hardening at the look in his eyes when he realizes what he's seeing.

"Step closer, baby," he orders.

I do as I'm told and hold perfectly still while he removes the protective tattoo film covering his gift. His eyes darken with heat when he pulls the film away.

Looking up to my eyes, he asks in a guttural tone, "You put us together on your body? Fuck, Ivy. Fuck, I love it. Love you. I want the same fucking tat on me."

I stand still while he studies the heavily shaded pigeon running up my ribs that has a string of ivy leaves trailing over one wing, across the body, and winding around a foot. It's not a large tattoo, but the detail in it is amazing. I loved it the second the tattoo artist was done, and I love it more now seeing the look in his eyes.

"Ivy leaves have many symbolic meanings, but I like to think these ones are for loyalty. Something you have from me and always will. A pigeon is best known for security, peace, and home. All of which you brought to me," I whisper.

"I have no words to explain what this means to me. You marked your body for me, with me, with us. It's permanent, and so are we. Lose the panties, honey," Pigeon rasps out.

I push them down and then step out of my panties, and Pigeon carefully, without touching my still tender skin, lifts and then lays me next to him.

"Ivy also symbolizes fertility. We going to have a lot of babies, wife?" Pigeon asks while tracing a finger down my body before circling my navel.

"Do you want kids?" I ask since it's not something we ever discussed.

"I want kids with you," Pigeon's answer is immediate and firm.

"Me too."

Pigeon's eyes flare with heat again, and while today was magical, our wedding night outshines everything I ever imagined.

Lola Wright

Chapter 15
Pigeon

Weeks have passed since the wedding, and I haven't quit smiling yet. That's not strictly true because we're no closer to finding Chubs than before, and the club is showing the strain. Other than that, though, life is good, and Ivy and I are happy.

Ted hasn't been seen since the day before our wedding, and Ivy relaxes more each day. We're finding our way as a married couple, compromising and working together when things arise. I've found that Ivy will speak her mind, but she's not one that likes to argue. She says what she thinks is important for me to hear but never demands her way. She listens to my viewpoints with an open mind and gives in when it's something important to me. Somehow, we've developed a perfect give and take relationship.

We've built trust with each other through respect and knowing the other only wants what's best for us.

Bailey did a deep dive into the ranch books and found what we knew she would. Ted had been skimming tens of thousands each year. It didn't take Rex long to locate where Ted had been stashing the money and left Ted with a zero balance of the stolen money. If he wants his money back, he'll need to admit how most of it found its way to his account in the first place. Ted was left with the inheritance he was given but not one cent beyond that.

The money that had been taken back has been tucked away for Ivy's future plans for the ranch. We'll need money to build the large indoor riding arena she requires and the addition she wants to add onto the bunkhouse. The only thing I pushed for and won was a new truck for Ivy. She's worked the ranch for several years without earning a dime from it, and I insisted she spend some on a reliable truck. I've never been comfortable with her making the long commute in her old truck, and now I worry less.

After our wedding, I drove Ivy to the rescue then explained that Thor was her other wedding gift from me. Ivy was so excited that she was speechless. Bringing Thor home with us, he's been adapting well. The heelers are patient with him and don't mind when Thor tries to help herd the cattle. He's horrible but enthusiastic at it, and the heelers simply clean up his mistakes when he bounds off to explore some new scent.

Thor's become Ivy's constant companion and seldom far from her side unless she's working. When Ivy's working, Thor hangs with me instead. At night, he has a bed in the corner of our bedroom. He sits outside the bathroom door whining while waiting for Ivy but moves quickly when Tabitha claims that space. He's becoming confident, and his social skills have improved dramatically.

Ivy's at work, so I'm hanging out at the clubhouse, killing time until Church. Sitting at the bar, I'm half-listening to Mac rant about Prissy. Mac has got a huge crush on Axel's little southern peach, and she couldn't care less. She's obsessed with Axel and no one else. Birds hate to be ignored, and Prissy has perfected the ability to get under Mac's feathers by doing just that.

"Gots to go," Mac says before making his way to the kitchen.

Axel said Mac's been sitting outside his front window, giving Prissy a wing-wave whenever she's on her perch in front of it. I'm guessing that's where the little feathered Romeo is headed now.

"How you feeling, Ava?" I ask as she walks out of the kitchen a moment later. "Shouldn't you be home, taking it easy?"

Ava and Taja are both nearing their due dates, and both women have a distinctive waddle to their walk now. Not that any of us, Axel included, is dumb enough to use those words out loud. Both have taken maternity leave, and everyone is on pins and needles waiting for their big days.

"I'm pregnant, Pigeon, not on my deathbed. Just doing a quick inventory of what the clubhouse needs before I head home."

I nod, knowing better than to say more about it. Ava's been short-tempered since Chubs came up missing, and I work hard at not lighting her fuse. The way I see it is that with all Ava does for her husband's club, she should be allowed to be angry and scared over Chubs being gone. He's her best friend, and her temper is coming from a place of fear.

When my phone rings, and I pull it out to answer, Ava walks back into the kitchen. Listening to Toes explain that there's a woman at the gate to see Ava, I put him on hold. Walking to the kitchen door, I push it open to see Ava leaning against a worktable, slowly working the kinks from her back.

"Toes said there's a woman at the gate for you."

"Yeah, she called the bakery about having us cater an event for her. They told her I'm off for a few months, but she insisted, so I told them to send her here," Ava answers.

Walking back to the bar, I tell Toes to send the lady to the clubhouse. When the door opens, I watch a lady walk inside, looking around before spotting me. She's probably in her early 50s but looks older. Harsher than she should at that age like maybe her life hasn't been easy. She was pretty once but not so much now.

"I'm looking for Ava, the owner of Sweet Angel Treats," she says while eyeing Mac skeptically.

"I'm Ava. Why don't we take a seat, and you can give me an idea of what you want for your event," Ava offers while taking a seat at a table.

The woman stands and stares at Ava long enough that I tune in to her mannerisms. She looks unsure, nervous, and that makes no sense for someone wanting to hire a caterer.

"You're pregnant," the woman states before asking, "Is this your first child?"

"Yes, I am, and, no, it's not. What can I help you with, Ms. Foster?" Ava asks.

The woman walks to the table and hesitantly takes a seat. Still staring at Ava, she asks, "How many children do you have?"

"This will be my fourth. I'm sorry, I'm not trying to be rude, but I have things to do. Can we get down to what you're here for?" Ava answers with a small bite to her tone.

"Yes, sorry, of course," Ms. Foster says but then says no more.

Ava waits a full minute before I notice she's trying to hold her temper in check.

"Maybe now would be a good time to tell Ava what type of event you want catered," I urge the woman.

"I don't have an event. I lied about that because I needed an excuse to meet you, and you're not at the bakery anymore," the woman finally says in a quiet voice.

I stiffen in alarm, and I watch Ava do the same. As I'm standing to walk to the table, the woman speaks again.

"I think I'm your mother."

Ava freezes instantly, even her breathing. I step between the two women's chairs while pulling my phone out.

"Why do you think that?" Ava calmly asks while laying her hands on her belly and caressing it with both hands.

When Gunner answers, I say two words before disconnecting. "Clubhouse. Now."

"I recently saw an old article about you and this club. It had a picture of you, and you're the spitting image of me when I was your age. Also, I left an infant girl on the street you were found on," the woman confesses.

"First, you didn't leave an infant. You placed it in a box at the bottom of a dumpster. You abandoned your infant in a way that shows you wanted her to die. Don't care who you claim to be, but you're not my mother. A mother would never do that," Ava replies, still in a calm manner.

"I can explain!" the woman rushes to say.

"No, you can't," Ava counters while standing up.

"I was on drugs! I was an addict, and I was too young to know how selfish I was being!"

"Not an excuse. Even animals will fight for their young. Why are you really here? Why now after all these years?" Ava asks with anger finally showing up in her tone.

"I just wanted to meet my daughter," the woman explains, but it sounds false even to my ears.

The kitchen door slams open, and Gunner, Petey, and Axel crash through it. Coming to a quick halt when they don't recognize an immediate threat. Gunner reads his wife's face, though, and moves to her side.

"I'm not your daughter! Don't use the words mother or daughter again! You don't understand the meaning of those words!" Ava shouts, placing her hands on the table and leaning into them.

Still standing between the two women, I watch as Petey's face ignites in anger, and Axel tenses, ready to defend his sister against anyone or anything.

"I understand why you'd be angry. I do. But if you would just listen—" the woman starts to say.

"Cut to it!" Ava orders as she slices a hand through the air. "Tell me what you want and why you're here. Do it now, or you'll be the one placed in a box at the bottom of a fucking dumpster!"

"Fine. I was telling the truth when I said you're my daughter. Here's a picture of me, taken before I gave birth to you. You can't deny the resemblance," the woman says while holding an old photo up in the air.

The woman in the picture could be Ava. The resemblance is uncanny, and it's obvious she's either Ava's biological mother or a very close relative. Ava's eyes glance at the picture before returning to the woman's face.

"How much do you need?" Axel barks, patience having run out.

"Things have been difficult for me lately. Being a business owner, I thought you might be able to help me out a little," the woman says without a lick of shame in her voice.

"Get her out of my sight," Ava says in a suddenly exhausted voice as she turns away and disappears into the kitchen.

"Stay away from my wife, my family, my club, or I'll make you wish you'd have died the day you tried to kill your own fucking infant," Gunner spits out in disgust before following his wife.

When I reach for the woman's arm to escort her out, Petey intercedes.

"Stand down, Pigeon. I've waited years to meet this cunt and have a few things I need to say."

Petey takes the woman by the arm and stalks to the door. The woman's feet barely have time to touch the floor due to the speed in which Petey's helping her exit. When Axel starts to follow, anger painted all over him, Petey holds up a hand.

"Go check on your sister, son. Tell Trudy I'll be late getting home and why."

We find Ava clinging to Gunner's big body, soaking up his support. Dry-eyed but visibly shaking, Ava's trying hard to keep it together. After another moment, they walk out the back door, Ava leaning heavily into Gunner's side. Looking to Axel, I see his expression of concern. Putting a hand on his shoulder, I say, "She'll be fine, Axel. After all she's survived. This won't keep her down long. Let Trudy know where Petey is, go home, and hug your daughter. We can postpone Church until tomorrow."

Axel takes my advice and leaves. I finish my beer and am planning on leaving when the door opens, and Horse strolls in. A few minutes go by, and Pooh enters, sees us, and moves to the stool closest to Horse. As more people show up, the room fills with club brothers and club family. Seeing Cash and Livi, Vex and Taja together is making me miss Ivy. Toes enters and walks behind the bar, coming to a stop in front of me.

"Who was that woman, and what did she do to make Petey that mad?" Toes asks.

"What's he talking about?" Pooh asks.

"A lady showed here, wanting to talk to Ava. Pigeon told me to send her to the clubhouse. Next thing I know, Petey's outside ripping the lady a new ass. Never saw him that angry before," Toes explains.

"Lady claimed to be Ava's mom," I add and watch everyone in the room go still.

Everyone knows Ava's history about being abandoned. I personally think the lady was lucky it was Petey and not Trudy who had words for her. Trudy's words would have been short before it escalated into a physical thing.

Axel enters the clubhouse, his daughter clinging to him, his other arm around Bailey, who has Prissy on her shoulder.

"Church is postponed until tomorrow. Gunner called and said Ava's holding strong, but he wants to stick close to her and the kids. Trudy's with them, and Pops hasn't returned yet. I may have to bail him out tonight," Axel says, then gives a small shrug, unconcerned about that possibility.

"Did the woman look like Ava?" Pooh asks.

"Yep. No doubt they're related," Axel states.

As nearly everyone in the club makes an appearance, Craig along with several of the pets, enters too. Mac immediately lands on a table and starts making cooing sounds, staring at Prissy. To her credit, Priscilla ignores him completely. When she leaves Bailey's shoulder and lands on another table, Mac flies over to stand beside her.

"Pretty lady," Mac says.

"Back off," Prissy warns.

Craig crawls onto the stool next to me, gives Toes a chin lift and waits for his root beer. Receiving it, he takes a long drink before wiping the foam off his lip with the back of his hand. Turning to look at the birds, he nudges my arm.

"They need to work this out," he says while watching the birds.

"Will it get worked out, or will one of them need a vet visit?" I ask with a laugh, then laugh again when Gee walks past wearing a shirt that reads, "Pig Phat."

Looking toward Pooh, he grins and shrugs innocently at my look.

Mac starts strutting his stuff in a circle around the table while Prissy looks away from him. He fluffs his feathers, extends his neck, and then wiggles his tail before making another loop. Axel stops next to them, drops a handful of pecans in front of Prissy, and takes a seat on a couch with Bailey.

"Hey, Freddy!" I shout.

"What?" he answers from across the room.

"You still have a houseguest?" I ask and laugh at the look on his face.

"No, Gunner took him home a few days ago. Ava finally admitted that she knew about Little A all along. Apparently, everyone knew about the pig. Gunner didn't realize that Ava raving about the little guy at the rescue was her way of getting him to notice the pig. He had a love at first sight moment, I guess. I think Ava just outsmarted him. Kind of quiet around my place now without the pig."

"The pig's got hair. Lots of it. How are we still calling it Little Axel?" Craig asks before laughing at his own joke.

Duffy strolls past Freddy's feet on his way to Taja, and Freddy makes the mistake of absently reaching down and stroking the fat cat's back while answering me. A hiss, growl, and then a swat, and Freddy's pulling back a bloodied hand.

"Was thinking of getting a pet, but it sure as fuck won't be a cat!" Freddy shouts while accepting a napkin from Bella to wrap his wound in.

When Taja bends to pick up the temperamental cat, Vex shakes his head no, risks life and limb, and does it for her. Setting Duffy in her lap, what's left of it with her large belly anyway, Duffy starts purring and rubbing his face over the large baby bump. Vex scowls because he's always got his hands on Taja's pregnant belly, but he doesn't push his luck.

"If you have time tomorrow, Freddy, I could use another driving lesson," Tessie says in a hopeful voice.

I grin because Freddy's face takes on a pallor usually reserved for a corpse, and we all watch him squirm.

"Yeah, Freddy. Didn't you say you had tomorrow off and nothing to do? Weren't you thinking of coming out to the ranch just to get out of town?" I ask, even though he'd never said any such thing.

"I could drive you there!" Tessie shouts, excited about the possibility.

"It's nearly an hour away. They'd never make it past the city limit sign," Pooh states with a wicked grin.

"At least the ranch would be safe from her," Toes adds.

"I'll take you driving tomorrow, Tessie," Lucy says while standing from her chair.

"Thank fuck!" Freddy shouts before dropping his head in relief.

"Lucy, honey, no. You don't want to do that," Taja speaks up.

"Got nothing else to do. The men haven't taught her shit so far. You know the old saying. If you want something done right... yada, yada, yada. Pick you up around noon, Tessie," Lucy says in a flat voice before walking toward the main door.

"Don't think that's a good idea, Lucy. Chubs wouldn't want—" I start to explain.

"Chubs isn't here, so he has no say in this. If he was concerned with my well-being, he'd be here but notice he isn't. I have nothing else to do, and I no longer care about fuck-all. Noon, Tessie. You'll learn, but you're not going to like my methods. Too bad," Lucy says with venom and then walks out the door.

While everyone sits, slack-jawed at Lucy's words, Craig sets his glass down and slides off the stool.

"Hold my beer. I got this," he says, then exits through the door Lucy just slammed behind her.

When Pooh steps off his stool to follow Craig, Axel waves him off.

"They're close. Maybe she'll listen to the little guy."

"Why are you guys always causing drama?" Tessie asks loudly to no one in particular.

"Yeah, we cause the drama. Not your driving," Horse mutters, and I bite back a grin.

"Drama will be happening in a big way if we don't find Chubs. Because come fall, someone's got to tell Craig that he'll have to attend regular school. I've already volunteered Trigger for that conversation," Pooh says while several of the adults laugh.

That's a conversation I want no part of because Craig's not going to take that well. The other kids work with Chubs on school things, but they enjoy attending regular classes too. Not Craig, and I'm thankful for not being the poor teacher that's going to have him in their classroom.

Picking Ivy and Thor up from the rescue, we make the drive home to the ranch. Ivy wanted Thor to have more time socializing, so he went to work with her tonight. He's doing great and even does well at the clubhouse with the pets. He keeps his distance from Duffy, but otherwise, he likes all the rest, especially the donkeys.

"Good day at work?" I ask as Ivy leans into my side.

"Not really. We lost a baby goat tonight. It was in bad shape from the day it came to the rescue and never recovered."

"Sorry, honey," I answer while dropping a quick kiss on the top of her head.

"I have to bring the trailer to work tomorrow and be there early. Two draft horses are being surrendered, and I'm going to pick them up."

"I have to be at the security office early, so I'll take my bike."

We pull into the ranch, and I park my truck. Turning Ivy's face my direction, I kiss my wife. I'm enjoying our moment when Thor whines. Ivy pulls back, opens her door, and lets Thor scramble over her to get outside. Shutting the door, she turns back to me. Climbing onto my lap, Ivy rests her back against the steering wheel, wraps her fingers in my hair, and tugs my mouth back to hers. Because I'm not the kind of man to ignore an invitation, I slam my mouth against hers. Placing my hands on her hips, I slide her lower half against mine. I groan when my cock responds to the heat from her body on mine.

"Need you in me, Pigeon," Ivy whispers against my mouth.

I open the door, help Ivy out and follow her. Slamming the door, I push her back against it and grind myself against her. Reaching down, I flick open the button on her jeans, unzip them, and slide my hand inside. Finding what I knew I'd find, I glide my finger through her wetness while Ivy moans deep in her throat.

Using my other hand, I push her shirt and bra up, exposing her to my eyes. Leaning down, I take a hard nipple into my mouth and suck. I've found that my wife loves nipple play, and that works for me because I have a major thing for Ivy's full breasts. Using my teeth, I bite gently. Ivy tugs on my hair, pulling my head back and then pulls my mouth to her other breast. I repeat my actions and revel in the sounds she makes.

"Inside, Ivy."

"No time, need you in me now," she answers while struggling to get one leg of her jeans off.

Somehow, we manage to get her half undressed, my jeans loose and hanging from my ass. Grasping her hips, I lift and then lower her onto my cock. Pressing her backside hard against the truck, I thrust deep. Ivy wraps her arms around my shoulders, drops her forehead to mine, and I fuck my wife.

When we finish, we don't bother righting our clothes any more than needed to get into the house. Laughing at each other's struggles, we make it to our bedroom and collapse on the bed. After a minute, Ivy says into the dark, "Love you."

"You only love my cock," I retort and listen to her snort, then laugh.

"I do, very much, but that's not all I love about you."

Standing to finish undressing, I ask, "What else do you love about me?"

Ivy, doing the same as me, answers, "Everything."

When we hear a dog barking, I realize we left Thor outside.

"Go clean up, honey. I'll let Thor in," I tell Ivy as I pull on a pair of boxer briefs and make my way back downstairs.

Pulling the back door open, I'm surprised that Thor isn't standing there. Looking out across the yard and barnyard, I finally spot Thor standing near the bunkhouse, sniffing around the door. Calling his name, he eventually lifts his head and trots to me. Letting him in, I kill the lights and head to bed.

The alarm goes off early, and I groan as I reach out a hand to silence my phone. I promised Rex I'd come in early because we have a couple of installs to do today, and neither are going to be quick jobs. Reeves is meeting me at the office, and I don't want to leave him waiting. Waking Ivy, we shower together and eat a quick breakfast of bagels.

"Thor going to work with you?" I ask.

"Yeah. Are you coming back here after work or meeting me at the rescue?" Ivy asks while looking out the window.

"I got Church first. Then I'll stop by and see you. After that, I'm coming back here. Trigger's probably coming too. He wants to bring the boys out and go fishing."

"Sounds good. When you brought Thor in last night, did you go inside the bunkhouse?" Ivy questions.

"No, he was down there, but he came when I called him. Why?"

"Huh. There's a light on in the bunkhouse, so I thought maybe you left it on," Ivy answers while walking to the garbage can and tossing out her napkin.

Walking to the window, I look at the outline of the bunkhouse in the darkness but don't see a light. Before I can tell Ivy that, a scratching can be heard at the door. Ivy opens it, and in walks the heelers. When Ted lived here, they stayed near the barn if Ivy wasn't around. Now that he's gone, and they're welcome inside, they often show up at the door. They aren't big on spending the night indoors, but they like the option they now have. Leaning down to give first Cody and then Annie a scratch, Ivy hands out a treat to all three dogs. Walking to her, I give her a kiss then make my way to my bike.

Walking into the security office, I stop at the front desk and glance through the work orders. Walking down the hall, I turn into Rex's office to find him sound asleep on the couch in the corner. While trying to decide what evil method of waking him I'm going to employ, Reeves stops next to me, peering inside.

Grinning at each other, we walk quietly to the couch. My idea of sitting on Rex and pinning him down goes out the window when I see Reeves pull something from his pocket. My eyes go wide at this new possibility, and I nod eagerly in agreement. Pulling my phone out, I get it ready. When I nod, Reeves puts his evil plan into motion.

Standing as far back as the length of his arm will allow, Reeves presses the prongs of the small handheld taser to Rex's jean-covered balls. Our poor boss's body jolts and stiffens straight, so painfully so that I feel a little of it too in what I call ball sympathy. Eyes fly open, along with his mouth, but no sound emerges. After about two seconds, Reeves pulls the torture device back, and Rex's body relaxes for a brief moment before he curls into himself. Body folding in half, both hands gripping his dangly parts, he moans long and loud. Body twitching, head thrashing, teeth chattering, he starts cursing. At first, his words are incoherent, incomplete sentences including words like murder, dead, and castrate before they become clearer.

"I'm going to fucking murder you dead after I castrate you fucking assholes."

I clearly heard that sentence more than once as Rex has a tendency to repeat himself. When his body finally stops violently reacting to what happened to it, his eyes find Reeves.

"Work van's loaded. Let's go, brother!" Reeves shouts as we both make a break for the front door.

Not bothering to shut it behind us, we sprint to the van, dive inside, and lock the doors. Looking out the window, I see Rex stumbling out the door, one hand holding his injured parts, the other holding a handgun.

"He's going to shoot us! Go! Go! Fucking go!" I shout to Reeves.

Reeves starts the van and floors it, spraying gravel as it slides sideways down the drive. When I hear a gunshot, metal striking metal, I duck instinctively. The fucker just shot at us and hit the van somewhere. Reeves never lets up on the gas, and while I hear a few more shots, none hit us. Nearly falling out of my seat from the wild turn Reeves makes, I hang on for dear life. Just as I start to relax, I recognize a new threat coming down the street toward us.

"Fuck me, we're going to die!" I tell Reeves in a panic.

"Nah, we're good. We're out of firing range now," he answers before starting to laugh hysterically.

"That's Lucy's car coming at us, and I think Tessie's the driver! Abort! Abort!"

Reeves, realizing I'm right, cranks the steering wheel to the right, and the van careens through the ditch, bouncing wildly, up the other side, through a fence, and stops when it strikes an electrical pole. I would have most likely had my head slammed through the windshield except that the wild ride through the ditch unseated me. Ending up on the floorboard probably saved my life. Looking to see if Reeves is alive, I see him still gripping the steering wheel, staring straight ahead.

Trying to unwedge myself from between the seat and dashboard, I hear a tap on the window. When the door opens, I see Lucy and Tessie standing in the opening, looking me over first and then Reeves. With Lucy being so short, we're on eye level with each other. I'm shocked speechless when she reaches out and thumps me on the forehead with her tiny fist.

"Why did you take to the ditch?" she asks Reeves, and I'm wondering why she's not thumping his forehead since he's the driver. I'm an innocent victim in all of this.

"Because Rex was shooting at us," Reeves answers.

When Lucy simply raises an eyebrow, Reeves continues to explain.

"Then we saw Tessie driving and chose the ditch over a head-on."

"That part, I understand. But why was Rex shooting at you?" Lucy questions while crossing her arms and, I should note, still blocking the door, so I am still stuck on the floorboard in the shape of a pretzel.

"We, uh, I, may or may not have tased his balls," Reeves admits honestly.

"Chubs thinks the world of his club brothers, but I'm finding it hard lately to understand why. Not a complete brain amongst the group," Lucy mutters, mostly to herself. "If the van is undriveable, we can give you a ride. Warning, though, Tessie's driving."

"No! The van's fine! Really, it is. We'll be fine," Reeves shouts.

"I can't breathe like this much longer. Can I get the fuck out of this position now?" I ask as nice as I know how when simply breathing is an effort.

Lucy and Tessie step back and pull the door open further. It's easier to extricate myself now, so I only required Tessie to tug on one leg a few times before I'm standing outside the van.

"Payback for all your comments about my driving. At least I've never deliberately drove into a ditch," Tessie says with a small sniff before walking back to Lucy's car.

Lucy stares us both down for another moment before following Tessie. Because one wreck is enough for one day, Reeves and I both stand on the far side of the van until Tessie has driven away. After some effort, we get the van started, backed out of the ditch, and are on our way to our first install. When steam starts rolling out of the radiator, without a word, Reeves turns toward the club's auto body shop.

Trigger, walking around the van, finally looks at Reeves.

"Someone run you off the road?" he asks while eyeing the bullet hole in the back door of the van.

Neither of us answer. I just hand Trigger my phone with the video paused. He looks at me first, then Reeves before he sighs and hits play. Viewing it, eyebrows so high they've joined his hairline, Trigger's body jerks in laughter before he hands the phone to Petey. Because Rex was shooting at us, I forgot to stop the recording, and you can clearly hear our conversation with Lucy and Tessie. The video of Rex is funny. The fear in our voices of seeing Tessie on the road isn't. Next time, I'll replay things before I let others view them.

"So, you weren't run off the road. You chose it over certain death," Trigger says with a snicker.

"You should up your life insurance, Pigeon. Having a shit ton of money will make it easier for Ivy to move on," Petey states before walking off, his booming laugh heard even after the door shut behind him.

We hang out with Petey while Trigger fixes the van enough for us to get to work. Reeves sticks close to the window, one eye watching the parking lot in case Rex shows up. Petey starts laughing every time a car or bike passes the shop, and Reeves snaps his head around to see if we need to hide or not. After about an hour of this, Reeves finally takes a seat and puts his boots up on a nearby bike seat. He nearly pisses himself when Rex's voice immediately comes over the security system.

"You two fuckers can run, but you can't hide. I have cameras every fucking where, and I'll strike when you least expect it! Get some fucking work done today!"

Petey, using the counter to stay standing, laughs until he's breathless. Reeves and I hustle to Trigger's work bay and prod him to hurry the fuck up. This only makes him laugh harder, but he gets the job done, and we get the fuck away from Rex and all his little eyes in the sky.

"We have Church this evening. Rex will be there. Maybe we should have Cash do a pat-down on him before he's allowed inside," Reeves suggests. "No guns should be allowed in Church anyway."

Agreeing, I shoot a text to Cash.

Cash: Why? What did you do?

I send the video and wait.

Cash: You fuck up, you pay up.

"We're going to die alone," I tell Reeves while I put my phone back in my pocket.

Church takes place, and Reeves and I survive. In fact, oddly enough, we're even more nervous since Rex never even looked at either of us. That doesn't mean I don't keep him in my sight afterward. I made sure to sit with my back to a wall, as did Reeves. The other guys find this highly amusing, and I'm fine with being their entertainment tonight as long as I leave here still able to pleasure my wife.

"Vex, did Tessie make it home today?" I ask.

"Yep. She drove into the yard, no damage that I could see to the car, and Lucy drove it away."

"Lucy never showed at the shop as we expected today," Petey adds.

"Maybe we hit the ditch unnecessarily," I say to Reeves.

"Maybe, but Tessie's driving has conditioned us all to take serious evasive maneuvers anytime she's spotted behind the wheel," he answers, justifying the ditch dive.

Nodding, I agree that our reaction was reasonable.

"We going fishing or sitting here waiting for Rex to kill off two members?" Craig asks as he and Luke stop beside my chair.

"How do you know, uh, forget it. You hear everything," I mutter. "Ready to head out, Trigger?"

"Yep, let's go, boys."

Standing in the kitchen, Trigger and the boys out fishing, I think back to what Ivy asked this morning. Walking out the door and to the bunkhouse, I open the door. Looking around, I don't see any lights on anywhere. I close the door and walk to the barn, heelers at my side.

Each stall has a small outside fenced-in area, so none of the horses are locked inside all the time. Ivy only keeps a few horses in the barn or the pasture close to it. The ones we ride regularly and the few mares that had foals this spring. The mares and foals are in a small field together now off the end of the barn, and I stand and watch the little ones play. All legs and attitude, they practice their big horse skills like running, bucking, and rearing. The mares graze peacefully nearby, knowing their baby isn't far. When my phone vibrates, I pull it out and answer with an irritated sigh.

"Yeah?" I answer abruptly.

"Not the proper way to answer a phone, but I guess I shouldn't be surprised," my father responds.

"My phone, I'll answer it however the hell I want to. What do you need?"

"Heard you got married. That true?" he asks.

"Yep, I did," I answer curtly.

"Elope?"

"No, we didn't elope, and we didn't have to get married if that's your next question," I answer while pinching the bridge of my nose.

"Thought maybe you eloped since we didn't receive an invitation. Church wedding then? Hurt your mother's feelings when she heard about your wedding," my dad says with reproach in his voice.

"Didn't figure you'd make the trip. Not for my wedding, anyway," I answer in a flat voice.

"We have to be in Denver day after tomorrow. Thought we could meet your new wife," he says, completely surprising me.

They've never once asked to see me when they've come to the Denver area before. I'm instantly suspicious as to why they're so curious to meet Ivy and not sure I want this meeting to take place. My wife has had enough shitty relatives to last her a lifetime, and I don't want mine to become another nightmare for her.

"Not sure that's a good idea, Dad."

"Why not? She's family now."

"How'd you hear that I got married?" I ask while ignoring his question.

"Your brother heard through a friend. Told us."

"I'll check with my wife, see what her schedule looks like, and let you know," I answer, being completely done with this conversation.

"Make it happen, Elijah. Only right we welcome our daughter to the family," my dad replies before hanging up.

Hitting Ivy's contact, I wait for her to answer. When she does, I know she's busy with something.

"Hey," she answers, breathless.

"You okay?"

"Yep, just flipping fabulous," she replies, then gives a little laugh.

"You sure?" I ask because her tone says otherwise.

"I'm fine, honey. Had a little issue with loading the draft horses, but I'm technically okay."

"Explain that a little more, wife," I order when I hear noises in the background that sound nothing like a barn. They sound more like a hospital.

"The first horse loaded fine. Second horse spooked and may have broken my foot. I'm waiting for an x-ray, but other than that, I'm good," Ivy answers in a quieter voice.

"Stay where you're at. I'll ride back to town with Trigger and come get you so I can drive you home."

"No, don't do that. It's my left foot so I can drive," Ivy argues.

"You're not driving. Be there in an hour," I answer before disconnecting.

Texting Trigger, I wait for him. While waiting, I send out a group text to find out if anyone can get to the hospital, so Ivy's not alone there.

When I get a text, I see it's from Horse.

Horse: I'm close to the hospital. I'll go find Ivy and wait with her until you get here.

Me: Thanks. Be there as soon as I can.

Trigger and the boys show up, and we leave for town. The boys are upset about Ivy but happy with their catches today. That includes Trigger, who talks non-stop about fishing during the drive. Arriving at the hospital, I see Ivy's truck and trailer parked at the back of the lot. I assure Trigger that he doesn't need to come inside too and wave them off.

Walking into the hospital, I get directions to the E.R. bay that Ivy's currently in and make my way down the hallway. I recognize their voices, so I follow them. Pulling back the curtain, I find her lying on the bed, foot elevated by pillows. Horse is in the chair next to her, and they're arguing.

"They're four-legged fur missiles that intend to eliminate all humans from this Earth," Horse states in an exasperated voice.

"It was an accident. He has feet larger than my head, and these things happen," Ivy answers in the same voice.

"Bikes are safer because they don't have a brain of their own," Horse argues his point.

"And neither do some of the other people on the road. At least riding a horse, I won't take a fall at speeds greater than about 50 miles per hour," Ivy counters while I lean my shoulder against the divider between bays.

"No horse can run 50 miles per hour, Ivy. I'm not a horse person, but I'm not that gullible either," Horse answers with a snort.

"No horse with you on his back can," Ivy mutters before noticing me.

"Are you implying I'm fat?" Horse asks in a truly offended tone.

"No, dipshit, she's taking a shot at your lack of riding abilities. You'd slow any horse down," I answer before walking to Ivy's side and leaning down for a kiss.

"I told you I didn't need a driver. Doctor is bringing in a boot for my foot, and then I'm out of here," Ivy says when I pull back.

"It's broken then?" I ask while looking at the foot in question. It's swollen and very bruised.

"Yep. Not much they can do with it but to put me in a boot until it heals itself. I hate to use an overused phrase, but this ain't my first rodeo with a broken foot," Ivy answers with a grin.

A doctor and a nurse enter our cubicle, and the doctor slides a boot over the injured foot and adjusts it. When he's done, he tells us the nurse will explain anything we need to know, and he leaves. The nurse does exactly that, and she patiently answers all my questions while Ivy rolls her eyes at me. The nurse hands Ivy a set of crutches and starts to explain how to use them when Ivy holds up a hand.

"I don't need these. I have a few sets laying around the ranch somewhere, and I'll find them if I need to use them."

"We'll take them and thank you for your help," I counter Ivy's answer.

The nurse grins, wishes us luck, and leaves. Horse stands, gives us a salute, and follows the nurse.

"Let's get you home," I say as Ivy stands then places the crutches under her arms at my pointed glare at them.

Once we clear the E.R. door, I tell Ivy to take a seat on the bench nearby, and I'll go get the truck. Trotting across the lot, I retrieve the truck and drive up as close as I can get to Ivy. Jumping out to help her, I find her already climbing inside the cab. I return to the driver's side, and we pull out.

"You hurting?" I ask as I reach for her hand.

"No, they gave me some painkillers, and I have a few extras, just in case."

"Hungry?"

"Starving," she answers with a grin. "We're close to the clubhouse. Why not stop there and raid the fridge? I'm sure Ava's got it stocked up."

"Uh, that might cause us to make a return trip to the E.R.," I admit. "Might be best to avoid the clubhouse for a few days."

"What did you do, and to whom did you do it to?" Ivy asks while shooting me a look.

"Why would you automatically assume I did anything? It was Reeves who caused the shitstorm. I just happened to be with him, so I'm guilty only through association."

Ivy snorts before turning her head away, but I can see her shoulders shaking.

"You don't believe me?" I ask incredulously.

"Not for a second, but it's your story. Stick to it, honey. Who's headhunting you?"

"Rex. The man has no sense of humor," I mutter.

"I'm hungry, and I have crutches. You can use them to defend yourself if needed, but maybe he'll take pity on me and not make me a widow yet."

"Fine, we'll stop at the clubhouse, but it's on you if I get jumped by a nerdy tech guy."

Turning into the clubhouse drive, I pull through the gate, waving at James on the way through. Stopping the truck near the clubhouse, I jump out and rush to Ivy's side of the truck. Of course, she's already out the door and cruising up the sidewalk. It's obvious she's well used to crutches, and I rush to keep up. Opening the door, I follow her to a table. Taking a seat, Ivy leans the crutches against the chair next to her. I pull another chair over and insist she props her foot on it before making my way to the kitchen.

I listen to her chatting with the members that are hanging out tonight while I make us a couple of sandwiches, grab a bag of chips and a couple of drinks. Returning to the table, I sit and set her food in front of her. Craig walks in and heads straight to Ivy's side for a hug. When he's done, he steps back, carefully pulls off his backpack, removes Bart, and hands him to Ivy. Ivy pushes her plate back and cuddles Bart close.

"He'll make you feel better. He always does for me," Craig says while he takes a seat.

"Thank you, Craig. I feel a little better already," Ivy answers.

"Where's Thor?" I ask, suddenly remembering that Ivy took him to work with her today.

"Livi's picking him up from the rescue and bringing him here," Ivy answers while taking a bite out of her sandwich one-handed. "She texted me just before you got to the hospital."

"So, that's why you insisted I risk my life by coming here?"

"Yep, and the food. I wasn't lying that I was starving," Ivy answers with a grin.

The door opens, and Livi enters with Snots and Thor on her heels. Thor bounds over to our table but stops near Ivy's foot and carefully sniffs it. Snots walks a few feet inside then tips sideways, asleep within seconds. Livi looks down at her dog in disgust but leaves him there.

"How you feeling, Ivy?" Livi asks as she pulls up another chair.

"Fine. Probably high on pain meds, though. Thank you for picking up Thor. Any trouble with him?"

"None, he's a really good boy. Your boss was at the rescue to let me in, so that was easy. Do you know if Thor likes to jog?"

"He loves to run. Why?" Ivy questions while taking another bite.

"Maybe we should swap dogs then. Mine's allergic to physical activity as much as James is," Livi mutters while eyeing her now snoring dog.

Livi's dog makes a liar out of her when the door opens, and Lucy walks in with Bailey. Snots lifts his head, eyes Lucy, bolts upright, and scrambles as fast as his chubby body allows him to across the room and behind a couch. Everyone laughs, but Livi just shakes her head in dismay at her dog.

Lucy and Bailey stop near Ivy, ask how she's doing, chat a minute, and move to another table. I finish eating and take Bart from Ivy so she can too. When she's done, I exchange the skunk for her plate and take our dishes to the kitchen.

"Let's get you home, babe," I say to Ivy.

She nods, and Craig takes Bart from her. Helping her stand, I hand her the crutches, and we say our goodbyes. When I open the main door for Ivy, I find Rex standing there. I jump backward and throw up my hands, but he ignores me, asks Ivy if she's okay then walks past us. Before we get out the door, Rex speaks again.

"Surprised your husband didn't know you got injured today, Ivy. With as much as he watches you on the security cameras at the rescue. Oh wait, that's right. He wasn't in his office much today."

I guide Ivy outside with one hand while using the other to flip Rex off. I never did tell Ivy about the cameras or my obsession with watching her on them. When I see her looking at me with raised eyebrows, I say, "Home first, then I can explain that comment." She finally nods in agreement, and I ignore her snickering at me, watching behind us as we walk to the truck.

Ivy pushes the console between our seats up and slides over to my side. Leaning against me, she's asleep within a few minutes. Placing my hand on her thigh, I drive my woman home while wondering if that's all the payback Rex is going to send my way. I doubt it, but a guy can always hope.

Carrying a sleeping Ivy into the house, I take her upstairs and lay her on the bed. The pain meds must be doing a number on her because she sleeps through me removing her boots, socks, and jeans. Tucking her under the sheets, I strip, prop her foot on a pillow, and climb in beside my slumbering wife.

"You can quit fussing with my foot, Pigeon. It's fine. I'm fine. Explain what Rex was talking about," Ivy asks while we're sitting at the table eating breakfast. I should say that I'm eating while she's nearly mainlining coffee. Woman likes her coffee. That's very evident if you open the right cupboard.

"Don't want to," I answer before taking a deep breath and diving into this topic. "When the first litter of puppies came up missing, Margie contacted the security company and asked about having cameras installed. None of the employees were told because she didn't know if it was an inside job or not. Turns out, it wasn't. It was the guys who snuck in the night you were there. They wanted puppies or kittens, but the puppies were easier to get to. Don't ask what they wanted them for because, believe me, you really don't want to know."

"So, that's how he knew when those men showed up? I always thought it was because I called your number first, and he just happened to see the call, assumed I was in trouble, and sent Cash."

"Yeah, he saw what was going on and called Cash and Horse since they were closer than I was."

"And he mentioned it last night because?"

"Because he wanted to put me on the spot. Rat bastard. I, uh, well, I watched the cameras at the rescue a lot, Ivy. I always insisted it was for the rescue's safety, but it was more than that. I fucking loved watching you and how you interacted with the animals. I told myself, and the guys, it wasn't you I was watching, just how you are with the animals, but that wasn't the whole truth."

"And what is the whole truth?" Ivy asks in a soft voice.

"You intrigued me, even before the cameras were installed. When the club would help with projects there, I volunteered because of you. I kept telling myself that I was too old for you, that it kind of made someone my age a pervert for watching you, but I couldn't not do it."

"We're almost 14 years apart in age, Pigeon. That's not a big deal, you know. Our age difference doesn't matter to me in the least, and I've never bothered to think about it. Stop letting it bother you."

I cup her chin with one hand, lean closer, and kiss my wife. When she suddenly jerks back, I wait for what I knew was going to come all along.

"Oh my God! I didn't know anyone could see me! Holy crap balls, I'm so embarrassed!" Ivy shouts then slams both hands over her mouth.

I wait, watching her wide eyes bounce around while she thinks of the times she thought she was alone at work. I grin when I see realization hit her eyes, and they stop moving and focus on mine. Dropping her hands, she lowers her face to the table. Resting her forehead on its hard surface, I listen to her horrified voice.

"I'm beyond mortified that someone—that you—watched me singing and dancing with the animals! I can't sing worth a crap and yet had an audience while doing it! Please tell me that no one else ever saw those videos!"

When I don't answer, Ivy lifts her head and stares at me. When I still remain silent, she covers her face again.

"Who else?" she whispers through her fingers.

"Rex and Reeves."

"Well, that's just effing peachy! I've already embarrassed myself with Reeves and the whole flashing incident, but now I can never face Rex again either!" she moans loudly.

Laughing, I pull her hands down and hold onto them. Giving them a squeeze, I wait until her eyes meet mine again.

"Yes, you can. You were amusing as hell, and they got a kick out of your antics. You enjoyed your job, and that's nothing to be ashamed of. I fucking love you and who you are with the animals, so don't ever change that about yourself. I'm so fucking proud that you're my wife because God knows I don't deserve you. That being said, embarrassing moments or not, I'm not giving you up."

I watch as Ivy's face softens, calms, and then she leans toward me. I meet her halfway; our lips meet, and I know she's going to laugh about the shows she put on someday. Maybe not today, but someday.

"If you ever want to see me naked again, you'll make those videos disappear before Axel finds out about them," she orders softly against my mouth.

I nod, agreeing with her because there's no way I'm going to allow Axel to keep me from seeing Ivy naked.

"Ivy!" I shout. "Where did you say the beer is? There's none in the fridge."

"I thought I put some in there a few days ago. Check the laundry room. Should be some there," she answers from the living room.

There isn't any there either, so I grab a Coke instead. Walking into the living room, I slide behind Ivy on the couch and stretch out. Pulling her tight to my front, I kiss her neck.

"Didn't find any?" she asks.

"No, it's fine. I texted Gunner and told him to bring some."

"When are they getting here?"

"In a couple of hours. Kids are excited as hell, so he'll give in and come a little earlier than planned," I reply.

Gunner, Ava, their kids, along with Pooh, Pippa, and Craig are coming to the ranch for their first riding lesson. Afterward, I'm grilling burgers, and Ivy made a macaroni salad and cut up veggies for the burgers this morning. She insisted she's fine to give them lessons, even with her foot still in a walking boot. She's been walking without the crutches for a few days now and thinks she can do everything she used to, but I'm fighting her on it.

I never returned my dad's many calls, and the day they were coming to Denver has come and gone. I have no guilt over doing that, especially with Ivy getting hurt. When I told her about his call, she told me that she'd meet with them if I wanted to, but she'd be fine with my decision either way. To be honest, if he hadn't continued calling, I would have completely forgotten about his request.

When Gunner arrives, I step outside to see several SUVs, trucks, and a couple of bikes come to a stop near the house. I laugh when I recognize that nearly everyone I know just pulled in our driveway. Doors slamming, kids screaming, and pets racing across the yard, I feel Ivy's arm wrap around my waist from beside me. I stiffen when I see the last vehicle in line. It's Lucy's, and Tessie is driving. When the car pulls to the side of Trigger's truck, stops without hitting anything, I breathe in relief. When Tessie emerges from it, she throws up a victory sign before giving a fist pump. I laugh.

"Had a few tag-alongs," Ava says as she makes her way up the deck stairs. "Hope that's ok."

"Of course, it's okay. We may need more burgers, though," Ivy answers with a laugh.

"We should have enough. Trigger's planning on bringing fish to the cookout," Bella says with a grin as she carries a large bowl past us and into the house.

"We all brought food and drinks in hopes of not being turned away," laughs Trudy as she follows Bella with her arms full of bags.

"You'd never get turned away, and thank you," Ivy replies before following Trudy.

The guys get busy setting up lawn chairs on the deck while the women put the food away. Joining us outside when they're done, I pull Ivy onto my lap and insist she props her foot up on another chair.

"You worry too much," she murmurs.

"Love you and want you to be healthy again, wife," I answer.

"They all think we're too delicate to survive without them," Ava says while several of the other ladies nod their heads in agreement.

Lola Wright

"Vex and Taja didn't come?" I ask Gunner.

"No, and talk about being overprotective. Vex refused to let Taja get this far away from the hospital. Said she's not going to be out of his sight or far from medical help until after the baby's born," he answers.

"After what happened before, I guess I can see his point," I mutter while Gunner nods in agreement.

"Ivy!" Trigger shouts from beside his truck.

"Yeah?"

"Can I use the side by side?"

"Sure can. Pigeon filled it with gas this morning, so it's ready for you. Have fun!" Ivy shouts back.

"Love you, girl!" Trigger hollers as he carries his gear to the side by side.

"Love you, too, Trigger!" I shout back as everyone laughs, but Trigger doesn't even respond. He's too excited to hit the fishing hole to care that I was being a smart-ass.

"Okay, kids! Let's hit the barn!" Ivy shouts, and the kids come at her at a run, even little Alex.

I help Ivy stand, and everyone follows us to the barn. Taking seats on the various bales of hay and any surface available, the adults sit and quietly listen. Ivy explains to Craig that her ASL is limited and asks if he'll help explain things to Luke if she can't.

"I got you, Ivy," he answers in a serious tone.

I'm surprised, along with most of the adults, when Ivy starts explaining the rules. I thought she'd pull Lucky out, pop a kid on, and walk them around, but she's not. She explains to the kids that there are rules for their safety but also for the horse's safety. Telling them what they are, each kid nods in understanding.

Showing the kids the various brushes and hoof picks, the twins squeal in delight.

"We always clean their hooves first, so if there are stones in them, we get them out, and the horse is comfortable while we're riding them," Ivy explains and then demonstrates.

Holding Lucky's hoof, she lets each kid use the pick to learn how to do it right. Moving on from there, she explains that while it's fun to brush a horse, it's also very good for them and explains why. Showing them how to use each brush and when to use them, she again demonstrates then lets the kids take a turn. She continues with explaining the tack, the various names of the basic pieces and then lets the kids halter Lucky. Lucky is a rockstar and stands like a statue when the kids are near him. Glancing over at Horse, I laugh. When he looks at me, I can't help but taunt him a little.

"That the jackhammer on steroids you were bitching about?"

"He must only hate adults," Horse complains while the rest of us laugh at him.

Ivy finishes up the demonstrations and then asks who wants to ride first. Every hand goes in the air except for Luke's. Instead, he pushes his way to Ivy's side and points at himself. Seeing this, I hear Ava suck in a breath and watch as Gunner wraps an arm around her shoulders.

I stand, pick up the saddle Ivy wanted to use today, and carry it to her. Placing the pad on Lucky's back, Ivy takes the saddle and sets it on the pad. Explaining what she's doing and why, she has Luke repeat her steps when she's done. He does each step perfectly, just as Ivy showed him. After Ivy checks the cinch, adjusts the stirrups, she hands the lead rope to Luke, signs that he needs to follow her, and we all walk back outside. We gather outside the round pen while Ivy and Luke walk inside, Luke leading Lucky. Helping Luke mount the tall horse, Ivy steps back while Luke's face lights up with his smile.

"Pigeon, could you please saddle Junior for me and bring him out here?" Ivy asks.

I do as she asks, and then I boost Ivy onto his saddle since her booted foot won't fit in the stirrup. I walk to the railing and lean against it. Watching her, I'm blown away at how good she is at this. Not just working with horses or kids, but in instilling confidence in Luke. He's like a whole new kid sitting on that horse. He's sitting straight, watching Ivy intently, and imitating her every move. He's no longer hanging to the back of the group or following Craig's lead. He's his own person when he's sitting on top of a large, gentle buckskin gelding. Glancing at Ava and Gunner, their faces show that they're seeing it too.

Ivy leads Lucky next to Junior and walks around the round pen, showing Luke how to sit a horse, how to move with it, how his heels need to be down, toes up in the stirrups. They continue making laps. Luke zeroed in on Ivy, his horse, and nothing else. When Ivy's comfortable with how much Luke has learned today, they come to a stop next to me. I help Ivy off Junior, and she shows Luke how to safely dismount. When he turns toward his parents, his smile has never been larger. I know then that we'll be seeing a lot more of Luke in the future.

Ivy goes through the same procedure with each child, except for little Alex, who rides in front of

Ivy on Junior. Each kid listens, and each kid gets off their horse standing a little straighter and smiling wide. The twins can barely contain themselves, but they follow Ivy's rules about not spooking the horses or running behind one.

"We need horses, Daddy," Zoe, or maybe it was Mia, announces.

Gunner groans while the adults laugh, but we all knew where this was probably going to go, and it went there.

"My balls wouldn't have been damaged for life if she'd have told me all this," Horse complains.

"Kids listen. Adults don't. Mere woman and all that jazz, so I let you learn the hard way," Ivy retorts. "Want to try now?"

"No! I'm never willingly putting myself through that again!" Horse shouts before getting shushed by the twins.

"Can I?" asks Livi, bouncing on her toes in excitement.

"Yeah, but the kid's saddle won't fit you. You can ride Junior instead," Ivy offers.

"I'm smarter than Horse. Way smarter because I was not born with a penis. So much so, I'll admit

I've been on a horse but never learned how to ride. I'd feel better if you'd lead me too."

I turn, walk into the barn, and return with another adult-sized saddle. Swapping them out, I help Ivy mount as Livi does the same. I adjust her stirrups to the length Ivy suggests, and the two women walk off.

"If Livi decides she wants a horse after this, we're moving in with you. One's not going to fit in my backyard," Cash says with a grin.

"I can't wait until this baby is born. Ivy promised me a day in the saddle then," Ava informs Gunner.

"Ivy's costing me a fucking fortune," Gunner complains but does so with an indulgent grin.

After Livi's turn, several others step up, wanting their ride. Ivy's patience is endless, and everyone, regardless of age, size, or gender, receives the same care from her.

Turning to Cash, I joke that Ivy doesn't own a horse large enough for him or Gunner to ride when I notice a look pass between Ivy and Livi.

"What was that? I saw a look," I ask Ivy as she passes, leading Lucky with Bella astride.

"There was no look," Ivy denies, but Livi laughs before turning away from me.

"I saw it too. I'm good at spotting looks, as you well know, Pigeon," Axel adds.

"Ivy Hayes! Stop right here and explain," I order.

She stops in front of me and then smiles.

"I may have done a thing," she admits.

"What kind of thing did you do?" I ask.

"I may have adopted a couple of horses that are large enough for Cash and Gunner to ride," she admits while everyone around us laughs.

"You may have?" I question while crossing my arms across my chest.

"Okay, I did."

"Would one of them be the reason you're injured right now?" I ask, already knowing the answer.

"Maybe."

"Maybe, Ivy?" I inquire while fighting back a smile.

"Definitely."

"Serves you right that your damn wife is costing you money too," Gunner mutters.

"When you're done losing this argument, can we go see the foals?" Craig asks.

Trigger returns beaming and holding up a string of fish in time to add them to our meal. Sitting on the deck, surrounded by friends, family, and good food, I look at Ivy. She may never realize this, but her fight to keep this ranch has already soothed broken souls. Mine, definitely her own, and there will be more in the future. Luke will only be the first of the many kids she's going to have an impact on.

Watching my club family interacting, enjoying their day, pets exploring, and racing around, I think about how all I ever wanted before Ivy was to party, sleep around, and generally cause havoc. I didn't want responsibility and avoided acting like an adult because I believed that was boring as fuck and couldn't possibly be any fun. I smile inwardly now because Ivy's unknowingly taught me that age really is just a number and that I wasn't too old to learn a new way. I fucking love this new way, being an adult and taking care of my responsibilities, being a husband to Ivy, and enjoying every second of it.

"What? Why are you getting stitches? Are you kidding me? Is Taja okay? The baby? Holy shit! I'll be there as soon as I can!" Tessie shouts while jumping to her feet and looking around wildly.

Tessie listens to whoever is on the phone for a few moments while she paces, and we shout at her wanting to know what's up.

"What's going on, Tessie?" Gunner questions loudly several times before snatching the phone out of her hand.

Tessie slaps at his arm and chest, trying to retrieve her phone, but Gunner ignores her physical attack like he's unaware she's waging one. He listens and asks questions to whoever is on the line with him. Everyone is sitting on the edge of their seats but relax when Gunner's face breaks into a huge smile, and he speaks into the phone.

"Congratulations, Vex! Give Taja and your little princess a kiss from us, and we'll get Tessie to the hospital in an hour. Tell Freddy congrats on becoming a grandpa."

Gunner disconnects and hands a glaring Tessie her phone before explaining to the crowd.

"Baby girl. Came a little early but with good working lungs from what I could hear. Taja's doing great, but I think Vex may need a few days to recoup," Gunner says with a laugh.

"You mentioned stitches?" Petey asks Tessie.

Giving Gunner an evil smirk, Tessie explains.

"Vex pulled a Gunner, lost his shit when Taja's water broke, and smacked his head on an open cupboard door. Five stitches and he'll still be gorgeous, but Taja had to drive them to the hospital. Head wounds bleed like hell. Don't they, Gunner?"

"Pulled a Gunner? What the fuck, Tessie?" Gunner snorts in disgust.

"Quit poking the oversized man, Tessie. They have to protect their reps and manhood, so he'll stand here all day arguing about the day the twins were born. I'll take you to the hospital so you can meet your niece," Lucy says calmly while holding her hand out to Tessie for the car keys.

The women leave, and everyone starts cleaning up while feeling relieved that all turned out great for the couple who most deserved it this time around. At Ivy's questioning look, I explain softly about Vex and Taja's first pregnancy. The look on her face is heartbroken for the couple but clears when I remind her that today had a different ending, thank God.

"Did Gunner really lose it when Ava went into labor?" Ivy asks quietly, disbelief clear in her voice.

"No, Gunner did not!" my club president snaps as he stalks past our chairs.

"I'll explain later, honey. Like, when he's not close enough to do great bodily harm to your husband."

"He did it twice, actually. When Bailey went into labor, Chubs had to deliver our daughter at the clubhouse. Gunner was fucking useless," Axel informs Ivy while laughing at the memory. "He brought random items to the room and tossed them at Chubs. Not towels or hot water, but gum and I think a porn video."

Ivy's laughing along with Axel and the rest of us when Gunner barks, "Quit gossiping like a little bitch and help us load shit so we can leave," and then tackles a laughing Axel off the deck and onto the lawn.

"I'm not breaking those two up again. I've had a fucking lifetime of doing that," Petey says while pulling out his wallet. "I'm putting $20 on Gunner winning this round, though."

"I'll take that bet. Axel's tired of being called a gossip," Trigger answers while pulling out his wallet.

"Is there anything you people don't bet on?" Ivy asks.

"Not really, darlin'. I have to make up the money I lost today on Horse. Thought for sure that fucker would prove he has some balls left by getting on that horse today. Kids were riding it, but, nope, Horse backed out with no shame," Petey says in disgust while keeping an eye on the current battle ensuing on the lawn.

Horse shoots Petey a dark look before stalking away while we laugh outright at his retreating back. Another fun day hanging with the brotherhood.

"Today was perfect," Ivy says with a sigh as she slides into bed next to me.

"You're amazing, honey. The kids loved you and the horses, but the look on Luke's face stole the show."

"You saw that too? I swear you could see his confidence grow."

"Everyone saw it. Ava could barely breathe because of it. A lot of kids could benefit from your program," I tell her while wrapping my arm around her and pulling her close.

"I want to talk to you about that. I don't want to wait to start this program. I want to get busy making the plans, getting things ready, and lining up clients. It's going to take a lot of time and work. Not sure I can do all that, keep the ranch running as it is, and work at the rescue. Even with your help, that's a lot."

"You have to make some choices, Ivy," I tell her.

"I'm going to quit the rescue. I hate doing that because I love it there, but I need to be here on the ranch. I'm also thinking about selling off a lot of the cattle. The money we'll make from them will go a long way toward making the necessary changes I need to make. Also, it'll cut down on the amount of hay we need to put up each year and the time spent moving herds from pasture to pasture. We have several ranch horses that will work out great for the program but a few that won't. Other than breeding a few mares a year to keep the herd the size I need, I don't need several studs anymore. I know a few ranchers that have wanted to add our bloodlines to their own remudas, so that's an easy decision."

"Why adopt the draft horses?" I ask.

"They're an awesome team, and they should stay together. Also, both are trained to ride and drive, so they're versatile. Hayrides are a great way to wind down a busy day for the kids, and they'll get to see more of the ranch than just the inside of an arena. Draft horses are incredibly gentle and sensitive animals, especially with people unfamiliar with horses. I don't want the program to be just about riding but about learning about a lot of different animals. Some kids may bond with an 1,800-pound draft horse, while another might do better with a donkey. I want to cover all bases," Ivy answers enthusiastically.

"So, I can expect to see donkeys, mules, mini ponies, and more hooved animals find their way here?" I ask with a laugh.

"Pretty much."

"Works for me. You do your thing, and I'll be standing right behind you all the way," I whisper in her ear before gliding a hand down to find a breast.

"Let's finish this conversation tomorrow. It's playtime," my wife states while placing her hand over mine and subtly asking for more.

Weeks have passed, and still no sign of Chubs. The club has exhausted every avenue we know of in trying to find a trace of him. Livi and James haven't found anything out at work except that the Feds are no longer hanging around or harassing them. This didn't happen overnight, though, and got especially tough on Livi. Being threatened with her job was bad enough, but the not-so-subtle threats against her incarcerated brother were more than Cash could tolerate.

Standing outside the police department, Cash and I waited, so he could speak his mind to the two federal agents that were going too far in their duties. In the dark, leaning against their car, they didn't spot us until they were standing right in front of our very large club enforcer. Cash did not mince words.

"None of us know where Chubs has disappeared to. Threatening Livi's brother isn't going to gain you knowledge that she doesn't have to give. It's dirty and about as low as a man can get but seems to be your M.O. Her brother committed crimes, while Livi has worked hard to prevent crimes. She worked with law enforcement even when it was against her brother. Leave her out of your games, or shit's going to go south."

"You making threats against federal agents?" one of them asks.

"Yes," Cash answers instantly while pushing off their car to stand towering over the agent.

"We can arrest you for that alone," the other states.

"Do it. Call for backup first, though, because you're going to need it," Cash answers calmly.

The agents wait a few beats, probably realizing it won't play out well for them, physically nor job-wise, if their methods come to light, and then back down.

"We're leaving Denver tonight to follow a new lead. If you find him before we do, you're legally required to contact us. You're willing to go to jail for someone you don't even know. Fucking bikers," the first agent says sarcastically before getting in their car and pulling away.

"I'd go to jail, prison, or hell to protect Chubs, but the fucking moron never realized Livi was the one I was protecting tonight," Cash says with a chuckle as we walk to our bikes. "Fucking feds."

Walking into the clubhouse, the mood is jubilant. Petey is standing in the middle of the room, holding up a full shot glass and making a toast. His smile's wide, face relaxed while Trudy has tears in her eyes. Stopping just inside the door, Cash and I wait.

"To Ava for giving me another grandchild to love and watch grow! A nine-pound healthy, happy baby boy! Mommy and baby Chasin are both doing great! Gunner, well, that's another story,"

Petey announces while everyone howls loudly then downs their drink.

Congratulating Petey and Trudy, I find my way to the bar and wait for my beer. Watching the backslaps and hugs being handed out, I realize how much I want babies with Ivy at some point. Not now. We have too much to accomplish yet, but someday. I want little girls with her kind heart and curls. Maybe a boy or two, if they don't act like me when I was younger. Ivy will make an amazing mother, and I'll do my best not to fuck up as a father.

"You and Livi want more kids?" I ask Cash.

"Fuck yeah, when the time's right," he answers immediately.

"Are we going to lose our shit like Gunner or be the nutjob dad that Axel is?" I ask.

"I'm going to be Livi's rock, not to steal Gunner's useless words. Nobody can be the nutjob Axel is, so we're safe on that count. You'll lose your shit when Ivy's in labor, though."

"Why would you think that?" I question loudly in an offended tone.

"Jesus, Pigeon. Her foot's been healed for weeks, and you're still trying to carry her everywhere," Cash replies with a smirk.

"Maybe I just like carrying my wife," I lamely defend myself.

The man needs to speak more and see less.

"Yeah, and that doesn't scream any indication of how you'll be when she's in pain, and you can't stop it? You can only stand by, watch, and know you're the reason she's being torn in half? Or that there's going to be time during the labor that she's going to hate you? With a fucking vengeance."

Maybe the man doesn't need to speak more.

"I liked you better when you were a silent fucker," I mutter and walk away, listening to his laughter.

Keeping one eye open for any sneak attack Rex might attempt, I take a seat on a couch. Rex still hasn't gotten even with Reeves and me, so neither of us are comfortable when he's in the room. I wish to hell the techy bastard would just do what he's going to do and get it over with. The waiting and watching for it is worse than whatever pain he'll inflict.

Glancing at my phone, I see the time and realize Ivy's really late. She was supposed to meet me here after she finalized the sale for two of her studs. She should have been here before me. Hitting her contact, I wait while it rings. When it goes to voicemail, I disconnect. Feeling uneasy but thinking over Cash's words, I ignore the feeling.

I force myself to wait ten minutes before calling her number again. Still no answer. Before I can panic too much, Mac distracts me. Standing on the table closest to the couch, he starts stomping his feet in a beat I recognize but can't name. I laugh out loud, though, when he starts singing, and I know why the beat was familiar. As Mac sings "Love Stinks" by the J. Geils Band, stomping out the drumbeats, he gains everyone's attention. Laughter from the men, sympathy from the women, Mac continues his unrequited love song of sorts.

Stopping abruptly, Mac asks me, "You have pecans? Fucking pecans?"

"Nope, buddy, sorry, I don't have pecans or fucking pecans."

"Chingalinga, my feathered ass. Mac's chingalinga!" he shouts in anger.

The strain of not gaining Priscilla's undying love is making Mac crack up. We have a dire situation of a bird going over the edge on our hands. Axel unknowingly happens to enter the room at the most unfortunate moment. Mac's head snaps his direction, and he takes flight. Axel's eyes widen as he sees Mac in full-on attack mode and headed directly for him.

Axel drops his bowl of cereal and makes a break for the door. Mac effortlessly changes direction and screams, "G.M.S., asshole!"

Axel makes some impressive moves trying to avoid Mac's attack, with the final one being a belly dive under a table. Mac lands on the floor in front of Axel and sticks his face close to the terrorized biker.

"Why you coming after me?" Axel asks loudly in confusion and, most likely, fear.

"Priscilla!" Mac screeches.

"Not my fault she loves me and not you," Axel taunts with a grin.

"Don't go that route, Axel," Petey advises.

"But it's the truth. Don't be a sore loser, Mac," Axel says, ignoring the great advice of his father.

Mac shakes his whole body and then attacks. Using his beak, he clamps down on Axel's chin and hangs on. Axel's head slams into the bottom of the table as he tries to get loose from Mac. The table crashes to the floor sideways. Male screams and bird screeches erupt at the same time as feathers flutter around them. Axel manages to break loose, but Mac's a persistent little fucker. As Axel tries to gain his feet, Mac attacks his unprotected ass. The large biker makes an ungodly sound, but the bite motivates his feet to get under him. Standing, upper-half turned around, Axel tries to pry Mac's beak loose, whining the whole time. When he manages to free his ass from the crazed bird, he grips both of Mac's feet in one hand and holds him at arm's length.

"What's going on?" Craig asks.

Shifting my eyes to the kid, I see Craig, Luke, and the twins leading Moose and Matilda through the main room.

"Mac's lost his damn mind!" Axel shouts.

"Why are there donkeys in the clubhouse?" Axel then asks in a calmer voice. Probably calmer now that Mac's incapable of inflicting more pain at the moment.

"We're practicing our leading skills," Craig answers like it's completely normal to do this in the dark.

The door flies open, and Bailey rushes in carrying Alexia, panicked.

When her eyes land on the four kids, her body sags in relief. When they switch to her man and his prisoner, her mouth drops open.

"I've been running all over this compound trying to find you kids! If you're going to leave the house, let me know!" Bailey shouts while fighting to calm down. "I was only on the phone for a few minutes, and poof, you all disappear."

"Sorry," the kids say in unison while Luke signs it, having figured out why Bailey looks so upset.

Turning to Axel, she asks, "Do I even want to know what this fresh kind of hell is all about?"

"No," answers several of the adults in the room before laughter rings out.

"Turn him loose and come home with me. I need a mommy break after tonight. Maybe a bath and a smoke, too. Bottle of wine or a valium even," Bailey says before turning back to the door. "Bring the kids and return the donkeys. The kids might be spending the night at our home, but the donkeys are not."

"Have you calmed your shit, Mac?" Axel asks skeptically. "And what does G.M.S. mean?"

"I be good," Mac answers, but I'm not sure any of us believe him.

"G.M.S.? Mac tell you to G.M.S.?" Craig asks before starting to laugh, leaning against Moose to stay standing.

When he regains control of himself, he explains.

"Prissy says that to Mac when he annoys her. It means gargle my sack. Southern slang, I guess."

"That's just rude, Mac!" Axel shouts.

"I be angry," Mac answers in his defense.

"I don't want to hear that phrase again from any of you. Not nice! All of you get moving and Axel, leave Mac behind. I don't need another fight breaking out in my living room," Bailey orders before her and little Alex leave the clubhouse.

"I don't do a thing wrong, and you still got me in trouble, birdman," Axel complains while carefully handing Mac over to Petey.

"Fuck my life," Mac replies.

I watch the kids, donkeys, and my VP exit the clubhouse, followed by Ava's other pets, minus Duffy. He's decided to adopt Taja and Vex's house as his own and spends most of his time sleeping next to their daughter Kalea. Ava's tried her best at keeping her cat at home, but after he shredded several window screens trying to escape,

Taja told her she likes Duffy spending his time with her and her tiny daughter. Vex isn't as thrilled about it but smart enough to not piss off the cat by stopping it.

My phone vibrates, and relief hits me when I see Ivy's name. Answering it, I know immediately that my relief was premature. At Ivy's words, I'm off the couch and running for my bike.

"I need you."

"What's wrong, baby? I'm leaving now."

"Ted," Ivy answers, and she's out of breath.

When my ass hits my bike seat, I stop for a moment to hear her words before I start the engine. Several of my club brothers are on their bikes too and waiting for me to explain what I need.

"Is he hurting you?" I roar.

"I got away from him. I'm on foot, trying to hide. Oh God, Pigeon! I think he shot the dogs before he came after me."

"Where are you? Are you somewhere safe yet?" I ask in a much calmer voice than I feel.

"I'm south of the house, still on ranch property. He's in the side by side, hunting me. I can see the headlights, and they're not far off. I don't have many places to hide. It's pretty wide-open land, not many trees, but I didn't have cell service until now. What do I do?"

"Whatever you have to do, do it. I'm on my way. Think about the land, Ivy. You know it better than anyone. Think of places that can give you cover," I answer, disconnect, then tell the guys what little I know.

James hands me a set of earbuds, and I connect them to my phone before starting my bike. Hitting open road, I twist the throttle and pray that nothing slows us down and then vow that nothing will. I think of nothing but getting to Ivy. To ensuring that she sees tomorrow, that we see thousands of tomorrows together. I don't think about Ted or what he's done or why. Only Ivy, and it keeps me focused on finding my wife.

As we get close to the ranch, I fish my phone out and call Ivy's number. Dangerous maneuver considering I'm on a bike at high speeds, but I need to hear her voice.

"Can't talk. He's close."

I push my bike to speeds I've never attempted before and barely slow in time to make the turn into the driveway. Rear tire sliding dangerously, I right my bike and gun it again. Sliding sideways to

a stop, I drop my bike and run for my truck.
Spinning it in a circle, I see my club brothers
jumping off their bikes.

"Take Ivy's truck and the other side by side! She's
somewhere south of here in one of the pastures!
She said Ted's close to where she's at, so watch for
the side by side!" I shout out the window as Cash
and Pooh vault into the bed of my truck. Not
waiting for the others, I drive down the small road
that leads south through the ranch.

Reaching down, I open the console and remove a
handgun. Checking to make sure it's loaded, I set it
on the seat beside me. I have one in the waistband
of my jeans. I'm sure Cash and Pooh are also
armed, but having more firepower is always a good
thing.

I drive the truck off the road and up a slope that
should give me a good view of a lot of land.
Stopping, I scan the dark, hoping to see headlights.

"Can't see anything. Keep driving," Cash hollers,
and I realize that him standing in the bed of the
truck gives him a better view than I have.

When I finally see lights, I drive toward them, but
it turns out to be Petey, Trigger, and Reeves in
Ivy's truck. They haven't seen anything yet either.
Listening carefully, I can hear another engine in
the distance, but when it comes into view and

drives our way, I know it's the wrong side by side. Toes and Freddy pull up and shut down the engine.

"Axel's on his way with Rex, James, and Livi. Called him. Told him what's up. Rex is working on a location using Ivy's phone GPS. We'll stay in touch with them," Freddy says before they drive off.

"Fan out," I order as I put the truck in drive.

Before taking my foot off the brake, I text Ivy.

Me: We're spread out in the southern pastures. Keep your phone on but muted. Rex is tracking it. Is Ted still close?

Ivy: Yes. I'm on the other side of a small herd of cattle. Trying to keep them between us.

Me: You stay safe. We'll find you.

I then shoot off a group text telling the others to watch for a herd of cattle because Ivy's close to one.

I drive for what seems like endless hours, but, in reality, was about one and a half when I spot Axel's truck coming my way. Stopping, he pulls up so our windows are next to each other.

"She's close, Pigeon. According to her phone, she's within about a quarter of a mile radius of us right now," Rex states while watching his laptop.

"Livi! Get in the truck with Pigeon," Cash orders, and she complies.

Shutting her door, Livi reaches over and grips my forearm.

"We'll find her, Pigeon. She's smart, and he's not."

I nod, feeling gutted but hopeful with her words.

"And when we do, if one of you don't kill him, I'm going to," Livi states calmly while checking her handgun before lowering it to lay on her thigh.

"Fuck me," Cash mutters but is clearly heard by everyone.

We get back to searching again, and it's not long before Trigger calls to say they've spotted a small herd of cattle in a gully. No sign of a side by side, but it's dark, and the gully is casting shadows. I whip my truck around and head their direction, forgetting that I have two men standing in the back. Livi looks over her shoulder then gives me a thumbs-up letting me know I haven't lost my passengers.

Killing my lights, I stop near Ivy's truck. Petey, Trigger, and Reeves are all belly-down along the edge of the gully. We join them, and I pull my phone out when it vibrates.

Ivy: I'm on the other side, behind the cattle, near the bank. Ted's somewhere below you on your side. Please tell me you're here too.

Me: Just got here. Stay down.

I tell the others what Ivy said, and all eyes peer down, trying to locate Ted in the darkness. It's black as hell on this side of the gully with the cattle barely outlined in the center with what available light there is shining on them. We put some distance between each of us as we move along the rim, hoping one of us gains an angle that shows his position. Ted must know it's no longer him hunting Ivy but us hunting him. With the arrival of Axel's truck and the side by side, he's far outnumbered, and his time of being free is coming to an end.

When the cattle start moving restlessly, I grow concerned that he's making his way to Ivy's side of the gully. Cash must too because he lets me know he's moving around the end of the gully. I pass it on and then follow him. We stay low but move quickly. Rounding the end where there's a path leading up and out, I realize this must be how the cattle got down inside the gully. The further around it we get, the better I feel knowing I'm closer to Ivy's position.

When a shot rings out, I freeze. Not able to determine the direction it came from because of the acoustics of the high slope on each side, I wait. My blood runs cold when I hear Ted's words shouted into the darkness.

"Let me leave, and I'll let her live."

"You're going to hide behind your own sister now, you fucking coward?" shouts a pissed-off Trigger.

Another shot rings out, and the nervous cattle start moving and bawling loudly. This time, I think I know where the shot came from, and it's not where I think Ivy's hiding. Turning to tell Cash, I see him nod before I even speak. He's thinking the same as me.

My next thought is if Ivy's in a position that puts her at risk if the cattle spook. I risk being seen, but I start moving quickly toward Ivy's side of the gully. When I stop moving, my phone vibrates. Hiding the light of the screen behind me, I find a text from Ivy.

Ivy: Someone's right above me.

Dropping my phone to the ground, I lay on the edge and look down. Nothing but blackness.

"Ivy," I say quietly, then take the first full breath I've taken in hours when I hear her voice.

"I'm here."

"I'm coming down to you."

"No, it's a big drop. I came from the end and climbed up to a small, uprooted tree. I think I have to come out the same way."

Our conversation ends when another shot rings out, and the cattle do as I worried they would. They spook and start running. Cash appears on one side of me, Axel on the other.

"Ivy!" I shout while swinging my legs over the edge and feeling for a foothold. Nothing. Flipping to my stomach, I grip the ground and try again.

The cattle must reach the far end and can't climb out that way because they circle back, running hard. Even though it's a small herd, they're causing the ground to shake.

"Pigeon!" Ivy shouts, terror in her voice.

Axel drops to his belly in front of me and grabs my arms. Holding tight, it allows me to go lower. Searching frantically for a place for my feet, I find nothing. Slamming the toe of my boot into the side of the gully, I make an unstable foothold.

Gripping wrists, Axel keeps me steady.

"Grab my legs, Ivy!" I shout, not knowing if she can yet or not.

When I feel her hands brush my leg, I encourage her upward. I don't hear anything but the thundering hooves and the sound of her breathing.

"Boots, then my belt. Keep climbing, baby. Use those work muscles. Grab my shoulders when you can."

Quicker than I expected, I feel her hand land on my shoulder before the other one follows suit. Wrapping them around my neck, she clings to my back.

"Hang on, honey," I instruct. "When you can, work your way to my shoulders, kneel or stand on them, and Cash can reach you then."

"Cash lets go of me, and we're all going down," Axel warns in a strained voice.

"Climb higher, Ivy. I'll grab you, girl," James says from above my head.

Knowing there's more hands available, I take a deep breath and urge Ivy to move.

She somehow scurries higher, using my shoulders, and then suddenly, her weight disappears. More hands grab my arms, and I'm pulled up to the rim. Laying on my belly, arms burning, I give Axel's ass a pat. He huffs out a laugh as Ivy's body collides with mine.

Rolling over, I pull her close and hold her against me.

"Anyone know where the brother is?" Livi asks.

"No idea. It's too fucking dark to know. The cattle found a way out and scattered. We need to get moving. We're too exposed out here. Maybe Freddy and the others have him," Petey says.

Standing, keeping Ivy close, we work our way back around the long gully to the vehicles. Everyone's on edge, guns held at the ready, but we make it there without incident. No one has seen Ted or the side by side. Everyone loads up, and Ivy guides us to the ranch in silence. There's plenty to say, but that can wait.

"We're further out from the house than I thought we were," Pooh says as the lights come into view.

"How long were you out there before you called me?" I ask Ivy.

"Hours. I couldn't call in the beginning because he was hot on my tail, and I was running. He got close enough a couple of times to try to run me over. When I finally could, I didn't have service," Ivy answers in a subdued voice. "If I could have made it to the barn or the horse pasture, I could have grabbed a horse to ride, and he'd never have gotten close."

Climbing out of the truck, I hold my hand out for hers when I get the first good look at her face. Gripping it gently, I turn her head so the truck's interior light gives me a better view.

"Holy fuck," Trigger mutters as he stops next to us.

"I'm fine. It's bruises, and they heal," Ivy insists before pulling away from me and walking toward the barn.

Realizing why she's going that way, I step in front of her. I don't want her to see whatever Ted did in there to any of her pets.

"Go to the house with Livi and James. I'll go to the barn," I order softly.

Hesitating a beat, she turns and lets James wrap his arm around her and lead the way to the house. Going into cop mode, Livi enters first, gun drawn. When she shouts "clear," James and Ivy enter and shut the door behind them.

"I hope to fuck he didn't have much time to spend with her animals," I mutter.

The guys follow me to the barn. Opening the door and flipping on the lights, the first thing I see is Annie. Dead, bullet to the head. While my stomach drops, I hear whining and know that someone has survived Ted's rampage.

Petey slides the stall door back, and I watch in relief as Thor and Cody rush out. Both appear uninjured, and I'm confused as to what Ted's plan was. Cash swears loudly from just outside the barn, and I turn to see why. He's standing next to four large gas cans that I've never seen around here before. Walking the length of the barn, I note that each stall door that exits outside is closed. Ivy's horses were locked inside their stalls, something she seldom does.

"Son of a bitch. He was going to torch the barn, probably other buildings too, with her animals trapped inside. The dead dog must have surprised him and got shot because of it," Petey states in a low, angry voice.

"I'll bury her dog. You guys open those stalls and let her horses out like she would want them to be," Cash says while picking up a shovel.

"Hey! I think he was hiding out here. We just walked through the other buildings and found empty beer cans in the bunkhouse," Axel says when he enters the barn.

Thinking back to Ivy mentioning the light in the bunkhouse, I remember other odd things that happened here lately. Things moved, beer missing from the fridge, food gone too. I never thought too much about those small things, but now they make my skin crawl. Knowing he was this close to Ivy, waiting for a chance to strike. Anger surges through me, and I sincerely hope we find him so I can end him.

Working together, we right the barn, feed and water the animals, and Cash buries Annie. By the time the sun is up, we're sitting around the kitchen table, sipping coffee. Exhaustion is evident in everyone's face, but no one's leaving until we find Ted. Angry energy blasts through the room when Ivy walks in. Her face is battered, as are her ribs, back, arms, and legs.

Livi and I had warned the men, but a warning doesn't matter when physical proof of her brother's brutality is standing in front of you. Having refused to go to the hospital, Ivy did concede to a warm bath and sleep. Livi helped her with the bath and attended her many bruises, scratches, and cuts. I laid with her until she fell asleep before returning to help the others in and around the barnyard.

Self-consciously, Ivy attempts to keep the worst parts out of view, but there isn't much left to see that doesn't show damage. I stand and point to my chair. Ivy sits, waits a minute before looking at each of the people in her kitchen.

"Thank you," she simply says, and there isn't much else to say.

Ted's crimes, not hers.

To stop the questions everyone has for her, Ivy looks to Petey and asks, "Livi said Ava and Gunner had their baby yesterday. Congratulations. Shouldn't you be with them?"

"Saw the baby and them yesterday at the hospital. I'll see them again soon enough. Trudy's with them, and Bailey and Tammy have the kids. They're covered, darlin'."

"Livi and James are staying with Ivy. Let's go," I say to the room.

We find Ted, still in the gully. He's nearly impossible to identify due to the amount of damage his body took from the cattle he spooked. Livi was right. Ivy's smart. Ted wasn't. She knew to do the best she could to be above the danger of a spooked, stampeding herd of cattle. Ted didn't and paid for that stupidity with his life.

In the light of day, it wasn't hard to find the side by side. Ted had parked it a ways off and walked to the gully. Most likely hoping to sneak up on Ivy in the dark. Leaving his body where it lies, Rex takes pictures and then video of the area, same as he did inside the barn last night. Petey drives the side by side back to the ranch, and we follow. After speaking with James and Livi outside, it was decided to contact the local police department and let them handle Ted's death. As James said, it happened during a crime he was committing, and it was obviously accidental.

I sat with Ivy and told her what we found. No expression on her battered face, she listens and then nods in understanding. I then broke the news about Annie and watched as her face crumbled. Holding her, I let her cry out her anger and grief. When the storm passes and the cops arrive, Ivy stands at my side and tells them what happened yesterday.

The cops take notes, listen carefully, and Axel and James take them to the gully. I send Ivy upstairs with her cat and dogs to rest and then wait for the cops to return. When they do, they tell us we'll hear back from them, maybe need to answer more questions, but that they didn't expect any problems. The ambulance with Ted's body can be seen in the distance as it turns onto the driveway but doesn't come our way. When they turn to leave, one cop stops and looks at me.

"I remember them in school. Ted was a dick even back then and apparently, didn't change his ways. He had a great life here, but it was never enough for him. Ivy was the opposite. Everyone liked her, especially the kids that she defended. I was one of those kids. My family was poor, and I got picked on for wearing second-hand clothes and not having a cell phone," the cop stops speaking for a minute and then laughs. "Ivy spent some time in the principal's office for her methods of sticking up for me. I heard the principal hollering at her one day, and Ivy responded by telling him she wouldn't have to slap idiots upside the head if he did his job and protected the kids."

I thank him for coming out, and he says, "Glad I got this call. I hope Ivy heals up and puts this behind her. He's not worth anyone's tears."

The cop car leaves, and shortly after, my club family does too.

Finding Ivy sitting in the kitchen, drinking coffee, I sit across from her.

"I don't want to have a funeral for him. We can have him buried in the family plot, but that's it. That's all I'm willing to do for him."

I nod, reach across the table, and clasp our hands together.

"Will you go with me to tell mom when the bruises fade? I'm not telling her anything other than he died when some cattle ran over him. That's it. She's too fragile, and it's unnecessary for her to know more than that," Ivy says in a soft voice.

"Of course, I'll go with you. I agree with what you're telling her. It's not her fault her son turned out the way he did."

Standing, I pull Ivy to her feet and walk us into the living room. Pulling her down on the couch with me, I stretch out and cuddle her close.

"No more thinking, Ivy. What we're doing right now is all we're doing for the rest of the day. Relax and know you're safe," I whisper in her ear.

Ivy's body relaxes, and she slips into sleep. It's a very long time before I follow.

Lola Wright

Chapter 16
Pigeon

Sitting in a lawn chair outside the clubhouse, Ivy in one next to me, I listen to Axel tell us about all the amazing things Priscilla can do and say. The man is truly enamored with his lady bird friend, and she is with him. Hearing the screech of the main gate, I again remind myself to oil it. Seeing Tessie's Jeep come into view, I bail out of my chair and start running for my bike.

"Pigeon! Stand down, brother!" Axel shouts.

Gauging the distance between me and my bike and Tessie's Jeep and my bike, I stop. I'm never going to get there in time to save it. Wanting to cover my eyes in fear instead, I hold my breath, not releasing it until the Jeep comes to a stop, still several feet from my bike. Not believing my eyes telling my brain that my bike's still whole, Tessie steps out of the Jeep.

"Really, Pigeon? I haven't hit anything in months! You guys are such unforgiving twats!" she hisses before stomping past me.

When I sit back down next to Ivy, I ignore her and Axel laughing at me. I look over to my bike and Tessie's Jeep, still amazed there wasn't a casualty.

"I don't know what Lucy did or said, but Tessie hasn't put a ding, dent, or scratch in anything since their lessons started," Axel informs me. "Trigger said he's got so much free time now because he's not fixing her Jeep every week that he's going to take a few weeks off from the shop."

"He'll be out to the ranch then to fish," I reply, glad to hear Trigger's finally taking some time off.

"More than that. He said he and Tammy want to stay for a few days. He wants to fish, of course, but he went on about helping with Ivy's riding clinic and rebuilding that wagon you bought for the hayrides," Axel explains.

"I would never have been ready to start doing the clinics if it wasn't for him and the rest of the club," Ivy softly says.

"Pippa's going to talk with you when she gets here too. She has a woman at New Horizons that might be perfect for helping on the ranch. The lady needs to stay out of sight and has ranch and riding experience. Might be the perfect solution for both of you," Axel continues.

"That's great! We've been thinking about hiring a few employees, and if the peace of the ranch can help this woman too, all the better. Be great if she could help with the cooking. If not, we'll need to find someone who can," Ivy says.

Bella, with Craig and Luke, take seats near us as we chat. Of course, that means we've now been joined by a large dog, Cain, and a skunk too.

"I wanted to ask about your clinics, Ivy. When you are running one, is there anything I can do to help? As you know, I'm just learning how to ride, and thank you for being a great teacher, but anything else I could do? Childcare, cleaning stalls, feeding the animals?" Bella asks. "I'm happy to do anything that gives you more time with the animals and kids."

"Absolutely," Ivy and I answer at the same time, then laugh because that happens a lot.

"Thank you! I already asked Mom and Pops, and they said they'd bring me out anytime."

"Love to have you, Bella, but you will accept pay for the hours you work. No arguing," I say, knowing that Bella's saving her money but still not knowing what for.

"I will if you insist, but I'm happy just helping out, too. I love being at the ranch. There's something peaceful and soothing about it and the horses. I can't explain it," Bella says with an embarrassed smile.

"You don't have to explain it, Bella. I get it. I really do," Ivy replies.

"I have a question. You two both grew up as country kids, but Ivy calls her home a ranch, and Pigeon says he was raised on a farm. What's the difference?" Axel questions.

"Ranches raise livestock. Farms raise crops," Craig answers.

"Ivy raises crops. Hay, corn, oats," Axel points out.

"Ranchers raise crops to feed their livestock. Farmers raise crops to sell either for humans or livestock to eat," Craig continues.

"Huh. That's interesting. Thanks, little man," Axel says

"Google knows these things," Craig admits with a grin. "I guess there's exceptions, but that's the basic difference."

Prissy comes flying around the corner of the clubhouse to land on Axel's thigh. Right behind her, in hot pursuit, is Mac. He lands on Axel's other thigh, and Prissy hisses loudly at him.

"Give back!" Mac hollers.

"Fitt'in to bitch slap a bird!" Prissy threatens, then slowly lifts her foot showing a cashew clasped in it.

"Fitt'in?" Mac asks with an adorable head tilt.

"Fixing to," Prissy answers before popping the cashew in her mouth and chewing slowly.

"Thief!" Mac shouts.

"Mac! Stop! I gave it to her. She didn't steal it," Ava says as she, holding baby Chasin, Gunner, and the twins, join our group. Loki, trailing them, flops down on the ground next to his own son.

"Oh! Can I hold him?" Ivy asks while holding her arms out.

Ava passes the baby to Ivy, and I peer down to see the chubby infant sound asleep. Gunner told me that Chasin has been super easy so far. After having twins the first time, I'm sure part of it is because there's only one infant to deal with this time around. But I have to admit, I have yet to hear him cry.

Vex and Taja approach, and I quickly hold my hands out for their daughter. With Axel busy keeping the birds from battling, we finally get a chance to hold the babies. Holding Kalea next to Chasin, I grin. He's larger by far but having half of his dad's genes in him, that's not surprising. Kalea is smaller, delicate, and a beautiful baby. While Chasin has Gunner stamped all over him, Kalea is a beautiful mix of both her parents. Meeting Ivy's eyes, I smile. This is our future. Being together, with our club family, holding our babies.

As more members show, our group grows. When we run out of chairs, it's decided to move inside to wait for our guest of honor. Cash and his family arrive, and Liam toddles his way to my side. Hefting the husky kid up in my arms, he immediately turns to Ivy and holds his hands out to her. Grinning, she takes him. All the kids gravitate to Ivy, and she loves it.

Everyone is sitting or standing, chatting, or drinking when James walks through the door. When a loud chorus of cheers go up, he stops, bewildered. Gunner hands Mia, or maybe it's Zoe, to Petey before walking across the floor to meet James in the middle.

"Time for Church," Gunner states as every patched member stands and walks to the room we hold Church in. "You too, James."

We take our seats while James, who is still a prospect, isn't allowed to sit in Church, so he leans against the wall. I can tell by the expression on his face he knows why we're here. What he doesn't know, though, is whether he's being patched in or told the vote went against him which would mean his time is done here. Glancing around at the members faces isn't going to help him determine which way this is going to go either.

"We're voting today on Prospect James. Yay to patch him in. Nay, if you don't think he fits in our club," Gunner announces.

Yay's are heard one at a time as the vote goes around the table. When the last vote reaches Gunner, our club President, he says yay and then bangs his gavel down.

"Vote falls in favor of James becoming a patched member of The Devil's Angels," he says. "Welcome to the club, Brother James."

When Gunner holds up our club colors, I watch as James realizes what this means. His head drops for a moment before he lifts it, removes his cut, and lays it on the table. Axel pulls out his knife and cuts the prospect patch from the back of it.

"Get your colors sewn on before you wear that cut again," Gunner orders, then pulls James in for a hug.

We take turns giving James a hug and congratulating him, welcoming him into the club as a fully patched member.

"I wasn't sure I'd get voted in," James says in a quiet voice while looking at his new patches laying in place on his cut.

"Why would you think that?" Petey asks in a concerned voice.

"Because I wanted it so much," James responds.

"Livi brought a sewing kit with her. Let's go get those patches taken care of and have a drink," Cash says.

"She brought one with her? She knew I'd get in?" James asks, surprised.

"No, she didn't know. She just had faith in you and in us to be smart enough to vote the right way," Cash answers with a grin.

Filing out of Church, cheers erupt again when James holds up his club patch.

"Let me do the honors, partner," Livi says after she hugs James and holds up the sewing kit.

"You voted for him, didn't you?" Ivy asks me when I put an arm around her shoulders.

"Of course. Was afraid if I didn't, he'd go through with the body cavity search he threatened me with before," I answer and laugh when Ivy's eyes go wide. "I'll explain that later."

We grab a drink and raise our glass to James, toasting his new status. Tossing my drink back, I take the seat next to Ivy, pull her body into mine and look around the room. Everyone that's important to me is in this room except for one.

Chubs' absence has affected our club in a fundamental way. He was always the heart and soul of The Devil's Angels, and he's sorely missed. His loss is like having a death within the club. We're all going through the steps of grief like denial and anger, but I don't know of a single person here that's reached the acceptance part. Not sure that will ever happen, even if he never returns.

Looking over at Lucy, my heart breaks for the tiny woman. If Chubs being out of our lives is this hard, I can't imagine how she's still standing. We've kept her close, even when she didn't want any of us around, and we'll always do that for her. She's earned our love and loyalty all on her own, even without Chubs at her side, and that will never end. Even so, we're a sad replacement for what she had with Chubs. Still not sure I believe God's ever heard my prayers before, I send up another one hoping he'll listen since it's about the best one of us.

"Please, God, hear my words. Bring Chubs back to Lucy, back to us, safely. He's needed here."

The End

Epilogue

"Your room is ready, Mr. Johnson. Second floor, turn right at the top of the stairs," the clerk says while handing me a set of door keys.

"Thank you."

Taking the keys, I make my way up the outside stairs to another nondescript motel room on the outskirts of the city. Rundown, depressed area, I won't be noticed because nothing about my clothes or car stands out. I've become adept at fitting in wherever I am, chameleon-like. If you look like the others around you, it's easy to blend in.

Setting my duffle bag on the floor and food bags on the foot of the bed, I strip down to my boxers before I look out the window to study the parking lot. I always memorize the lay of the land, wherever I'm staying. Taking a moment to check all avenues for an escape or attack, I move to take a seat on the bed. Leaning my back against the headboard, I flip on the TV and listen idly as I open the take-out food bags. It's been hours since I ate anything substantial, and I'm starving.

After eating and licking my fingers clean, I take a shower and pull-on clean boxers. Returning to the bed, my interest is piqued at the news story coming from the TV.

"Seven men were found dead today. The bodies were badly beaten and mutilated, and identification hasn't been made as of yet. According to a source from the police department, the men were not killed at this location but were dumped there. Identifying them may be difficult since fingers, teeth, other parts of the bodies are missing. The police are not, at this time, looking at this as the work of a serial killer but rather a deal-gone-bad type situation," the news anchor says.

"Sounds gruesome," states the other news anchor while giving a fake shudder.

"Genitals were all missing too, so yes, very gruesome," responds the first news anchor. "We'll keep following this story and will report any new updates as soon as we have them."

I grin because I know who those seven men were. Good riddance, the world's a better place with them no longer a part of it. I pick up my burner phone from the nightstand when it rings. Answering, I don't have to look to see who the caller is since only one person has this number.

"You have a hand in that? What's on the news?" the voice on the other end asks.

"Played a small part," I answer and jealously listen to the sound of a potato chip bag being opened.

"Are you close yet?" my brother questions.

"Yeah. I'll be busy for a few days, so if you don't hear from me, don't worry."

"Aria's worried about what's been happening around here, but Mom's solid. Aria may never forgive you. You know that, right?" my brother asks with concern in his voice.

"I know. I can't change the past, so I'll have to deal with it if she doesn't," I answer in a low voice.

"Deal with it? As close as you two were? You were inseparable! I think you're underestimating her capacity for anger and the resentment she'll feel at being left in the dark," my brother warns. "She mourned your death, brother. We all did, but it nearly killed her. She hasn't been the same since, and now to find out you were never dead?" my brother trails off.

Aria has been my biggest regret, and knowing it changed her kills a part of me for real this time. Life is all about the choices you make, but I had few to choose from. Aria got caught in the crossfire, as did my mom and brother, and I've never stopped regretting that fact.

"I just hope we're all alive in the end to argue about who was right and who was wrong," I say.

"Yeah, me too. I've got to go. Talk later, brother," my brother says before disconnecting.

Setting my phone down, I think of the challenges I'm facing in the next few days. I have to survive them because I have more life to live, far away from my current location. I have a lot of people to explain my decisions to and to beg for forgiveness from. One in particular, and that's the one person who deserves everything I've got to give.

Standing, I pull on my jeans and hoodie, pulling it up to cover my head, grab the hotel keys and my wallet. Opening the door, I carefully search the parking lot for threats. Seeing none, I hustle down the stairs and to the vending machines I saw tucked into a corner under the balcony. Pulling cash from my wallet, I start the long process of buying enough snacks for a day or two.

I hope you enjoyed Ivy and Pigeon's story!

The next book in The Devil's Angels MC Series is Book 7—Chubs.

Lola Wright

About the Author

Lola Wright currently lives in the great state of Michigan with her husband. She has enjoyed living in several different areas of her home state and the USA, but Michigan is home. Her kids are grown now, and between them, her grandchildren, and numerous furry family members, Lola keeps busy. When Lola has free time, she will most likely be found outside riding her horses or being entertained by her rescued minis, her dogs, and cats. Lola has a passion for feeding the wildlife and enjoys watching them come and go on her property. If indoors, Lola is usually cooking up new recipes, reading, or is in front of her computer dreaming up who she hopes is the perfect couple.

Amazon
In the Kindle Store on the Amazon site, search for "Lola Wright"

Facebook
On Facebook search for "Lola Wright, Author" to find *Lola's Profile*, *The Devil's Angels Page*, *Lola's Angels Group Page*, and the *Angels Spoilers Group Page*.

Twitter
@LolaWri47124635

Join Lola Wright's Mailing List for the latest news on her books! Go to the **Lola's Home page**—https://www.lolawright.store—and scroll to the bottom of the page.

Also by Lola Wright

The Devil's Angels MC Series

The Devil's Angels MC: Book 1 - Gunner

Ava

Left to die as an infant, Ava Beaumont has not had an easy life. Being raised by the system has taught her to be independent, hardworking, and cautious. When Ava becomes a victim, she uses her inner strength to put it behind her and move forward. Now she lives a good life with the family she's created through adopting pets that were also throwaways, including a smart-mouthed parrot and a skateboarding pig. When Ava meets Gunner, she realizes what her life is lacking but does she have the courage to trust a big, rough biker enough to let him into her safe little life?

Gunner

Being the President of The Devil's Angels MC was not something Gunner asked to become, but through the loss of his dad, the job was thrust upon him. While he loves his club and club brothers wholeheartedly, Gunner wants his club to move in a better direction. And when Gunner spots bakery owner, Ava, he realizes that's not the only change he wants to make in his life.

Nothing worth having is easy to acquire.

This is an MC story with a heart. Come meet the crazy pets and even crazier club members of The Devil's Angels MC.

The Devil's Angels MC: Book 2 - Axel

Bailey

I'm the sensible, independent, quiet, and hardworking accountant girl next door. My life is safe, sane, predictable, and boring. My biggest concern is dealing with my free-spirited, wild-child parent.

Until it's not.

The day I see something I shouldn't have and crash into the crazy lives of The Devil's Angels MC is the day my life changes forever. That's the day I looked into the bluest eyes I have ever seen and knew nothing would ever be the same.

Axel

My life is perfect. I'm the Vice President of my club, The Devil's Angels MC, and we've moved the club in the right direction. I manage the club's gym, own my own home, and have women around that are always up for a night of fun. I have my club brothers, the world's best dad and a new sister. Family is everything in my world, and I have a great one. What more could a guy want or need?

That question is answered when a tiny, little woman slams her way into my life. I never saw her coming, but I'm not letting her leave.

The Devil's Angels MC: Book 3 - Pooh

Pippa

Owning and operating a home for victims of domestic violence doesn't leave a woman wanting a man in her life. Not a permanent one anyway. Having been a victim myself, I chose to open this refuge to help others that are in a similar situation that I had been. I was one of the lucky ones because my foster mom was always my rock, my safe haven. It was never me alone against the world. We decided, together, that we wanted to be just that for others. New Horizons is born, and we are on a mission to save all that we can.

Pooh

I'm restless, bored, and I want more. I want what some of my club brothers have found. I want that one woman that is meant to be mine.

The problem is I don't know any women that qualify. Being in a motorcycle club brings women around in flocks, but they're not meant to be mine when they're clearly everyone's girls.

Then I meet her. The One.

Now the problem is that she is not interested in me or a relationship and not a big fan of men in general. She's a strong, independent woman, and a little spitfire when it comes to protecting those she's sworn to keep safe.

She will be mine, and I'll prove to her that men like me and my club brothers from The Devil's Angels MC are nothing like the men she's known before.

The Devil's Angels MC: Book 4 - Vex

Vex

I've lived my life free and easy. No attachments, no entanglements. I easily move on after an evening with a woman. For a night, they get all I have to give. After that, it's time to go. They're warned ahead of time, so tears and ploys have no effect on me. I love my MC family, The Devil's Angels, and my bikes. Not much else. Certainly, none of the various women I've known.

Then I meet someone who changes all my rules, thoughts, and beliefs. But as luck would have it, she's the unattainable one. She seems immune to my charm, and that tweaks my ego. After being warned away from her, I try to push her to the back of my mind. She doesn't stay there for long, though. Now I'm determined to have my night with her, consequences be damned.

Taja

Trying to raise my sister, working any job I can while fighting to keep a roof over our heads, I don't live the life of a normal woman my age. I don't have time for dating, sex, or men. Especially a member of an MC. My father's an MC President, and I want nothing to do with that lifestyle. Not even for the gorgeous biker whose nearly golden eyes follow my every move. Common sense tells me he's in it for a night, and that's not my style. Best to keep my head on straight and ignore what my body's craving.

Actions have consequences, and fate has a way of messing up the best-laid plans.

The Devil's Angels MC: Book 5 - Cash

Livi

Being a female in a male-dominated career can be daunting, but I refuse to allow others' attitudes to deter me. I always try to be professional, compassionate, and non-judgmental. Through hard work, I have earned respect within my department. Wearing a badge and uniform, I've seen the best and worst of humanity. Heartbreaking, dangerous, hectic, or hilarious, I approach each shift and person with an open mind.

As all cops know, the partner you're teamed up with makes all the difference in the world, and I struck gold. Work partners and best friends, James and I have a tight, unshakable bond. We're each other's support system when things get rough and defend each other's right to wear the uniform against anyone who believes otherwise.

Cash

Muscled, tall, tatted, and The Devil's Angels MC Sergeant at Arms, some see me as an intimidating man. Others see me as quiet, thoughtful, and dedicated to my blood and MC families. I'm the first call everyone makes when things are going sideways. Whether it's bullets or fists flying, I'm the man you want at your back. Highly respected within my club, I live by a strict biker code.

When a life-altering event occurs in my life, I will not waver in doing what's right. With the love and support of my two families, I'll face my new circumstances with determination.

The Devil's Angels MC

More books to follow in this series!

Printed in Great Britain
by Amazon